"Sherry Thomas has done the impossib... [P9-DXM-545] ...new version of Sherlock Holmes. From the carefully plotted twists to the elegant turns of phrase, *A Study in Scarlet Women* is a splendid addition to Holmes's world. This book is everything I hoped it would be, and the next adventure cannot come too soon!"

—Deanna Raybourn, *New York Times* bestselling author

PRAISE FOR THE NOVELS OF SHERRY THOMAS

"Enchanting . . . An extraordinary, unputdownable love story."

—Jane Feather, *New York Times* bestselling author

"Sublime . . . An irresistible literary treat."　　　—Chicago Tribune

"Thomas continues to be a refreshing voice in the genre with her lively plots, witty dialogue, and intelligent characters . . . She compels readers to think, feel, laugh—and, ultimately, heave a deep sigh of satisfaction."

—*RT Book Reviews* (Top Pick)

"Thomas tantalizes readers . . . An enchanting, thought-provoking story of love lost and ultimately reclaimed. Lively banter, electric sexual tension, and an unusual premise make this stunning debut all the more refreshing."　　　—*Library Journal* (starred review)

"[A] masterpiece . . . A beautifully written, exquisitely seductive, powerfully romantic gem of a romance."　　　—*Kirkus Reviews* (starred review)

"Deft plotting and sparkling characters . . . Steamy and smart."

—*Publishers Weekly* (starred review)

"Historical romance the way I love it."　　　—All About Romance

"[A] truly enjoyable historical romance with funny characters, beautifully written prose, and a satisfying ending."　　　—Dear Author

"Sherry Thomas's captivating debut novel will leave readers breathless. Intelligent, witty, sexy, and peopled with wonderful characters . . . and sharp, clever dialogue."　　　—The Romance Reader

"Layered, complex characters . . . Beautiful writing and emotional punch."

—Smart Bitches, Trashy Books

A Study in Scarlet Women

Sherry Thomas

BERKLEY

New York

BERKLEY
An imprint of Penguin Random House LLC
375 Hudson Street, New York, New York 10014

An application to register this book for cataloging has been submitted to
the Library of Congress.

ISBN: 9780425281406

First Edition: October 2016

Printed in the United States of America
3   5   7   9   10   8   6   4   2

Cover art by Shane Rebenschied
Cover design by Alana Colucci
Book design by Tiffany Estreicher

To the beautiful person and constant delight that is Sean

ACKNOWLEDGMENTS

Kristin Nelson, who never met a book of mine she couldn't sell.

Wendy McCurdy, who believed the Lady Sherlock series had potential.

Kerry Donovan, who worked tirelessly on this book.

Janine Ballard, who went over the manuscript with a fine-toothed comb.

Shellee Roberts, who kicked my ass when it needed kicking. Traci Andrighetti, who restored my confidence after said ass-kicking.

My husband, who can always be counted on to hold down the fort, deadlines or not.

Everyone who ever cheered on the idea of a female Sherlock Holmes.

And you, if you are reading this, thank you. Thank you for everything.

Prologue

DEVONSHIRE, ENGLAND
1886

Had anyone told the Honorable Harrington Sackville that the investigation into his death would make the name Sherlock Holmes known throughout the land, Mr. Sackville would have scoffed.

He had never heard of Sherlock Holmes. But more importantly, he despised the idea of death. Of his death, to be precise—others could die as they wished.

He loathed old age almost as much: that long, vile decline into help-lessness halted only by the final breath, falling like a guillotine blade.

And yet his reflection in the mirror made it increasingly difficult to tell himself that he was still a young man. He remained a fit man, a handsome man, but the skin beneath his jaw sagged. Deep grooves cut into the sides of his mouth. Even his eyelids drooped, heavy from the passage of time.

Fear hooked through him, cold and sharp. Every man was afraid of something. For him, death had long loomed as the ultimate terror. A darkness with fangs.

He turned away from the mirror—and the unwelcome thoughts that always simmered these days a scant inch beneath the surface. It was summer. The glow of twilight suffused the house. From his perch on the headlands, the bay blazed with the flame of the setting sun. A hint of salt fragranced the breeze that meandered in; the top note of that perfumed air was tuberose, bulbs of which he had imported from Grasse, in the south of France.

But a storm was coming; inky clouds gathered at the edge of the sky . . .

He inhaled deeply. No, he must not let his mind wander to shadowy places. Recent weeks had been difficult—the events in London particularly distressing—but in time things would improve. He had many good years left to relish life, and to laugh at death and its still distant grasp.

No premonitions crossed his mind that death was to have him by morning.

But have him it would—and the last laugh.

One

On the day Mr. Harrington Sackville met his darkness with fangs, certain parties in the know were bracing for—and eagerly anticipating—a major scandal involving the youngest member of the Holmes family.

Lord Ingram Ashburton did not share in their anticipation. The idea that such a catastrophe could come to pass had haunted him for days. He did not yet know that Holmes was already doomed, but a sense of dread had been growing in him, a tumorlike weight on his lungs.

He stared at the envelope on the desk before him.

Mr. Sherlock Holmes
General Post Office
St. Martin's Le Grand
London

Any idiot could see the frustration that seethed with every stroke of the pen—at several places the nib had nearly torn through the linen paper.

The writing on the note next to the envelope was equally agitated.

Holmes,

Don't.
And if you must, not with Roger Shrewsbury. You will regret it relentlessly.
For once in your life, listen to me.

He dropped his forehead into his left palm. It would be no use. Holmes would do as Holmes pleased, carried along on that blitheness born of extraordinary ability and favorable circumstances.

Until disaster strikes.

You don't need to let it happen, said a voice inside him. You *step in.* You *give Holmes what Holmes wants.*

And then what? Then I carry on and pretend it never happened?

He stared out of the open window. His unimpeded view of the sky appeared as if seen through a lens that had been smudged with a grimy finger—a polluted blue, a fine day for London. Peals of irrepressible mirth rose from the small park below—his children's laughter, a sound that would have brought a smile to his face on any other day.

He picked up his pen.

Do not do anything without first consulting me again.
Please.

Was he acquiescing? Was he jettisoning all caution—and all principle as well?

He sealed the unsigned letter in the envelope and walked out of his book-lined study, envelope in pocket. He was scheduled to give an archeological lecture in the evening. But first he wanted to spend some time with his daughter and son, rambunctious children at the peak of their happy innocence.

After that he would decide whether to post the letter or to consign it to the fire, like the dozen others that had preceded it.

The front door opened and in came his wife.

"Afternoon, madam," he said politely.

"My lord." She nodded, a strange little smile on her face. "I see you have not heard about what happened to your favorite lady."

"My favorite lady is my daughter. Is anything the matter with her?"

He kept his voice cool, but he couldn't stop the hair on the back of his neck from standing up: Lady Ingram was not talking about their child.

"Lucinda is well. I refer to . . ." Her lips curled with disdain. "I refer to Holmes. *Your* Holmes."

"How dare you humiliate me this way?" Mrs. Shrewsbury rained down blows on her husband. "How dare you?"

The painted French fan, folded up, made for a surprisingly potent weapon—a cross between a bolt of silk and a police baton. Roger Shrewsbury whimpered.

He didn't understand the way her mind worked.

Very well, he had committed an unforgivable error: The night before he'd been so drunk he mistook his wife for Mimi, his mistress, and told the wife what he was going to do this afternoon with Charlotte Holmes. But if Mrs. Shrewsbury hadn't wanted him to deflower Miss Holmes, why hadn't she smacked him then and there and forbidden him to do anything of the sort? Or she could have gone 'round to Miss Holmes's and slapped her for not having a higher regard for her hymen.

Instead she had mustered a regiment of sisters, cousins, and friends, set his *mother* at the helm of the entire enterprise, and stormed the Bastille just as he settled into Miss Holmes. So how could she accuse *him* of humiliating *her*, when she was the one who had made sure that a good dozen other women saw her husband in flagrante delicto?

He knew better than to give voice to his thoughts. After twenty-six years as Lady Shrewsbury's son and three as Anne Shrewsbury's husband, he'd learned that he was always wrong. The less he said, the better.

The missus continued to hit him. He wrapped his arms around his head, made himself as small as possible, and tried to disappear into a nice memory, a time and a place in which he wasn't a bounder twenty-four hours a day, three hundred and sixty-five days a year.

—————❦—————

Lady Shrewsbury frowned mightily at the young woman who sat opposite her in the brougham. Charlotte Holmes was still, her face pale but composed.

Eerily composed, given she was now ruined beyond repair.

So composed that Lady Shrewsbury, who had been prepared for any amount of hysterical sobbing and frantic pleas, was beginning to feel rattled—a sensation she hadn't experienced in years.

Lady Shrewsbury had been the one to throw a sheet over the girl. She had then ordered her son to go home with his wife, and the rest of the women to disperse. Miss Holmes had not trembled in a corner, her hands over her face. Nor had she stared numbly at the floor. Instead she had watched the goings-on as if she were a mere bystander, one whose own fate had not in the least taken an unthinkable turn. As Roger was shoved out by his wife, Miss Holmes glanced at him, without anger, loathing, or any reflection of his helplessness.

It had been a sympathetic and apologetic look, the kind the

ringleader of a gang of unruly children might give one of her follow-
ers, after she had got the latter into unlimited trouble.

Lady Shrewsbury had fully expected this bravado to disintegrate
once the others had gone. She was famous for her sternness. Roger,
whenever he found himself alone with her, perspired even when she
hadn't planned to inquire into what he had been doing with himself
of late.

But her formidableness had no effect on Charlotte Holmes. After
the gaggle of eyewitnesses departed to spread the salacious story in
drawing rooms all over London, Miss Holmes, instead of dissolving
into tears, dressed and ordered a considerable tea service.

Then, under Lady Shrewsbury's increasingly incredulous gaze,
she proceeded to polish off a plate of plum cake, a plate of cherry
tartlets, *and* a plate of sardines and toast. All without saying a single
word, or even acknowledging Lady Shrewsbury's presence.

Lady Shrewsbury controlled her vexation. Silence was one of her
greatest weapons and she would not be goaded into abandoning that
strategic advantage. Alas, her magnificent silence had no effect on
Charlotte Holmes, who dined as if she were a queen and Lady Shrewsbury a lowly lackey, not worthy of even a spare glance.

When the girl was ready to leave, she simply walked out, forcing
Lady Shrewsbury to catch up. Again, as if she weren't a strict moral
guardian escorting a fallen woman to her consequences, but a simple-
minded maid scampering behind her mistress.

The silence continued in the brougham. Miss Holmes studied
the carriages that clogged the street—shiny, lacquered town coaches
jostling for space amidst long queues of hansom cabs. From time to
time her gaze fell on Lady Shrewsbury and Lady Shrewsbury had
the distinct sensation that of the two of them, Miss Holmes considered Lady Shrewsbury the far stranger specimen.

"Have you nothing to say for yourself?" she snapped, unable to stand the silence another second.

"For myself, no," Charlotte Holmes said softly. "But I hope you will not be too harsh on Roger. He is not to blame for this."

——— �֍ ———

Inspector Robert Treadles of the Metropolitan Police always enjoyed an outing to Burlington House, especially to attend Lord Ingram's lectures. They had met via a shared ardor for archeology—Lord Ingram had sponsored Treadles's entry into the London Society of Antiquaries, in fact.

But this evening his friend was not himself.

To the casual observer, his lordship would seem to command the meeting room, thorough in his knowledge, eloquent in his presentation, and deft with a touch of dry humor—his comparison of the ancient family strife caused by variation in size and ornateness of each member's jeweled brooches with the modern jealousy aroused by the handsomeness of a sibling's new brougham drew peals of laughter from the audience.

To Inspector Treadles, however, Lord Ingram's delivery had little of its usual élan. It was a struggle. A futile struggle, moreover: Sisyphus pushing that enormous boulder up the hill, knowing that it would roll away from him near the top, condemning him to start all over again, ad infinitum.

What could be the matter? Lord Ingram was the scion of a ducal family, an Old Etonian, and one of the finest polo players in the world. Of course Inspector Treadles knew that no one's existence was perfect behind closed doors, but whatever turbulence Lord Ingram navigated in his private life had never before been made visible in his public demeanor.

After the lecture, after the throng of admirers had dispersed, the two men met in a book-lined nook of the society's soaring library.

"I'd hoped we could dine together, Inspector," said Lord Ingram. "But I'm afraid I must take leave of you very soon."

Treadles was both disappointed and relieved—he didn't think he would be able to offer Lord Ingram much consolation, in the latter's current state.

"I hope your family is well," he said.

"They are, thank you. I'm obliged to pay a call on short notice, that is all." Lord Ingram's words were calm, yet there was a hollowness to his tone. "I trust we shall have the pleasure of a more leisurely meeting in the not too distant future."

"Certainly, my lord."

Inspector Treadles did not mean to delay his friend, but at that moment he remembered his other purpose for being at Burlington House this evening. "If it isn't too much trouble, sir, may I ask you to convey a note to Holmes? I'm most grateful for his assistance on the Arkwright case and wrote a few lines to that effect."

"I am afraid that would be impossible."

Inspector Treadles almost took a step back at his friend's expression: a flare of anger that bordered on wrath.

"I understand that you are engaged this evening, my lord," Treadles explained hesitantly. "My note requires no haste and needs be relayed only at your lordship's convenience."

"I didn't make myself clear," said Lord Ingram. All hints of rage had left his countenance. His eyes were blank, the set of his jaw hard. "I can't—nor can anyone else—convey any notes to Holmes. Not anymore."

"I—I don't—that is—" Treadles stuttered. "Has something terrible happened?"

Lord Ingram's jaw worked. "Yes, something terrible."

"When?"

"Today."

Inspector Treadles blinked. "Is . . . is Holmes still alive?"

"Yes."

"Thank goodness. Then we haven't lost him completely."

"But we have," said Lord Ingram, slowly, inexorably. "Holmes may be alive, but the fact remains that Holmes is now completely beyond my reach."

Treadles's confusion burgeoned further, but he understood that no more details would be forthcoming. "I'm exceedingly sorry to hear that."

"As am I, to be the bearer of such news." Lord Ingram's voice was low, almost inaudible.

Treadles left Burlington House in a daze, hounded by dozens of unhappy conjectures. Had Holmes leaped from a perilous height armed with nothing but an unreliable parachute? Had he been conducting explosive experiments at home? Or had his brilliant but restless mind driven him to seduce the wrong woman, culminating in an illegal duel and a bullet lodged somewhere debilitating but not instantly lethal?

What had happened to the elusive and extraordinary Sherlock Holmes?

Such a tragedy.

Such a waste.

Such a shame.

Two

"The shame. Oh, the shame!" Lady Holmes screeched.

From her crouched position before the parlor door keyhole, Livia Holmes glared at the young maid peeking around the corner. *Back to your duties*, she mouthed.

The girl fled, but not before giggling audibly.

Did no one understand the concept of privacy anymore? If there was any spying to be done in the midst of a reputation-melting scandal, it ought to be left to a member of the family.

Livia returned her attention to the *sturm und drang* in the parlor. Her view through the keyhole was blocked by her mother's skirt, a ghastly mound of heliotrope silk that shook with Lady Holmes's outrage.

"How many times have I told you, Sir Henry, that your indulgence of the girl would prove to be her undoing? How many times have I said that she ought to have been wed years ago? Did you listen? No! No one heeded me when I warned that letting her reject perfectly suitable gentlemen one after another would only serve to make her unfit for marriage and motherhood."

Her mighty bustle oscillated from side to side as she lurched forward. She lifted her arm and brought down her hand. An explosive *thwack* reverberated. Livia flinched.

She and Charlotte, the recipient of this resounding slap, had once discussed their mother's talents, or lack thereof. Livia was of the view that a segment of the population was inherently middling. Charlotte, of a more charitable bent of mind, believed that even those who appeared incurably undistinguished must possess some hidden skills or aptitudes.

Livia, not convinced, had brought up Lady Holmes as an example of utter mediocrity, a person who was unremarkable in every observable trait. Charlotte had countered, "But she has an extraordinary technique at slapping, the backhand especially."

Now Lady Holmes produced just that, a dramatic backhand the force of which wobbled the lace trimmings on her skirt. "The worst has happened. No one will marry her and she can never show her face in Society again."

It was the eleventh time she had spat out these lines this evening. Livia's neck hurt from the strain of crouching so long before the keyhole. How many more iterations before Charlotte would be allowed to escape to her own room?

"You haven't only caused your own ruin, Charlotte. You have also made us laughingstocks the rest of *our* lives." Lady Holmes was still plowing through the remainder of her tirade, though her voice was becoming hoarse. "You have perpetrated a crime against Livia's chances at a decent marriage. If Henrietta hadn't already secured her Mr. Cumberland we would have nothing but a passel of spinster daughters."

The contempt in Lady Holmes's voice—spinster daughters might as well be thieving whores. Livia lived with that scorn daily, a woman of twenty-seven, eight Seasons under her belt and no marital prospects whatsoever. Still she winced.

If history was any indication, Lady Holmes would storm toward where her husband sat and berate him some more. Then the entire diatribe would begin again.

Lumbering bustle in tow, Lady Holmes marched on, clearing the line of sight from the keyhole to Charlotte.

— ❋ —

It never failed to astonish Livia that, after having known Charlotte all her life, sometimes she was still surprised by her sister's appearance. Especially at moments like these—well, there had never before been a moment quite like this, to be sure, but Charlotte had been dumbfounding her family for as long as Livia could remember.

When Livia was six and Charlotte four, one cold but clear Saturday afternoon on a family stroll around the village green, they'd come across a drawing that had been pinned to the noticeboard. There were four images on the piece of paper: a well, a horseshoe, the Virgin, and a kitten that was only half the size as the other images, a round, quizzical head floating on the top half of the paper.

Lady Holmes had sniffed. "How strange."

"Rather interesting, I should think," replied her husband.

"But what is it?" asked Henrietta, the eldest of the Holmes girls, her voice high-pitched and whiny.

"It's a message, of course," Livia told her impatiently. "Must be something about the children's Christmas party."

"What about that party? I don't see how that can be."

How anyone could live to be ten years old and still remain so thick Livia had no idea. "The Virgin gave birth to baby Jesus at Christmas. The other drawings are games that will be there."

Henrietta looked doubtful. "What kind of games?"

Before Livia could enumerate her guesses, Charlotte said, loudly and clearly, "It isn't about games. It's a proposal."

All attention immediately turned to her.

Charlotte did not speak. In fact, their mother had been fretting for some time that Charlotte might turn out to be the same as Bernadine, the second oldest Holmes girl. At nine, Bernadine was no longer taken on family outings: She'd become too disconcerting, a lovely child who paid no attention to anyone or anything. If she had any thoughts at all, she never shared them with a single person.

Charlotte, with her blond ringlets and big blue eyes, resembled Bernadine almost exactly. But whereas Bernadine was rail-thin—nothing Cook made ever agreed with her—Charlotte was a roly-poly dumpling, her cheeks full, her limbs round, her hands adorably chubby.

A cherubic girl, one who was as silent as the small hours of the night. She nodded, shook her head, and pointed, if necessary. Cook insisted that one time, in answer to the question *How many pieces of apple fritter do you want, Miss Charlotte?*, the girl had given a beautifully enunciated *Twelve*. But no one else had ever heard her say so much as *Mamma*.

One time Livia had overheard Lady Holmes weep about her family being cursed. *Not only can I not have sons, but half my daughters are imbeciles!* Livia had come away feeling both relieved that she herself wasn't an imbecile and heartbroken that Charlotte, whom she found darling and hilarious—she never failed to smile at the sight of Charlotte attacking her food—might someday become as unreachable as Bernadine.

But now Charlotte had spoken her first full sentences. Livia would have been indignant had anyone else corrected her so unceremoniously, but *Charlotte* had spoken and Livia had—no, not butterflies, but a whole stampeding herd of wildebeest in her stomach. With everyone else still dumbstruck, she shook Charlotte's mitten-clad hand, which she held in her own, and asked, "Do you mean a proposal of marriage, Charlotte?"

"Don't be ridiculous, Livia," Lady Holmes scoffed. "She doesn't know what that is."

"Yes, a proposal of marriage, Mamma," Charlotte answered. "I know what that is. It is when a gentleman asks a lady to become his wife."

Again, stunned silence all around.

Sir Henry got down on one knee, a feverish gleam in his eyes. "Charlotte, my dear, why do you say these images constitute a proposal of marriage?"

Charlotte cast a critical eye at the picture, her expression amusingly grown-up. "It isn't a very good one, is it?"

"Maybe not, poppet. But why do you say it's a proposal in the first place?"

"Because it says *Will you marry me*. Actually, it says *Well you marry me*."

"I can see a well. And I can see that the horseshoe opens up and looks like a U. And the Virgin's name is Mary," said Sir Henry. "But how is the cat 'me'?"

"Exactly," Henrietta joined in. "That makes no sense."

Livia would have liked to shove a snowball deep down the front of Henrietta's frock. But Charlotte didn't seem to mind. "The cat is in the middle of a meow. But since there's only half a cat, it's half a meow. And half a meow is 'me.'"

Henrietta pouted. "How do you know half a meow isn't 'ow' inst—?"

"Henrietta, shut up." Sir Henry placed his hands on Charlotte's pink cheeks. "That is remarkable, poppet. Absolutely remarkable."

"Are you sure?" said Lady Holmes. "She might be making things up and—"

"Lady Holmes, kindly shut up, too."

"Well!" Lady Holmes sputtered. But she wasn't as easily silenced as Henrietta. "But you must tell Charlotte that since she is able to speak, she may no longer be so rudely silent."

Sir Henry sighed. "Do you hear your mother, poppet?"

"But Papa, why should I talk when I've nothing important to say?"

Sir Henry barked with laughter. "Why, indeed. You're wise beyond your years, my dear poppet. And you have my blessing to be as silent as you'd like."

This was said with a glance at Lady Holmes, the corners of whose lips turned down decidedly. With an exaggerated half bow, Sir Henry offered his wife his arm; she flattened her lips further but took it. Henrietta grabbed his other arm. Livia and Charlotte resumed walking hand in hand.

The next day was Sunday. After the sermon, the vicar announced from the pulpit that Miss Tomlinson had made him a very happy man by consenting to be his wife. Soon news was all over the village that those odd pictures on the noticeboard had been the vicar's way of proposing, as he and Miss Tomlinson were both fond of puzzles and rebuses.

Sir Henry pranced around the house, looking delighted and smug. Livia was happy for Charlotte, a little jealous that she wasn't the one to decipher the message, and strangely despondent. It would take her a long time to understand that the asphyxiated feeling in her chest had nothing to do with Charlotte but everything to do with their parents.

Sir Henry disdained his wife as Lady Holmes disdained her daughters. They weren't happy together but Lady Holmes was the far unhappier one.

It had been frightful for Livia to understand this. Her mother had seemed immensely powerful, an Olympian figure striding about her fine country house, emanating command and superiority. But she was impotent before her husband's contempt.

Nor was she, in the end, the kind of household authority figure that Livia had first believed. What control Lady Holmes exerted was largely illusory, maintained tenuously and with frequent outbursts of anger and violence—that extraordinary slapping technique had not come about without assiduous practice. The servants despised her, Livia barely tolerated her, and Bernadine's condition was always worse when she was near. The only one with whom she got along was Henrietta, who happily flattered and even emulated her.

Once in a while Livia came upon this domestic despot sitting by herself, in a corner of the parlor, looking pale and lost. But then Lady Holmes would see her and shout at her for being a disagreeable sneak who never knew when she wasn't wanted and Livia's sympathy would evaporate as she broiled in humiliation.

She was twelve when she realized that the same could happen to her. That she, too, could marry a handsome, well-liked man and still be miserable.

That very same week Charlotte made her observation about Mrs. Gladwell.

Mrs. Gladwell was the widow of Sir Henry's cousin, a stylish, vivacious woman in her late thirties. She lived twenty miles away and occasionally called on the Holmes household. Mrs. Holmes didn't care for her. She sniffed whenever Mrs. Gladwell's name was brought up and deemed her "common." "Vulgar," even, sometimes. Sir Henry, however, always insisted that Mrs. Gladwell be made to feel welcome, since she was family.

Mrs. Gladwell spent part of the year in Torquay, a balmy seaside resort. Upon her return she would call upon the Holmes girls, gifts in tow. For that reason, even Henrietta, otherwise a reliable ally for Lady Holmes, couldn't disapprove of Mrs. Gladwell with any kind of sincerity.

In the course of that particular visit, Henrietta, who loved her wardrobe, received a chic new straw boater. To Livia, who wrote copiously in her diary, Mrs. Gladwell gave a handsome journal with an image of the Devon Coast on the cover and a bottle of novelty ink that was a beautiful lilac. And Charlotte, whose one true love was food, but whose diet Lady Holmes carefully watched for fear she would balloon to an unacceptable size, got a scrapbook of preserved seaweed, with dozens of delicate feather-like specimens ranging from pale green to robust maroon.

That evening, the girls were home alone with their governess, Sir Henry and Lady Holmes having gone out to dine at Squire Holyoke's. While Miss Lawton was supervising Bernadine at her bath—Bernadine suffered from occasional seizures and could not be left alone in a tub of water—Charlotte had taken Livia by the hand and pulled her into Sir Henry's study.

"We're not supposed to be here!" Livia had whispered, her heart thudding. She liked a minor dose of the forbidden as much as the next girl, but Henrietta was home and Henrietta lived to snitch.

"Henrietta is changing," said Charlotte.

"I guess that's all right then." Henrietta, at sixteen, dined with their parents when the latter were home and otherwise alone at the big table. She loved the ritual of changing into her dinner gown and could be counted on to spend forever coiffing her hair and trying on different petticoats until she found one that best complemented the shape of the dress. "But why are we here? What do you want to show me?"

Charlotte lifted a paperweight from Sir Henry's desk and held it out toward Livia.

"I've seen it." Livia, too, sometimes snooped around Sir Henry's study. "He got it from that place he went to in Norfolk on the trip with his classmates."

Twice a year Sir Henry went on a gentlemen-only excursion with old boys from Harrow. He'd returned from the latest one three days ago and Livia had peeked in on the paperweight when it was still sitting in a box that declared *A gift for you from Cromer is within.*

"Look closer," said Charlotte.

Charlotte was no longer the mute she'd once been, but still she didn't utter much beyond what was required, the "Morning, Vicar" variety and the occasional "How do you do?" to people she was meeting for the first time. So when she did speak, Livia paid attention.

She gazed down to the photographic image at the bottom of the glass paperweight, which depicted a large building, several stories tall. "Isn't this the hotel he stayed at when he was in Cromer?"

Charlotte pulled out a postcard from the pocket of her blue frock. "I found this in the book of preserved seaweeds."

On the postcard was a near replica of the image in the paperweight. *The Imperial Hotel, Torquay,* said the caption. Livia sucked in a breath. That Mrs. Gladwell had such a postcard was hardly surprising, since that was where she'd holidayed. But for Sir Henry to have come back from his trip with a keepsake smacking of Devon, when he should have been several hundred miles away on the coast of the North Sea . . .

"How did he get a souvenir from Torquay?"

"Either he was given one by someone who had been there or he was there himself."

"Why did he put it in a box that said it was from Cromer?"

"Why does Henrietta lie about finding a length of ribbon in her trunk when she bought it?"

Livia's stomach rolled over: It was because Henrietta knew she was doing something she wasn't supposed to.

"But what was Papa doing in Torquay? And why didn't he take us there with him?" Insight burst into Livia's head with the force of an explosion. "Good gracious! He was there with Mrs. Gladwell."

Charlotte didn't appear in the least surprised. Livia realized that her sister had already come to that conclusion and that was why she had wanted to show Livia the evidence.

"You mustn't tell Mamma, Charlotte. You understand?"

"I won't say anything, but I think Mamma knows. Or suspects, at least. You know she rifles through Papa's study, too, when he's not home."

Livia stared at Charlotte's round, pink-cheeked face, cherubic as ever. Was this why Lady Holmes so disliked Mrs. Gladwell? And dear God, did Sir Henry mean to leave this paperweight where Lady Holmes was sure to see it, and then have a postcard bearing the exact same image come into the house—something the girl who found it would probably display in her room—thereby rubbing his seaside holiday with his mistress in his wife's face?

Was *that* what Charlotte had wanted to tell Livia?

"Do you think he's in love with Mrs. Gladwell?"

Livia couldn't decide which would be worse, that their father loved someone else or that he was unfaithful to their mother with a woman he didn't even love.

"No," said Charlotte decisively. "Come here."

There was a box inside the bottom drawer of Sir Henry's desk, a box secured with a dark bronze, strange-looking lock, which Livia guessed to be some sort of Chinese antique. Its shape was a barrel formed by five rotating disks, which bore Chinese characters that had once been painted with gold lacquer but had now faded almost to the point of illegibility.

Livia knew about the box. She'd understood instinctively that the lock would open if she lined up the correct characters. But when she'd tried on a previous occasion, with their parents out of the house, she'd become frustrated after dozens of unsuccessful attempts.

Charlotte, however, peered at the lock and turned the disks one by one with great confidence.

"You tried enough times to find out the correct combination?" Livia marveled.

"No. Papa doesn't read Chinese any more than we do. If you look at the lock in strong light, you can see smudges of pencil marks around some of the characters. And when you line those up—"

Charlotte drew back the pin, set the lock aside, and held out the now open box to Livia.

The first thing Livia saw was a newspaper clipping, which announced Sir Henry's engagement to someone named Lady Amelia Drummond.

Next came a wedding invitation. "But this can't be right. The wedding was on—that's the day of Mamma and Papa's wedding. You don't suppose Mamma is secretly Lady Amelia Drummond?"

Charlotte shook her head and gestured Livia to lift the invitation. At the very bottom of the box lay a small photograph, of a young Sir Henry and a handsome and very superior-looking young lady who was most certainly not Lady Holmes.

Livia stared at the picture. "Did this Lady Amelia jilt Papa? And did he marry someone else on the original wedding day to spite her?"

Charlotte locked the box again and put it back carefully. Then she went to the door, peered out, and beckoned Livia to follow her. Once they had ascended the stairs to their room, Livia sat on the bed, her head in her hands, and tried to cope with the day's revelations.

"Do you think Mamma found out that he married her on the day he was supposed to marry Lady Amelia?"

"Yes."

"Before or after?"

Charlotte thought for a minute. "After."

That made sense. Lady Holmes's parents had been respectable but short on funds; without the means to afford a Season for their daughter, they might not have kept up with the flood of matrimonial news coming out of London.

Not to mention, Lady Holmes wouldn't be so disillusioned if she'd known what she was getting into in the first place.

"I wonder why Mamma doesn't have the equivalent of a Mrs. Gladwell. Do you think she wants to?"

At Charlotte's placid question, Livia bolted upright. "Have an affair? I've no idea if she wants to, but I'm sure Papa would be extremely cross if she were to."

"Why? He does it. And he doesn't seem at all ashamed about it."

"I can't explain it. I just know he'd be angry."

Charlotte considered this, her face as serene as that of an angel on a Christmas card. "That's not fair, is it?"

"Of course it's unfair but that's how it is."

"I don't like it."

"Neither do I. I hate it. But we have to live with it."

Charlotte was silent. Down the passage Henrietta's door opened. The heels of her evening slippers clicked forcefully as she descended to dinner.

"Must we?" asked Charlotte.

This question, somehow, shocked Livia more than the ones that preceded it. She tossed the postcard into the grate and set it on fire. "Yes, we must. There's nothing else to do but to live with it."

The matter of Sir Henry's romantic liaisons and their effect on Lady Holmes wasn't mentioned again until two years later, when Henrietta, at eighteen, became engaged before the end of her first Season.

Shortly afterward Livia and Charlotte met Mr. Cumberland, her fiancé. With every last ounce of her self-control, Livia managed not to roll her eyes during the encounter—Mr. Cumberland wasn't nearly as insufferable as Henrietta, but good gracious that man was dumb as a post.

"That poor idiot," she said to Charlotte as soon as they were alone.

Charlotte opened the drawer of her nightstand and took out her contraband, a large piece of plum pound cake that she'd smuggled out of the kitchen. "I agree."

Livia huffed. "Anybody willing to marry Henrietta has to be an idiot."

Charlotte nodded absently, her attention on the cake. Lady Holmes was unhappy that for all the restrictions placed on Charlotte's diet, the latter had not become any less tubby. Livia used to delight in the trafficking of buns and puddings for Charlotte, as much to defy her mother as to savor Charlotte's inexpressible joy as she sank her teeth into forbidden fruits. But lately Livia was beginning to be remorseful about her role as Charlotte's abettor and procurer: The prevailing fashion was unforgiving and Charlotte was going to be awfully uncomfortable in those whale-boned, steel-ribbed corsets the only purpose of which was to manhandle a woman's body into a wasp-waisted figure.

Well, provided that someday Charlotte could be persuaded to abandon her dedication to her blue broadcloth frock, the only dress she had worn for years, remade every eighteen months or so to accommodate for her growing height.

"Well, don't just assault your cake," Livia went on. "Tell me why *you* think Mr. Cumberland is an idiot."

It was possible to hold a minor conversation with Charlotte these days, if one was willing to prompt her at every turn. Charlotte didn't seem to mind being asked to speak, though she often volunteered to take Henrietta's shift with Bernadine: One didn't need to say anything, sitting with Bernadine. In fact, the opposite was true—the less one tried to talk to Bernadine, the less frustrating those sessions were.

"He doesn't lack for money," said Charlotte, "but the fit of his clothes is terrible—he clearly doesn't know how to choose a tailor. And he thinks one showy knot of the necktie makes up for bad shoes and trousers that are too short. Besides, his valet is robbing him blind."

"What?"

"The diamond on his stickpin is paste. Since he wouldn't have bought a paste stickpin, his valet probably sold the original and put in a cheap replica."

Livia had been half reclining on their bed. She leaped to the floor. "Shouldn't we tell Henrietta that he employs a thief?"

"Henrietta was the one who showed me how to tell a real diamond from paste," Charlotte said, as placid as she always was when she dropped these bombshell observations. "She knows. She'll make sure the valet's gone soon."

"But to knowingly accept a proposal from this moron—I almost feel sorry for Henrietta."

"Don't. He's exactly what she's been looking for. Henrietta isn't stupid. She isn't going to marry someone like Papa. She wants someone she can control and now she has one."

Livia grimaced. "Are we sure that he does have sufficient funds? Not like us—all appearances."

Charlotte had first pointed out, a year earlier, that Cook wasn't putting the correct amount of butter in her pound cake anymore, which led to the discovery that the allowance Cook had for purchasing ingredients had been significantly reduced. But it was Livia who took the audacious step of steaming open a letter for Sir Henry from his bank, and that was how they found out that the house was heavily mortgaged and their parents deep in debt.

(It was around the same time that Bernadine's nursemaid was let go and the task of keeping an eye on her fell to her sisters, whose governess was also relieved of her duties, with Lady Holmes declaring that the girls were old enough to not need one anymore.)

Livia, already disillusioned with her parents, became even more so: If they must make a mockery of their marriage, couldn't they at least be responsible stewards of their finances?

"Henrietta was careful," said Charlotte. "Remember when she and Mamma went on that two-day trip to visit Mamma's sick aunt— or so they said? I found punched tickets from their journey and the destinations weren't anywhere Mamma had relations. But Mr. Cumberland mentioned all those places today—locations for his family's holdings. That's what Mamma and Henrietta did—they investigated those holdings on the ground, to make sure they were in sound shape."

"Huh. I didn't give Henrietta enough credit."

"Henrietta has always been clever where her own interests are concerned."

"But she's still marrying an idiot," Livia flopped back down on the bed. "Though I suppose it's better to marry an idiot than someone who thinks you're an idiot."

Charlotte's attention returned to her cake. Livia stared at the ceiling, swarmed by pessimistic thoughts. She was startled when Charlotte spoke again, as much by the fact that Charlotte wished to continue their conversation as by Charlotte's actual question.

"You won't marry an idiot, will you?" asked Charlotte.

"I certainly hope not," Livia answered glumly. "Or at least with my eyes open if I do. What about you?"

"I don't want to marry."

"But how will you live? You know there won't be enough money to keep us as spinsters."

"I can earn money. If I were a boy, and there were no money in the family, wouldn't I be expected to have a profession?"

"Yes, but you aren't a boy. Mamma will have a fit at the idea of one of her daughters . . . working."

"Mamma doesn't need to agree."

Livia sighed. "You're deluding yourself if you think Papa will."

She was unsentimental about Sir Henry, since Sir Henry had no use for her. But Charlotte was his pet—he was vastly amused by her combination of great intelligence, great oddity, and great silence. He regularly took her for walks, just the two of them. He bought contraband sweets for her. And he read her his favorite poems and was tickled that she could immediately recite them back to him.

"What makes you think he won't?" asked Charlotte.

"The same reason I think he'd fly into a rage if he found Mamma having an affair. He might appear congenial, but he isn't at all liberal in his thinking. Keep that in mind."

Charlotte nodded, looking rather sadly at the empty plate before her.

It was the last time Livia saw Charlotte consume such a quantity of cake—or of any comestible, for that matter—in one sitting.

———— ❊ ————

The next few years brought a slew of unforeseen changes on Charlotte's part. For one, she began to take an active interest in her wardrobe—studying fashion plates, trying on different combinations of petticoats and stockings, accompanying Lady Holmes to browse selections of lace and feathers.

By extension, she paid far greater attention to her figure and stopped eating until she couldn't swallow another bite. The day she asked for a second helping of carrots and then forewent pudding at the end of the meal, Livia drew her aside and asked whether she was ill. Charlotte shook her head.

Much to Lady Holmes's relief, her youngest child also exerted a heroic effort in the direction of small talk. Instead of startling and discomfiting visitors with such comments as "I see you no longer write in your journal" or "I'm sorry the trip to Bath wasn't as successful as you'd hoped it would be," she learned to smile, nod, and chat about the weather.

This last was not accomplished without trial and error. In the beginning she had a tendency to correct old squires' exclamations of "We haven't had so much rain since I was a boy in short breeches" by quoting concrete records from the parish registers, which demonstrated that there had been far greater precipitation a mere five years ago. It was after a fair bit of practice and no shortage of awkwardness that she at last grasped the point of all that persiflage, which was merely to avoid the silence of people having nothing to say to one another.

The uncomfortable silence, in other words. But since there was no such thing as an uncomfortable silence for Charlotte, it was as difficult for her to understand as it was for a man with vertigo to master the Viennese polka.

Sometimes, as Livia stood beside her, perspiring on her behalf and making every attempt to convey the correct response via telepathy, it struck her how much Charlotte resembled a foreigner who found native customs baffling and, on occasion, patently ridiculous. One time, in the middle of reading a magazine article about the possibility of life on Mars, it occurred to Livia that Charlotte was more akin to an interplanetary alien: It wasn't only the habits and conventions of the English she found perplexing, but that of all humanity.

But eventually Charlotte cleared that hurdle. She not only learned the stark difference between asking after an old lady's cold versus her problem with incontinence, she became adept at navigating these formerly treacherous shoals, even though Livia could tell, at times, that she was herding a situation through an internal algorithm, trying to generate an appropriate response.

But overall, her transformation appeared complete. The little girl who insisted on wearing the same dress year in and year out had been replaced by a young lady in ruffles and plumage. Instead of the *Encyclopedia Britannica*, she now read *Burke's Peerage* and *Cornhill Magazine*. And while she never slimmed to an elegant svelteness—she retained a hint of a double chin and the buttons of her bodice always seemed in danger of popping open—her tendency toward plumpness worked very well with her wide eyes and rosy cheeks.

She wasn't beautiful, but she was darling. People responded to her the way they would a nursery rhyme character all grown up and come to life. Boys and young men became tongue-tied, their eyes busily darting from her pink, pillowy lips to the firm rise of her breasts.

Livia was half envious of this response her little sister evoked from the gentlemen and half . . . mournful. Who was this girl swaddled in flounces, who put honey on her face and coconut oil in her hair? What had happened to the Charlotte Livia remembered, that noted odd duck who was the only person with whom Livia felt comfortable, the only person Livia trusted?

And then, the day before they were to leave for London for their first Season together, Charlotte said to Livia, "I spoke with Papa today."

They were walking in the fields on the outskirts of the village. The day was sunny but still cool. The countryside was a fresh, sparkling green. And Charlotte's cream-colored dress, dainty with lace and passementerie, offered an impossibly pretty contrast against this backdrop of brightly lit nature.

Livia was feeling downhearted at the likelihood that the new Charlotte would swim in proposals by the end of the Season. Livia's chances on the matrimonial mart were nowhere as favorable. She was a misanthrope—rare was the man or woman who didn't deeply disappoint her. That was bad enough for a young lady, but to make matters even worse she was a misanthrope who didn't know how to pretend not to be one.

If Charlotte were to accept a proposal, Livia would be left all alone at home.

She sighed. "What did you and Papa talk about?"

"Do you remember the day we met Mr. Cumberland? I said I didn't want to marry."

"You told Papa you don't want to marry *today*, right before we are to leave for London?"

"No, I spoke to him the day after we met Mr. Cumberland."

Livia blinked. That would have been five years ago.

"I told him I did not think the institution of marriage would suit me very well. I said I wished to look into other means of livelihood."

"And what did he say?"

"He said that he believed I was too young to make any permanent decisions. He encouraged me to look into aspects of being a girl that I hadn't explored at the time—fashion, etc.—to experience more fully the traditional path for a woman before I rejected it altogether."

This sounded shockingly reasonable and wise—Livia could scarcely believe they were talking about Sir Henry.

"I did as he asked. As it turns out, fashion is rather enjoyable. And so is talking to people—amazing how much they'll tell you if you only inquire. And I imagine there should be something interesting to a London Season as well. But none of it changed my mind about marriage, since none of it changed the economic and political equation that is marriage. I do not like the idea of bartering the use of my reproductive system for a man's support—not in the absence of other choices."

Livia's eyes bulged. The old Charlotte had never gone anywhere; she'd been but reupholstered in fine muslin and a jauntily angled hat! Livia was ashamed that this simple camouflage had fooled her completely.

"And you told him that?"

"That he already knows. What I told him today was that I'd settled on a choice of career: I believe I will make a fine headmistress at a girls' school. If I achieve that position at a reputable school, I can earn as much as five hundred pounds a year."

Livia sucked in a breath. "That much?"

"Yes. But I cannot become a headmistress overnight. I must attend school, undertake the required training, and then work my way up the ranks. I asked Papa to foot the expenses until I can pay him back."

"And he is amenable to it?"

"Our agreement is that I will wait until I'm twenty-five. If by then I still haven't found anyone I wish to marry, then yes, he will sponsor my schooling."

Livia was flabbergasted. "I can't believe it."

"He gave his word as a gentleman."

A man's word was no trifling matter, so Livia shook her head. She supposed she must believe now that Sir Henry had made a serious promise. "But it'll be a long time before you turn twenty-five, almost eight years. Anything could happen in the meanwhile. You could fall in love."

"That's what Papa is counting on, no doubt. But romantic love is . . . I don't wish to say that romantic love itself is a fraud—I'm sure the feelings it inspires are genuine enough, however temporary. But the way it's held up as this pristine, everlasting joy every woman ought to strive for—when in fact love is more like beef brought over from Argentina on refrigerated ships: It might stay fresh for a while under carefully controlled conditions, but sooner or later its qualities will begin to degrade. Love is by and large a perishable good and it is lamentable that young people are asked to make irrevocable, till-death-do-we-part decisions in the midst of a short-lived euphoria."

Livia's jaw hung open. She, too, had doubts about love and marriage, but they centered largely around her fear of coming across as arrogant and off-putting to potential suitors—and on whether she'd be able to choose better than Lady Holmes had. It had yet to occur to her to form large-scale judgments on the entire system.

"But what about the Cummingses? They've been married thirty years and they're still happy with each other."

"And there are the Archibalds and the Smalls, too. But we mustn't be sentimental about the success of those marriages. We must look at it mathematically, the number of long-term happily married couples in proportion to all married couples. By my estimation that comes to less than twenty percent among our acquaintances. Will you bet on that kind of odds?"

Livia blinked several times. "I take it you won't."

"Those wouldn't be bad odds at all if we were at a horse race. And they aren't such terrible odds if we consider that the prize is decades of contented companionship. My problem lies with the stake I'm required to put up: my entire lifetime. Not to mention, unless I bury my husband or divorce him, I can play only once. And of course if I were to divorce my husband, my parents can never show their faces anywhere again—I'll have effectively done them in, too. So, no. Given the exorbitant costs and constraints, I am not willing to take this gamble."

She tugged at Livia. Belatedly, Livia realized that they'd come to a stop some time ago and that she stood in the way of an oncoming dogcart. She allowed Charlotte to guide her to the edge of the dirt lane and nodded mechanically at the village doctor who drove past, tipping his hat.

"I take it you plan to wait for your twenty-fifth birthday, then thumb your nose at society and go to school," she said, when they resumed walking again.

"More or less. Papa asked me to make a good-faith effort to let a man sweep me off my feet and I've agreed. But I don't know why he thinks I'll weigh contributing factors differently when I'm off my feet. Sometimes I feel I must conclude that Papa doesn't know me at all."

That was a deduction that needed no comment. It was Livia's opinion that Sir Henry still viewed Charlotte as an amusing oddity— or at least still hoped she'd return to being such if he ignored her radical thinking long enough. And it certainly didn't help matters that Charlotte looked as she did, so emphatically, and one might even say extravagantly feminine, all rotundity and softness, not a sharp angle anywhere.

"Well," said Livia, "I've heard that kissing does affect a lady's thinking."

"I've been kissed. It's very nice, but I—"

"*What?* Who kissed you? When? And where?"

"It was several years ago. But I've pledged to never divulge the gentleman's name—which means I also can't tell you where the kiss took place, since that would narrow the list of likely candidates."

Several years ago? Charlotte would have been only thirteen or fourteen at the time. "You never said a thing!"

"You never asked."

"I—" Livia decided she had better shut up before she blurted out that she could scarcely have wondered whether Charlotte was kissing boys when she had half suspected Charlotte had been sent from Mars to investigate the cultural observances of Earthlings. "How did it happen? Did it take you by surprise?"

"Not at all. I set it in motion."

"Charlotte! Were you in love?"

"No, I wanted to know what it felt like."

"But how did you pick the boy? Surely you didn't draw a name out of a hat." Livia gasped. "Or *did* you?"

"I didn't do that. But I can't reveal the circumstances that led me to choose him, since that would also give clues to his identity."

Livia tried a few more times, but Charlotte remained amiably tight-lipped. Livia gave up. "Look at you. You had a 'very nice' kiss—*and* you've got a plan of action for your life. That makes me feel completely aimless."

"Usually one feels aimless because one isn't sure yet what one wants—until one does, a proper strategy can't be formulated." Charlotte studied Livia a moment. "But in your case, it's possible you know exactly what you want, but you're afraid to want it, let alone pursue it."

Livia swallowed. She didn't ask Charlotte what or how she knew; she didn't say anything at all. They walked in silence the rest of the way.

As they approached the house, Livia wrapped her arm around Charlotte's shoulders. "What if everything Papa promised was only to mollify you temporarily? It gives me no pleasure to say this, but our father isn't terribly farsighted—he'd be happy to postpone a problem for another day, let alone another eight years. What if when the time comes, he reneges on his word?"

"I don't know. Not yet, in any case—I'll have plenty of time to consider my response." Charlotte took Livia's hand in her own. "But if our father should prove a man of his word and sponsor the necessary education and training for me to earn a living, will you allow me to do the same for you in return?"

Livia squeezed Charlotte's hand, suddenly close to tears. Charlotte seldom initiated physical contact—this was as solemn an offer as the queen could make standing in the middle of Westminster Abbey.

"Yes," she said. "Yes, please do."

She allowed herself to be briefly carried away by visions of this impossible future, two sisters, united in a most gratifying independence.

Would they have a little cottage? Or a nice, spacious suite of rooms at the girls' school that Charlotte would direct? She could see them sipping tea together on Sunday afternoons, Charlotte with a plate of her beloved plum cake in front of her, looking out to a small garden reserved for their private use.

It was a more appealing future than any she'd imagined yet.

But pessimist that she was, she couldn't let the occasion pass without a word of caution. "Remember, Charlotte, Papa doesn't like women. He'd feel a lot more hesitation breaking his word to a man—but you aren't a man."

"He had one fiancée who jilted him because of his character flaws. And the woman he married to spite the fiancée dislikes him because he used her with little regard for her feelings. What reason does he have to dislike all women? Does he disdain all men because his father was an ass and his solicitor made a soup of his affairs?"

"By your standards it isn't rational, I know. But you can't expect to be treated rationally when you are a woman, Charlotte. I can't explain why—that's just how it is. And you must learn to accept it."

Charlotte was quiet. Livia thought that perhaps for once, she'd put some sense into her little sister's head. But as they walked back into the house, Charlotte turned to her and said, "I will try to understand why. But I will not learn to accept it. Never."

—❈—

Livia had long suspected that Sir Henry would not hold to his promise. And yet when it happened, when he broke his pledge, she was far angrier than her sister.

"It's unconscionable, what he did. To lie to you so baldly, to ask you to act in good faith when he hadn't the slightest intention of upholding his end of the bargain—" She sputtered, unable to go on.

Charlotte sat at the edge of their bed, the slow tapping of her fingertips on the bedpost the only sign of her agitation.

After a long minute, Charlotte said, "My timing was less than ideal. I didn't know it before I spoke to him, but Lady Amelia Drummond was found dead this morning. Papa was in a minor state."

Livia's hand came up to her throat. "Oh."

Charlotte played with a bow on her skirt. "This isn't to say that he would have kept his word otherwise. If he meant to keep his word, he would have, whether or not Lady Amelia still breathed. But had there been any vacillation on his part, any remote chance that he might have changed his mind at the last minute . . . as I said , my timing wasn't ideal."

"Will you ask him again?"

"Do you think that would be any use?"

"No."

"Neither do I."

"Then what are you going to do?" Livia was fuming again. "Please tell me you won't swallow this appalling deceit. Papa will feel no remorse. He will only be endlessly smug that he got away with this kind of disgraceful chicanery."

Charlotte wrapped her hands around the bedpost. If it were Livia, she'd be imagining the bedpost to be Sir Henry's throat. But Charlotte retained her usual tranquility as she replied, "No, I won't let it pass without a suitable response."

"Good!" cried Livia. Then, a little less certainly, "But what kind of response would do the trick? How can you both punish him and still extract the necessary funds for your education?"

"I have an idea. I will think about it."

"Can I be of help?"

"It'll be best if I handle it myself."

Livia was taken aback. "You aren't going to—you aren't going to put arsenic in his tea or anything like that, are you?"

"No, of course not. Besides, his death would offer no financial advantage to us at all. That's when his creditors will pounce. Mamma will have to sell the house to satisfy them and I will not receive a penny for my education."

"Then what?"

"I'll tell you when it's done."

A chill ran down Livia's spine: Her sister could be ruthless in her own way. "Will you at least tell me when you'll implement this diabolical plan of yours?"

"Soon. Within weeks, I should think."

Livia took Charlotte by the shoulders. "Don't do anything you'll regret."

Charlotte's lips stretched into a smile that did not reach her eyes. "Would that someone had given Papa that warning."

—⁂—

In the following days, Livia pestered Charlotte for more details about The Plan. But Charlotte only smiled, shook her head, and carried on as usual. It was the Season, with its attendant rounds of afternoon garden parties and evening dances. The whirl of merrymaking, however, had long ago lost what little appeal it had for Livia: The ultimate purpose of this yearly assembly wasn't fun and games; it was for unmarried ladies to find husbands and married ones to jostle for social prominence.

Livia wouldn't say she'd never met any gentlemen who appealed to her. But those of lofty enough qualities to interest her never seemed to be interested *in* her. And those who did bother to pay attention to her failed to spark the least reciprocal warmth on her part.

A sorry outcome, to say the least. After Charlotte's thoroughly unromantic analysis of the institution of marriage, Livia had been on guard against runaway emotions that might lead to regrettable choices. But this resolute *lack* of runaway emotions was dispiriting in its own way. One ought to fall in love at least once, oughtn't one? If only to understand what Elizabeth Barrett Browning had meant when she'd written, *The face of all the world is changed, I think / Since first I heard the footsteps of thy soul.*

Yet this common, practically universal experience evaded Livia everywhere she went. And of course for her mother, Livia's failure to garner a single proposal in seven and a half Seasons was a shameful burden to bear, a burden that Livia must hear of weekly, sometimes daily.

Lady Holmes's latest tirade lasted the entirety of their ride home—they were alone in the carriage, it being Charlotte's afternoon at the Reading Room of the British Museum, and the brougham was stuck in one of London's horrible traffic logjams that took an hour to clear. Livia was exhausted by the time she escaped to her room. She feared she was coming dangerously close to the point when she would begin to encourage anyone, anyone at all, with a matrimonial interest in her—to get away from her mother, if nothing else.

If Charlotte would only succeed somehow in her endeavor. But every passing day sapped Livia's confidence that any good would come of Sir Henry's betrayal, that Charlotte would somehow rise triumphantly, phoenixlike, from the ashes of her hopes.

The sound of metal tires coming to a stop drew her to a window. Charlotte usually walked home from the British Museum and the hour for ordinary calls was well past. Who could be pulling up to their front door?

An unfamiliar town coach disgorged Charlotte, followed by . . . what in the world was Charlotte doing with the Dowager Baroness Shrewsbury? Lady Shrewsbury was the last person who would set foot in the Reading Room, so Charlotte couldn't possibly have met her there. And even if she had, ever since Charlotte had turned down a marriage proposal from Lady Shrewsbury's son, Lady Shrewsbury had been chilly toward the Holmeses, finding it an outrage that a girl from a family of lesser pedigree and standing had decreed her Roger to be not nearly good enough.

From her vantage point, Livia hadn't been able to see Charlotte's face properly, but something in her posture didn't feel right. Livia opened the door of their bedroom, but there was no indication that Charlotte was coming upstairs. What could Lady Shrewsbury possibly want with Charlotte?

Below, her parents were headed for the parlor, exchanging whispered words with each other, sounding just as baffled as to Lady Shrewsbury's presence: After all, Roger was now married—all the baroness's sons were married—so she couldn't have good news to announce involving Charlotte and any kinsman of hers.

They entered the parlor. Lady Shrewsbury's voice called firmly for the door to be closed. She also instructed the footman that there would be no need for tea. Livia's heart dropped a few rungs. What was going on?

She took a deep breath, tiptoed down the stairs, and sidled as quietly as she could to the door of the parlor.

". . . an absolute disgrace. What girls these days think I have no idea. To turn down Roger's proposal, only to indulge in a shameless affair with him six years later—as an unmarried woman, no less!"

Livia covered her mouth. Dear God, no. This couldn't possibly have been Charlotte's response to Sir Henry. Lady Shrewsbury raged on, her words sloshing in and out Livia's hearing, a tide of undifferentiated syllables, carrying no meaning except wrath and ruin.

At some point Lady Shrewsbury stopped and Sir Henry spoke, his words too soft for Livia to hear. Lady Shrewsbury laughed derisively. "Keep it from spreading? No, my good sir, that horse has bolted the barn. By dinnertime tonight everyone in London will know what your daughter has been caught doing today. But even if that weren't the case, *I* would make sure that she is shunned from every respectable drawing room in the land. Her conduct is beyond the pale and no good family should tolerate any association with a girl of such abominably loose morals."

"My daughter has committed an unforgivable sin," said Sir Henry, his voice tight yet defeated. "But has your son fared any better? No gentleman would take up with an unmarried young lady from a good family. Does he not share some of the blame?"

"He does." Lady Shrewsbury sounded as if she were speaking through a mouthful of sand. "And he will hear from his wife and myself. But men are creatures of unbound lust. It is the duty of good women to keep them in check. For your daughter to lure my son from home and hearth, for her to—"

Livia turned and ran back upstairs, so that she wouldn't kick in the door, grip Lady Shrewsbury by the front of her bodice, and start screaming. What luring of her son from home and hearth? Roger Shrewsbury already kept a mistress in St. John's Wood. Had kept a string of mistresses there over the years, one of the reason Charlotte turned him down.

In the room she shared with Charlotte Livia paced, her footsteps heavy and frantic. She sat down for a while, rocking back and forth at the edge of a chair, before leaping up to pace again. When Lady Shrewsbury drove off in her carriage, she rushed downstairs, only to find the parlor door still closed and her mother shouting inside.

Ever since she'd been waiting for Lady Holmes to stop yelling.

At last a small silence fell. Lady Holmes trudged to a chair at the far end of the room and sank into it with a graceless *whomp*. Charlotte sat, very primly, with her hands folded together in her lap. Her face was splotchy with Lady Holmes's hand marks and her coiffure appeared slightly askew, as if missing a few pins that would have better kept it in place. But otherwise she looked calm and collected, not at all like a woman about to be shunned by everyone she'd ever met.

Did she understand what had happened?

Or had this been her plan from the very beginning?

Sir Henry spoke for the first time since Lady Shrewsbury's departure. "Is this what you intended, Charlotte, to bring discredit and reproach upon the entire family?"

Is this your retaliation for my failure to keep my word?

Or at least that was what Livia heard.

Charlotte looked in Livia's direction, as if she knew exactly who was on the other side of the door and what questions tumbled about in Livia's head. "No. My plan involved no publicity whatsoever. Despite my longstanding wish to seek education and respectable employment, despite promises some in this room have made to me, in the end it became clear that I was not to be allowed any path except matrimony, which is an eminently unsuitable choice for me. So I decided to take the logical next step: remove my maidenhead and therefore nullify my marital eligibility."

Lady Holmes leaped to her feet. "But that is the most stupid, absurd, and—"

"Lady Holmes, we have heard enough from you today," Sir Henry growled. "Charlotte, continue."

"I needed a man. Moreover, I needed a man who cannot be compelled to marry me, therefore a married man. This presented some difficulty, as most married gentlemen I know would refuse me on grounds of either principle or caution. So I had to settle for someone who is both amoral and somewhat reckless.

"Mr. Shrewsbury fit my criteria perfectly. Unfortunately, he is also an idiot. Yesterday evening he returned home roaring drunk from a birthday celebration, mistook his wife for his mistress, and proceeded to tell her all about our agreement, time and venue included."

Lady Holmes gasped loudly. "But that is reprehensible. Why did not Mrs. Shrewsbury or Lady Shrewsbury come to us then, so that we could prevent your execrably ill-considered plan from going forward?"

"Why indeed? But you need not be so outraged, Mamma: You would have done the same thing, keeping the intelligence quiet until such a time when you could appear with a regular jury box of witnesses to catch the offending couple in flagrante delicto."

"I— You— It is—" Lady Holmes sputtered. "Oh, I see. You don't think you did anything wrong, Miss Charlotte, do you? Are you so selfish that you cannot think beyond yourself? Who will marry Livia now, with the family's reputation dragged through mud?"

Livia had to restrain herself from throttling her mother. Charlotte's life had been ruined. Would no one think of *her*? What would *she* do for the rest of her life?

"Well, you will have plenty of time to contemplate it now!" Lady Holmes's voice was once again climbing rapidly in pitch and volume. "You'll spend the rest of your life in the back cottage at home. No one will call on you. No one will write you. No one will care in the least whether you live or die."

"Yes, I suppose," said Charlotte softly, almost inaudibly.

Livia couldn't control herself anymore. She threw open the door. "Charlotte!"

Charlotte rose, a wan smile on her face. "Livia."

Livia ran to her sister and embraced her. "Oh, Charlotte. What a horrible day."

"For her?" said Lady Holmes sharply. "It is you who will pay the price for her infamy."

"You think I give a farthing for that?" Livia took her sister by the elbow. "Come upstairs, Charlotte. I'll ring for a tray of tea. You must be hungry."

"You won't take her anywhere. I am not finished with her."

"Yes, you are. For the rest of the evening, at least."

Lady Holmes wore an almost comical look of surprise. Livia was the Holmes daughter most likely to scowl, but she was rarely openly disobedient.

Taking advantage of her mother's momentary stupefaction, Livia made off with Charlotte.

Three

Inspector Treadles had first heard of the name Sherlock Holmes two years earlier.

The Treadleses had joined Lord Ingram for a dig on the Isles of Scilly—it never failed to surprise Treadles that he was affiliated with a man of such elevated circumstances, but their friendship was as warm as it was unlikely.

The excursion had been an especially good one, the days balmy and clear, the landscape a heart-stopping green against a shallow sea that was almost turquoise at times. At each meal, the companions luxuriated in conversation and camaraderie. And late at night, conversation and camaraderie continued in private between the inspector and his wife in their tent, augmented by tender lovemaking.

The pearls came up one evening.

Not long before, at Easter dinner with his wife's family, Mr. Barnaby Cousins, Treadles's brother-in-law, had complained bitterly about a pair of expensive earrings he had bought for his wife and which had disappeared ten days prior, shortly before Mrs. Cousins dismissed her maid. Mr. Cousins simply could not understand why the matter hadn't been handed to the police.

"If a servant steals a spoon," he had thundered, "you dismiss her without a letter of character. Those pearls cost a fortune! Of course one never wants one's door darkened by a constable, but this one could have used the service entrance and the housekeeper could have taken care of the matter."

Remembering himself, Mr. Cousins had nodded stiffly at Treadles, then still only a sergeant. "Present company excepted, of course."

"Of course," Treadles had replied.

Mr. Cousins berated his wife for another five minutes. Treadles would have had more sympathy for Mrs. Cousins if she weren't as disagreeable as her husband—and he'd have forgotten the matter if Alice, his wife, hadn't commented later how odd it was that Mrs. Cousins hadn't turned to the law.

"She abhors any hint of criminality on the part of staff. I would have expected her to at least have said something to me, in order that word would reach your ear. And I did visit at the time—remember? She was so upset Barnaby demanded that I call on her."

Lord Ingram, as was his wont, listened carefully to their account. Two nights later, he asked Alice whether Mrs. Cousins frequently suspected wrongdoing on the part of her staff.

"And how," answered Alice. "I should hate to be in service in her house."

"You wouldn't by any chance have noticed any strong odors when you visited her, shortly after the disappearance of the earrings?"

Alice leaned back in surprise. "Now that you mention it, I do remember thinking that my sister-in-law's rooms smelled pungently sour. But how did you know that, my lord?"

"*I* hadn't the least inkling, Mrs. Treadles," replied Lord Ingram, a rather mysterious expression on his face. "But I know someone named Holmes, who enjoys such little puzzles. I sent a note—with all references to names and locales redacted of course—and a reply came today with these questions to ask."

"How interesting. Will you now write back to Mr. Holmes with the answers to his questions?"

Lord Ingram's eyes gleamed. "That will not be necessary. Holmes had instructed that should the answers to both questions be yes, I may go ahead and tell you that it is Holmes's theory that Mrs. Cousins's suspicions got the better of her sense. More specifically, she became convinced that her maid had stolen her precious pearls and replaced them with a pair of replicas, French imitations which are said to be able to fool the eyes of an expert. To prove that it was indeed the case, she dropped the earrings into a container filled with hot vinegar—ergo the odor in her rooms—because paste pearls would not dissolve in vinegar."

Alice gasped. "And the pearls must have dissolved, fully or partially, which proved her maid's innocence but destroyed the expensive earrings!"

"No wonder she needed to take to her bed!" exclaimed Treadles. "And no wonder she couldn't have her maid charged with any crime when her own stupidity was her undoing."

"Oh but she did dismiss the poor woman without a letter of character. After seven years of service!" Alice set her hand on her husband's sleeve. "We must find her so that I may provide a letter of character for her—and to amend for my sister-in-law's unkindness."

"Consider it done, my dear." Treadles turned back to Lord Ingram. "But this Holmes fellow is marvelous."

"Holmes's mind has always been a thing of beauty," said Lord Ingram with a slight smile.

Two months later, while dining out with Lord Ingram in town, Alice related a tragic but curious case that came to her via her physician, Dr. Motley, who had learned of it many years ago from a colleague. The colleague had attended a prominent family. The daughter of the house, who was about fourteen at the time, had suffered for a while from a deep melancholia. One morning, by all appearances, she passed away peacefully in her sleep. The parents, though devastated, believed it to have been an act of God, that their child was now in a much better place. The family physician, however, could not bring himself to put faith in such a fairytale.

He dared not voice his thoughts aloud to the parents, but did confide in Motley his suspicion that the girl had committed suicide, even though he couldn't find any evidence to that effect. She had on occasion taken a sip of her mother's laudanum to help her sleep, but the draught was always measured out carefully by the mother, drop by drop. No empty bottles of morphine or chloral lay by the girl's bedside. No signs of suffering or struggle that would have betrayed the involvement of arsenic or cyanide. She had said good night to her parents a perfectly healthy young woman and in the morning they had found themselves sobbing over her inert body.

"Perhaps your friend Holmes can solve this terrible riddle, my lord," Alice had said to Lord Ingram.

The next evening Inspector Treadles received a note from Lord Ingram. He had a question from Holmes. Was soda water made on the premises for the consumption of the household?

As it so happened, Alice, calling on her father, whose health was deteriorating, had run into Motley the following day. She took the opportunity to pose the question. A surprised Motley had answered in the affirmative: Yes, he believed that the staff at the house did procure canisters of liquid carbon dioxide to make soda water.

Treadles passed on the intelligence to Lord Ingram. An answer came in due time. According to Holmes, as relayed by Lord Ingram, the girl had died of self-inflicted hypercapnia. When liquid carbon dioxide evaporated, the process dramatically lowered the surrounding temperature, so that some of the liquid carbon dioxide froze into a solid—a phenomenon someone in the house might have shown her.

On the night of her death she could have replicated that process, smuggled the resulting solid pieces to her room, and then, when she was drowsy from the laudanum, set the frozen carbon dioxide on her bed and drawn the bed curtains. In the morning there would have been no trace of the frozen gas, which would have sublimated completely in the intervening hours, suffocating her in the process. And if any excess carbon dioxide had been in the air, it would have dissipated by the maid opening the door, the windows, and the bed curtains.

"But why?" Treadles exclaimed after he'd read the note. "Why go to such extraordinary lengths?"

"So that her parents would think exactly as they did, that their daughter perished by the will of God, and not her own hand," said his wife sadly.

They held on to each other for a while. At the end of this silence, Alice murmured, "Do you think, my dear, that Holmes is perhaps not a real person, but an entity Lord Ingram made up so that he wouldn't intimidate us with his vastly superior intelligence?"

"That is brilliant, my dear. Why have I not thought of it before?"

"Oh, because it's brilliant?" She laughed. He pulled her to him for an affectionate kiss.

Mere weeks after that Treadles plucked up his courage and wrote to Lord Ingram to request help from "Holmes." His career was on a healthy path. Had he married a woman of his own social class, he would have been content to let promotions come in time. But Alice had given up a life of luxury to become his wife. He was never going to be a rich man; the least he could do was to become highly successful and respected in his profession—in as little time as possible—and make her proud.

The case in question concerned a body discovered aboard a P&O liner that had set sail from Port Said. The passenger was identified as an Egyptologist named Rendell. He had been dead at least a day and by his side was a note that, according to his family and friends, was most certainly written in his own hand.

The note read,

The curse of the pharaohs is real. Wilkinson has leapt overboard in a fit of madness and now I feel its grip on me. A darkness descends. I can't breathe. Can no one help me?

The mummies that had been brought back in the cargo did not look particularly menacing to Treadles, as far as mummies went. And the sarcophagi that contained them seemed pedestrian, remarkable in neither beauty nor worth.

One of the ship's officers recalled that approximately thirty-six hours before the steamer's arrival in Southampton, an agitated Rendell had demanded that the vessel be turned around to search for his friend. He declared that Wilkinson had been in a state ever since Gibraltar and had remained confined to his room, shaking in terror at the mummies' specters. But now he was nowhere to be found and Rendell was convinced he was bobbing in the Atlantic.

The officer had pointed out that Wilkinson might have been nothing more than seasick. And perhaps, having recovered, he had taken to shipboard society with fervor, to make up for lost time. It was scarcely unheard of for passengers to be found inebriated in nooks and crannies—or in the company of friendly widows. Rendell, miffed that his concern wasn't taken seriously, stormed off. And the officer was now experiencing remorse. Perhaps he ought to have believed the poor man.

Treadles was not one to dismiss the supernatural out of hand, but neither was he convinced that malevolent spirits lingered for millennia, waiting to ambush hapless Egyptologists.

He sent Rendell's body to the coroner and laid out the facts of the case for Lord Ingram to pass on to Holmes. A response came the next day.

Dear Inspector,

I have received the following from Holmes, quoted verbatim.

It is possible there is more than one intrigue at play.

The first involves a deception. Two young men set out for Egypt with high hopes of a tremendous find. They returned with sadly ordinary artifacts. There would be no fame and fortune waiting in England, only the disappointment of fathers who had financed the expedition. What to do? Ah, yes, the curse of the pharaohs. If they could stage something dramatic——Rendell comatose and Wilkinson missing——the public might be intrigued enough to pay to see those objects, the removal of which incited the wrath of the spirits.

Rendell's conversation with the ship's officer was clearly meant to give the impression that Wilkinson had leapt overboard. Since no one saw that happen, the possibilities are twofold: One, Wilkinson disembarked in Gibraltar; two, he did so at Southampton.

The likelihood is that Wilkinson remained on the ship to tamper with the draught Rendell was to take. Rendell went to his death in blithe ignorance of his friend's treachery. Wilkinson then disembarked with the rest of the crowd, before Rendell was found dead.

As for why Wilkinson cooked up this entire elaborate scheme to do away with Rendell, since no financial trouble or professional jealousy has been mentioned, let us say, Cherchez la femme.

Wish you success in your endeavor,
Ashburton

The dead man's fiancée turned out to be a very beautiful young woman. Wilkinson was found in Southampton, waiting for an opportune moment to pretend to have lately reached England. And Holmes was almost exactly right about how it had been done, except that the curse of the pharaoh had been Rendell's idea, which Wilkinson co-opted for his own purpose.

The case had firmly secured the favor of his superiors for Treadles and he had very much wished to thank Holmes. But Lord Ingram had refused all offers of gratitude on Holmes's behalf. "Holmes wants only an occupied mind. Everything else is secondary."

"What does Holmes do then, when there aren't perplexing riddles to be solved?"

"You do not wish to know," said Lord Ingram. And then, after a moment, "Perhaps I should have said, '*I* do not wish to know.'"

An answer that did nothing to dispel Inspector Treadles's conviction that Lord Ingram and Holmes were most likely one and the same.

Since then, he had consulted Holmes, via Lord Ingram, two more times, still surprised on each occasion by the resolute agility of the mind on the other end of the correspondence. Holmes was becoming— had become, if Treadles were entirely honest with himself—an institution in his life.

A venerated institution.

And now that institution had crumbled.

Treadles pushed aside the evening newspapers littering his desk and pinched the bridge of his nose. He'd found no article about any Holmes suffering from a carriage mishap, a tumble into the Thames, or a botched medical procedure. A discreet inquiry to his colleagues had yielded similarly barren results: no dispute taken too far, robbery gone wrong, or attempted murder that left a man in a deep coma.

For that had to be it, hadn't it, a deep coma? What else could

Lord Ingram possibly mean by Holmes being alive, yet completely beyond his reach?

His wife, in a lilac dressing gown printed with a paisley pattern, came into the room. "Nothing, eh?"

He shook his head. "Nothing."

Alice sighed. "Poor Mr. Holmes. Whatever could the matter be?"

Treadles could only continue to shake his head. As an investigator, he had decent instincts. And his instincts told him that he was in the wilderness with regard to the misfortunes of Mr. Sherlock Holmes, not even near the right track, let alone following it.

"And I've certainly been put into my place," Alice went on, "given that Lord Ingram and Mr. Holmes aren't remotely the same person."

"Well, I for one thought your hypothesis was remarkably elegant. It really is too bad that sometimes inconvenient facts surface to thumb their noses at remarkably elegant hypotheses."

"Poo to inconvenient facts." She came around and laid a hand on his shoulder. With her other hand she turned the pages of the papers. "Ludwig the second of Bavaria found dead. Fire destroys nearly one thousand buildings in Vancouver, British Columbia. What an age we live in—bad news from the entire world delivered right to our doorsteps."

She selected a different paper. "Not that news from home is much better. Recriminations over the failure of the Irish Home Rule bill. Police still looking for suspects in the fire in Lambeth that destroyed a building and killed two."

"I know about that building in Lambeth," said Treadles. "Every last inspector in Scotland Yard got letters about it—and it isn't even a copper hell, but a bookmaker's. You close one down and it opens right back up two streets over."

She flipped a page. "Even society news is no help: Lord Sheridan's birthday celebration canceled due to a death in the family."

"It would be a newspaper that turns no profit if it reported only fires that didn't burn any houses and parties that took place as expected." Treadles kissed the palm of her hand. "Fortunately for me, whenever I see the mistress of my household, I feel as if I have received an abundance of good news."

She smiled. "Ah, Inspector Treadles. I do love you. Come, lay aside the mysterious fate of Mr. Sherlock Holmes for the moment. For you know this much flattery will lead nowhere, sir, except straight to the marriage bed."

Inspector Treadles needed no further prompting to serve his lady.

Four

"Thank God for Great Aunt Maribel," Livia said thickly.

Great Aunt Maribel, a spinster, had lived to be eighty-three. When she died, she left Livia an entire crate of her own creative endeavors—embroidery, glazed pottery, and watercolor paintings, all amateurish work that displayed little talent and even less effort. Livia, unpacking the crate, had grown increasingly dismayed: Was this really how life was lived for a spinster, full of long, idle hours that must be filled with useless crafts?

Halfway through the contents, she'd come across an envelope addressed to her, with a note inside.

Ha, you thought I'd wasted decades on this lot of rubbish, didn't you? No, my dear. I have been well satisfied with my life and hope you will be, too, in time. But until then, a bit of consolation to assist you in getting through those more trying years. I don't know about you, but I always need a stiff drink after a visit with your parents . . .

The bottom of the crate, underneath all the artistic flotsam, was lined with liquid gold: whisky from every distillery on the Isle of

Islay, calvados, madeira, sherry, good vintages of claret, even two bottles of absinthe.

Livia had carefully stowed this most marvelous bequest. She had since been frugal with it—she didn't want to squander her only source of wealth before her most desperate hour.

Well, this was somebody's most desperate hour. She'd say it was Charlotte's, but Charlotte was holding herself together rather well. Instead it was Livia who couldn't stop swallowing gulp after gulp of sweet madeira, Livia who couldn't stop shaking and weeping, Livia who ranted and cursed.

"He's such an imbecile, that Roger Shrewsbury, such an utter, irredeemable, muttonheaded dolt." She waved the bottle for emphasis. "Oh, God, Charlotte, of all the amoral and reckless married men to be had in London, why did you pick him?"

Charlotte sat on the windowsill, her feet on top of a packed suitcase. Livia had hours ago shed her blouse and corset to swaddle herself in an old, comfortable dressing gown. Charlotte remained in her day dress, a summery confection of cream silk printed with roses and climbing vines. Livia preferred her garments as unadorned as possible, but Charlotte relished a good ruffle, yards of lace, and the most dramatic tassels swinging from the shiniest cords of braided silk.

You are more upholstered than a dowager's boudoir, Livia had once said to Charlotte, exasperated by the latter's more-is-always-better taste. And Charlotte had laughed and countered, *Didn't I tell you? Great Aunt Maribel always said that I reminded her of her favorite needlepoint footstool.*

Tears welled in Livia's eyes. She drank directly from the bottle. "I'm going to smash something into Roger Shrewsbury's face the next time I see him."

"Oh, I can't condone that," said Charlotte. "Mr. Shrewsbury's face is his only contribution to humanity. I recommend you instead smash something into his derriere, which is rather ordinary and not as worthy of preservation."

Livia gasped in shock—and hiccupped at the same time. "You saw his derriere?"

"I saw his everything."

"Even the . . ."

"Even the parts usually covered by a fig leaf in the British Museum."

"Did it . . . did it hurt?"

"If you speak of the act of penetration, it wasn't exactly pleasurable but it was no agony. Far more unpleasant was the fact that I had to go through such extreme measures in a bid for a modicum of freedom."

Livia rubbed her eyes. "Do you really think that would have got you what you wanted? Our parents don't strike me as the sort to reward what they'd consider gross misconduct with what they weren't willing to provide when you were being an obedient daughter."

"Which is why I'd have blackmailed them."

Livia choked mid-swallow. "What? How?"

"By threatening to reveal to the general public that I'd been ruined—and hope that they'd cough up enough hush money for me to be educated."

The audacity of Charlotte's plan made Livia lightheaded. Or was it the madeira? She set down the bottle. "Oh, Charlotte."

The tears that had long stung the back of her eyes at last spilled down her cheeks. "You won't be all alone in that horrid cottage, Charlotte, I promise you. I'll come around every time Mamma and Papa aren't looking. I'll bring you books and newspapers. I'll bring you cake. I'll bring you—"

Charlotte peered at the curtain gap. "Papa is leaving to visit Mrs. Marsh."

Mrs. Marsh was Sir Henry's current paramour. She, like Mrs. Gladwell, enjoyed rubbing the fact that she was sleeping with Sir Henry in Lady Holmes's face.

"I hope she gives him something dreadful," said Livia vehemently.

"No, then Mamma might get it too, and that wouldn't be fair to her." Charlotte looked back at Livia. "Anyway, Papa going out means Mamma has taken her laudanum and gone to bed. Will you please check to make sure she's fast asleep, Livia?"

Livia rose unsteadily to her feet. "I can, but why?"

"Can you check first, please?"

Livia did as she was asked, her brain foggy. But there was no doubt about it: Lady Holmes was snoring.

She reported her findings to Charlotte, who led her to a room at the back of the house. There Charlotte opened a window. "Moo as loudly as you can, please."

"What?" Livia was extraordinarily good at imitating animal sounds—a most useless talent for a lady except for entertaining her baby sister when they were little. She hadn't mooed in years.

"Please. It'll be a signal to Mott."

Mott was their groom and coachman—and gardener, too, when the family was in town.

"But why do you want to signal Mott?"

"I'll explain. But please hurry. It'll be past his bedtime soon and I don't want him to go to sleep thinking he's no longer needed."

Livia wondered if she were roaring drunk. Or perhaps Charlotte was. The *moo* emerged with surprising vigor, if also plenty of unintended tremolo.

She moaned. "I sound like the bovine version of a fishwife, toward the end of an argument."

"But a victorious one," said Charlotte.

An unconvincing *baaa* came back from the mews. Charlotte nodded. "Mott's heard us."

"Now will you tell me what's going on?"

"All right," said Charlotte, guiding Livia back to their room. "But you must promise not to say anything to anyone."

"I promise. What is it?"

Charlotte shut the door and began to unbutton her dress. "I'm leaving."

"I know that." Her suitcases had been packed for the rail journey on the morrow that would see her confined to the country for the foreseeable future. "I wish Mamma didn't have such a bee in her bonnet about my staying put for the rest of the Season. To prove what point? I'd rather we be locked away in the country together."

"We will neither of us be locked away in the country," said Charlotte. "Mott is bringing round the carriage. He'll take me to one of the bigger hotels near Trafalgar Square, where the clerks won't find it so strange that an unaccompanied woman comes to ask for a room at this hour. Tomorrow I'll find a place in a boardinghouse."

Livia shook her head. Was she hearing things? "You can't be serious. You're running away?"

"I am not. I am of age. I am free to leave my parents' home and set up my own establishment. It only appears as if I'm running away because I don't want our parents interfering with my plans."

"My God, you're running away."

For the first time, Charlotte raised the glass of madeira Livia had poured for her hours ago, an odd little smile on her face. "All right, I'm running away. I prefer being on my own to being locked up in the country."

"But Charlotte, how will you know where to find a boardinghouse? Or which ones are suitable for a lady?"

"*Work and Leisure* publishes a curated list from time to time—it's a magazine aimed at women who work or are seeking employment. I've memorized the most recent list, since we only hire a house for the Season and I knew I must live in London year-round if I was to be educated here."

Of course Charlotte would have committed such a list to memory. But the discussion made Livia feel as if she were suspended high in the air by nothing more than embroidery threads: Neither she nor Charlotte knew anything firsthand about life outside the boundaries of their upbringing. "But—but you'll have to pay to be lodged, won't you?"

"Yes. I have a few pounds put away. But I also plan to find work."

"What kind of work? You've become notorious, Charlotte. You won't ever become the headmistress of a school. You won't even be able to work as a governess or a lady's companion."

"True. But there are positions that do not require me to take charge of other people's daughters—or pollute someone else's home with my infamy. Plenty of firms need typists. And more women have become secretaries of late. I can type. I've practiced shorthand on my own for when I'd have to transcribe at school. I'm qualified for many positions."

Livia squeezed her eyes shut for a moment—the idea of Charlotte's flight into the wilds of London was utterly overwhelming. "I don't doubt your qualifications, but—"

"Then there's nothing to fear." Charlotte stepped out of her summery frock and reached for a traveling dress of russet velvet. "I'll be fine. I should have done this long ago, as soon as I came of age."

"But Charlotte, how much money do you have? A few pounds won't get you very far if you don't find employment right away."

Livia hoarded the miniscule allowance she received from Lady Holmes, but Charlotte had a tendency to spend hers on books, bonbons, and odds and ends like a typewriter or a chemistry set.

If she had more than five pounds to her name, Livia would be shocked.

"I'll be fine, Livia. I expect the process to move quickly."

There wouldn't be "the woman question" if it were so easy for a female to leave her home and achieve independence. Granted, Charlotte's mind had to be one of the finest in the land, but she was and would forever be a woman who had lost her respectability. A pariah. That had to be a monumental impediment, even away from the froth and vanity of the Upper Ten Thousand.

That said, Charlotte's steely confidence was inspiring. Good old Charlotte, who knew everything, observed everything, and deduced the rest, if there were still anything left to be deduced. If anyone could succeed at this mad endeavor and live—no, prosper—to thumb her nose at her hidebound parents, it would be Charlotte Holmes.

However, at the thought of their parents . . . "What about Mamma and Papa? What will they do once they learn that you've run away?"

"Mamma will be hysterical. Papa will be furious. Mamma will wish to tear the city apart to find me, so she can slap me some more. Papa will agree with her initially, that I should be brought home to be firmly dealt with.

"But whether he decides to confide his troubles to the police or a private investigator, before he's dressed to go out, he'll change his mind. Why should he take the trouble to haul me home when I'll most likely run away again? Why not let me be defeated by London—and life outside his sphere of protection? That way, when I come knocking, in helpless despair, he'll be sure I'll stay put in the country for the rest of my life."

Livia clutched at her temples. "That's heartless."

"That's logical and our father considers himself a clever man. Besides"—Charlotte marched to the window and peered out, straightening her cuffs as she did so—"Mott's here. It's time."

━━━❉━━━

While Mott secured Charlotte's luggage to the top of the carriage, Charlotte said her good-byes to Bernadine. Livia wasn't sure whether she would have taken the trouble: All Bernadine ever did was spin things, spools on a wire, wooden gears, paper windmills. She never spoke to anyone and Livia sometimes wondered if she could distinguish members of her family from strangers on the street.

She watched Charlotte with Bernadine, but for only a moment. It always made her both dejected and angry—at God himself, perhaps—to see the futility of anyone trying to interact with Bernadine. Charlotte was less bothered by Bernadine's condition and spoke to her softly and calmly, an adult to another adult.

Livia waited in the passage until Charlotte was done. Then she accompanied her sister to the carriage—and climbed in first. "If you think I'll limit myself to saying good-bye here—"

"I never thought that."

During the ride Charlotte told Livia about the registries and societies that helped women find employment, lodging, and companionship, which was somewhat heartening—Livia had no idea there were so many resources available. But all too soon they came to a stop before the hotel where Charlotte would spend the night.

Panic assailed Livia. She gripped Charlotte's wrists. "Are you sure, Charlotte? Are you sure you can do this?"

Charlotte nodded. In the light from the carriage lanterns, she seemed to be made of granite, all cool, solid strength.

Livia pressed a small pouch into her hand. "Take this."

In the pouch were a crumpled pound note, several shillings, and three pairs of gold earrings. "This is all the money I brought with me to London. I have more in my bank account. If you're in trouble, let me know. I'll funnel you funds."

Charlotte blinked several times in rapid succession—and looked as if she wanted to say something. But in the end she only embraced Livia. "I'll be absolutely fine. You'll see."

—⁂—

So rushed, their good-byes. So complete, the silence and emptiness of the carriage. Livia stared at the sidewalks, crowded with wide-eyed tourists and insouciant young men in evening attire, strolling toward their next venue of diversion.

Her mind was sinking into a dark place. Sister, companion, refuge, hope—Charlotte was everything Livia had in life. Now she was gone, and Livia had nothing.

Nothing at all.

The carriage took a turn—a few more minutes and she would be back at the house her parents had hired for the Season, where there would be more silence and greater emptiness.

She would be alone. She would be alone for the rest of eternity.

Before she knew it, she'd yanked hard on the bell pull.

"Yes, miss?" came Mott's voice through the speaking slot.

"I'm not going home," she said. "I have a different destination in mind."

Five

The pain behind Livia's forehead corroded the backs of her eyes. Her tongue felt as if she'd used it to clean the grate. And when she tried to move, it became clear that a maniacal sprite was drilling holes into her temples.

It was morning and she'd spent the night in the guest room—in order to be able to lie more convincingly about not knowing when Charlotte had escaped.

She kept dreaming of Charlotte's sweet, sad face. And for some reason, Charlotte's features insisted on turning into Lady Shrewsbury's, all pinched lips and jutting cheekbones. Livia had screamed at the hateful woman for ruining Charlotte's life.

For ruining all their lives.

Groaning, Livia staggered out of bed: She needed to go down and delay her parents' discovery of Charlotte's absence for as long as possible.

She barely made it to the top of the stairs when Lady Holmes stomped up, a wild expression on her face. "You will never guess what happened!"

Her voice scratched across Livia's skull. A wave of nausea pounded her. "Wh—what happened?"

Had Lady Holmes already found out that Charlotte was gone?

"Lady Shrewsbury is *dead*."

Livia braced a hand on the newel post, her incredulity shot through with an incipient dread. "How can that be?"

"They found her expired early this morning. The doctor's already been and declared it an aneurysm of the brain. But *I* think it's divine justice. The way she came and shoved all the blame on us, when it was her own son who was the cad and the bounder? She deserved it."

Livia shuddered at her mother's callousness. "I don't believe the Almighty strikes anyone dead solely for being petty, or even hypocritical."

"I happen to be convinced that sometimes He does." Lady Holmes's tone was triumphant. "And maybe this is the year He smites those who have been thorns in my side."

It took Livia a moment to realize that Lady Holmes was referring to Lady Amelia Drummond. That name had never been brought up in the Holmes household, certainly not in Livia's hearing. But Lady Amelia's abrupt death—she'd been in perfect health and vigor only the day before—had been quite the topic of gossip for the past fortnight.

Lady Holmes shoved past Livia.

"Wait. Is that all you know? Are there no other details?"

Lady Holmes stopped and thought for a moment. Then she snorted. "Mrs. Neeley said Roger Shrewsbury is devastated. Said he is sure his disgrace sent his mother into an early grave. How typical of a man, to think the world revolves around him."

"Wait. Is—"

Lady Holmes marched on in the direction of Livia and Charlotte's room. "When will you learn to be quiet, Olivia? I have other things to do than standing there and answering your questions—especially today."

The silence, as Lady Holmes threw open the door, was thunderous. Her question, when it came at last, deafened. *"Where* is Charlotte?"

—⋇—

Charlotte had been everywhere in London this day, or at least it felt that way to her throbbing feet.

By midmorning she—or rather, Miss Caroline Holmes from Tunbridge, typist—had secured a room at Mrs. Wallace's boarding-house, a very respectable place at a very respectable location near Cavendish Square.

The rest of her first day of freedom was spent whittling away at her scant funds. She was obliged to acquire a tea kettle, a chipped tea service, a spirit lamp on which to heat water, silverware and flatware, tooth powder, towels, and bed linens—plus a number of other miscellany that a young woman accustomed to living at her parents' house never needed to worry about.

She tried to think of her purchases as an investment for the future, for when she and Livia—and Bernadine, too—would have a place of their own and direction over their collective existence.

But that dream was taking its last labored breaths, wasn't it, all alone in a ditch somewhere?

Bernadine might not care much one way or the other, but Livia, Livia who was so proud, so fragile, and so constantly doubtful of herself . . .

Livia who mistrusted humanity yet feared being alone.

Charlotte had been Livia's companion; she listened when Livia wanted to talk and remained quiet when Livia wanted to hear herself think. And Charlotte, too, had been a target of Lady Holmes's wrath, with her refusal of proposal after proposal. But now Livia was unsupported and unshielded. Now she was all alone before both a scornful Society and a pair of livid parents with no other outlet for their anger.

Charlotte passed Cavendish Square, the trees and shrubs of which were dingy with soot. The air in London had always been terrible, but far more so for a woman who must walk all day long than one who had a carriage at her disposal. By midday, as she stood before the mirror in her new room at Mrs. Wallace's, the top of her ruffled collar was already marked by a ring of grime on the inside. She didn't want to think of its advanced state of soil after several more hours out and about.

Turning onto Wimpole Street, she made a stop at Atwell & Dewsbury, Pharmaceutical Chemists. Mrs. Wallace had recommended the place for the purchase of incidentals. Charlotte had visited the shop earlier in the day to buy bathing soap and matches—and to take a look at the selection of books that customers could borrow for a penny apiece.

But of course she hadn't thought of everything. This time Mr. Atwell kindly sold her some stationery. And a package of one hundred perforated pieces of tissue for the water closet, wrapped in brown paper and without either of them ever mentioning it by name.

As she stepped out of the shop, a dapper older gentleman sauntered past on the opposite side of the street. He looked so much like Sir Henry she came to a dead halt.

Had she been angrier at him or herself? The latter, most likely. Livia had warned her repeatedly not to trust their father's promises. But she had been deaf to those warnings—willfully deaf. Not that she thought Sir Henry the kind of paragon he most emphatically wasn't, but because she believed that her good opinion and good will meant something to him.

They probably did, but not enough, in the end, to make any difference.

—❧—

Mrs. Wallace's place was around the corner. When Charlotte walked in, most of the boarders were milling about in the common room, socializing before supper.

"I'll bet the girl's mum is having a right laugh this minute," said a vivacious brunette. "Goodness knows I would, if the old woman what caught my daughter and acted so hoity-toity about it is found dead the next morning."

Charlotte's ears heated as if a curling iron had been held too close.

"You don't think the girl's family had something to do with it?" said another woman. She was no more than twenty-one and looked excitable.

"Which old woman?" asked Charlotte.

The brunette turned toward her. "You must be the new girl. Miss Holmes, is it?" she asked, her demeanor friendly.

"Yes. Nice to meet you, Miss . . ."

"Whitbread. Nan Whitbread, and this is Miss Spooner."

They all shook hands.

"I didn't mean to interrupt, but what you were talking about sounded fascinating."

"Oh, it is. My cousin works at one of the fancy dressmakers on Regent Street," said Miss Whitbread. "And she kept hearing about it all day from the clients. They weren't talking to her, of course, but among themselves, about the lady what caught her married son having a go at this young lady, hung the young lady out to dry, and then woke up dead the next morning."

Lady Shrewsbury was dead? *Dead?*

"Oh, my," Charlotte mumbled. "Just like that?"

"That's what they say. Can't remember the name for it, the condition what makes you bleed in the head."

"An aneurysm of the brain?" Charlotte supplied.

"Sounds about right. First-rate story, ain't it? Oh, I mean, isn't it?" Miss Whitbread lowered her voice. "Mrs. Wallace don't like us using 'ain't' around here. Says it isn't ladylike."

"And if you got a young man who's sweet on you, don't ever mention it to her—or Miss Turner," added Miss Spooner. "We aren't supposed to have any gentlemen friends at all."

"'Specially not a young man like Miss Spooner's. He takes her out to tea shops and feeds her suppers," said Miss Whitbread with a wink.

"Shh," warned Miss Spooner, laughter and alarm alike dancing in her eyes. "Speak of the devil."

Mrs. Wallace came into the common room. She was in her mid-thirties, a tall, broad-shouldered woman with a clear look of authority. Behind her followed a thin, short woman who must be at least five years older but was obviously a lieutenant, rather than the captain. Miss Turner then.

Mrs. Wallace greeted her boarders and introduced Charlotte. The company duly proceeded to the dining room, where Miss Turner said grace, and the women helped themselves to a supper of boiled bacon cheek and vegetable marrow.

Charlotte's meals were very important to her. But this evening she noticed nothing of the food she put in her mouth. With half an ear she listened to Miss Whitbread tell her about the rules and customs of the house. The only question she asked was, "Do you think I'd be allowed to go out and buy a newspaper?"

"Oh, you don't need to. Mrs. Wallace don't like any of us going out after supper so she has the evening paper delivered."

When Charlotte reached the common room after supper, Miss Turner already had the evening paper in hand. She read aloud from its pages as the other women knitted, mended hose, wrote letters, or played games of draughts.

"Now listen to this advert, ladies. *Seeking, sincerely and urgently, girl infant left behind on the doorsteps of Westminster Cathedral, on the night of the twenty-third of November, 1861.*" Miss Turner peered over the top of the paper at the other occupants of the room. "This is why you must always be careful and not be led astray, or the same could happen to you—become a sorry woman looking for her child twenty-five years too late."

The date sounded familiar. Charlotte searched her memory and recalled that there had been an awful pea-souper on that day in 1861. She sincerely doubted anyone would choose to venture out in such weather to abandon a baby, of all things, but she didn't say anything.

At precisely nine o'clock Miss Turner laid aside the paper. All the other women rose and prepared to vacate the room.

Charlotte took the paper.

"Miss Holmes, lights-out is at half nine," said Miss Turner officiously. "You should not read past that."

"I won't," Charlotte promised.

In her room, a small but faultlessly clean space, she quickly found the death notice for Lady Shrewsbury. So Lady Shrewsbury truly was dead. When she'd been energetic and vigorous only the day before.

Lady Shrewsbury had seemed a great deal more upset at Charlotte than at her own son. But could she have been furious about him, rather than merely peeved? Could that fury have led to her perishing in her slumber?

Charlotte rubbed her temples, wishing she'd bought a cache of foodstuff. The portions at supper might have been enough for a woman of smaller appetites, but Charlotte had never been one of those women.

What was really going on? And would people think *Charlotte* might have had something to do with it?

Charlotte,

You liar!

You swore up and down that all would be well, that you would have no trouble landing a post in short order. How inebriated I must have been, to have taken you at your word.

I have since skimmed through your stacks of books and magazines having to do with female employment. I ended my reading with a pounding headache and a heart that cannot sink any lower.

The vast majority of avenues open to gentlewomen seeking work are for those who already possess the necessary educational and professional qualifications. Of which you have none. And those other opportunities you mentioned? Most require a period of apprenticeship, for which you have to pay a premium with money you do not have. The only positions that do not demand either education or apprenticeship pay so little they are only suitable for young girls working to supplement the family income, not for a grown woman trying to live on her own.

And I have not even brought up the Working Ladies' Guild, which you described as so very helpful. It requires that a member personally vouch for you before you can seek employment via its registry. May the Almighty strike me dead for saying this to my own sister but Charlotte, no woman alive will risk her respectability to recommend you to any association or employer.

Not anymore. Not ever.

You knew all this. And you lied through your teeth. And I aided and abetted you in this hopeless venture. If I had shoved you in front of an oncoming omnibus, I could not have done worse as your sister.

Oh, what have you done, Charlotte? What have we done?

Livia

P.S. I wrote the above shortly before luncheon, but have not been able to leave the house to post it. I hope I will have better luck in the afternoon.

P.P.S. You were right about our parents' reactions. Mamma was in a state and Papa coldly angry—and he changed his mind after first saying he would bring you back, exactly as you had predicted.

P.P.P.S. As you instructed, I told them I did not know when or how you had left. I said I had too much to drink and went to bed early in a stupor and you must have stolen out at night. I do not know how much Mamma and Papa believe me. They questioned Mott, too, and Mott turned out to be a tremendous liar: He looked them in the eye, and his expression remained frank and naive throughout.

P.P.P.P.S. Mamma has forbidden me to leave the house. I will try to entrust this letter to Mott.

P.P.P.P.P.S. An awful realization: If I cannot leave the house, then I cannot withdraw any money from the bank. Charlotte, promise me you will not let yourself starve to death on the streets—or worse. No, forget that. There is no worse fate than your starving to death on the streets. Do not let your pride be your end. If things go ill, come home. Please.

Charlotte met Miss Whitbread, who carried a heavy-looking satchel, outside Mrs. Wallace's.

"Why, hullo, Miss Holmes," said Miss Whitbread. "Back home early?"

"Yes," Charlotte answered, opening the door for Miss Whitbread. "I have my own typewriter and the firm doesn't mind if I brought some work home."

Charlotte had always been a good liar. According to Livia, her expression didn't change at all as she slipped between truths—having her own typewriter, for example—and falsehoods—in this case, having a firm that paid her for clacking away at said typewriter.

"That's capital. I'm doing the same here—bringing work home." Charlotte remembered that Miss Whitbread painted silks and cards for a living. "My employer's got only the shop on the Strand— everybody who works for him takes their pieces home. It's nice in a way, but to tell you the truth I wouldn't mind if he had a studio somewhere, so I've a place to go during the day and people to see."

"Yes, staying put in your room all day can become tedious." Charlotte didn't mind it so much, but Livia became antsy if she couldn't get out for a daily walk.

"That, and not having anyone around for a good chinwag 'til supper." Miss Whitbread set her satchel on a chair in the empty common room and rolled her shoulders. "That's why I stopped to see my cousin today. We had a cup of tea and she gave me the latest about the scandal."

Charlotte's hand tightened on her reticule. "Do tell."

Miss Whitbread needed no further prompting. "You won't believe it. Apparently, the girl's sister had a flaming row with the dead woman only hours before she died. A *flaming* row. They said she told the woman to her face that she, even more than her son, deserved to die for ruining her sister's life."

Charlotte felt as if she'd been hit in the stomach by a cricket bat.

"Oh, dear," she said, praying her suitably interested face was holding together.

"That's what I said." Miss Whitbread nodded sagely. "I told my cousin, 'Abby, this is going to be interesting before long. Real interesting.'"

⁕

The moment Charlotte had finished reading Livia's letter, a weight had settled in her stomach. Not because of Livia's dismay and anxiety at the realities of Charlotte's employment prospects, but because the former had not said a word about Lady Shrewsbury's death.

Now she knew why.

Just as she had concealed the truth from Livia, Livia was concealing the truth from her.

She didn't believe Livia would be in any trouble from the law: Even if the Shrewsburys suspected that something might be awry, they would not let matters proceed to an inquest, where under questioning Roger Shrewsbury's seduction of a virgin he could not possibly marry would become a matter of public record, carried in all the papers of the land.

Lady Shrewsbury would return from the dead first.

But Livia did not need to be wanted for murder to suffer. If rumors and speculations persisted long enough, Society would come to believe that she had *something* to do with Lady Shrewsbury's death. And that would be enough for her to become marginalized, if not outright ostracized.

At least this time Charlotte had some food on hand. She had asked for an extra sandwich when she'd bought her lunch—and also some apricots sold at a discount because they'd been bruised during their travels.

She finished the sandwich first, washing it down with a cup of weak tea. The apricots came wrapped in crumpled newspaper. By habit she scanned the columns of print. Her eyes widened. She read the small article again, this time more attentively.

Mr. Harrington Sackville of Curry House, Stanwell Moot was found unconscious yesterday morning, from an apparent overdose of chloral. Unfortunately, he could not be revived and was pronounced dead on the scene.

He was a well-respected gentleman, said to have been in good health and spirits before his passing.

An inquest will be held in two days.

Charlotte frowned. She had very few talents that her mother found useful. In fact, she had only two: one, she knew most of *Burke's Peerage* by heart; two, after her first Season in London, she developed a clear understanding of the myriad alliances and sometimes enmities that connected those families listed in *Burke's*. Therefore, she knew exactly who Mr. Harrington Sackville was, and how he was related to two others who had also passed away recently and abruptly, and whose deaths were even more inexplicable than his.

Maybe she could yet do something to break the siege for Livia.

She sat down and pulled out a piece of stationery she'd bought at Atwell & Dewsbury, Pharmaceutical Chemists.

Six

"Ash," called Roger Shrewsbury. "Ash, a minute of your time, please."

Lord Ingram Ashburton turned around. "What can I do for you, Mr. Shrewsbury?"

They had known each other since they were children. Lord Ingram had never called his old school chum Mr. Shrewsbury, except when he presented the latter in formal introduction. Shrewsbury swallowed: He understood the rebuke for what it was. He understood that Lord Ingram no longer considered him a friend.

They were at the private cemetery on the Shrewsbury estate, on a high bluff above an inlet of River Fal, not far from the southern coast of Cornwall. Overhead the sky lowered ominously; rain was imminent. Lady Shrewsbury was already in the ground, and the mourners were fast dispersing, hoping to find shelter before the storm unleashed.

Shrewsbury hesitated. Lord Ingram did not further prompt him. Shrewsbury's gloved hand opened and closed around the top of his walking stick. Opened and closed again.

One of their classmates walked by and inclined his head. They both nodded in return. Thunder rumbled, then cracked. Shrewsbury jumped. Lord Ingram remained stock-still.

Shrewsbury cleared his throat. "Ash—that is, my lord—"

He had never before called Lord Ingram "my lord," except jokingly. But this was no jest. This was Shrewsbury acknowledging his new place, that of a mere acquaintance no longer accorded the privilege of addressing Lord Ingram as an intimate.

"My lord, I wonder if you would—ah—possibly—be so kind as to pass on a word for me."

Lord Ingram only looked at him.

Shrewsbury put a hand at the back of his neck and cleared his throat again. "You see I feel terrible about what happened. I feel even worse now that I heard Miss Charlotte Holmes has run off on her own.

"Most of London is no place for a genteelly brought up young lady. It's bone-chilling, thinking about the mishaps that could befall her. I want to help—or at least mitigate my part in the whole . . . fiasco. But I can't approach her family or any of her lady friends—you know how it is. So I thought, well, perhaps she might come to you for aid. You two used to be thick as thieves, even if that was a while ago."

"I have not heard from Miss Holmes since the fiasco," said Lord Ingram.

"But you might in the future, mightn't you? If you do, please let her know that I'll be more than happy to put her up in a safe place and, well, look after her."

"And how would she reciprocate your kindness?" Lord Ingram's words were even, almost good-natured.

"She was . . . she was willing to be my . . . paramour before. I . . . ah . . . I assume that hasn't changed."

"I see," said Lord Ingram, his tone even more kindly. "Should Miss Holmes seek my help, I will remember to point her in your direction. Would that be all?"

Roger Shrewsbury's throat moved. "I know you want to punch me. Why don't you? Go ahead!"

Lord Ingram lifted a surprised brow. "Mr. Shrewsbury, I'm a married man. I don't know about Mrs. Shrewsbury, but Lady Ingram would not care to hear that I brawled over another woman."

Roger Shrewsbury flushed to the tops of his ears. "Of course. Of course. Please forgive me."

Lord Ingram nodded. "My condolences."

He turned and walked away.

Roger Shrewsbury would never know how close he had come to being thrashed within an inch of his life.

Lord Ingram looked up from his cufflinks. "Yes, Cummings?"

"I've saved the article on Mr. Holmes from the paper," said his valet. "May I assume you'll have no more use for the rest of it, my lord?"

Lord Ingram stilled. He had purchased a West Country paper before his return journey, which had sat next to him on the train, unread, as he stared out of the window for hours on end. He vaguely recalled leaving Paddington Station with the paper in hand.

"You may dispose of the paper as you see fit."

"Very good, sir. I have left the article in your dressing room."

Lord Ingram waited until his valet had left before heading to the dressing room. Cummings handled the posting and collection of his correspondence from time to time, so it wasn't surprising that he would remember Sherlock Holmes. But why in the world was there an article about Holmes in the paper—a West Country paper, no less?

The newspaper clipping had for its headline

INQUEST ADJOINED AWAITING FURTHER EVIDENCE.

Lord Ingram frowned as he read the opening account of Mr. Harrington Sackville's death. Sackville. He had heard the name in passing at Lady Shrewsbury's funeral. Lord Sheridan's long-lost brother, whom no one had seen for many years. Lord Ingram didn't know the man, but the general reaction seemed to have been surprise— of the so-he-was-still-alive-as-of-recently variety.

Inquest testimonies from physicians and Sackville's household retainers were recorded verbatim in the paper; everything seemed more or less straightforward—and nothing had anything to do with Sherlock Holmes.

Had Cummings clipped the wrong article?

At the end of witness testimonies, the coroner read the following letter from Mr. Sherlock Holmes of London.

Lord Ingram swore.

Dear Sir,

It has come to my attention that Mr. Harrington Sackville's death, by apparent overdose of chloral, may not be an isolated incident: Lady Amelia Drummond preceded him in death by a week and a half; the Dowager Baroness Shrewsbury followed a mere twenty-four hours later. Lady Amelia was first cousin to Mr. Sackville's elder brother by the same father, Lord Sheridan, and godmother to one of Baroness Shrewsbury's children.

All three deaths were unforeseen. As was true in Mr. Sackville's case, Lady Amelia and Lady Shrewsbury, too, had been in excellent health and spirits. They all perished overnight. The only difference is that Mr. Sackville's maid came across him while he still drew breaths, albeit weakly, which gave the household sufficient time to fetch a physician and for the physician to diagnose an overdose of chloral, even if that diagnosis came too late for anything to be done.

Had the maid not tried to rouse him, he would have been found dead, and the cause of death would most likely have been given as failure of the

*heart or an aneurysm of the brain—causes set down on the death
certificates of Lady Amelia Drummond and Lady Shrewsbury,
respectively. And his passing, however unexpected, would have been treated
much in the same manner as theirs, attracting its share of gossip and
speculation but no legal notice.*

*Each death, taken singly, may be accepted as unfortunate but not
suspicious. However, the proximity of all three, not only in time, but in
their social and familial connection, becomes difficult to ignore.*

I urge you, sir, to share this intelligence with your jury.

Yours truly,
Sherlock Holmes

Lord Ingram swore again. By tomorrow the news would be in all
the London rags. Holmes never once mentioned the word, but how
long before speculations leaped from mere suspicious deaths to the
most conspiratorial of murders? He didn't want to imagine the bed-
lam that would be unleashed.

Was this circus but a sleight of hand on Holmes's part, to draw
the glare of unwanted attention away from a certain beleaguered
relation? No. If a diversion had been all that was required, Holmes
would have accomplished it without provoking a public uproar.

He read the letter again, pressing two fingers against the center
of his forehead. Holmes believed that something was wrong—
believed it enough to write from the wasteland of exile, in the hope
of influencing the outcome of the inquest.

Lord Ingram closed his eyes, but it was no use. He was too accustomed to giving Holmes everything he could, always with a sense
of urgency. And a sense of futility: What Holmes wanted most was
beyond his power.

Some people never meet the right person in life. They, on the other hand, met when they were too young to realize what they had found in each other. And when they did at last see the light, it was too late.

He tossed aside the newspaper clipping and headed for the front door.

❖

"My lord!"

Inspector Treadles found himself a little uncertain at the appearance of Lord Ingram in his parlor. It wasn't yet late, but it was after dinner and he hadn't anticipated any social visits, let alone one from his lordship.

Lord Ingram inclined his head. "Mrs. Treadles, Inspector, I hope I haven't disturbed you in your hour of repose."

"Of course not." Alice rose from her seat and shook Lord Ingram's hand. "Do please sit down and let us know what brought you here."

"This brought me here." Lord Ingram handed over a large-ish newspaper clipping that had been carefully folded. "If you will do me the honor of reading the article to the end."

Alice rang for tea. Then she and Treadles sat down with the article. They gasped at almost the same time, upon the first mention of Sherlock Holmes. Treadles sucked in another breath as he reached the conclusion of the letter.

"Does this mean that Holmes is well again?" he asked. "Or is this from before his misfortune?"

"I have no way of ascertaining—Holmes remains beyond reach." Lord Ingram's gaze strayed to the mantel and lingered on a photograph of the Treadleses and himself, taken on the Isles of Scilly, in those days when Holmes was only a quick note away. "But it doesn't take a mind of extraordinary caliber to deduce that this must be important to Holmes.

"I understand Mr. Sackville's death took place outside the Metropolitan Police's district of authority. But I also understand that it is not unusual for county police to request help from the C.I.D., especially in case of suspicious deaths, where there isn't enough local expertise to handle the investigation." He looked back at Treadles. "Inspector, may I ask that you personally inquire into the matter?"

Treadles glanced at his wife, who gave a small nod. "Certainly, my lord. I will send a cable to some friends serving with the Devon Constabulary first thing tomorrow morning."

Lord Ingram exhaled. "Thank you, Inspector. I am most obliged."

My Dear Lord Ingram,

As soon as I arrived in Scotland Yard this morning, I learned that the Devon Constabulary has requested assistance from the C.I.D. with regard to Mr. Sackville's case. I have volunteered my services.

I can only hope I shall not disappoint Sherlock Holmes.

Your servant,
Robert Treadles

Seven

"No letters for you, miss," said the post office clerk to Charlotte. Charlotte thanked him, yielded her place, and walked across the cavernous, impersonal interior of the post office. She was fine until she reached the third pillar from the door, and then her lungs collapsed.

She couldn't breathe. She couldn't move. Her nails dug into the palms of her hands as she broke out in a cold sweat. Imminent heart failure—she recognized all the symptoms. Dear God, what would happen to Livia? And what would the man she couldn't stop caring about think, when he learned that she'd met her end at the General Post Office on St. Martin's Le Grand, of all places?

Two minutes later, still very much on her feet and not lying in a heap on the floor, she began to realize that what ailed her wasn't the spear point of mortality, but the onset of panic.

She had never felt panic in her life. Livia sometimes did, when she imagined, in excruciating detail, ending up an indigent old maid unwanted by any and all relations, spending her days in a grimy boardinghouse, subsisting on only bread and boiled cabbage.

When Livia fell into one of her states of uncontrollable anxiety—or climbed into one, as Charlotte sometimes thought—Charlotte would bring her a heaping plate of buttered toast and hot tea laced with brandy. She would rub Livia's back. And then she would read aloud passages from *Jane Eyre*, Livia's favorite book, a work Charlotte couldn't otherwise get through, finding it too dense with high emotion and melodrama.

But even though she did all these sisterly things, she never did feel any of Livia's fear and anguish. It had seemed utterly incomprehensible that a future decades distant, built of nothing but worst-case scenarios, should hold such sway over the here and now.

Until this moment.

Until the weight of all her choices descended upon her with the force and tonnage of a landslide.

What if the investigation into Mr. Sackville's death unearthed nothing? What if the truth remained obscured and Livia was forever branded an unprosecuted murderer because of a drunken spat?

Fear swelled, crushing her organs to make room for more of itself. It squeezed the air out of her lungs. It coiled, pythonlike, around her stomach. It forced its way up her windpipe, pushing, expanding, blocking every last sliver of open passage.

She had always been certain that she'd be able to take care of Livia in addition to herself. She never thought she would wreck both their lives simultaneously.

She had not made up out of whole cloth the more numerous opportunities open to women these days. Nor had she conjured from thin air those societies that existed to connect women in need of employment with employers in need of positions filled.

But a good portion of those organizations, for all their good and noble intentions, were thinly funded. Two of those she visited had already closed permanently, with another still nominally in operation, but taking applications only by post. The ones that appeared to be in more robust shape all required letters of character written by ladies of good standing—those Charlotte would never have, but those didn't concern her so much: She was passable at imitating handwriting and did not consider it a moral failing for a woman in her situation to forge her own recommendations.

Of a far greater worry was that to receive help from those societies, she had to first pay a subscription fee, which her already thin wallet could ill afford—not if she wanted to eat and have a roof over her head, too. And then, were she determined enough to pay the fee, she could expect to wait weeks, possibly months, before a suitable position turned up.

She didn't have that kind of time.

It wasn't so dire yet. Not at the moment. But just as Livia looked down the years and saw nothing but misery and loneliness at the end of the road, Charlotte could not get rid of this stone-hard dread of coming to the last of her pennies.

Her room and board was nine shilling six a week. After paying for the first two weeks, she had five pounds three and ten left, including what Livia had given her. That amount had been further reduced after the purchase of the daily necessities—not to mention she had to provide for her own lunches.

The money would not last forever. It would not even last very long. And then what? If she couldn't look after herself, how would she begin to help Livia?

"Are you all right, miss?"

An almost comically resplendent creature stood before Charlotte, in a polonaise of lustrous Prussian blue silk, worn over an elaborately ruffled white underskirt. Her hat was narrow brimmed and high crowned, laden with sprays of ornamental grass against which nestled a . . . a stuffed blue-breasted parrotfinch, if Charlotte wasn't entirely wrong about her ornithology.

She realized that she'd been standing with her back against a forty-foot-high column, her hand over her chest. She dropped that hand. "Yes, I'm fine. Thank you, ma'am. It's the weather, a bit hot today."

"It *has* been rather warm lately," said the woman. Her voice was of a startling loveliness, rich as cream, with a barely perceptible hint of huskiness. "Should I ask someone to fetch you a glass of water, miss? Or find you a place to sit down for a minute, in peace and quiet, away from nosy old ladies such as myself?"

The woman chuckled at her own joke. Until she did so, Charlotte had thought her in her mid-to-late thirties. But her mirth revealed webs of crow's feet around her eyes and deep channels to either side of her lips: She was a woman at least fifty years of age.

Her money was new: No one who'd been raised to follow the unspoken standards of Society, not even a woman with Charlotte's "magpie tastes," as Livia called them, would sport so elaborate and fanciful a confection for an outing to the post office.

She wore no wedding band. But that, Charlotte decided, was not because she had never been married. The parrotfinch on the hat was perched on a little nest made of black crape. The same material formed a most discreet border around the blue reticule the woman held in her hand.

Women only wore black crape if they had lost their husbands. And the woman here, despite her extravagantly exuberant day dress, wished to honor her late spouse in a subtle manner, nearly invisible expressions of grief and remembrance woven into her daily attire.

Charlotte shook her head at herself, at her ingrained tendency to observe those she came across to the very last detail. She enjoyed it and she was good at it. But what use was it?

What use was a woman with a mind and a temperament that would be odd and borderline worrisome even in a man?

She forced a smile. "Thank you, ma'am, but I really am quite all right. Nothing is the matter with me at all."

After the woman sashayed away to conduct her business with the post office—her progress followed by all the men and most of the women in a twenty-five-foot radius—Charlotte pulled herself together and left.

Perhaps it was nothing more than hunger. Feeling the pinch of imminent penury, she had saved two slices of buttered toast from breakfast. But she had wanted to see whether she would still be able to function as usual without eating them for lunch. It had been a long day of walking about London, and she had two and a half more miles to go before she reached her little room at Mrs. Wallace's. She grew increasingly sure that if she could only set a kettle to boil, and put the slices of toast in her stomach where they belonged, she wouldn't feel nearly so dispirited.

Not to mention that Miss Whitbread had kindly loaned her a half dozen magazines. Charlotte had already found two interesting travelogue pieces—one on the fjords of Norway and the other about the Canary Islands. A cup of tea, a bite to eat, even if it was from morning, and a chance to forget her troubles by vicariously living another woman's holiday—

"A penny, mum? A penny please?"

The plaintive cry of a child beggar yanked Charlotte back to the unhappy here and now. The girl was small and hollow cheeked. Her face and her outstretched hand were coated with grime, her frock such a hodgepodge of brown and grey patches that Charlotte couldn't tell what its original color had been.

But it was the woman holding on to the girl's shoulder who made Charlotte's chest constrict. She had seen beggars in London, but never one like this. The mother wore a black patch over one eye, her other eye the milky blue of the blind. Her face had the vacantness of a North Sea beach in the dead of winter; her arms, held close to the sides of her body, the stiffness of a marionette.

She did not look defeated. To look defeated was to suggest that one had recently strived for something. This woman was drained, whatever hope and energy she'd once possessed long ago permanently depleted.

The husk that she'd become was far more frightening than the sight of the down-on-their-luck-but-still-saucy beggars Charlotte was more accustomed to seeing, ones who accosted their passersby with a combination of pathos and bravado.

"A penny for me supper, mum?" The little girl, not yet entirely diminished by life, asked again.

Charlotte opened her reticule and pulled out not only a coin, but the two slices of toast, wrapped in brown paper. "Here's a sixpenny bit for you. You look after your mum. Make sure she has her supper, too."

The little girl looked with incredulity at the coin that had been dropped into her palm. She raised her face to Charlotte, let go of her mother's hand, and wrapped her arms around her benefactor. And only then did she accept the toasts.

Charlotte walked on, feeling a little less in despair.

—❈—

Her relief that she could still do something for someone evaporated before the display windows of Atwell & Dewsbury, Pharmaceutical Chemists. She had never walked so much in her entire life; her feet were in agony. She probably couldn't afford to buy plasters for her blisters, but at least she could inquire into their prices.

She patted the hidden pocket on her skirt. In her reticule she kept only minor change, but in her pocket she had a pound note.

Mrs. Wallace's place seemed safe enough and the lock on Charlotte's door was sturdy. But what if the place burned down while Charlotte was out seeking employment? She didn't want to lose all her money, along with all her other worldly possessions. The pound note in her pocket served as a crude form of insurance.

But it was not there. Through the broadcloth of her dress, she couldn't sense the small but very real presence of that precious piece of paper, folded into a square. Surely she was mistaken. She dug her fingers harder against the fabric. Nothing. All she felt was the bulk of her petticoat—and beneath that, the form of her limb.

The little beggar girl who had embraced her. Charlotte should have known—she should have known that instant something was wrong. The girl hadn't been anywhere near as emaciated as her face would suggest. And she hadn't smelled of the sourness of lack of washing.

No, Charlotte should have known *before* then. The girl hadn't left her mother's hold—it had been the other way around. The mother had signaled her to go for the easy prey. The eye patch hadn't covered some unsightly deformity: It had covered her good eye, the black cloth thin enough for her to make out something of her surroundings in good daylight.

Charlotte was vaguely aware that she was drifting along the street. At some point she might have entered Mrs. Wallace's boarding home. Did someone attempt to speak to her? She had no idea. Nor could she be sure whether she had responded.

She did remember locking the door of her room before she lifted up a wide band of lace ruffle on her skirt to check the opening of the pocket. It had two buttons, both securely fastened when she'd left the house. Now one button was open, leaving more than enough room for small, nimble fingers to reach inside and extract the pound note.

Which accounted for nearly forty percent of her remaining funds.

All at once she became aware that someone was banging on her door. "Miss Holmes. Miss Holmes!"

She opened the door to Mrs. Wallace's resident sycophant. "Yes, Miss Turner?"

"Miss Holmes, are you suffering from deafness? I spoke to you downstairs—you didn't even react. And I've been knocking for at least two minutes now."

"Is everything all right?"

"Mrs. Wallace would like a word with you in her parlor at the earliest possible moment," said Miss Turner with a smug mysteriousness.

Why would Mrs. Wallace wish to speak with Charlotte? She was paid up until the end of next week and she had come nowhere near the house rules, let alone broken any. "Certainly. I'll be right down."

At the far end of the corridor was a simple galley, open for two hours every afternoon, where Mrs. Wallace's boarders, who weren't allowed to do more than boil water in their rooms, might fry some sausages or heat up tinned beans to have with their tea. Today someone had scrambled eggs and the rich aroma made Charlotte's stomach tremble in longing. She had skipped both lunch and tea—an unprecedented event in her life.

Her brain was dull from hunger. When she looked at Miss Turner, she saw few of the details that usually leaped out at her, except to note that the woman, a good fifteen years older than Charlotte, was practically skipping down the stairs.

A gong went off in her head. When a woman who adored authority and revolved as close to power as she could became this excited, it was probably because authority and power were about to be put to use—to someone else's detriment.

To Charlotte's detriment.

———※———

Mrs. Wallace had a small apartment on the ground floor, consisting of a parlor, a bedroom, and most likely a private bath. This apartment was accessed via a corridor that led out from the common room. A door barred the way a few feet into the corridor. On the wall next to the door was a bell and next to the bell a sign that read, PRAY DO NOT RING AFTER 8 O'CLOCK IN THE EVENING, EXCEPT IN CASE OF EMERGENCY.

The door had been left ajar. Miss Turner ushered Charlotte past to another door, which led to Mrs. Wallace's parlor.

Charlotte had stepped into the parlor once before, for her initial interview with Mrs. Wallace. She had been very ladylike and Mrs. Wallace had declared herself pleased to offer the vacancy to Miss Holmes.

But this Mrs. Wallace did not look at all pleased with Miss Holmes. Her expression was forbidding, which seemed to only further excite Miss Turner.

"I've brought Miss Holmes, ma'am," she announced breathlessly.

"Thank you, Miss Turner," said Mrs. Wallace. And then, after a moment, when Miss Turner showed no inclination to depart, "I will see you at supper."

"Of course, ma'am."

When she was gone Mrs. Wallace commanded, "Have a seat, Miss Holmes."

Charlotte sat down—then stood up again. She walked to the door and yanked it open. Miss Turner stumbled into the parlor, unembarrassed. "Do excuse me. I wanted to ask Mrs. Wallace a question about her policy for the washings. I'll come at a more convenient time."

Charlotte accompanied her as far as the barricading door in the middle of the corridor, which she locked before coming back into the parlor and closing the door firmly behind herself.

She did not bother to take a seat again. "Is something the matter, Mrs. Wallace?"

Mrs. Wallace considered her a minute. "Miss Holmes, you have deceived me."

Charlotte took a deep breath. "Have I?"

"Miss Whitbread's cousin, Miss Moore, called on her this morning—and saw you leave as she came in. Miss Moore works at a Regent Street dressmaker's and told me that she had seen you more than once at Madame Mireille's.

"Unfortunately she also told me that you are not Caroline Holmes of Tunbridge, a typist newly arrived in London, but Charlotte Holmes, daughter of Sir Henry Holmes, who was recently caught in a compromising position with a married man. Do you deny that?"

How ironic. Mrs. Wallace's establishment in the West End had not been Charlotte's first choice. There was a more highly recommended place in Kensington and Charlotte had passed on it because she hadn't wanted to run into anyone she knew. West End, a relatively safe, well-maintained district, with a large population of doctors and other professionals, but with Society having decamped decades ago to more fashionable addresses further west, promised greater anonymity.

It would appear that she had chosen badly in everything.

"Well, Miss Holmes?"

"I can see that your mind is already made up, Mrs. Wallace. Any denial on my part would only lead to further accusations of dishonesty."

"In that case I have no choice but to ask you to leave immediately. I must have a care for the reputation of my establishment. This is a house of virtue, of good Christian respectability. There is no room for you, Miss Holmes. There never was."

"Very well. You will have no trouble from me, Mrs. Wallace. Return me the sum I've paid in advance, minus the portion deducted for the nights I've spent here, and I'll be gone within the hour."

"I'm afraid I will be keeping your rent." Mrs. Wallace's tone was firm. "You were plainly informed that any misrepresentation or misconduct on your part would lead to a forfeiture of rent already paid."

Charlotte folded her hands together. "Then what about misrepresentation on your part, Mrs. Wallace?"

"I beg your pardon?"

"You said that this is a house of virtue, of good Christian respectability. But you yourself entertain, on a regular basis, a man to whom you're not married."

Mrs. Wallace recoiled. "Where did you hear such a malicious rumor? I will have you know—how dare you—" She paused to exhale. "I will have you know there are absolutely no such shenanigans going on here!"

"I must disagree. You have a strict no-gentlemen policy for the house. Your boarders, even if they have brothers or fathers in town, are expected to meet them at tea shops and other such venues. In the common room there are no antimacassars on the furniture, yet in this, your own private parlor, I see an antimacassar on every chair except one, yours."

"Some women do use macassar oil in their hair," Mrs. Wallace said heatedly.

Charlotte scanned the room and made for a door to her right. Beyond the door was a small anteroom, with a mirror, an umbrella stand, a coat tree, and, of course, a doormat.

She looked back at Mrs. Wallace, who was beginning to look hunted. "True, some women do use macassar oil. But why would a woman leave muddy prints in the shape of a pair of men's shoes on the doormat just inside the private entrance to this apartment?"

Charlotte walked across the room to Mrs. Wallace's writing desk. "Furthermore, you are right-handed, but the ink blotter was on the left-hand side of the desk when I came for my interview. You had asked me to write down the name and address of my next of kin, in case of emergency. As I stood over your desk, almost directly above the wastepaper basket, what had I seen but a rectangle of discarded blotting paper, with the words *Cordially yours, George Atwell*, in reverse, just discernable at the corner.

"I asked then whether you had any family in town or visiting regularly. You replied that your parents are no more and that your only surviving sibling, a sister, lives with her husband and daughter in India. Mr. Atwell, therefore, cannot be a father or a brother. And unless you are impersonating a man by post, a problematic activity in itself, Mr. Atwell sat here at this very desk recently and dashed out a message before he left.

"That was when I decided to look for the private entrance I knew must exist. And when I found it in the alley behind the house, what should I see, almost directly opposite, but the service door to Atwell & Dewsbury, Pharmaceutical Chemists.

"I visited the shop and met Mr. Atwell. When I mentioned that I am a new boarder at your establishment, he had nothing but the most effusive praise for you as a woman of substance and character. It really is too bad that he is already married."

Mrs. Wallace's face turned red, then pale, then splotchy. "Unfounded accusations, one and all."

"Perhaps. But your other boarders will no doubt be curious as to the reason behind my hasty departure. I can disseminate a great many unfounded accusations during the hour you allotted for my packing."

"You—you would destroy my reputation as you destroyed your own?"

"To the contrary, I have no intention at all of besmirching your good name, publicly or privately—notice I kept Miss Turner of the long ear and eager tongue far away from our conversation. I know nothing of Mr. Atwell's domestic situation, but it is evident he and you have arrived at a comfortable state of affairs. There is your ongoing chess game in the corner. The bottle of Pimm's on the shelf you probably enjoy together. And I can see him reading those William

Clark Russell sea novels, should you be busy with business matters in the evening. I would not wish for anything to upset your cozy arrangement.

"But in return, I'd like you to extend a similar consideration to me. You should be able to deduce that I am in difficult circumstances. I will not blackmail you to let me remain under your roof—you do have your reputation to consider—but it is reasonable to ask for the rest of my money back."

Mrs. Wallace's jaw worked. A second later she rose, unlocked a drawer under the writing desk, took out a cash box, and returned Charlotte her money.

Charlotte pocketed the coins carefully. "Thank you, Mrs. Wallace. Your secret is safe with me. And . . . if I were you, my next move on the chessboard would be king rook to b4—if you wish to win, that is. If you prefer to let Mr. Atwell win, put your queen rook pawn to a5."

Eight

Devonshire

Even in death, Mr. Harrington Sackville was a handsome man. He was fifty-five, but his salt-and-pepper hair was still thick, his waist still trim, and his musculature that of a man twenty years younger. There was a bluish cast to his skin, but not so much that Inspector Treadles couldn't tell that in life he had enjoyed a hale complexion, lightly tanned from time spent outdoors.

His expression was solemn. Peaceful. Had he died of natural causes, his would have been a much-admired corpse at the funeral, eliciting genuine lament that a man of such health and vigor should have been taken so abruptly.

Dr. Merriweather, the pathologist who was frequently engaged by the coroner's district for his medical expertise, trailed behind Treadles and Sergeant MacDonald, also of the Criminal Investigation Department, as the latter two made slow circles around the body.

"As you can see, Inspector, there are no signs at all of a struggle. No bruises around the throat or anywhere else on the skin. No wounds or injuries. And since chloral was the culprit, I made a careful inspection of the entire body. There isn't a single puncture mark to suggest the use of a syringe. Nor is there any evidence that chloral was administered rectally."

The pathologist's tone was professional and brisk. But Treadles heard a trace of vexation—that what should have been a straight-forward inquest returning a verdict of accidental overdose had been unnecessarily prolonged by the involvement of that busybody Sherlock Holmes.

And now, of Scotland Yard.

At the same time, however, Treadles discerned a hint of excitement. Dr. Merriweather, like most men, was intrigued by the possibility of a truly unusual crime, one so subtle that even someone of his considerable knowledge and experience could not identify, let alone fathom, it.

Treadles had confessed the same excitement to his wife. What he had not told her was the tremulous hope in his heart that such a closely watched case—the C.I.D. had been bombarded by reporters hounding for the latest developments—might make his name known to the public. He cared little for fame, but he wanted those friends of Alice's who had become mere nodding acquaintances after her marriage to a policeman to read about his exploits in their morning papers. They would never envy her, but perhaps someday they would no longer disdain her for her choice of mate.

He knew that she had no regrets about becoming his wife. He only wanted that she never would.

"And chloral is absolutely the culprit?" he asked.

"Absolutely," said Mr. Smythe, the young chemical analyst for the county. He hadn't Dr. Merriweather's detachment before dead bodies, and had remained in a corner of the room as the policemen and the pathologist inspected the cadaver, but now he warmed up to his subject and launched into a detailed explanation of the tools and procedures used to ascertain that it was not chloroform or antimony found in the tissue, but chloral hydrate and only chloral hydrate. "I performed the assays myself, each step repeated multiple times. There can be no mistake."

"Thank you, Mr. Smythe," said Treadles. "And thank you, Dr. Merriweather."

Dr. Merriweather was correct: there was no trace of foul play to be seen on Mr. Sackville's body. And Treadles had no reason to doubt that the enthusiastic Mr. Smythe wasn't just as meticulous at his work. From afar it had been easy to imagine all kinds of overlooked details that, once observed, would lead clearly and triumphantly to a conclusion of criminality. But up close such had not turned out to be the case at all. In fact, Mr. Sackville's death appeared more and more what it had seemed at first glance: a simple matter of accidental overdose.

He sighed inwardly—so much for his dreams of a most publicized success.

Well, on to the house.

Per Treadles's request, a capable constable had been dispatched to Curry House—and the nearest village—to gather general information ahead of Scotland Yard's arrival. The report had been waiting for Treadles when he reached Devon, as had a copy of the official transcript from the inquest.

Mr. Sackville did not own Curry House. It belonged to a widow named Mrs. Curry, who, upon remarrying and becoming Mrs. Struthers, moved to her husband's home in Norwich and put up the house for let.

Seven years had passed since Mr. Sackville took over the lease of Curry House. No nearby squires, however, could claim anything beyond a nodding acquaintance—Mr. Sackville had been a recluse. That said, he'd enjoyed a gentlemanly reputation in the area: He might not have cultivated close ties with anyone, but he was never too proud to acknowledge the villagers he came across on his walks, be they vicars or simple farm wives.

And though he had not participated in the civic life of the village, he could be counted upon to give generously to any and all causes, whether it was for a new altarpiece in the old Norman church, coal and windows for the village school, or funds to purchase titles for the circulating library.

He was, in other words, not beloved, but respected and admired. No one thought it particularly odd that he chose to keep to himself; the great families of the land were well-known to produce eccentric sons.

Not that the villagers knew which great family had produced Mr. Sackville—they had no copy of *Debrett's* to consult. It was simply their instinctive conclusion that his origins lay not with the gentry, but the nobility.

Curry House, too, added to that impression.

The Devon Coast was a lovely place. The cliffs that met the sea were high and dramatic—an almost startling reminder that Britain was but an island. The headlands along this stretch of the coast were a green patchwork of fields and sheep-dotted pastures. Curry House stood one and three-quarter miles outside the village of Stanwell Moot and was reached by a narrow path, hemmed in on both sides by hedges of hawthorn and field maple.

The house was relatively recent, built at the beginning of the century, with a slender, almost delicate silhouette, its stucco exterior bright white under the sun—and impossibly clean against a backdrop of limitless blue skies. The two policemen were more accustomed to the soot and grime of London, where it was easier to find a unicorn than a set of such immaculate walls. Sergeant MacDonald whistled softly.

Inside, the house was no less immaculate: clear, white-framed windows, pastel blue walls, and thick oriental rugs adding a welcome splash of color and texture. The woman who received them could not be said to be as elegant as her surroundings: Mrs. Cornish, the housekeeper, had a ruddy complexion and a somewhat lumpy build. But her black dress had been skillfully pressed and her large, white cap perfectly starched.

Not as elegant, but certainly as spotless.

After politely inquiring into their trip, she offered them tea. Inspector Treadles accepted, but asked to see the house first, particularly the bedroom in which Mr. Sackville had drawn his last breath.

The airy refinement of the house extended to the upper story. Mr. Sackville's bedroom commanded a spectacular panorama of the coast—the house was less than half a mile from the sea and boasted one of the highest vantage points in the surrounding countryside.

"A most favorable view," murmured Treadles.

Sergeant MacDonald nodded. "Probably why the house was set here in the first place."

Treadles turned his attention to the room itself. "Are these the same sheets on which Mr. Sackville died?"

"No, Inspector. The sheets have been changed. But they haven't been sent out to launder yet."

"I will need to see them. And the rest of the room has been cleaned too, I suppose?"

"Yes, Inspector. Top to bottom, on the day itself."

Had Mr. Sackville died of natural causes, he might have been allowed to remain undisturbed on his deathbed for a while—or transported no further than the dining room table and laid out. But such had not been the circumstances and a conscientious housekeeper, faced with an unexpected death, had no doubt wished to return the house to its usual state of order and orderliness.

Treadles could not argue with the caretaker of a fine property duly discharging her duties, no matter how much he wished the room had been better preserved.

He and Sergeant MacDonald examined the windows and asked Mrs. Cornish about the various ways one could enter the house. She was certain that Mr. Sackville's windows had been closed that night, as after dinner there had been a thunderstorm. The exterior of the house, smoothly plastered, would have been difficult, if not impossible, to climb up.

"Were the windows firmly latched?"

"Yes, Inspector. I unlatched them to air the room after Mr. Sackville was taken away."

"And where does he keep his supply of chloral?"

Mrs. Cornish opened a nightstand drawer to reveal a small vial with two white grains inside.

"This was the quantity of chloral left the day of Mr. Sackville's death?"

"Yes, Inspector. Dr. Birch asked to see it and I remember this was how much was left inside then."

On top of the nightstand were several very recent periodicals—everything from literary weeklies to penny dreadfuls—Mr. Sackville had a catholic taste. "Did these come by post?"

"Yes, Inspector."

They moved to the other upstairs rooms. Besides the private facilities, there were two more bedrooms, a sitting room, a study, and the valet's room. "Mr. Hodges lives up here because we are all women below," Mrs. Cornish explained.

Treadles nodded. "The windows in these rooms were also secured that night?"

"I unlatched them the next day—we aired out the entire house."

Her responses were concise and to the point—Mrs. Cornish was not a talkative woman. But something in the way she held herself—a tightness in her jaw, the hard clutch of her fingers around one another—belied her apparent composure.

She was deeply unsettled to be speaking to the police. But whether it was because the entire affair was upsetting or for some other reason, Treadles could not decide.

"And the doors?"

"I check them every night at nine."

"Is it possible for someone to slip into the house unnoticed before nine o'clock?"

"I suppose it's *possible*." But her tone indicated that it was so improbable, the very thought was ridiculous.

If the deaths of Mr. Sackville, Lady Amelia, and Lady Shrewsbury were related, then an outsider—or more than one outsider—must be involved. But that theory of interconnectedness appeared ever more tenuous, now that Treadles had seen for himself the isolation of the house—and of the nearest village. This was the kind of place where a stranger would be immediately noticed. Or, likewise, a local doing something out of the ordinary.

Tourists did come through the area, tramping along the edge of the coast and taking in the views. But the preliminary report listed only two sets of guests at the village pub-and-inn in the preceding week: a traveling photographer and his assistant, who had stayed overnight and left five days before Mr. Sackville died, and some friends of the vicar's brother, who'd come with the brother for a visit and slept at the pub, rather than cramming into the crowded vicarage.

Treadles and MacDonald were now back on the ground floor. "Would you mind showing us the rest of house, Mrs. Cornish?"

Kitchen complexes at large country houses were often separate from the main building, to reduce the risk of fire. Here, however, the kitchen was on the ground floor, separated from the drawing room and dining room by two sets of heavy, green baize–covered doors.

The corridor led past the larder, the pantry, and the scullery before coming to the kitchen proper.

Stairs at the end of the corridor led down to other domestic offices, as well as to the servants' hall and staff quarters. Mrs. Cornish showed Treadles where the linens from Mr. Sackville's bed had been stowed, and they might as well have been freshly laundered, given how pristine they were.

"We changed the bedding frequently," said Mrs. Cornish, not without a note of pride.

Another avenue of inquiry shut off. But Treadles was a patient man. He would find his openings.

"Will you take your tea now, Inspector, Sergeant?" Mrs. Cornish went on.

"We will," answered Treadles. "Most kind of you, Mrs. Cornish."

The housekeeper hesitated a moment. "Inspector, Sergeant, you are visitors to this house and by rights ought to be received abovestairs. But I wouldn't feel right sitting down in the drawing room . . ."

"We'll use the drawing room for our interviews but we'll be happy to take tea where you'll be comfortable, Mrs. Cornish," said Treadles.

They had tea in Mrs. Cornish's small office, next to the storeroom. Two-thirds of the entire floor was below ground level, but enough light came through windows set high on the wall that the room didn't feel subterranean.

Mrs. Cornish poured tea. Treadles took the opportunity to ask some questions. From the preliminary report, he already knew that Mrs. Cornish had been at Curry House the longest, fourteen years, taking over the housekeeper's position while the former Mrs. Curry was still in residence.

Mrs. Cornish confirmed that, as well as information about the rest of the staff. The cook, Mrs. Meek, was the newest, arriving on the Devon Coast little more than a month ago. There was also a valet, a housemaid, a kitchen maid, and a lad who looked after both the garden and the horses.

With the exception of the valet, Hodges, the servants were paid by the owner of the house, who charged higher rents for a property that came with a full implement of competent staff. Mr. Sackville's solicitors had agreed that his estate would continue to foot the lease—and Hodges's wages—until their client's death had been properly investigated.

Treadles didn't doubt the lawyers were irked when the inquest didn't immediately return a verdict of accidental overdose.

"Will you tell me something of Mr. Sackville's daily routines?" he asked Mrs. Cornish.

Mrs. Cornish did so readily. On an ordinary summer day, Mr. Sackville would have taken his morning cup of cocoa in bed at half past six. Then he bathed and dressed. At quarter past seven he rode. Breakfast was at half past eight, when he returned. He liked to spend some time in his study after breakfast. Luncheon was at one. He often went for a long walk afterward, returning home to take tea at half past four, and dinner at eight. Twice a month he traveled to London after luncheon and didn't return until tea time the next day.

Inspector Treadles knew about the London trips from the preliminary report—Constable Perkins of the Devon Constabulary had been thorough at his task. He also knew that the visits were a source of curiosity in the village. Some thought he went to visit friends, some speculated that he gambled, and a few more were of the opinion that Mr. Sackville simply wished to get away regularly—that they would, too, if they had his wealth and freedom of movement.

"Do you happen to know, Mrs. Cornish, what had been his purpose for those trips?"

"Not at all, Inspector."

"He did not speak of them when he returned?"

She shook her head. And of course a self-respecting servant would never think to interrogate her employer on his private affairs.

"Which train did he take?"

"The 3:05 from Barton Cross."

Barton Cross was the next nearest village. Treadles had studied the local railway timetable. The 3:05 from Barton Cross didn't arrive on a mainline until almost four o'clock in the afternoon. And even if Mr. Sackville caught the next express to London, it would be well past business hours by the time he pulled into Paddington Station.

Not the kind of itinerary a man would choose, if his primary intention was to see his agents or solicitors.

"Did he always leave on the same days?"

"The second and fourth Thursday of each month."

The London theatrical season ran from September to the end of July. But the regularity of Mr. Sackville's visits didn't suggest the jaunts of a theater lover. It also seemed unlikely that he went to see friends—members of his social class congregated in London during the Season and spent the rest of the year in the country, where the air was far more salutary.

"You are certain London was his destination, Mrs. Cornish?"

"Mr. Hodges said so. He went through Mr. Sackville's pockets before his clothes were sent out for laundering. And he always found punched tickets issued from Paddington Station, from Mr. Sackville's return trips."

Mrs. Cornish blushed slightly, as if embarrassed that she'd gossiped about her employer with the valet.

"I see. I understand Mr. Sackville's London trips became a little more irregular in the weeks before his passing."

"Gastric attacks," Mrs. Cornish replied with great authority. "They happened twice in April. Once he never left the house, the next time he began to feel poorly while he was on the train. He got off at the next station and spent the night at the railway hotel."

This was in accordance with what the ticket agent at the Barton Cross railway station remembered.

"A fortnight after that he did go."

"He did, but he came back the next morning, earlier than usual. And two weeks after that he didn't go at all, even though he was well."

"Were those two times in April the only occasions he suffered from gastric attacks?"

"No, Inspector. He'd had them for as long as I've worked for him. I think there was once before when he didn't go to London because he wasn't feeling up to it."

Once in seven years and then twice in a month. Curious. Not curious enough to suggest outright foul play—the nature of random events was that they were random—but noteworthy, nevertheless. "Did he say anything about why he came back early that time in May?"

"No, he didn't."

"How did he appear when he arrived back at Curry House?"

"He kept to himself that day and didn't want to be disturbed."

"He also went to church, I understand, before he returned home that day. The vicar saw him, as well as some other villagers."

This for a man who had never attended service the entire time he had resided at Curry House.

"I heard the same."

"Were you surprised the Thursday a fortnight later, when he didn't head for London at all?"

"I . . . I was, but not terribly so."

"Why not?"

"He had a resigned air about him."

This had not been part of the village gossip. Inspector Treadles frowned slightly. "How resigned?"

Mrs. Cornish thought for a moment. "Disheartened, I'd say. Restless, too. His habits used to be regular. But in those last few weeks, he'd disappear a whole day at a time. And once he came back drenched in rain—and it'd been raining even when he left."

The information did not bode well for Sherlock Holmes's conjecture. The relevant dates for Mr. Sackville failed to line up with Lady Amelia's sudden death, which came too late to explain his downheartedness. The most likely hypothesis would be that Mr. Sackville had a mistress in town whom he visited with clockwork regularity. And then what happened? Had she left him for greener pastures? Or perhaps accepted a proposal of marriage from another smitten man?

It was hardly unheard of for a man in the throes of heartache to be overly generous with substances that offered him a few hours of oblivion and forgetfulness.

Inspector Treadles pressed on. "Please describe for me the household activities in the twenty-four hours preceding Mr. Sackville's death."

"There isn't much to tell, Inspector. It was a half day. I had the Anglican Women's meeting in the afternoon. Then I went to Bideford, had myself a spot of tea, walked around the shops a bit, and came back at half past seven. Everyone else returned a little before eight—except Mr. Hodges, he was out on his annual holiday.

"We had our supper in the servants' hall and then brought back the dishes from the dining room—on half days Mrs. Meek, the cook, left Mr. Sackville a cold supper. At nine I took him a cup of tea, a plate of biscuits, and the evening post and asked if there would be anything else. He said no, I might retire. And that was the last I saw him conscious."

"Can you recall what came in the post for him?"

"A magazine or two and maybe a few pamphlets—he liked to send for those from time to time," Mrs. Cornish said rather reluctantly, as if finding it distasteful to admit that she'd guessed the contents of her employer's mail.

"And how did he look?"

"A bit tired, but not in a way to alarm anyone."

Had he any idea those would be his final hours?

"You were at the inquest. You heard the letter read from Mr. Holmes, connecting Mr. Sackville's death to those of two ladies in his circle. What did you think of that?"

"I'm sure I don't know what to think of it at all," answered Mrs. Cornish, her expression as circumspect as her words.

"Have you ever heard Mr. Sackville mention either Lady Amelia Drummond or Lady Shrewsbury?"

"No, sir."

"Did he write to them?"

"I have never seen an envelope with either of those names."

"Whom did he correspond with?"

"His lawyers, mostly."

"And the morning of the discovery? Please give an account."

Mrs. Cornish thought for a moment. "Before Mr. Hodges went on his holiday, he gave the task of Mr. Sackville's morning cocoa to Mrs. Meek. But that morning she was busy in the kitchen so Becky Birtle, the housemaid, carried it upstairs."

"According to Becky Birtle's testimony at the inquest," said Treadles, "she set down the tray and wished Mr. Sackville good morning. And when he didn't respond, she spoke louder. And when he still didn't respond, she shook him by the hand, only to feel that his hand was alarmingly cool."

Mrs. Cornish nodded, her brow furrowed. "She went to Mrs. Meek—and Mrs. Meek came to me. The three of us went to Mr. Sackville's room together. He was still breathing then. Mrs. Meek said it didn't look good for him. Becky started shaking. I ran to find

Dunn in the stable. He rode to the doctor's house, but Dr. Harris wasn't home. He had to ride another four miles to Barton Cross to fetch Dr. Birch.

"When Dr. Birch finally came and examined Mr. Sackville, he asked me whether Mr. Sackville used chloral. I said I'd seen some about. He said that if he'd had a better description of Mr. Sackville's condition, he'd have brought strychnine. He and Dunn rushed off to Dr. Harris's house, raided his dispensary, and came back with strychnine. But by then it was too late. Mr. Sackville, he'd stopped breathing several minutes before."

Mrs. Cornish's voice quavered slightly at the end of her recital.

"I have an unpleasant question that must be asked," said Treadles. "Do you know of anyone who might wish Mr. Sackville harm?"

"No!" The housekeeper's answer was instant and fierce, the strongest reaction they'd seen from her this day. "No one. Well, certainly not anyone in these parts."

"Thank you, Mrs. Cornish. I have no further questions for you at the moment," said Treadles.

Mrs. Cornish inclined her head, her breaths still noticeably shallow.

"The next person I'd like to see would be Becky Birtle, the maid who found Mr. Sackville," Treadles went on. "But Constable Perkins reported that Becky Birtle is no longer at this house. Can you elaborate on that, Mrs. Cornish?"

"The whole thing upset the girl terribly. And the letter from that Holmes man even more so. After the inquest she begged to be let go so she could return to her parents. She's still a child and I didn't have the heart to say no."

There was a faintly mulish set to Mrs. Cornish's mouth, as if daring Inspector Treadles to question a decision she'd made out of compassion.

"Of course you were right to think of her, Mrs. Cornish," he said mildly, rising. "Sergeant MacDonald and I will remove to the drawing room upstairs. Please inform Mrs. Meek that we would like to speak with her next."

❖

Mrs. Meek, the thinnest cook Inspector Treadles had ever come across, turned out to be a much more voluble witness.

"I think it was food from the pub—those two gastric attacks in April. You see Mrs. Oxley, who was cook here before me, she had to leave end of March to look after her orphaned nieces. Until I came, folks here had to make do with what the inn could supply. Now Mrs. Pegg at the inn is a fine woman and serves ample portions, but her food is a bit rough around the edges, if you know what I mean.

"But me—before I came here, I worked at Mrs. Woodlawn's Convalescent Home in Paignton. For ten years I did nothing but cook for ladies with the most worrisome digestions in the whole country. I'm proud to say that Mrs. Woodlawn's was awful sorry to see me go—I helped make the reputation of her establishment."

"And your food agreed with Mr. Sackville?" asked Treadles, though that was obviously Mrs. Meek's point.

"I had no complaints. But then again, I didn't cook very long for him, did I?"

"I'm sure your work was most satisfactory. Now, if I may have your description of the twenty-four hours before Mr. Sackville was found comatose—and your account of the events of that morning."

Mrs. Meek took a long swallow of her tea. "Certainly. The day before was our half day. I was busy in the kitchen most of the morning. There was luncheon to be thought of and cold suppers for everyone, but we were also making jam that day—Tommy Dunn has a green thumb and we had strawberries and gooseberries coming in by the boxful from the kitchen garden. When the washing up from luncheon and the jam-making was done, I walked Jenny Price, our scullery maid, to her parents' place. They are lovely people, the Prices. I had a chat with Mrs. Price. We had tea together. And in the evening we were sent back in the dogcart.

"After dinner that night I made sure the kitchen was all tidylike and went to bed. I was in the kitchen again at six in the morning, as usual. Mr. Hodges was out, so I made Mr. Sackville his cocoa, and Becky Birtle took it to him.

"A few minutes later she was back in the kitchen, all alarmed like. 'Mrs. Meek, I don't think Mr. Sackville is all right. He's cold.' My heart rather did a turn. 'You don't mean he's dead, do you?' I asked her. 'No, he's breathing. But real cold. Come and see for yourself, please.'

"I was about to rush upstairs with her, but then I thought Mrs. Cornish ought to know. So I jogged down to her room. She was still in her dressing gown. She gasped when I told her what Becky told me and we all ran up together. And there Mr. Sackville was, like Becky described, still breathing but cold as a bucket of water kept in the cellar.

"We opened the curtains for a better look. And I said to Mrs. Cornish that whatever it was, I didn't think Mr. Sackville was going to make it. Becky started whimpering and shaking. Mrs. Cornish told me to look after her; she herself ran out for help.

"I slapped Mr. Sackville a few times, took him by the shoulders and shook him, but he didn't even twitch. Becky started to cry. I remembered then that Jenny Price was in the kitchen alone and that if I wasn't there to supervise, she'd eat what I'd cooked for the master, or add goodness knows what to the pot. So I told Becky to come with me to the kitchen but she said she didn't want Mr. Sackville to be all alone.

"I went down to the kitchen by myself. I heard Mrs. Cornish

coming back in and running upstairs. She came down after a while and said Tommy Dunn was gone to fetch Dr. Harris and she supposed there was nothing we could do except wait. I still had everyone's luncheon to see to so I kept working, or at least I tried to. But every few minutes I'd stick my head out of the door and see if I couldn't hear anyone coming.

"When finally someone came, it wasn't Dr. Harris but a different doctor. When he'd worked out that it was chloral, he shouted at us to get some hot water bottles next to Mr. Sackville so that he wouldn't keep getting colder. We were in a mad scramble. Becky, that silly child, filled the pot with too much water and then she was crying again that it wasn't getting hot. Jenny Price thought we were playing a game and almost got herself burned. Mrs. Cornish had to drag her out of the kitchen and lock her in her room."

This was a much more detailed and dramatic account of the events. Inspector Treadles found himself leaning forward in his seat, even though he knew the eventual outcome.

"We tucked in several hot water bottles around Mr. Sackville. Then Mrs. Cornish took his pulse and said, 'I can't feel anything.' That was when Dr. Birch and Dunn came pounding up the stairs with strychnine. 'I can't feel any pulse,' Mrs. Cornish said to Dr. Birch.

"Dr. Birch rushed to Mr. Sackville. He felt and listened and held out his card case in front of Mr. Sackville's nose. Then he let out this tremendous groan. 'I might have been able to save him if only I'd known what was ailing him.'

"He wrote down the time of death. Mrs. Cornish offered him tea and asked the rest of us to return to our duties. I suppose that's what we've been doing since, carrying on."

"What did you think when you heard about the possible connection to the deaths of Lady Amelia Drummond and Lady Shrewsbury?"

"I'm sure I've never been more amazed. But it couldn't have been more than a coincidence, could it?"

"That's what we're here to find out," said Treadles, a faint note of apology to his voice. He sympathized with those whose lives were disrupted by the appearance of policemen—especially in a case like this, when it could very well turn out to be much ado about nothing. "Have you ever heard of either of the ladies?"

"Never. I barely saw Mr. Sackville himself and I didn't have anything to do with the post coming or going. Mrs. Cornish and Mr. Hodges will know more."

"Can you think of anyone who might have carried a grudge against Mr. Sackville—or wished him harm?"

Mrs. Meek shivered. "No, not at all. But I'm the wrong person to ask—I've been here only a month and hardly stepped out of the kitchen."

"Thank you, Mrs. Meek, you've been most helpful. If you could ask Mr. Dunn to spare a minute for us, it would be very much appreciated."

"Of course, Inspector." Mrs. Meek rose to leave. But she turned around at the door. "Do you really think, Inspector, that there was foul play here?"

Anxiety tinged her voice—but even more than anxiety, dismay. The dismay of someone fearing the shattering of innocence, fearing to find herself embroiled in the cold-blooded killing of one person by another.

"We're here because certain irregularities have been pointed out. Our goal is only to determine whether there is sufficient cause to warrant further investigation."

"I hope you'll determine that it's all just happenstance. And that Mr. Holmes who wrote the letter a mischief-maker with nothing better to do than rousing groundless suspicions and inconveniencing innocent people."

She spoke with surprising vehemence. After she left, Inspector Treadles and Sergeant MacDonald exchanged a look.

"Do you think she might have a point, sir?" asked Sergeant Mac-Donald, gently blowing over his notebook page to help the ink dry faster. "This Mr. Holmes, from everything you've said, Inspector, sounds rather extraordinary. But you know how it is with extraordinary men. They aren't always right in the head all the time."

There was most certainly something rather not right with Holmes at the present. Treadles liked to think that true genius couldn't be easily obliterated. But with Lord Ingram so tight-lipped about Holmes's actual condition, Treadles had little to go on except his faith that his friend wouldn't waste his time by personally requesting a fruit-less pursuit.

"Let's have a little more patience," he said. "We haven't even spoken to all the witnesses yet."

Whereas Mrs. Meek had been loquacious, Tommy Dunn was taci-turn almost to the point of muteness.

He had been working at the house for three and half years. Never had any trouble with Mr. Sackville or any of the other servants. For his half day he went for a walk and sat on a rock in a nearby cove and watched the sea until it was time for supper in the servants' hall.

"You have no family nearby to visit, Mr. Dunn?" asked Treadles.

"I'm an orphan, Inspector."

"I see. Go on."

"I went to bed after supper. Was sweeping out the stables in the morning when Mrs. Cornish came running. I rode to Dr. Harris's but he wasn't home. Rode to Dr. Birch's and fetched him. He needed strychnine so we rode back to Dr. Harris's. When we came back it was too late. Mr. Sackville, he was dead."

With further prodding from Treadles, Dunn added that he knew nothing of Lady Amelia Drummond or Lady Shrewsbury, and could think of no one who might have wanted to harm Mr. Sackville. He had, however, noticed Mr. Sackville's low spirits in the weeks leading up to his death.

"His mind was somewhere else. Once I saddled his favorite mare. He stood there for a bit, holding on to the reins, and then walked off." Dunn clenched his hands. "I should've asked what was the matter, even if it wasn't polite. We lived in his house. We lived on his money. We knew he didn't have no one else. And not one of us bothered to ask him if everything was all right."

This was the first emotional response to Mr. Sackville's death Treadles had encountered. He gave the young man a moment to pull himself together before asking gently, "I take it he was a good master?"

"The best," said Dunn. "He gave me one of his own watches my first Christmas here—had it engraved with my initials, too."

"May I see?" asked Treadles.

The watch Tommy Dunn produced was very fine, of comparable quality to the one Treadles had received from the late Mr. Morton Cousins, his excellent and much lamented father-in-law. And on the cover of the watch, a large letter D with a small T to the left and a small E to the right.

"A very generous gift, indeed."

"And he gave me a new fob for it last Christmas, but it's so fancy I only wear it to church."

"The others who were in his service, did they receive as handsome gifts?"

"Mrs. Cornish got nice vases and picture frames. Hodges got silver cufflinks. And Penny Price got huge puddings and cakes that she didn't have to share with anyone."

"Mrs. Meek and the young one, Becky Birtle?"

"They ain't been here long enough. Becky came in spring and Mrs. Meek even later than that."

They thanked him and asked him to fetch Hodges.

Treadles had anticipated a trim, natty man, in the mold of his late father-in-law's valet. Hodges, however, was wide-shouldered to the point of burliness—and his nose must have been broken a few times in his youth. But he was well turned out and when he spoke, he sounded much more polished than his smashed nose would have suggested.

He couldn't help the police with what happened during the days and hours immediately preceding his employer's death, since he'd been away on holiday to the Isle of Wight. But he did confirm that Mr. Sackville had suffered gastric attacks for many years—"Since when he was in school, I believe." He complimented Mrs. Meek on being a skilled and caring cook—"She was always conferring with me about how he looked and trying to ferret out what foods to avoid." And he firmly declared that in five years of working for Mr. Sackville, he'd never had a harsh word from his employer—and couldn't think of anyone who would want to harm a man who never gave any trouble at all.

Treadles thanked him and requested that he convey word to Jenny Price that she was wanted for questioning.

Hodges's eyes widened. "But Jenny Price is a half-wit."

"Be that as it may, we still must speak with her."

Jenny Price wasn't a young girl, as Treadles had assumed, but a heavyset woman in her mid-thirties. She looked worried when Mrs. Meek, who brought her in, left the drawing room, but her eyes lit with pleasure as she discovered the plates of biscuits, cakes, and sandwiches that had been laid out for the visitors from London.

She moved astonishingly quickly—and polished off several biscuits before Treadles recovered from his surprise.

"Ah, Miss Price, we have some questions for you."

She looked at him blankly while chewing on a piece of seed cake.

Treadles tried again. "Jenny, is it?"

She nodded.

"Can you tell me anything about the day Mr. Sackville died?"

"They took 'im away."

"Do you remember anything else from that day?"

She shook her head.

"Nothing at all?"

Jenny Price, her mouth now full of anchovy sandwich, didn't bother to respond. Treadles asked more questions about Mr. Sackville, life at Curry House, and her work in the kitchen. And managed to receive not so much as a mumble in response: Jenny Price had no more answers to give.

Treadles and MacDonald admitted defeat and escorted her back to the kitchen. Mrs. Cornish happened to be in the kitchen, talking to Mrs. Meek. Treadles asked the housekeeper to show him the rest of the rooms belowstairs, to make sure that they did not make for easy entries.

Mrs. Cornish agreed, but with visible reluctance. Treadles gave an apologetic nod—he wouldn't want the police to inspect his home either. But suspicious deaths had a way of trumping the wishes of the living.

The housekeeper's private quarters consisted of a small parlor and an even smaller adjoining bedroom. Above the fireplace in the parlor hung a framed photograph of the staff—an older batch, before the arrival of Mrs. Meek and Becky Birtle. Another framed photograph, of a vivaciously pretty young woman, sat on Mrs. Cornish's nightstand.

Treadles nearly made the mistake of asking whether the young woman was a niece before he realized she was none other than Mrs.

Cornish, from half a lifetime ago. It occurred to him that the house-keeper wasn't that old now—likely younger than Jenny Price.

"May I ask, Mrs. Cornish, why you gave a place to Jenny Price?"

"Oh, I didn't, Inspector. Mrs. Struthers—the former Mrs. Curry—she took Jenny in about ten years ago."

"And why did Mrs. Struthers make that choice?"

"The Prices are yeoman farmers. Lots of men trudging about, especially during planting and harvest. And Jenny, well, I'm sure you wouldn't, Inspector, but there are men who would take advantage of a girl like that. Her parents tried to lock her in her room, but she gets in a bad way if she's locked up all the time."

Mrs. Cornish opened the door to the maids' room. Two neatly made iron beds were arranged in the shape of an L. The one that presumably belonged to Jenny Price had a pair of slippers under-neath. Inspector Treadles noted the bars on the window and the padlock on the door.

"Mrs. Struthers offered to take Jenny in," Mrs. Cornish continued. "She was a widow then and except for the man who took care of her horses and her garden there was no other man on the property—and he lived above the stables, not in the house. Jenny can only manage simple tasks, but she works hard and Mrs. Struthers didn't have to pay her. In fact, to this day the Prices supply a good portion of the food-stuff that goes into the kitchen."

"But with Mr. Sackville's arrival there were men in the house."

"At first there was only Mr. Sackville himself—Mr. Hodges came later. It was when we knew that the house had been let to a gentleman that I put the lock on the maids' door—and the bars outside the window. I wasn't so much worried about anyone getting into Jenny's room as that she'd be lured out. But I needn't have wor-ried. Mr. Sackville wasn't that kind of man—and neither is Mr. Hodges."

They were now in Mrs. Meek's room. A photograph of *her* younger self sat on a desk. She had not been nearly as pretty as the young Mrs. Cornish, but she beamed with confidence.

"I haven't asked you this, Mrs. Cornish. What is your opinion of Mr. Sackville as a man?"

Mrs. Cornish was taken aback. "He was a gentleman, of course."

"Many men are born gentlemen, but not all are worthy of that term."

"Well, he was a true gentleman. He was always courteous to everyone. And considerate. We used to do all our own washing here, in the house. When Mr. Sackville saw how hard and rough the work was, he told me to have the laundry sent out—he'd pay for it." Her voice cracked a little. "Now that was real kindness, that."

Her anecdote left an impression on Sergeant MacDonald. As they walked away from the house, after saying good-bye to Mrs. Cornish, he said, "A shame this Mr. Sackville died. He seemed a real gentleman."

"It would appear so. But if experience has taught me anything, those who knew the deceased are unlikely to speak ill of him so soon after his passing—especially not to a pair of police officers."

From Curry House, they were to head back to the village to call on Dr. Harris. But Treadles exclaimed softly, turned around, and rang the doorbell again.

Mrs. Cornish opened the door. "Inspector, did you forget something?"

"I did indeed, Mrs. Cornish. I forgot to ask where the Birtles live." He and MacDonald could easily pay Becky Birtle a visit while they were in the area.

"They live in Yorkshire."

"*Yorkshire?*" Young girls in service tended to find work nearby. Or they departed for the big cities via connections with family and friends. For Becky Birtle to travel from Yorkshire to a barely on-the-map village four hundred miles away was unusual, to say the least.

"I worked in Yorkshire years ago and knew the Birtles. When Becky was old enough to work, they asked me if I had a place for her—they said they'd feel less worried if someone they trusted kept an eye on her."

"I see. Did you inform Becky that the police would like a word with her?"

"I wrote her parents as soon as I heard. But I don't expect to hear back from them before tomorrow."

"I see."

Treadles collected the Birtles' address from Mrs. Cornish and made a mental note to find someone from the district's constabulary to speak with Becky.

Sherlock Holmes had better be uncannily brilliant in his conjectures about these deaths—or at least about Mr. Sackville's. Or he and Treadles would both end up looking very silly.

Very silly indeed.

———— ✺ ————

At Dr. Harris's home, Treadles and MacDonald were pleasantly surprised to find not only Dr. Harris waiting for them, but also Dr. Birch, the physician who had attended Mr. Sackville on the latter's deathbed.

"Dr. Birch, Miss Birch, Mrs. Harris, and I play whist together quite often," said Dr. Harris. "So we thought we'd make a party of it today, and save you gentlemen a trip to Barton Cross."

"Your thoughtfulness is most appreciated," said Treadles.

"I assume you will wish to speak to Dr. Birch first, since his intelligence is more germane to your case?"

"That will suit us very well."

They were shown into Dr. Harris's study. Dr. Birch was a lively man with a gleam in his eye. He responded to Treadles's questions with quick, to-the-point answers. Yes, his doorbell had rung shortly after seven that day and he had to dash off a quick note to the proprietor of the village inn, where there was an elderly traveler waiting for him, in pain and in need of morphine. And since his dogcart was already hitched, he drove, following Tommy Dunn to Curry House.

"It really was too bad that young Dunn couldn't tell me anything relevant about Mr. Sackville, except that he couldn't be roused and appeared to be in a bad way. Or I'd have been better prepared."

"You'd have brought strychnine?"

"Most likely, if I'd suspected an overdose of chloral. And I would have if I'd been told about Mr. Sackville's body temperature—that is a telltale symptom of chloral poisoning."

"Isn't strychnine a deadly poison in itself?"

"One of the deadliest. Administered to a healthy person, strychnine would cause fatal muscular convulsions. But that property makes it an effective antidote to chloral: It stimulates the heart's function and stops the slide of decreasing body temperature."

"Now, doctor, do you believe the chloral that killed Mr. Sackville to have been self-administered?"

"Dr. Harris and I spoke about it and we saw absolutely no reason why it shouldn't have been so," Dr. Birch answered confidently. "The chloral that Dr. Harris prescribed for Mr. Sackville was in the form of grains. It is very difficult to force a man to ingest anything he doesn't wish to—and there were no signs of violence anywhere. The only explanation that makes sense is that Mr. Sackville miscounted the number of grains and paid for his mistake."

The bespectacled Dr. Harris was more deliberate in his demeanor than Dr. Birch. But he confirmed without hesitation that Mr. Sackville's gastric episodes had been ongoing, nothing unusual. And that he had indeed prescribed the chloral, for Mr. Sackville's insomnia.

"When was the last time you saw Mr. Sackville in a professional capacity?" asked Treadles.

"Six weeks ago. He had a persistent cough and was worried that it might turn into pneumonia."

"It didn't, I presume?"

"No. Once the weather turned warmer, the cough cleared."

"He didn't consult you about his gastric attacks?"

"He mentioned them from time to time, but he was resigned. He'd been suffering from them since he was a young man and had accepted that they would continue to plague him for as long as he lived."

"I see," said Inspector Treadles.

He was about to ask another question when Dr. Harris said, "His new cook showed far greater interest in his digestion than he did. She came and conferred with me once, on her half day no less. Interesting woman. She wanted to cure Mr. Sackville of his 'tummy aches' by modifying his diet to exclude those items that could be proven to irritate his innards.

"Her plan was to start with one item known to be fine for him to eat and then add in other items one by one, with at least forty-eight hours between each addition, so that any single item that set him off could be pinpointed and eliminated right away—very sound methodology, that. But Mr. Sackville scoffed at her suggestion. He might suffer abdominal turmoil once in a while but he was still a man who like a good supper and a proper pudding with every meal. Having so limited a diet for any length of time was unthinkable for him."

"So Mrs. Meek attempted to enlist the weight of your professional opinion in persuading Mr. Sackville to change his mind?"

"Precisely. I commended her for her dedication and initiative—I wish my own cook thought half so much of my digestion. But if I've learned anything in my years of dealing with patients it's that it is nigh impossible to change a grown man's habits. I told her I'd put in a word with Mr. Sackville the next time I saw him—but I never did see him again."

"A shame," said Treadles. "Let me now ask you the same question I posed to Dr. Birch. Do you believe that Mr. Sackville died because he took the wrong number of chloral grains?"

Dr. Harris took off his spectacles and polished them with a handkerchief. "Let me tell you a secret, Inspector: Dr. Birch is a terrible player at whist—he would be hopeless if it weren't for his sister, who is formidable on a green baize table. But as a physician, he is thoroughly observant and exceptionally competent and would have made a successful name for himself in the city if he didn't greatly dislike city life. So if he tells me that there was no sign the chloral got into Mr. Sackville by force or trickery, then I will gladly take his word for it."

Treadles sighed inwardly. With every interview, Holmes's first foray onto the public stage looked more likely to be a stumble rather than a triumph. So much for the hope that his genius would carry Treadles to widespread acclaim, thereby bolstering Alice's social standing.

"On the other hand," Dr. Harris went on, "as much as the most obvious explanation seems the most logical and likely, I am uneasy about accepting the theory of miscounted grains of chloral."

Treadles sat up straighter. "Oh?"

"Years ago, while I was still a student at medical school, a good friend of mine committed suicide by ingesting chloral. His death left a lasting impression." The physician donned his glasses again and looked meaningfully at Treadles. "In my own practice I never dispense vials with more than eight grains of chloral inside."

Treadles's fingertips tingled: He remembered the vial in Mr. Sackville's nightstand, still with two grains of chloral left. "I take it eight grains do not amount to enough to kill a man."

"Precisely. Mr. Sackville's insomnia was sporadic rather than frequent. He sent for a vial a few times a year. If one assumed that he sent for more when he'd run out, then there wouldn't have been enough chloral at Curry House to harm him."

Sergeant MacDonald, who had been largely bent over his notebook, glanced at Treadles, surprise and excitement in his eyes. Treadles felt that same flutter in his stomach. "Is it reasonable to assume that he sent for more only when he ran out?"

"Reasonable enough, since I could dispatch a vial back within minutes."

"But in the end there was more than enough chloral at Curry House," Treadles pointed out, doing his best to keep his voice even.

Dr. Harris set his hands at the edge of the desk and leaned forward. "Which to me suggested two possibilities. One, he had been purposefully accumulating chloral. Keep in mind though, the last time he had a vial from me was shortly after I saw him six weeks ago. Is it not odd, if he planned to kill himself, to wait that six weeks? Not to mention he never struck me as a man who had the least desire to die before his time."

Treadles exchanged another look with Sergeant MacDonald. "And the other possibility?"

Dr. Harris exhaled and clasped his hands together. "Let's just say that I for one was not sorry that Mr. Sherlock Holmes of London took the trouble to write to the coroner."

Treadles's breaths came faster. He had to remind himself that he mustn't get carried away—not yet. "You made no mention of your unease at the inquest, doctor."

"I was never asked any question except whether I'd prescribed chloral for Mr. Sackville."

"Given your misgivings, Dr. Harris, do you believe that it is a coincidence that Mr. Sackville happened to die on a day you were away?"

"That did give me pause." Dr. Harris looked down for a moment at his hands. "I haven't told anyone this, but at the inquest, had the letter from Mr. Holmes not been read, I would have said something about my suspicions, even though I was most reluctant to do so."

"Of course. I understand that reluctance—it's a small village and the glare of the public would immediately focus on those closest to Mr. Sackville."

Dr. Harris nodded. "I was both baffled and relieved when Mr. Holmes connected Mr. Sackville's passing with deaths in the wider world—since that would exonerate members of his household."

"Would someone who isn't from around here know that you'd be gone that day?"

Dr. Harris blinked. "I can't be sure."

"But people from the village would know?"

"They know that I travel to London once a month to meet with old friends from medical school, have dinner together, and talk about interesting cases we've come across—they more than I. Afterward, it's usually late enough that I stay overnight and start back early in the morning."

"Does it always happen on a fixed day?"

"Usually it falls in the middle of the month and I put a note on the church bulletin to that effect. Dr. Birch looks after my patients in my absence, as I do in his. But this isn't the sort of place where one expects to hear frantic knocking on the door in the middle of the night. In fact, the unfortunate circumstances surrounding Mr. Sackville's death were the first time Dr. Birch had cause to bestir himself for one of my patients when I was away in London."

They thanked him and walk out of his house.

"I see you've something in mind, Inspector," said MacDonald, after taking one look at Treadles.

"I hope you still have ink in your pen, sergeant," replied Treadles. "We are going back to Curry House."

———✤———

Mrs. Cornish's brows shot up as she opened the door to Inspector Treadles and Sergeant MacDonald one more time.

"Inspector. Sergeant. Did you forget something after all?"

"No, indeed, Mrs. Cornish. More questions came to mind after we spoke to Dr. Birch and Dr. Harris. Would it be all right for me to take a few minutes of Tommy Dunn's time—and a few minutes of yours?"

"Certainly. Tommy is in the garden, I believe. Should I have him come in?"

"No, we'll be happy to speak to him in his natural habitat."

Mrs. Cornish pointed the policemen in the direction of the walled kitchen garden. Tommy Dunn, digging in a corner of the garden, was surprised but not alarmed to see them. "Something I can do for you, Inspector?"

"Yes, Mr. Dunn. Do you remember what exactly Mrs. Cornish said to you, when she came to ask you to fetch Dr. Harris?"

Tommy Dunn thought for a moment. "She said, 'Quick. Get on that horse and go get Dr. Harris. Mr. Sackville is badly off. We can't wake him up and I don't think there's much time.'"

"Anything else?"

"No."

"Did she mention Mr. Sackville's temperature?"

"No. She came running in her dressing gown and she was out of breath. So I knew something must have happened. I'd ought remembered if she told me he was really cold. I wouldn't forget."

"Did it not occur to you that Dr. Harris wouldn't be home? From what I understand, he posts the date he'd be gone to London on the church noticeboard."

"Can't say I read the church noticeboard on the regular. It's all about on which days the altar flower ladies meet and whatnot."

They thanked him, returned to the house, and followed Mrs. Cornish to her office. As they passed before the kitchen, Mrs. Meek stuck her head out, a worried expression on her face. "Everything all right?"

"Inspector Treadles has a few more questions, that's all," answered Mrs. Cornish, if a bit tightly.

As she offered Treadles and MacDonald seats and tea, she didn't seem so much nervous as rattled—perhaps it had not occurred to her that the matter was serious enough to merit a return visit.

"Mrs. Cornish," said Treadles, "would you mind recalling for us exactly what you told Tommy Dunn, when you tasked him to fetch Dr. Harris?"

The housekeeper frowned, whether in surprise or concentration Treadles could not tell. "I can't promise I remember what I said word for word, but it would be along the lines of 'Hurry! Jump on that horse and go get Dr. Harris. Mr. Sackville is in a bad way. We can't wake him up, he's going cold, and there's no time to lose.'"

"You are certain you mentioned his temperature?"

"Yes."

Treadles felt a glance from MacDonald. "Dr. Birch specifically laments that he wasn't told of it and that was the reason he was ill prepared to deal with an overdose of chloral."

Mrs. Cornish's frown deepened. "It must have slipped Tommy Dunn's mind then."

"You think so?"

"He's young and not used to handling emergencies. I wouldn't be surprised if his mind went blank after he'd heard that Mr. Sackville was in a bad way—he thought the world of Mr. Sackville."

"I see. Now did it not occur to you that Dr. Harris wouldn't be home? I believe the day and time of his absence is posted on the church bulletin."

Mrs. Cornish sighed. "That's one thing that's nagged at me ever since that day. I did realize it, but not until Tommy Dunn was at least five minutes gone. The thing was, Dr. Harris didn't go at his usual time of the month. We're used to him being gone around the middle of the month. But this time he was gone at least a week ahead of his regular day. And it was only after Tommy Dunn was too far to hear me shout that I remembered reading about the change on the noticeboard the day before, on my way to the railway station."

"When was the change announced, did you know?"

"Must have been after Sunday, or the vicar would have said something from the pulpit."

"Thank you, Mrs. Cornish." Treadles rose and inclined his head. "This time we are truly going, I promise."

—❈—

"So one of them is lying?" asked Sergeant MacDonald, as they made their way back to the village of Stanwell Moot.

They rode on bicycles that they had brought from London. The bicycles eliminated the need for the local constabulary to provide transportation for Scotland Yard, but more to the point, cycling happened to be an activity Treadles greatly enjoyed, and which was much more difficult to indulge in London. Here in the country the breeze was fragrant, the sun pleasantly warm, and there were no mobs of pedestrians or speeding carriages to contend with.

There were, however, occasional mud puddles to avoid and Treadles guided his bicycle around one before answering MacDonald. "I don't think one of them has to be lying. It's quite possible, as Mrs. Cornish said, for a young man unaccustomed to emergencies to not hear everything he's been told. My mother used to say that if she sent me to the shop to get five things, she'd be lucky if I returned with three."

MacDonald reached out a hand and let his fingertips brush the bright green leaves of the hedge. "So after a whole afternoon of interviews, we've Dr. Harris's suspicions and nothing else."

"But that's a very fine set of suspicions."

MacDonald was unconvinced. "Is that enough to get the coroner's jury to return a verdict other than accidental overdose?"

It was patently not enough.

"Well, we still have a few days left for that." They were near the village. The hedgerows dropped away and a wide vista opened up, green fields and shining sea, with the village's church tower rising up to an unblemished sky. "And if all else fails, we've got ourselves a holiday on the Devon Coast."

Nine

Charlotte,

You bloody fool.

(I hope Mamma never sees this. Or it would be off with my head for such blasphemous language—if not already for writing to you behind her back. But my word, you bloody fool!)

This morning Mamma took to her bed and Papa was abroad. I snuck out of the house to Mrs. Wallace's boarding home, hoping to run into you—and reassure myself you were still in tolerable circumstances. Needless to say, every single one of my nightmares came true in that woman's parlor.

I came home to a letter that Mott had smuggled in for me—he had been calling for my letters at the Charing Cross post office, since I am watched closely. The postmark let me know without a doubt that the letter was posted after you had been evicted. But you said nothing of it. It was full of falsely cheerful observations of life at Mrs. Wallace's!

I am drenched in fear. Steeped, marinated, macerated in it. I beg you to please tell me what is going on. The truth cannot be worse than the dreadful scenarios barging through my head.

Or at least tell me that you are not lying in a ditch somewhere, though how I am to believe you after all the lies I do not know.

Livia

P.S. Come home, Charlotte. Come home.

—❊—

Sherlock Holmes's letter had caused a sensation. The tone of coverage suggested a willingness on the part of the newspapers—and most likely, by extension, on the part of the public—to entertain the possibility that Lady Shrewsbury's death had been part of a sinister larger plan. Which ought to have made Livia breathe easier, as she'd rarely crossed paths with Lady Amelia and had never met Mr. Sackville.

Had probably made things better for Livia, which explained how she could have slipped out—and discovered the reality of Charlotte's current situation.

My Dearest Livia,

My apologies for not having been entirely truthful earlier. I am not lying in a ditch somewhere and things are not hopeless. Yet.

Charlotte

—❊—

The eviction from Mrs. Wallace's boarding home cast a long shadow. Charlotte felt marked. Even if her situation were to improve drastically, the danger remained that at any moment she could be recognized, her disguise stripped away, and her scandalous past brought to the fore to condemn her all over again.

But to be banished from her place of domicile, as bad as it had been, was not as awful as the possibility that the same might happen to her at her place of employment.

Should she ever have a place of employment, that is.

The inside of Miss Oswald's Employment Agency smelled of ink and overbrewed tea. The place was mentioned by two of the sources Charlotte had studied, not so much in recommending it as begrudgingly admitting its legitimacy.

Their distaste, as far as Charlotte could discern, stemmed from the fact that Miss Oswald's aim was less to help other women and more to make a living for herself. Charlotte had no objection to that goal. Moreover, she entertained hopes that Miss Oswald would, one, recognize that Charlotte would be a valuable worker and, two, prove more efficient than the charitable societies and registries for which greater efficacy would not bring more profits, only more work.

Squinting behind her thick glasses, Miss Oswald perused the letter of character Charlotte had brought. Behind her, a small window set high on the wall offered a rectangular slice of what passed for clear blue sky in London.

Livia lived for days like this. When sunlight wasn't just warm on the skin, but seemed to have a soft, blanketlike weight. She would sit outside and turn her face up—the risk of becoming unfashionably tanned be damned—and soak in all the heat and brightness.

Charlotte had never told her this, but she had planned to take Livia to the south of France someday. To spend a few weeks, or perhaps an entire winter, bathing daily in that lemon-colored sunshine.

"You were . . . a typist for Broadbent, Lucas and Sons in Tunbridge," said Miss Oswald, a hint of disbelief in her voice, as she set aside the letter of character.

"Yes, ma'am."

There was nothing amiss with the letter Charlotte had forged, which had been typed on proper stationery: The letterheads had been ordered from a good stationer's, and the signature was masterful, if she did say so herself.

Unfortunately, she had hesitated at the expense of acquiring new clothes that would have completed the illusion. The clothes wouldn't be costly in absolute terms—they were meant to make her look like a young woman who must contribute to her own support. But compared to how little money remained to her, every price was dauntingly exorbitant.

So she'd come to the interview in her own clothes—a jacket, a blouse, and a skirt—which, while not extravagant, were still of a level of quality and workmanship far exceeding what a typist ought to be able to afford.

Were she observing herself, she'd draw the obvious conclusion that there was something incongruous about her, that she might not be the humble position seeker she claimed to be. Why should Miss Oswald, whose business depended on accurately judging the trustworthiness of the applicants, come to a different verdict?

"And what is the reason you moved to London?"

"My parents are no more and my aunt asked me to come live with her."

"Where does she live, your aunt?"

"Lambeth, ma'am."

After losing her pound note to the girl beggar, a rundown boarding home in Lambeth was the best Charlotte could do. The district was grey, industrial, and in constant danger of flooding, but safe enough during daylight hours—and an acceptable place for a typist's aunt to live.

Except Charlotte wasn't dressed like a typist at all. This was what she would have worn for a day at the Reading Room of the British Library—and no one there had ever treated her as anything but a lady.

Miss Oswald pursed her lips. "Your typing speed, Miss Morrison?"

"Forty-five words a minute. I'm also familiar with Pitman's system of phonemic orthography." An honest answer. In her former life, she had many, many hours to fill—learning shorthand was as good a way to pass time as any. "If there are employers willing to have a female secretary, I'm sure I can handle the demands."

"Indeed," said Miss Oswald coolly. "I shall be astounded if you aren't equal to the task, Miss Morrison. But first I must get in touch with Broadbent, Lucas and Sons."

Charlotte sucked in a breath. The reason she'd gone to the trouble to counterfeit a law firm's stationery was so that its authenticity wouldn't be questioned.

"We've had word of a lady journalist masquerading as an applicant," Miss Oswald continued, "trying to dig up dirt on those of us in the business of matching qualified women with reputable employers. I'm not saying that you are she—of course not—but you will understand why I have no wish to unwittingly assist in such muckraking."

"Naturally not."

"It will take me ten days or so to complete the check and to review my openings. You may return Friday of next week to see whether I have found anything appropriate to your background and skills."

If Miss Oswald had heard about such a lady journalist from others in the business, then no doubt she would pass along that she had encountered the very woman, one who dressed too well for an applicant and bore with her a letter of character from Broadbent, Lucas and Sons.

Her stomach clenched, Charlotte rose, said her thank-you, and left.

Inspector Treadles, back at his desk at Scotland Yard, scanned the papers for their coverage of the Sackville case. Speculation was rampant, as much regarding the mysterious Sherlock Holmes as concerning the identity and motives of those dastardly individuals who might have done away with Mr. Sackville, Lady Amelia Drummond, and Lady Shrewsbury.

Theories on the deaths were wildly inventive—everything from dangerous secret societies to the testing of a new, untraceable chemical. About Sherlock Holmes, opinions were sharply divided. Some insisted that he was no relation to Miss Olivia Holmes, the young woman who had quarreled with Lady Shrewsbury the night before the latter died—Holmes was hardly a rare surname. Others pointed out that one was far more likely to find this man by searching more obscure branches of the family tree than among the general public: Didn't it make more sense for a kinsman, however remote, to come to the aid of the beleaguered Olivia Holmes?

"Your post, sir," came Sergeant MacDonald's voice. "Something from Inspector Waller for you."

Before Inspector Treadles left Devonshire, he had sent a cable to Inspector Waller of the West Riding Constabulary, calling in a favor. "Excellent!" he exclaimed, accepting the letter from MacDonald. "Any further response from Lord Sheridan's secretary?"

"Not yet." MacDonald pulled out his watch. "But the next post is only fifty-five minutes away."

He sauntered off. Treadles looked fondly at his retreating form, remembering himself as a bright-eyed young sergeant, eager to learn the tricks of the trade.

With a wistful shake of the head, he returned his attention to Inspector Waller's missive.

Dear Treadles,

Enclosed please find a transcript of my interview with Becky Birtle.
Constable Small, who came with me, takes excellent shorthand. You may
be certain of the accuracy of the document.

    The girl was a bit of an odd bird. Thinks very highly of herself. The
parents are all right, solid, salt-of-the-earth sorts. They were befuddled by
the whole affair and sought reassurance several times that their daughter
wasn't in any trouble.

    Anyway, glad to render a service—delighted, in fact. Let me know if
there is anything else I can do for you.

Waller

Treadles picked up the transcript. Becky Birtle's version of events didn't accord in every detail with those given by Mrs. Cornish and Mrs. Meek—a good thing, or it would lead him to think she had been tutored in her answers. But all three women's accounts agreed enough that minor disparities could be attributed to the vagaries of human memory.

Her description of the twenty-four hours before also did not differ too much from everyone else's: household duties, an afternoon spent with the vicar's wife, who organized activities so that girls in service didn't get into trouble on their half days and Sundays, and a return to Curry House in the evening for supper and bed. She complained about Mrs. Meek's food, "so bland, but she's a nice woman," and about being locked in nightly with Jenny Price, "as if we was chickens in a coop, with weasels prowling outside." And she'd have had more to say about Mrs. Cornish's strictness, but Inspector Waller moved on from the subject.

An exchange toward the end of the interview caught Treadles's eye.

Now most likely your Mr. Sackville died of an accidental overdose, but since we can't be sure yet, I have to ask you this: Do you know of anyone who might wish him harm?—You mean someone killed him? I knew it. I knew it the moment I heard that letter at the inquest.

I implied nothing of the sort. He could have committed suicide, for all we know.—Not him, not Mr. Sackville. He told me he wanted to live to a hundred twenty.

He did? When?—Not long ago.

Under what circumstances did he tell you that?—I took a walk one Sunday afternoon, a couple of weeks after I started working at Curry House, and he did the same. We ran into each other right above the cove. I said I was sorry that it happened, but he said not to apologize. He said of course I'd want to have a stroll on a beautiful spring day. Said he looked forward to every spring. More so now that he was older and there wouldn't be as many springs left for him. I told him he was going to live to a hundred. And he said he much preferred carrying on another twenty years past that.

I see. So you would swear on a Bible that he wouldn't take his own life.—I would, Inspector. I'd swear on a stack of Bibles taller than me.

Then do you know anyone who might have a grudge against him?—I say them what be good and generous always have people who hates them.

Anyone specific?—His brother.

His brother?—Yes.

Have you met his brother?—No, his brother is some high
and mighty lordship.

Then how do you know?—Mr. Sackville told me, of course.
He said his brother would be happy if he were dead.

—❊—

Ever since Treadles took on the investigation, he had been trying to
arrange an interview with Lord Sheridan. And the next of kin to
Lady Amelia Drummond and Lady Shrewsbury.

The ladies' relations flatly refused to have anything to do with
the police. Lord Shrewsbury—Lady Shrewsbury's firstborn son and
the current baron—went so far as to call Sherlock Holmes "a ghoul-
ish, depraved rumormonger" and characterized Treadles's professional interest as "shamelessly intruding on a family's private
grief." But after some more back-and-forth with Lord Sheridan's
secretary, Treadles did manage to gain an appointment with the
man's employer.

The Sheridans' address, unless Treadles was mistaken, placed
their dwelling close to Lord Ingram's, though not on the same street.
Treadles had never seen Lord Ingram's town house and found himself curious.

But first, business.

The Sheridan residence was third in a row of town houses, in white
stone and stucco, with wrought-iron railings and a small portico above
the entrance. A dour-looking footman opened the door and conducted them to a study.

The sight of an entire wall of books, as always, was delightful.
As for the rest of the room—Treadles was no expert on the furnishing of houses, but even to his relatively untrained eye, the study
appeared . . . threadbare. Literally so, in places. The two padded

chairs set against the far wall should have been reupholstered years ago. The curtains, too, looked sorry. The carpet, which had once probably cost a fortune, was now in its most heavily trod areas barely thicker than a tea towel.

The footman left to fetch his master.

Sergeant MacDonald scooted closer to Treadles. "Thought I'd be afraid to set me bum down in a place like this. But I never guessed it'd be because I don't dare put any more wear and tear on the chairs."

Treadles answered in a similar whisper. "It's the price of crops. They've been dropping a good long while and these old families who depend on the land for their income, well, that income has been dropping, too."

"Then why doesn't his lordship sell this house and live someplace smaller and cheaper, so he can at least afford new chairs?"

"Not so simple. The house might be entailed. In which case he can't sell it even if he wants to, not without first petitioning Parliament or something equally complicated."

"Huh, fancy that. But now he won't be as poor, not with his dead brother's money coming his way."

The day before, Sergeant MacDonald had paid a visit to Mr. Sackville's solicitors, who had confirmed for him that Mr. Sackville, despite his regular visits to London, had seldom called on his men of business. MacDonald had also obtained a copy of Mr. Sackville's will: There were various odds-and-ends bequests, but the bulk of his fortune had gone to Lord Sheridan.

Which meant that Lord Sheridan, unlike everyone else involved with the case so far, had a motive that passed muster. He needed a great deal of funds; and by getting rid of his brother, he would come into a great deal of funds.

Men had killed for much less.

138 · *Sherry Thomas*

The door of the study opened again and their best suspect walked in. Lord Sheridan, a man of about seventy, was short and bald, but his eyes were sharp and his movement spry. He greeted the policemen and bade them to take seats before the big desk.

"My secretary tells me you have questions for me, concerning my brother's death."

"We hope you can shed some light onto the circumstances of Mr. Sackville's passing, sir. You have heard of the connection that has been made between his death and those of Lady Amelia Drummond and Lady Shrewsbury?"

"It is one of the leading topics of the day," said Lord Sheridan with distaste. "That and the identity of this meddlesome Sherlock Holmes. Harrington retired from Society decades ago. The younger generation does not even know who he was. And now all manners of unfounded speculations circulate and multiply.

"But no, I cannot help you. My brother and I had not spoken in many years. I am unfamiliar with what his habits and inclinations had become."

"Can you give us some knowledge as to why he retired from Society?"

"No, I cannot."

Cannot or will not? Lord Sheridan spoke with a casual impatience that was surprisingly difficult to decipher. "And is that related to the reason the two of you became estranged?"

"You leap to conclusions, Inspector. My brother and I were not close, but I never suggested that we were estranged."

This gave Treadles the opening he had been looking for. "My apologies, my lord. My perceptions might have been colored by having read a statement, made by someone in Mr. Sackville's employ, that you would be glad if he were to drop dead."

Lord Sheridan's expression did not change. "I recommend that you give no credence to such statements, Inspector. I took no delight in Harrington's passing. I was much older than he—at one point I was his guardian—both father and brother. There is no joy to be had at the death of someone I watched growing up. Now, if you have no more questions . . ."

His tone carried more than a hint of sternness. Treadles pressed on. "I do happen to have one more. Forgive me if the question borders on vulgar, my lord, but if I understand correctly, in families such as yours, the eldest son inherits the bulk of the family wealth. Yet the impression I receive seems to be that Mr. Sackville had been the one with the larger fortune."

"Your impression is correct. Harrington is my half brother. His mother brought a great deal of wealth into her marriage. But while tens of thousands of pounds from her dowry were used in shoring up the estate, upon her death she willed almost all of her remaining assets to Harrington, her only child. So yes, he was wealthier and his wealth was never bled by the ancestral pile."

His recitation of facts was . . . smoother than his avowal that he found no pleasure in his brother's death. But how should Treadles interpret this observation? Was it because Lord Sheridan was not an accomplished liar—or was it because it in fact distressed him to have lost someone who had once been both brother and son?

"Would you happen to know, sir, who would benefit most from Mr. Sackville's will?"

"His lawyers have informed me that I stand to inherit his fortune."

"Did you know that before he died?"

Lord Sheridan's expression turned forbidding: He was quick—too quick, perhaps?—to realize the thrust of the question. "Of course not. We are finished here, gentlemen. I trust you will see yourselves out."

—❧—

"Not worried about what the law might think of him, is he, Inspector?" asked Sergeant MacDonald as they walked out.

"He is a peer. He can only be tried in the House of Lords *and* he enjoys privilege from arrest. If I were him, I also wouldn't burden myself too much with what a pair of lowly policemen might think of my statements."

MacDonald scratched his reddish, slightly scraggly beard. "So who do you think is lying then about how happy he'd be to see his brother dead, his lordship or the dead man?"

"Hard to say, without knowing what had made them grow apart in the first place. That is, provided the girl wasn't making it up out of whole cloth."

Treadles wished now he'd done the questioning himself. So much could be gleaned from face-to-face observation. Nuances in tone, changes in expression, and postures of the body added up to a rich symphony of information, as opposed to this thin, tinny tune derived from typed words.

To Sergeant MacDonald's surprise, instead of leaving the premises altogether, Treadles led them down to the service entrance and knocked. But his ambush of Lord Sheridan's staff, though successful in one sense—he managed to speak with both the butler and the valet—did not yield any useful information in the end.

Except in the negative category: His lordship did not leave London in the time period of interest to Inspector Treadles. In fact, he had attended a wedding and a dinner in the twenty-four hours immediately preceding his brother's death, not to mention went to sleep and woke up in his own bed.

This time, when they left the Sheridan house, they walked away—and turned onto the street where Lord Ingram lived. It was of a similar arrangement to Lord Sheridan's, a row of elegant town houses all of the same style and construction, except these houses faced a small park surrounded by a hedgerow, with swings and a duck pond in its interior.

They were approaching Lord Ingram's home when a gleaming brougham drew up by the curb and disgorged a beautiful and stylishly dressed woman. At the same moment Lord Ingram stepped out of the house. They greeted each other with cool nods. Treadles would have thought the woman was perhaps a neighbor Lord Ingram did not know very well, until his lordship said to the coachman, "I will need the carriage at seven tonight."

The woman was Lady Ingram.

Treadles did not move in Lord Ingram's circles. Nor had Alice ever done so, though her father had been a wealthy industrialist. It had not struck Treadles as particularly odd that Lady Ingram did not accompany her husband on digs or attend his lectures at Burlington House—he'd simply assumed that things were different for the very upper echelons of Society and that she must have been busy with her own duties.

That greeting between spouses, however, implied such a vast distance. What Treadles was looking at was not any kind of upper-class stricture against displays of affection, but a resolute lack of affection altogether.

Lord and Lady Ingram were two strangers who happened to live under the same roof.

This was probably not news to anyone who knew the couple. But Treadles still felt as if he'd witnessed something he ought not to have—an insight into Lord Ingram's marriage that the latter had not chosen to share with him. Embarrassment further pummeled him when he realized that he and MacDonald were too close to turn aside, that he might put Lord Ingram in a situation of having to introduce a pair of coppers to the lady wife.

Lord Ingram spied him. "Inspector, what an unexpected pleasure."

They shook hands. Treadles, praying his face wasn't as red as he imagined it must be, introduced Sergeant MacDonald to his lordship, who then turned to his wife. "Lady Ingram, allow me to present two of the Criminal Investigation Department's finest, Inspector Treadles and Sergeant MacDonald."

"A pleasure, I'm sure," said Lady Ingram with a fixed smile. "I will leave you gentlemen to discuss important affairs. Good day, Inspector. Good day, Sergeant."

Treadles and MacDonald bowed. Lord Ingram inclined his head. When Lady Ingram had disappeared into the house, Lord Ingram asked, "Are you on duty, gentlemen?"

"We are, but we have completed our interview—for now."

"Excellent. If you have a moment, I'd like my children to meet you. They are in the park."

The children, an elfin girl of about five and a sturdy-looking boy maybe a year younger, were busy building what looked to be a miniature tent with small twigs, under the supervision of a nanny. At the sight of their father they rushed toward him and excitedly told him about their castle.

Lord Ingram did the honors. The two policemen and the two Ashburton children shook hands, warmly on both sides, for the children were friendly, curious, and full of pep.

Lord Ingram promised his children that he would return and help them with the castle, and then he walked the police officers out of the park.

"Any headways in your investigation, Inspector?"

Treadles shook his head. "I'm afraid not. A few tantalizing glimmers here and there, but nothing that translates into solid evidence that would persuade any jury in the land."

Lord Ingram looked disappointed, but not surprised. "This was never going to be an easy case. I can't thank you enough, Inspector, for taking it on."

"For Sherlock Holmes, it's the least I could do," said Treadles, feeling warm and bolstered by Lord Ingram's words.

"If there's anything I can do to help, please don't hesitate to let me know."

"There is, in fact." If Treadles had not run into Lord Ingram, he would have sent round a note very soon. "I'd be most obliged if a discreet inquiry could be made to the cause behind Lord Sheridan and Mr. Sackville's estrangement. The families of the deceased ladies have categorically refused to be of any help. So Mr. Sackville is our only opening."

Lord Ingram thought for a moment. "There is someone I can approach for this purpose."

"Thank you, my lord." Treadles had every faith Lord Ingram would see to the matter promptly. "Have you any news from Holmes, by the way?"

Treadles had asked to see the letter to the coroner while he'd been in Devon. While the letter itself was undated, the postmark was two days after Holmes's misfortune. Most likely, someone close to him had discovered the letter afterward and dispatched it to its intended recipient. But Treadles still held out hope that Holmes might have recovered.

"No, I've had no news at all from Holmes," said Lord Ingram. Then, for the first time in their acquaintance, he asked of Treadles, "And you, Inspector? Have you heard from Holmes?"

Treadles shook his head. After he'd taken on the investigation,

144 · *Sherry Thomas*

he had indeed sent a note to Holmes—to the General Post Office, as Lord Ingram once mentioned he had. The letter might as well have been dropped into the Thames, for all the response he'd received. "But I plan to carry on and do as much as possible."

In the little time that remained.

"I am most grateful." Lord Ingram shook Treadles's hand. "And Holmes would be, too, if Holmes but knew."

Ten

Charlotte did know of Inspector Treadles's involvement—she'd received his letter—but sometimes gratitude wasn't enough to get a woman out of bed.

She had not packed an umbrella when she left home. Of course not. A parasol was an accessory for a lady. An umbrella, not so. When she'd had a bit of money in reserve, there had been no precipitation. And now that one cloudburst followed another, she could no longer afford any rain gear.

Or so she told herself, for an excuse not to go out to be met with further disappointments.

All the better options had been taken from her. Had she prowled the city with energy and determination, she'd still have returned footsore and empty-handed. The schools were closed to her. The professions were closed to her. Just about anything that had a possibility of a satisfying career was closed to her.

She could go into domestic service, but her age factored against her: Women who spent their working life in service often started when they were eleven or twelve. Someone as old as she should have already worked her way up to the position of a lady's maid or an underhousekeeper. She didn't mind scrubbing pots and pans alongside tweenies, but that didn't mean the person who did the hiring, the housekeeper or the cook, would want her about.

Which meant she must lie and pretend to have experience and references. She had read Mrs. Beeton's *Book of Household Management* from end to end. She knew that turpentine could remove stains from clothing and that spirit of wine was good for cleaning pokers.

But domestic service had its own drawbacks. In smaller households she might be harassed by her employer or other servants. In larger households, run with military precision, she was safer from unwanted attention—she might never see her employer except once a year at the servants' ball. But she faced a greater risk that someone might recognize her, leading to her expulsion—or to being blackmailed.

Was it any wonder she had spent most of the day staring at the ceiling? Why expend the energy—and wear out the soles of her boots—just so she could spend the next several years on her knees cleaning out grates while fearing either the son of the house or a sharp-eyed fellow servant who might have seen her from her pre-scandal days?

Much better to stay put. That way she'd at least be less hungry.

But when the rain stopped, she left for her daily pilgrimage to the General Post Office, in the hope that there would be a letter from Livia or Inspector Treadles—she hadn't heard from him again after he embarked on his investigation.

Temperatures had dropped. Unlike Livia, Charlotte enjoyed leaden skies and daylong drizzle. Even better if they coincided with raw winds that rattled roof tiles, while the last few brown leaves shivered on bare, swaying branches.

But winter was a pleasure only for those who could afford it. Who could sit before a blazing fire, a steaming mug of mulled cider in hand, and watch the storm pelt against windowpanes while nibbling on a slice of still-warm plum cake.

Winter would not be at all enjoyable for a woman who didn't even possess a winter coat anymore. Who had only enough money to last her two more weeks in the city, provided nothing untoward happened in the meanwhile.

At the end of those two weeks, if she hadn't experienced a sudden reversal of fortune, she would need to swallow her pride and go to a man.

Besides her father, there were two men she could call on. One she didn't want to visit because she wasn't sure whether he would help her. The other gave her pause because he would—and she would rather not need his help if she could at all avoid it.

No good choices. But then, what had she expected? Even before she ran away from home, she had reached a point where every choice was unhappy and every decision costly.

When summer ended, it would be an eternity before summer returned again.

As if to further emphasize how far she'd fallen from grace, it poured anew, forcing her to seek shelter beneath the awning of a printer's shop, so that the rain wouldn't ruin either her hat or the hem of her dress.

A long quarter hour to stand in place and stare into a future the unknowns of which were becoming all too grimly clear.

The rain lightened and became scarcely damper than mist. Charlotte set out again. She took a different route to the post office these days, since she was coming from a different direction, bypassing the spot held by the mother-and-daughter beggar-and-thief team. But whenever she was in the vicinity, she still looked about, not so much afraid of being stolen from again as fearing the mortification if she were to run into them.

The beggars were nowhere in sight. But the man who had waited out the rain across the street from her was twenty feet behind.

Was he following her?

She hadn't feared for the safety of her person in broad daylight. But now unsavory possibilities bombarded her. After a minute, she looked again. But he was no longer there.

Had it been a figment of her imagination? Had the man simply been on his way to his own destination?

She turned onto St. Martin's Le Grand and stopped under the side portico of the post office's façade. If the man were following her, he would catch up to her at some point and she'd see him.

She saw no one who resembled the man, but the beautifully overdressed woman from the other day walked past, staring down at a stack of mail in her hand. With every step, she shuffled the letter on top to the bottom, a sharp line creasing her lovely brow.

A herd of men came around the corner, obscuring Charlotte's view of the woman. She studied the men: None of them proved to be the one she suspected of following her.

When they had all passed, she saw a letter lying at the edge of the portico. When no one rushed back to claim it, she picked it up.

The letter, in a less-than-handsome script, was addressed to a Mrs. Jebediah. Mrs. Jebediah herself was already some distance away. Charlotte called after her; she didn't turn around, but headed inside a tea shop.

Sometimes Charlotte wondered what women did, before tea shops came along and provided venues where an unaccompanied female could dine respectably in public. She could only be thankful that this, at least, wasn't one of her problems.

The tea shop had a fair crowd, comprised mostly of those leaving work from the post office and other nearby establishments having a bite to eat before they set out for home. Against this backdrop of somberly attired men and women, Mrs. Jebediah was as easy to spot as a toucan among pigeons.

A waitress in a black dress and a long white apron hurried past, carrying a tea tray toward a table full of clerks. The aroma of eggs scrambled in plenty of good butter assaulted Charlotte.

She could not in good conscience complain about her current boarding home. It still clung to respectability—tooth and nail—and maintained a semblance of hygiene. For the price she paid, it was a miracle that any meals had been thrown into the bargain at all. She went to each supper full of gratitude, left still mostly hungry, and filled her tummy the rest of the time with two-day-old bread bought at steep discount from the bakery down the street.

So she wasn't starving—yet. But she also wasn't very far from crawling over broken glass to get to that plate of scrambled eggs and falling face-first into it.

She stared at the tea tray another moment before resuming her progress toward her quarry, who looked up in surprise as she approached.

"Mrs. Jebediah?"

"Y-yes?"

"I'm sorry to intrude, ma'am. But I believe you dropped this outside the post office."

Mrs. Jebediah rose. "Why, yes. Thank you, Miss . . ."

Charlotte hesitated—she'd been brought up to be wary of introductions performed without a reliable third party known to both sides. "Holmes."

"Delighted to make your acquaintance, Miss Holmes." Mrs. Jebediah smiled and gestured at a chair. "Please, won't you sit down?"

Charlotte's eyes widened. "Thank you, but no. I couldn't possibly impose."

"Oh, poppycock, Miss Holmes," said Mrs. Jebediah with gentle exasperation. "You can see plain as day that I am an old lady hoping for a bit of companionship. Now if you have pressing matters or more interesting friends awaiting your attention—or if you routinely run from women past their prime who still dress like peacocks—let me know and we will say our good-byes. But if you only fear to impose, then shove a few useless rules of etiquette to the side and sit down."

The wildest thought echoed in Charlotte's head. She felt as if she'd met her mother. Her real mother.

But still she hesitated.

A waitress came by and placed on Mrs. Jebediah's table a plate of scrambled eggs exactly like the one that had seduced Charlotte a minute earlier. And a ham pie. And a ramekin of potted chicken. And finally, luxury of luxuries, red ripe strawberries accompanied by a jug of fresh, rich cream.

Charlotte's bottom found the chair quite on its own. "In that case, I shall boldly impose."

"Excellent! Tea and a place setting for the young lady," Mrs. Jebediah instructed the serving girl.

"Right away, mum."

"As you can see, Miss Holmes, I've ordered too much. When I'm hungry, I want one of everything, somehow never remembering that I will be stuffed after two bites. But then food comes and I'm full of self-recrimination—how I hate letting anything go to waste. Would you mind sparing me those twinges of conscience?"

Charlotte once again surveyed the bounty before her. "I stand ready to undertake my duty to queen and country, ma'am. And your conscience, too."

Mrs. Jebediah grinned. "I shall be in your debt, Miss Holmes."

The waitress came back with plates and cutlery for Charlotte, and an empty cup. Mrs. Jebediah poured for her. "Milk? Sugar?"

"Yes, both." Charlotte never thought she'd salivate over a cup of tea—and how. "I wish I had your problem of feeling full early and often. For me, it's the opposite. I can't remember the last time I ate until I was completely satisfied."

Mrs. Jebediah stilled. "Oh, my."

Charlotte realized that her words might be misconstrued. "Please don't think that my circumstances stand between me and a full stomach." At least not until lately. "It has been all for vanity, of course. I can sustain somewhere between one point five and one point six chins. But the moment I have more than that, my looks suffer catastrophically."

Mrs. Jebediah laughed, startled. "But surely you exaggerate, my dear."

"I assure you I do not. Via scientific trials, I have determined the precise weight, to the ounce, at which the shape of my face changes to my detriment."

Mrs. Jebediah laughed again. "Goodness, Miss Holmes, but you are diverting to speak with. I am confident that at the moment you are at least a stone below that dreaded point on the scale. So shall we fall upon our feast?"

Her hostess, Charlotte was relieved to note, did not peck like a sparrow, but ate steadily if sedately—otherwise Charlotte would have felt conspicuous, gobbling up everything in sight.

The potted chicken, spread on richly buttered toast, had to be absolutely the most delicious thing she had ever eaten in her life. Until she reached the strawberries and cream, that was, which happened to be the most delicious thing to have ever existed in the history of the universe.

There were three strawberries left when Mrs. Jebediah asked, "Do tell me, Miss Holmes, what is it that you do with your rigorous and exacting mind? Surely you haven't devoted all your waking hours to experimenting with your chins and your intake of food."

152 · *Sherry Thomas*

"Not all, but a good portion. At the moment, though, I'm trying to find a position as a typist."

"But that would be a waste! Why not seek work that demands more of your abilities? I should hate to see you with your belly full but your mind criminally underused."

"Most positions for women that use their minds rather than their labor require education and training, which eliminates me from consideration as I have none. And the rest, well, given what other positions are there, I'd consider myself lucky if I could become a typist."

"You mustn't be so defeatist, Miss Holmes."

"But I am being optimistic in hoping for a typist position. There are so few good positions and so many young women who must support themselves."

"Ah, the woman question. But tell me, Miss Holmes, what do you think you are most well suited to do?"

Charlotte blinked in astonishment—no one had ever asked her that. "May I tell you a secret, ma'am?"

"Yes, I adore secrets."

"I've always told my sister and my parents that I wished to be headmistress of a girls' school. But that's only because I'm greedy and a headmistress earns five hundred, possibly seven hundred, quid a year. The truth is I've no idea what on earth I could possibly do with my particular talent."

Mrs. Jebediah leaned forward. "And what *is* your particular talent?"

"I'm not sure how to describe it. Or even that it is a talent, rather than a nuisance. In fact, I learned early in life not to practice it in public. Or in private, for that matter—people I know well are just as easily disconcerted by it."

"Practice what, Miss Holmes?"

"Discernment, I suppose." Charlotte took a deep breath. "I can tell more about you, for instance, than you would want me to know."

Mrs. Jebediah raised a brow. "I thought by dressing as I do, I already tell those I encounter everything they could possibly want to know about me."

"I do not believe you thought, that by dressing as you do, you would broadcast how much you still mourn your husband's passing."

Mrs. Jebediah became very still, her gaze fixed on Charlotte.

"My apologies, I shouldn't have—"

"No, no, please don't. I was unprepared, that's all. I'd like to hear how you came by your observation, Miss Holmes."

It was not a request, but a command. Charlotte complied. "The black crape on your hat and your reticule—I saw them the other day. You have on a different hat and a different reticule this afternoon, but they each still incorporate a square inch or so of the same fabric. The queen wears her widow's weeds for all to see. You wear your slivers of black crape only for yourself."

Mrs. Jebediah shook her head slowly. Once. Twice. "What else? What else do you know about me?"

"You were on the stage. And successfully so."

"And how do you know that? A stage performer does not have the equivalent of black crape to give her away."

"Your attire. I suppose I could interpret it as that of a parvenu, but it isn't so much ostentatious as it is intentionally theatrical, which leads me to conclude that you belong to the demimonde. My mother would have me believe that all the women of the demimonde are prostitutes who will die penniless and alone. But it's my understanding that the demimonde is broader than that—and includes others who live unconventional lives without necessarily resorting to cyprian means to support themselves.

"At first, however, I was inclined to think that you've been a courtesan at some point, on account of the trace of rouge I see on your lips and cheeks. There's also a substance that reflects light beautifully and gives your skin a smooth appearance. Rice powder, perhaps?"

"Arrowroot powder."

"I see." Charlotte made a mental note. She didn't understand the arbitrary line that declared only loose women resorted to rouge, whereas ladies must pinch their cheeks to achieve a rosier appearance. "Yes, given that, I'd first assumed you to be a courtesan—or a former courtesan.

"But your dress changed my mind. You're clearly conveying your status as a demimondaine, yet the manner in which you achieve it is curious: You are signaling not the men, but the women. Were you aiming for the notice of the gentlemen, a higher hemline and saucy boots with cutout patterns would be much more effective. Most of them do not quite grasp that your dress, beautiful as it is, is de trop. It is left to the ladies, who have been schooled in such things from the moment they can walk, to understand that you are doing them the favor of letting them know they would not wish to associate with you, not without provoking strong disapproval in their own circles.

"If you weren't a courtesan, then most likely you were a performer. Your voice, your movement—they speak of training and control. But just as important, your posture speaks of pride in your accomplishments. Which speaks of success. Yet not so much success—or success of sufficient duration—that I would have recognized you from having seen your photographs elsewhere."

With a thoughtful look on her face, Mrs. Jebediah lifted the lid on the teapot, peered at the contents inside, and then replaced the lid. "What else do you know about me?"

"That your husband was young when he died."

The older woman nearly came out of her seat. "How can you possibly deduce *that*?"

Customers at nearby tables turned toward them. Mrs. Jebediah settled back and took a sip of her tea. They waited for their neighbors' curiosity to dissipate.

"Well, Miss Holmes?"

Charlotte turned her teacup a few degrees on its saucer. "Gentlemen in their prime, hampered by the opinion of the public and often constrained by already being married, take mistresses from the stage. It is usually the young and the old who do not give a farthing, who have the audacity to pledge their hand to a woman who has entertained the public.

"And when an old man dies, no matter how well loved he is, it is easier to accept: death has been in the wings for a while. But when a young man perishes unexpectedly, his devoted wife, who has had every expectation of many more happy years together, suddenly finds herself profoundly alone—and descends into a powerful grief that lasts for years upon years."

Mrs. Jebediah's throat moved.

"I do apologize," said Charlotte quietly. "It has been pointed out to me that once I start, I do not know where to stop."

Mrs. Jebediah exhaled. "I can see why you refrain from regularly practicing this absolutely remarkable talent of yours. But please go on."

"Are you sure, ma'am?"

"I am."

"Well, with one exception, there isn't that much more I can tell, other than minor details such as that you've spent some time in India."

"I wouldn't call that a minor detail. But what is this exception you mentioned?"

"Your name is not Mrs. Jebediah. Or at least that isn't your only name."

Mrs. Jebediah chortled. "What gave it away?"

"The letter you dropped. It was to be called for not at the General Post Office, but at the one in Charing Cross. I can well understand why a resident of London might wish to have mail delivered to the post office, rather than her private home. But to be calling for letters at two different post offices? I can only assume that you are running a scheme of some sort, Mrs. Jebediah. Not a criminal one, necessarily, but a scheme nevertheless."

"At this point, Miss Holmes, I am only shocked that you haven't told me the exact particulars of my scheme."

"I believe it involves newspaper advertisements pointing those interested to write to you. Other than that, not so much."

"Goodness gracious," murmured Mrs. Jebediah. "Knowing everything you do about me before we'd even exchanged a word, the lure of the scrambled eggs must have been powerful indeed."

"It was the strawberries and cream that did me in, I believe." Charlotte glanced at the three remaining strawberries before looking back at Mrs. Jebediah. "Please do not feel that you owe me any explanations, Mrs. Jebediah. Your great kindness has been enough."

Mrs. Jebediah didn't answer for a while. Charlotte began to wonder if she shouldn't take her leave, when Mrs. Jebediah tucked a nonexistent stray strand of hair behind her ear and said, "But will you listen to an explanation?"

"Of course."

"As you've so capably deduced, I am a woman widowed before my time. And it was all the more bitter because my husband had not only been young, he had been a good eleven years junior to me—one of the reasons I resisted his entreaties of marriage, from near and far, for as long as I did. I was younger then, but I dreaded the day when he would still be in his prime, and I would have already descended into old age.

"Even when I finally decided to throw caution to the wind, I did so while making jokes about being mistaken for his mother one of those days—or at best, his dear old aunt. I never thought . . . I never thought God would take him first. That instead of dreading the appearance of each new wrinkle, each new white hair, I could only wish he were here to witness my inevitable aging."

Charlotte found herself with a lump in her throat. She ate another strawberry.

"In the six years since he passed away, I've kept myself busy looking after my niece, who had lived with me all her life. But last year she moved to Paris to study medicine. And while I couldn't be more proud of her, I am alone in a large house and at a loss over what to do.

"Not that there aren't things to do, but I don't wish to do them all by myself. And of course I have no plan to recall my niece—this is her time to spread her wings. So I thought I'd find myself a companion.

"I wrote to a few registries and was sent some candidates to interview. But the moment they saw my photographs from my days on stage, gallivanting in hose and breeches, they couldn't swallow their tea and get out fast enough. Mustn't have their respectability tampered by association. And then they'd storm back to their registries and fume about my disrepute."

She spoke lightly, but Charlotte couldn't imagine that it would have been easy for her to swallow the rejections.

"After that, I had no choice but to advertise in the papers."

"But how can you be sure that your candidates will be suitable?"

Lady Holmes always suspected the servants to be full of sloth and thievery. Livia, as great a pessimist as ever lived, simply assumed that the staff, like the rest of the world, despised her on sight and would inevitably take advantage of her. Charlotte didn't share their views, but seeking a lady's companion directly via the back of the newspaper was probably not the best way to find qualified candidates. And if she were a qualified candidate herself, she'd be leery of such an advert, wondering why a potential employer didn't obtain recommendation from friends or use the service of a registry, wondering whether it wasn't instead the work of a confidence artist.

"Well, I placed another advert, this one for finding a long-lost daughter, and I made sure the two adverts are set close together—in the same region on the page, but in different columns," explained Mrs. Jebediah who wasn't really Mrs. Jebediah. "And of course, the two adverts direct potential applicants to write to two different women at two different post offices."

Charlotte clapped her hands together. "Aha! At my previous boarding home, one of the women read aloud your lost-daughter advert. I see your ruse: If a candidate answers both adverts, then she is clearly not to be trusted."

"Precisely."

"And has this method helped you eliminate some candidates?"

"All of them, except one. That is, one woman who hasn't written about the lady's companion position, but seems to be most sincerely seeking her mother, which makes me feel terrible for possibly having given her hope where none existed." Mrs. Jebediah smiled a little. "You are correct, Miss Holmes. I am running a scheme, only not a successful one. At least not for me."

A fine carriage drew up before the tea shop. "Oh, that's mine," she said, "which reminds me that I have an appointment to keep."

She rose. A look of alarm must have crossed Charlotte's face, for she added, "And the bill has already been settled. I would not dream of saddling you with it, my dear."

Charlotte's face heated. She didn't believe Mrs. Jebediah was the sort to indulge in such frauds, but then again she had read the mother-and-daughter beggar team completely wrong, too. "The thought never occurred to me. Thank you most kindly for tea, ma'am."

"I'm sure we will run into each other again at the post office, Miss Holmes."

Mrs. Jebediah swept out and entered the carriage, the gaze of everyone in the tea shop and half of the pedestrians on the street affixed to her person. Charlotte was full—what a marvelous feeling—but she remained at the table and, without any hurry, polished off the last small clumps of scrambled eggs, the last crumbs of the ham pie, and the last two divine strawberries. Alas the potted chicken was already all gone, the inside of the ramekin as empty as Charlotte's appointment book.

Only as she finally rose did she see Mrs. Jebediah's reticule, left behind on a chair.

Eleven

The woman who wasn't named Mrs. Jebediah stood before her wedding photograph, gazing at the radiant bridegroom who would remain forever young. Her hand trembled slightly as she lifted a glass of sherry to her lips.

Mears, her faithful butler, walked into the room. "Ma'am, a young lady to see you. She said—"

"You may show her in."

She could very well regret it before the night was out, but Mrs. Not-Jebediah had come to a decision.

An important decision.

She set aside the sherry glass and took a seat in her favorite chair. Footsteps came up the stairs. The young woman who entered in Mears's wake, however, was not Miss Holmes, but someone she had never seen before.

"Miss Hartford," announced Mears—and withdrew.

Miss Hartford was about the same age as Miss Holmes, but the similarity ended there. She was thin, hunched, and remarkably dowdy for one so young: ill-fitting dress, drooping bonnet, and spectacles that insisted on sliding down her nose.

"Mrs. Jebediah?" she asked tentatively.

Mrs. Not-Jebediah blinked. She was only Mrs. Jebediah in the
advert for the fictional long-lost daughter and she had never given
her private address in that context, not even to the newspaper.

"Mrs. Jebediah, my name is Ellie Hartford. I'm mighty sorry to
call so late but I work as a cook's assistant at the Dog and Duck in
Bywater and they didn't let me out any sooner."

"Oh."

"A few days ago, the barmaid at the pub showed me the paper.
'Ain't you always said you was dropped on the doorsteps of Westminster Abbey, luv? Well, here be a lady looking for her baby what
was—'"

"You may stop right there, Miss Hartford," came another voice.
Miss Holmes.

Miss Hartford glanced at Miss Holmes. And then she stared, as
if unable to believe such a severe command could issue from someone who looked as if she'd freshly stepped off a Valentine card, all
wide eyes and blond ringlets.

"What right you got to tell me to stop? There ain't other babies
left at Westminster Abbey. There—"

"For a woman who works as a cook's assistant in a pub, you
certainly arrived in a very nice carriage, which is waiting for you
around the corner, with a well-dressed gentleman sitting inside."

Miss Hartford took a step toward Miss Holmes. "You're lying.
You'll do anything to claim Mrs. Jebediah as your own mum, won't
you?"

"I certainly wouldn't. I happen to know exactly where my mother
is and she would be very cross with me—not that she isn't already—
if I dared to find myself a new mother."

"Then what are you doing here?"

"I came to return Mrs. Jebediah's reticule, which she left behind
when we took tea together."

"Oh," said Miss Hartford, at a loss for further words.

"I believe you intend to show yourself out, Miss Hartford," said Miss Holmes, her voice cool.

Miss Hartford lifted her chin. "I sure ain't staying for more insults."

She flounced out with great vigor. Mrs. Not-Jebediah stared in the direction of her departure, still not sure what had taken place.

"I apologize for shooing off your caller, Mrs. Watson," said Miss Holmes softly. "It is Mrs. Watson, is it not? Mrs. John Watson?"

Mrs. Watson realized she was on her feet—and slowly sat down again. "How did you find out, Miss Holmes?"

"I enjoy fashion. I recognized that your hats are from Madame Claudette's on Regent Street. Chances are, not that many clients ask to have little black crape details appended to their millinery. So I went to the shop, knocked on the living quarters, and told the women inside that I'd met you on the train, that you'd left your reticule behind with no address to be found inside, and that the only way to return it was to identify you via your hat. They were very glad to help."

"Thank you for taking the trouble." Mrs. Watson sounded tremulous to herself. As if she were the woman in dire straits who'd been helped, rather than the other way around.

"I should be the one to thank you, for taking the trouble."

"I'm sure I don't know what you mean."

Miss Holmes smiled. She had dimples. Of course she did—the Good Lord went to ridiculous lengths to make sure that one of the finest minds in existence was housed in a body least likely to be suspected of it.

"I can accept that a kindhearted woman would want to feed a stranger a good meal," said Miss Holmes. "But when she also leaves her reticule behind, a reticule that contains far too much money for a trip across town, in far too usable a combination of coins and notes, I begin to ask questions. I begin to wonder whether it is merely my luck—or your design."

The butler returned with the tea service.

"Thank you, Mr. Mears," said Mrs. Watson.

Mears left silently.

Mrs. Watson poured for her guest, her fingers tight around the handle of the teapot. "Both milk and sugar, if I recall correctly, Miss Holmes."

"Yes, please."

Mrs. Watson couldn't remember the last time she saw anyone's face light up at the sight of a cup of tea. Miss Holmes half closed her eyes as she took that first sip.

"Some macaroons, perhaps?" asked Mrs. Watson, gesturing toward the plates of comestibles that had been brought in with the tea. She had appeared before audiences of thousands—and yet now she was nervous before an audience of one. "And if you like cake, the madeira is very good. But if I do say so, my cook makes the best plum cake I've ever tasted."

"I don't believe I've ever turned down plum cake in my life—and I certainly won't start now," answered Miss Holmes, helping herself to a slice. "Oh, you are right. This is scrumptious. Absolutely scrumptious."

Mrs. Watson smiled with some effort. "I'm glad you agree."

She took a macaroon, so that she, too, would have something to do while Miss Holmes polished off her slice of cake. When Miss Holmes finished, she sighed. Mrs. Watson half hoped she would take another slice—the girl certainly had the appetite for it. But Miss Holmes set down her plate and folded her hands neatly in her lap.

"Thank you. You are so very, very kind," she said, gazing fully upon Mrs. Watson.

Her eyes were clear and remarkably guileless. Mrs. Watson, blood pounding in her ears, braced herself for what was coming.

"You know who I am, don't you, Mrs. Watson?" asked Miss Holmes. "You know my story."

——— ❊ ———

Charlotte watched as Mrs. Watson stirred her tea.

Here in her own home, she was dressed more plainly, in a russet velvet dress that Livia might almost approve of, if not for the gold piping that trimmed the flounces of the skirt. The interior of the house was also conservatively furnished, without the wild prints and eastern influences that one often associated with more Bohemian décor.

In fact, if it weren't for the stage photographs, a caller might think herself in the drawing room of an ordinary, respectable widow. A kind and beautiful one, but otherwise unexceptional.

The photographs told a different story altogether. Charlotte, no stranger to flouting conventional mores these days, was more than a little taken aback by images of a young Mrs. Watson in "hose and breeches." A woman's lower limbs were always enshrouded by layers of skirts. Even bloomers, worn by the brave and athletic few, were purposefully billowy, to hide the exact form of the wearer.

Of course there were postcards of scantily clad actresses. But to see the sight of one's hostess's calves and thighs so obviously and deliberately outlined—she could only imagine the shock of those applicants who had come hoping to become Mrs. Watson's companion.

Mrs. Watson followed Charlotte's line of sight. "The public considers all women on stage to be of questionable morals, if not outright whores. But the serious Shakespearean actresses console themselves that at least they aren't involved in the vulgarity of musical theater. And those of us in musical theater congratulate ourselves on not being involved in the pornographic nonsense that is the burlesque. I don't know to whom the burlesque performers compare themselves, but I'm sure they feel superior to *someone*."

Charlotte sighed. "My sister fears becoming an impoverished old maid. Sometimes I think that more than eating boiled cabbage in a dilapidated boardinghouse, she fears becoming the most pathetic person she knows—to have no one before whom she could feel the least bit superior."

Mrs. Watson set aside her teacup without drinking from it. "What do *you* fear the most, Miss Holmes?"

"I . . ." Charlotte exhaled. She knew what she feared, but she wasn't accustomed to voicing it aloud. "I fear always being beholden to someone else. I want to be independent—and I want to earn that independence. But now I can no longer believe that fortunate state of affairs will ever come to pass, not with all the mistakes I've made."

"Is there someone specific you have in mind—that you don't wish to be beholden to?"

Charlotte hesitated. "My father has a natural son."

It wasn't common knowledge. Charlotte only found out because she wanted to know why Lady Amelia had, in the end, jilted Sir Henry. This might not be the only reason, but for someone of Lady Amelia's lofty background, marrying a mere baronet would already be a step down. That he had sired a child out of wedlock, hardly an unforgivable sin under normal circumstances, might have tilted the balance against him.

"Oh," said Mrs. Watson.

"My half brother lives in London and works as an accountant."

"And you consider him your last resort?"

Charlotte hesitated again. "I don't know anything about him. Though I dare say he has no reason to feel any sympathy for me: I didn't have the hurdles of illegitimacy placed in my path and yet I've managed to bungle everything."

She blew out a breath and eyed the plate of plum cake. Was it appetite or gluttony that made her want to reach out for another slice?

Or was it fear and fear alone?

She looked back at Mrs. Watson. "I guess you've answered my question, ma'am. You do know who I am."

Mrs. Watson picked up a piece of macaroon and took a delicate nibble. "It must have been three years ago that I first noticed you at the opera. I remarked that you were probably the most darling young woman present. In return, I was told that you were in fact the greatest eccentric in that crowd of thousands. As you can imagine, that left an impression.

"I've seen you a few times since, at the park or coming out of the modiste's with your mother. After the scandal erupted . . . Well, the separation between Society and the demimonde has always been porous and I quickly learned of your misfortune. And when I walked into the post office a few days ago and saw you looking pale and distressed, I decided that if I came across you again, I would try to help you."

"I cannot tell you how much I cherish your generosity. But it's no pittance that you left me in that reticule. And I'm not in such desperate straits yet that I can simply take the money without second thoughts."

Mrs. Watson smiled. "I cooked up my little scheme before I truly knew anything about you. The moment I stepped out of the tea shop, I realized that it wasn't going to work. I'd left no identifying information in the reticule. But you knew so much about me from a look—it would be only a matter of time before you discovered my address."

"I didn't mean to call upon you—my intention was only to ring the doorbell and give the reticule to a member of the staff. But as I approached the house, I saw Miss Hartford emerge from a carriage far too grand for her supposed station in life. She turned around and said to someone in the carriage, "Ow do I sound?' and a man's voice replied, in a similarly exaggerated accent, 'Like a proper Cockney, luv.'

"It made me uneasy. She was still some distance ahead of me.

When I turned the corner and saw that she'd been admitted into your house, I went back to the carriage, knocked, and asked for directions to the Strand, claiming to be lost."

"I imagine the young man in the carriage must have bent over backward to help you."

Charlotte smiled slightly. "He was very chivalrous and even brought out a map of London to help me orient myself. After I spoke with him, however, I became even more suspicious about his purpose here. So when I did knock on your door, instead of merely handing over the reticule, I asked to be brought to you. And a moment outside the drawing room was enough to let me know what Miss Hartford wanted."

"I did think her accent was put on," said Mrs. Watson. "She's a talented mimic, but she'd entered into it with too much enthusiasm and sounded as if a *Punch* caricature had come to life."

"Perhaps it would be a good idea to retract the advert. I imagine you wouldn't wish for any more young women to show up at your door trying to claim you as a mother, whether they are sincere or intent on swindle."

"You are right," said Mrs. Watson. "The experiment has run its course."

Something in her tone struck Charlotte. Mrs. Watson of this evening was different from the exuberant woman she had been earlier in the day: quieter, more solemn, and more . . . apprehensive.

She rose from her seat and walked to the mantel. There she stood with her back to the room, studying a row of framed photographs. Many featured a dark-haired young man with a steady, but mischievous, gaze.

He was in uniform in their wedding photograph—the army then. Dead six years, according to what Mrs. Watson had told Charlotte—and six years ago there had been a war with Afghanistan.

Distant colonial wars that one read about in the newspapers were like theatrical plays: vivid and dramatic. One could get caught up in the excitement of the battle, the unexpected turns of events, the high passions in the halls of Parliament. But in the end, they didn't seem quite real.

At least they had never felt real to Charlotte before this moment. Before she stared at Mrs. Watson's elegant back and saw thousands of dead men strewn across a harsh, brown landscape.

Mrs. Watson turned around. Charlotte half expected to see the very embodiment of grief and fragility. Instead she was reminded of the reason she had intuited that Mrs. Watson had been successful on the stage—she exuded a sturdy confidence, that of a woman who trusted herself because of a lifetime of good choices.

"Shortly before you arrived, I came to a decision," said Mrs. Watson, her voice soft, her tone firm. "I knew it wouldn't be long before you called, bearing my reticule. And that would be an excellent opportunity to offer you the position of a lady's companion."

This development Charlotte had entirely failed to foresee. Her lips flapped a few times before she managed a reply. "Me? To you?"

"We do have a lack of respectability in common, don't you think?"

"It isn't your disregard of my scandalous recent past that astonishes me, ma'am. Most people tend to want nothing to do with me after I enumerate what I see about them."

In fact, it had been a singularly effective means to persuade a gentleman to withdraw a proposal of marriage.

Mrs. Watson smiled wryly. "I can see why. It was extraordinarily uncomfortable to be laid so bare. But in my case . . . in my case it was also a tremendous relief.

"I stopped wearing mourning after the regulation period. I had a young girl under my care and I wanted her to see that life went on. That the loss of a man, even if he had been the love of her life, was not the end of a woman's existence. That such a loss was something she could recover from, with both courage and grace. But now that my niece is away in Paris, now that I have no audience for whom to perform this role of the merry widow, I—"

She pulled out a handkerchief that had been tucked into her sleeve, straightened it, and then tucked it back in. "In any case, I thought, let me try it. Let me try having as a companion someone before whom it is useless to pretend that everything is all right. Let me try living without hiding my grief, because to her that grief would already be plain as day."

For a minute, neither of them said anything.

Mrs. Watson retook her seat and looked at Charlotte. "Will you take the position, Miss Holmes?"

Would she?

Charlotte left her seat and walked to a window. It gave onto the same street where Miss Hartford's carriage had been parked, waiting for her return. The carriage was gone, but in its place, a man stood underneath a streetlamp, reading a newspaper.

At first she thought he was the man from the carriage. Instead, she recognized him as the one who had waited out the rain across the street from her earlier in the afternoon.

The one she'd suspected of following her.

She was not alarmed: Whoever had commissioned the man's service had not done so with the intention of harming her, but to keep an eye on her.

This did not make her happy—she did not care to be closely monitored. She wasn't angry at the person responsible for this surveillance—in his place she might have done the same. Nevertheless, she wished her secret guardian hadn't felt compelled to be so positioned as to be able to effect a rescue at any moment.

It implied that such a rescue was not only necessary, but imminent.

That she couldn't in good conscience—or cold logic—disagree with the assessment made it feel as if the air was slowly leaking from her lungs.

Of course she would have preferred to pull herself out of her difficulties by her own competence alone. That, however, was not the world in which she lived. If accepting the kindness of a stranger would stabilize her situation and give her another chance at ultimately improving not only her own lot but Livia's, too, then she must set aside her pride and do what was necessary.

She turned around. Mrs. Watson was still working on the same macaroon. She glanced up at Charlotte, her gaze kind but uncertain.

"You are absolutely sure you wish to have me as a companion, ma'am?" Charlotte asked.

Mrs. Watson set down the remainder of the macaroon. "Yes, I am."

"Then I will accept the position. Gladly and with much gratitude."

❖

Dearest Livia,

I have a position.

And not just any position, but one that provides good wages, light duties, and excellent accommodation. In fact, I am sitting in my new room, which boasts of a four-poster, silk-draped bed, a painting of a lovely and abrupt seacoast that must surely belong to the Impressionist school of works, and a view of Regent Park outside my window—not that I can see much now, it being late in the evening.

My belongings have been conveyed from the boarding home where I had been staying. They fit perfectly into my new wardrobe. Nothing looks out of place—my brushes on the vanity, my typewriter on the desk, even my magnifying glass on the nightstand. It is as if this room has been waiting for me to arrive and make myself at home.

I am a lady's companion.

And now that you have gathered yourself from where you had fallen on the floor, allow me to repeat myself. I am a lady's companion. Not a Society lady, obviously. And most definitely not a matron or rich spinster of the grand bourgeoisie—they care more about respectability than even we do. But a lady of the demimonde, a former stage performer, comfortably off and most amiable.

Please do not worry that I might have been ensnared into some scheme. My new employer is both sensible and kind and I have found not only employment but acceptance. My only worry is that I shall manage to repel her, when I have every intention to the opposite.

For the moment I will not set down my new address. The last thing I want is for this letter to fall into the wrong hands and Mamma to show up at my benefactor's front door, in a fit of trembling outrage. You know she would, whatever Papa's orders to the contrary, if she heard that I, in my exile, had taken up with an actress.

I will post this letter first thing in the morning, and hope that by afternoon, when I go to the post office on St. Martin's Le Grand, I will already have a response from you. God bless the eleven-times-a-day delivery in this great city and may it bring your words to me at the very earliest hour.

Charlotte

———

Charlotte had, as usual, chosen to paint an optimistic picture for Livia.

To put it mildly, she was ill suited to acting as a lady's companion. It hadn't been merely greed that had made her decide on becoming a headmistress at a girls' school. It had also been the autonomy, the authority, and last, but not least of all, the relative isolation of power. A headmistress made all the decisions—*and* she was not expected to make friends. To be paid five hundred pounds a year to be aloofly in charge—well, it would have been earthly paradise.

A position as a lady's companion offered none of what she sought to gain in employment. A lady's companion was a professional appendage. The spare legs to walk upstairs to fetch the needlework. The extra voice to read the paper aloud in the evening. The additional body in the house so rooms didn't echo with emptiness.

In her specific case, however, it wasn't this impersonal servility that concerned Charlotte, but her new employer's lack of prior experience with other companions and her general high opinion of Charlotte's mind. She was worried that Mrs. Watson would think it demeaned Charlotte to be asked to fetch needlework or read out loud from the paper. That she would, in the end, have too little to do.

And Mrs. Watson—she also worried about Mrs. Watson.

Charlotte was an acceptable conversationalist when the conversation revolved around weather, fashion, and the goings-on of the Season. But the deepest feelings of others were always a mystery to her. Not that she didn't know what sentiments were and how to read them, but she herself didn't seem to experience life in quite the same emotion-driven manner.

Her days were catalogued as facts and factual observations. She sometimes thought of herself as a combination of a phonographic cylinder and a motion picture camera—which inventors were still working on—that moved through life recording everything she saw and heard.

Sometimes she mentally annotated certain moments; most often she let them pass into memory without comments, as only sounds and moving images. It was in her adolescence that she discovered most people's memories worked nothing like hers. For them the only indelible elements in the dossiers of a life were the emotions. They might not remember when, where, or with whom something happened—or be reliable in their recall—but by God that joy, that anguish, that stab of pure hatred, the emotions lost none of their power and potency.

She accepted it. She couldn't understand it viscerally, but she accepted that she was the odd man out and that in this, as in most other respects, the norm did not remotely describe her experience.

How could someone like her comment on Mrs. Watson's grief, if she were ever asked to? Therefore, she was more than a little relieved when Mrs. Watson made no mention of her late husband the next day.

Mrs. Watson also gave no list of regular duties Charlotte was to perform. "It's new to me, too, such an arrangement," she said apologetically. "I'm sure in time we will arrive at a state of affairs that suits both of us."

Charlotte debated whether to mention her great willingness to fetch items—and decided to wait a day or two. Mrs. Watson did formally introduce her to the staff: Mr. Mears, the butler; Madame Gascoigne, the cook; Polly and Rosie Banning, a pair of sisters who shared housemaid and kitchen-maid duties; and Paul Lawson, Mrs. Watson's groom and coachman.

Mr. Mears painted in his spare time. Madame Gascoigne was Belgian, not French—and not from the French-speaking part of Belgium. And while the Banning sisters might have grown up in the same household, they were not actually related by blood.

All of which was fine, except . . .

"I'm not sure whether it's my place to bring it up, Mrs. Watson," said Charlotte when she and her employer took a walk in Regent Park, "but I'm strongly persuaded that Mr. Lawson has spent some time in a penitentiary."

"And so he has," replied Mrs. Watson, not at all alarmed. "Into many lives a little irregularity must fall."

Considering the amount of irregularities that had fallen into her own life of late, Charlotte could only nod. "How right you are, ma'am."

Post-lunch Mrs. Watson took a nap, giving Charlotte plenty of time to write another letter to Livia. She also attempted to draft a letter to a different recipient, but gave up after half a dozen attempts.

Later that afternoon, Mrs. Watson had herself and Charlotte driven to the General Post Office. In the morning Mrs. Watson had already written to the papers, instructing them to stop printing her adverts, but she expected it would be a few days before inquiries stopped arriving.

Charlotte had nothing from Livia—her letters arrived in fits and starts, whenever she could get them to Mott and whenever Mott could post them. There was, however, something from Inspector Robert Treadles of the Metropolitan Police.

"Miss Holmes," asked Mrs. Watson, as their carriage rolled away from the curb, "did I hear you call for letters for a certain *Sherlock* Holmes?"

There was only curiosity on Mrs. Watson's face. Charlotte decided to tell the truth. "Yes, you did."

Mrs. Watson leaned forward. "Would that happen to be the same Sherlock Holmes who wrote the letter to the coroner that has all of London Society in an uproar?"

"That's the alias I used."

"*You* are Sherlock Holmes?" Still no censure on Mrs. Watson's part.

"I thought calling myself Charles Holmes would have been too obvious. Sherlock is similar enough to Charlotte without being its exact masculine equivalent."

Mrs. Watson leaned back in her seat. "This makes perfect sense now. You wrote the letter to lift the siege around your sister."

"The best way to prove her innocence is to discover the truth."

"Do you really believe that those three deaths are part of a larger scheme?"

"I could not convince myself that they were all simply a coincidence." She glanced down at the letter in her hand. "I hope Inspector Treadles has some good news for me."

"You know someone in Scotland Yard?"

"I don't know him personally, but Sherlock Holmes has consulted for him a few times, via a mutual friend."

"Then why don't you read his note? You must be anxious to know what it says."

Charlotte did not need to be urged again.

Dear Mr. Holmes,

I have been looking into the Sackville case at Lord Ingram's request. But while I have come across tantalizing clues and insights, I have unearthed nothing concrete—nothing that would convince a coroner's jury, let alone be deployed as Crown's evidence.

Time is running out—the inquest reconvenes tomorrow afternoon. I need hardly state that if you have any special insights that would aid me in the investigation, sir, it would be well to convey them at your earliest convenience.

Sincerely yours,
Robert Treadles

P.S. My best wishes for your speedy recovery.

"The news is not encouraging, I take it," said Mrs. Watson. Charlotte handed over the letter for Mrs. Watson to read herself. Mrs. Watson scanned the lines. "What will you do now?"

Charlotte pressed a finger against her lips. "His letter is dated today, which means there is still time before the inquest reconvenes. I must arrange a meeting with him."

"As yourself?"

"Not at this crucial moment, I don't believe." Men had a tendency to discount a woman's thinking, even men who were otherwise open-minded. "Our mutual friend might have properties around town that I can borrow. Since he seems to have given Sherlock Holmes a condition, it would be doable to tell the inspector that Sherlock Holmes is in the next room but cannot receive him in person and that I, Miss Holmes, must be the conduit through which information passes."

If she started preparing this very moment—and everything went her way—she should be able to pull off the meeting, if only just. "May I have some time to make the arrangements, Mrs. Watson? Of course you must deduct—"

"I have a better idea," said Mrs. Watson. "I have some properties on Upper Baker Street, right behind the house. One of my tenants moved out two weeks ago. The flat has been cleaned and made ready but not yet put up for let again. What do you say that you receive your inspector right there?"

Charlotte did not debate long with herself. "In that case, would you mind asking Mr. Lawson to stop at the nearest post office? I'd like to send a cable to the inspector and ask him to meet me tonight."

Charlotte had accepted Mrs. Watson's offer because she needed it— time was of the essence. But as they went about staging the flat on Upper Baker Street, she saw that she'd have done Mrs. Watson a disservice if she'd declined her help.

Mrs. Watson had come alive.

The flat was already furnished, but she immediately set to work to make it look lived in. Potted plants and plump seat cushions were hauled over from her own house. Books by the gross went on the shelves. Several days' worth of newspapers and half a dozen magazines were stuffed into a canterbury next to the fireplace.

But Mrs. Watson was far from finished: They needed to create the illusion that a man lived on the premises. She set a decanter of whisky on the sideboard, hung hats and a pair of men's coats, and placed three walking sticks into the umbrella stand by the door.

A tobacco pipe was lit and left to smolder in an ashtray. Cups of steaming tea were allowed to sit and cool, for their fragrance to diffuse. And then, in a moment of inspired attention to detail, she simmered water over a spirit lamp and added a few drops each of cough syrup, camphor, and linseed oil, along with a handful of dried herbs. Immediately the flat took on the smell of convalescence, of many tinctures and compounds poured out and administered to a loved one.

She walked about the parlor, checking it from various angles, her brow furrowed. Charlotte, who had been placing a few of her own books onto the shelves, followed her line of sight. Knickknacks and souvenirs populated the top of the shelves. A vase of roses sat on the seat of the bow window that looked down onto Upper Baker Street. In the adjacent bedroom, a bolster had been placed under the cover of the fully made-up bed; the pair of men's slippers peeking out from beneath the bedstead served as the perfect detail, for someone stealing a glance into the room with the door open a bare inch.

"No photographs," said Charlotte.

"I knew it," exclaimed Mrs. Watson. "I knew something was missing. Would you happen to have any?"

"A few." She had brought a small album with her. "But none of them show me with anyone who can pass for a brother."

"Good enough. We'll say Sherlock Holmes has an aversion to cameras."

They adjourned to Mrs. Watson's house for a late tea. Afterward,

Charlotte went to her room to fetch the photographs. But as she returned to the corridor, she nearly bumped into Mrs. Watson, whose expression immediately made her ask, "What's the matter, ma'am?"

"I hate to tell you this, Miss Holmes, but I just learned that—that your father quarreled with Lady Amelia the evening before she died. A bad quarrel. And—and he was heard to make threats on her life."

Twelve

L ord Ingram stood on the curb, studying the solidly constructed redbrick edifice with a singular concentration. Unlike Inspector Treadles, his lordship didn't seem to approve of the place. But more surprisingly, Treadles could not detect any trace of gladness in his lordship's countenance.

Treadles, on the other hand, had leaped from his desk upon the arrival of Holmes's cable, gasping with marvel.

> Mr. Sherlock Holmes will be delighted to receive
> you at seven tonight and discuss the Sackville Case.
> 18 Upper Baker Street.

Taking advantage of Scotland Yard's telephonic systems, he had immediately rung Lord Ingram. His lordship was not at home, but a message had come for Treadles not long after: Lord Ingram had heard from Holmes and would meet Inspector Treadles at 18 Upper Baker Street this evening.

The two men shook hands. "My lord, you seem more concerned than pleased. But Holmes's recovery is terrific news, is it not?"

"I'm afraid the news is less optimistic than you believe, Inspector."

"So he *hasn't* recovered?"

Lord Ingram exhaled. "Not by any standards you and I would consider recovered."

"Then . . ."

"We'll know more inside."

They rang the bell. Treadles held his breath. Despite Lord Ingram's less-than-sanguine words, he remained excited at the possibility of meeting the great Sherlock Holmes.

A large, stooped woman in a starched white cap answered the door. She peered up at them through a pair of wire-rim glasses perched at the tip of her nose and said in a broad Yorkshire accent, "You'll be the gentlemen Miss Holmes is waiting for. Come in, then."

Miss Holmes? Inspector Treadles mouthed to Lord Ingram, as they followed the woman's plentiful behind up the stairs.

The sister, Lord Ingram answered.

This surprised Treadles. Of course Holmes was at liberty to have any number of sisters, but Treadles had always envisioned him as a solitary creature, not someone who shared a house with female relations.

They were brought into a cozy-looking parlor, with rose-and-ivy wallpaper, chintz-covered chairs, and a grandfather clock ticking away quietly in the corner. Miss Holmes, who had been standing before the window looking out, turned around at their entrance.

Treadles's eyes widened—he had *not* expected Holmes's sister to resemble an advertising illustrator's idea of ideal femininity. He glanced at Lord Ingram. The latter appeared unmoved—but of course he would have met Miss Holmes before, since he was acquainted with the latter's brother.

Miss Holmes came forward and shook hands with her callers. "Good evening, my lord. Good evening, Inspector. A pleasure to make your acquaintance."

"Likewise," said Treadles. "I'd have dearly wished for us to meet under happier circumstances but I'm nevertheless encouraged that Mr. Holmes is well enough to be consulted."

Miss Holmes sat down and folded her hands in her lap. "My brother's health has long been a burden to him. This latest episode was the most terrible yet—we truly lost hope at one point. Even at the moment he is barely able to communicate."

"Still, thank goodness."

"Yes. It's truly a miracle that he has recovered as much as he has," said Miss Holmes with feeling. "Unfortunately he is bedridden and therefore not able to receive you in person."

"Oh." Treadles hoped his disappointment didn't show too plainly. "Then he will not be able to discuss the case with us."

"While Sherlock will not be able to *discuss* the case, he will most certainly be able to contribute—we have rigged this room in a discreet manner so that he can see and hear everything from his sickbed."

The woman who had opened the door for Treadles and Lord Ingram returned, carrying a tray of tea. Miss Holmes poured a cup and handed it to her. "Will you take this to my brother, Mrs. Hudson? And will you stay with him to make sure he's comfortable?"

"Yes, miss," said Mrs. Hudson.

She waddled off with the cup of tea. Lord Ingram stared after her, a strange grimace on his face.

Miss Holmes poured for the rest of them and passed around a plate of curious-looking biscuits, fluted like seashells. "Madeleines," she said. "They are very good. The recipe is said to come from Madame Durant herself."

Treadles had no idea who Madame Durant was, but the biscuits were indeed good. In fact, by his third bite, he realized they were spectacularly delicious. He looked down at the plate and wondered whether it would be possible to pilfer one undetected to take home to Alice.

"I understand time is short," said Miss Holmes. "We are ready to proceed whenever you care to start, Inspector."

Treadles glanced toward the room that held the invalid. "You are certain, Miss Holmes, that this arrangement will prevail?"

"I have no doubt."

"But Mr. Holmes, if he is as indisposed as I imagine him to be—what if our discussion should prove too taxing? Out here I would not know when to stop."

"Mrs. Hudson would let us know if we have gone on too long for him."

Treadles lowered his voice, though he had the impression he was only being silly, rather than discreet. "I hate to ask this, Miss Holmes, but the episode, has it affected your brother's mind?"

Miss Holmes smiled—was it an ironic smile? "Allow me to assure you, Inspector, that although the episode negatively affected many aspects of Sherlock Holmes's life, it mercifully spared his mind, which remains as eccentric and intractable as ever."

Was Treadles imagining things or did Lord Ingram let out an almost inaudible snort?

"You are still unsure, Inspector," said Miss Holmes. "Would you like to know for certain that Sherlock's powers of observation and deduction are very much intact?"

"I would take the lady at her word," said Lord Ingram as he studied the rim of his teacup.

It occurred to Treadles that his lordship hadn't looked directly at Miss Holmes since they arrived.

"The choice is yours, Inspector," said Miss Holmes.

Treadles hesitated some more. "My lord, have you seen Miss Holmes's brother face-to-face since his episode?"

"No, I have not."

"Then, with all due apology, as this is a matter of public trust, I would like to be assured that Mr. Holmes's capabilities are what they were."

"Of course," said Lord Ingram.

Oddly enough, his lordship's voice contained no trace of annoyance, only the faintest hint of pity.

"If you'll excuse me for a moment." Miss Holmes went into the next room and closed the door.

Treadles turned to Lord Ingram. "My lord, I hope I have not given offense in following my own counsel."

"Not at all. Were I you, I would have made the same choice." Treadles exhaled.

But then Lord Ingram added, "And were you me, you'd have issued the same warning."

———⁂———

Miss Holmes returned with a bright smile for her visitors. She took her seat and arranged her skirts with practiced ease.

"This is what Sherlock has to say about you, Inspector."

Him? Treadles glanced again at Lord Ingram, who seemed once again fascinated by the shape of his teacup.

Miss Holmes pulled out a small notebook from a pocket in her skirt and consulted it. "You come from the northwest. Cumbria. Barrow-in-Furness. Your father was employed by either the steelworks or the shipyard. The shipyard, most likely. He was Scottish, your mother wasn't. He did well enough to send you to a good school, but unfortunately he died young and you weren't able to go to university."

Treadles stared at her. Had Sherlock Holmes learned all this from Lord Ingram? But he couldn't remember ever telling his lordship what Angus Treadles had done for a living.

"You began your career in Cumbria but came to London before too long. Here you were married. A happy union—many congratulations. Your father-in-law was a well-to-do man. And like Lord

Ingram, he appreciated your intelligence, industry, and decency. Unfortunately, he is no more and his heir, who is not a man of as exceptional caliber, does not feel nearly the same affection toward either you or your wife. Finances have become strained, but your wife is a resourceful and resilient woman, and your domestic contentment has not been adversely affected."

Inspector Treadles, with some effort, closed his mouth. He was sure he had never mentioned his finances to Lord Ingram, who now wore an expression of mild apology.

"Mr. Holmes knows all this from having listened to me speak ten words?"

"You have spoken closer to one hundred words, far more than necessary to pinpoint your general place of origin and your level of education. Although in your case it is a bit more complicated, with the trace of Scottish brogue in your vowels—which, on the other hand, made it easier to conclude Barrow-in-Furness, with its large Scottish population attracted by work in the industries. As for whether it is the steelworks or the shipyard, your own expression gave away the correct answer.

"The rest is fairly obvious. You're still a young man; to have risen to your current position indicates that you started early, but also possess a drive to succeed. Yet you are not one of those men for whom ambition is everything, or Lord Ingram wouldn't have taken any interest in your concerns."

She cast a look at Lord Ingram, who stirred his tea with great concentration.

"Indeed not," said he.

Even in the midst of his own astonishment, Inspector Treadles was beginning to wonder at the nature of the association between Lord Ingram and the Holmeses. Between his lordship and Miss Holmes, especially.

Miss Holmes smiled again. "Does that answer your question?"

Treadles had to think for a moment to remember what his question had been: How Holmes could know so much about him from so little. "Not entirely."

"Ah, your domestic situation. It is infinitely more likely that you left Barrow-in-Furness before you were married than after—you appear too prudent a man to marry early and of course it is far easier to relocate as a bachelor than with a family in tow. As for your late father-in-law's comfortable circumstances, the fabric and cut of your garments indicate that they were made by a tailor whose work Lord Ingram's valet would not have disdained—in other words, your late father-in-law's tailor.

"But for all that exquisite material and equally exquisite workmanship, your clothes are two years behind fashion. The buttons have been recently replaced and the cuffs rewoven. Perhaps most tellingly, your shirt has a detachable collar. Lord Ingram, does your shirt have a detachable collar?"

"No," said his lordship. "It does not."

"Lord Ingram has no need of detachable collars because he can afford to launder dozens of entire shirts at a go. But a man who wears a detachable collar underneath a jacket made by one of London's finest tailors—either he stole the jacket or his circumstances have been reduced. Since wages at the Metropolitan Police Force have not suffered a noticeable decline, one can only conclude that Mrs. Treadles's income had been drastically cut and it seems reasonable to conclude that instead of a generous father, she now has a much less generous brother.

"With regard to her devotion to you . . . She is being punished for marrying down by that ghastly brother of hers, and yet you look impeccable—the care and skill that went into the repair of your garments nearly equals that which went into their creation. Whatever sacrifices she has had to make in the running of the household, she has made sure that they affect you as little as possible. If that is not love . . ."

Throughout her explanations, Inspector Treadles had to restrain his facial muscles from expressions of dismay and stupefaction—to have his domestic situation laid bare like this by a stranger, and before an esteemed friend, no less! But now he found himself fighting back unexpected tears.

"I am extraordinarily fortunate in Mrs. Treadles."

"Yes, you are, Inspector," said Miss Holmes, taking a sip of her tea.

Inspector Treadles did the same, to help recover from his sudden onset of sentiments. Dear Alice. Dear, dear Alice.

"Well, Inspector, do you feel more confident now that my brother's abilities have not been diminished by his recent misfortune?"

Treadles wasn't sure whether *confident* was the correct word. He was awed, as well as rattled. "I—yes, Miss Holmes."

She smiled again. "Excellent. Let us proceed."

Treadles gave a quick account of his investigation thus far. "After I left Lord Sheridan's residence, I happened to run into Lord Ingram. Taking advantage of that, I requested his help in finding out what lay behind the estrangement between the brothers."

"It took me a little longer to hunt down my quarry than I'd anticipated," said Lord Ingram. "When I received word that you had telephoned, Inspector, I had just spoken to Lady Avery."

"Lady Avery, of course," said Miss Holmes. She turned to Treadles. "Lady Avery and her sister Lady Somersby are Society's most accomplished gossips. They possess an encyclopedic knowledge of every affair, every snub, and every spat from the past fifty years. If anyone alive knows the reason for the estrangement, other than Lord Sheridan himself, it would be one of these ladies."

"Unfortunately, even Lady Avery has never been privy to the

particulars of that alienation," said Lord Ingram. "She did, however, pinpoint the last time the brothers were seen together, which was in August of fifty-nine, twenty-seven years ago. The previous summer the Sheridans' only child had died. For a year afterward the parents did not move in Society. That August marked their first outing at a house party. Lady Avery was there in person and remembered the brothers being very affectionate.

"Later that year she heard that Mr. Sackville had left for an extended stay in the south of France. She thought nothing of it. He was a wealthy bachelor and south of France a fashionable place. It was quite some time later that she noticed he had not returned. Then rumor had it that he did come back but not to the bosom of the family. She tried to pry some information out of Lady Sheridan, but Lady Sheridan was apparently in the dark as well. She was under the impression that Mr. Sackville had suffered severe personal trials and was hurt that he didn't come to the family to seek comfort and succor, but rather shut himself away, locations unknown.

"And that was all she was able to tell me. That and something that may or may not be related to the case. Inspector, you said you had verified that Lord Sheridan had been in town throughout the time period of interest. But did you ask about Lady Sheridan's movements?"

"No, I did not. It didn't occur to me."

"Lady Avery mentioned that she recently saw Lady Sheridan at Paddington Station, getting off a train by herself, without a maid in tow. She is sure that was the day Mr. Sackville died."

Paddington Station served all points west of London, including Devon. It would be *very* interesting if Lady Sheridan's travels had taken her to the vicinity of Stanwell Moot. But again, a tantalizing clue that did not amount to concrete evidence.

"Anything else, gentlemen?" asked Miss Holmes.

Inspector Treadles produced all the transcripts and reports that had been generated in the course of the investigation, from the inquest onward.

"I will take this to my brother. Please excuse me."

They both rose as she departed. Lord Ingram remained on his feet and moved slowly about the room, examining the furnishing. Treadles, without thinking about it, reached for the notebook she had left behind.

It was new. And almost completely blank except a single word on the first page: *Barrow-in-Furness*, his place of origin, written in an unfamiliar hand.

He frowned and set the notebook down again.

Lord Ingram was before the mantel, looking at framed photographs, his brow furrowed. Treadles moved to the bookshelf and picked up a slim volume lying on its side, by none other than Lord Ingram himself, titled *A Summer in Roman Ruins*. Treadles remembered his lordship mentioning that he'd explored the remnants of a Roman villa on his uncle's estate. He didn't know Lord Ingram had also produced a written account.

The book was dedicated to "that wellspring of warmth and good sense, my friend and ally, J. H. R." The next page bore an inscription, *To Holmes, Long may you carry on as a reprobate of the first order. Ash.*

"Holmes dictated that inscription," said Lord Ingram from across the room.

Treadles chuckled. He'd read only two pages when Miss Holmes said, a hint of mirth in her voice, "Oh, the twists and turns in the plot of Lord Ingram's archeological adventure."

Treadles returned the book to its place. "Mr. Holmes has read everything?"

"Yes."

"And does he have any fresh insights?" asked Treadles, almost embarrassingly eager to receive what bounty of perspicuity Holmes might have to impart.

"He noticed a discrepancy about the curtains in Mr. Sackville's room."

"Oh?"

"Becky Birtle, the maid who first found Mr. Sackville in an unconscious state, said in her testimony at the inquest that she opened the curtains as soon as she went to Mr. Sackville's room. But in your interview with Mrs. Meek, the cook, she is recorded as saying that she and Mrs. Cornish, the housekeeper, opened the curtains after they reached the room, to have a better look at Mr. Sackville."

Treadles hoped his disappointment didn't show. "I noticed that as well, but I attributed it to the vagaries of memory—witnesses almost always recollect the same events with noticeable differences. What does Mr. Holmes see as the significance of that discrepancy?"

Miss Holmes glanced at Lord Ingram. "With regard to the reconvening of the inquest tomorrow, nothing. It will be easily dismissed as vagaries of memory, as you said. Overall Sherlock concurs with your assessment that there isn't enough evidence to persuade the coroner's jury to return a verdict that will allow you to carry on with the investigation."

This time Treadles didn't bother to hide his dismay. "Is there nothing we can do then?"

Miss Holmes tapped the tips of her fingers against one another. "You can test the bottles of strychnine in Dr. Harris's and Dr. Birch's dispensaries."

Had he misheard? "Strychnine? Mr. Sackville died of chloral."

"We, however, are operating on the assumption that his death was not an accidental overdose, but a murder that is meant to appear as an accidental overdose." Miss Holmes leaned forward an inch. "Were you the systematic executor who could pull off multiple murders that appear otherwise, Inspector, what would *you* have done ahead of time to make sure that Mr. Sackville wasn't saved by a dose of strychnine delivered just in time?"

It was the first time that anyone had, within Treadles's hearing, referred to the deaths of Mr. Sackville, Lady Amelia Drummond, and Lady Shrewsbury as murders. A chill ran down his spine. "Are you implying, Miss Holmes, that I would have tampered with the supply of strychnine in the vicinity?"

"Yes. So that even if help reached Mr. Sackville before the point of no return, that help would have been administered in vain."

Treadles let out a breath. "That is both diabolical and brilliant."

"It is, let's face it, quite a reach," said Miss Holmes modestly. "But at this point, Inspector, what do you have to lose?"

"True, nothing. But I must make haste, if I hope to achieve anything in time."

Cables needed to be sent immediately to have the evidence gathered for testing. He had planned to leave for Devon first thing in the morning, but now it would seem that he had better be on his way as soon as possible, to be there in the morning and urge matters along.

He rose. "Thank you, Miss Holmes. And please convey my gratitude to Mr. Holmes. I will see myself out."

"Inspector?"

"Yes, Miss Holmes?"

Miss Holmes smiled a little. "My brother advises that you request the chemical analyst to also test Mr. Sackville for every poison for which he has an assay. If the strychnine turns out not to have been tampered with, then this will be our last hope, to find something in Mr. Sackville's system that couldn't have arrived there accidentally."

Thirteen

A silence fell at Inspector Treadles's departure.

Charlotte moved to the window seat and poured a little water into the vase of roses. She was surprised to see raindrops rolling down the windowpanes. A shower fell, quiet and steady. A carriage passed below, hooves and wheels splashing, a yellow halo around each lantern.

She had expected Lord Ingram to stay longer—they were friends of long standing, having known each other since they were children. She had very much looked forward to a word in private with him. But she forgot, as she usually did, the silence that always came between them in these latter years, whenever they found themselves alone.

The sensation in her chest, however, was all too familiar, that mix of pleasure and pain, never one without the other.

She could have done without those feelings. She would have happily gone her entire life never experiencing the pangs of longing and the futility of regret. He made her human—or as human as she was capable of being. And being human was possibly her least favorite aspect of life.

"More tea, sir?" she asked, remembering that they weren't truly alone. Mrs. Watson was in the next room, the door to which was open a crack.

"No, thank you," he said quietly.

"Nibbles?" He hadn't touched the madeleines.

"Most kind of you, but no."

She returned to her seat and took a madeleine herself—she didn't understand how anyone had the willpower to say no to madeleines. Then again, the man before her said no to the vast majority of her suggestions, whether they concerned tea cakes or life-altering courses of action.

Other young ladies she knew enjoyed the construction of an ideal man for themselves. Charlotte never understood the point of such an exercise: She'd yet to meet a woman who thought her house perfect, and unlike men, houses could be planned, expanded, and redecorated from top to bottom. But had she indulged in intellectually devising her own perfect match, she would have come up with someone substantially similar to herself, an aloof observer, a creature of silence, a man happy to live life entirely inside his own head.

Whereas with Lord Ingram, she was always first struck by his physicality. She was aware of the space he occupied, his motion, his weight, the cut and drape of his coat, the length and texture of his hair—even though she had never touched his hair. She found herself observing, intensely, the direction of his gaze, the placement of his hands, the rise and fall of his chest with every breath.

He was not the only fine male specimen of her acquaintance. Roger Shrewsbury, for one, was considered handsomer and more stylish. But Lord Ingram possessed something else, a vitality with a jolt of sensuality and an undercurrent of hostility to the world at large, which made for a masculinity magnetic to both men and women.

When he was younger, that hostility had been more evident. But at some point, the troublemaker reformed and became thoroughly integrated with the rest of the Upper Ten Thousand. He was a member at all the expected clubs, friends with all the right people, and of course his polo matches featured as some of the more notable highlights of any given Season.

Another ten years and he'd be called a pillar of Society.

But . . .

Somewhere beneath all the respectability and sociability still lurked the boy who preferred long, solitary hours among relics to almost anything else. And he remained the only person she had ever met who did not mind her tendency toward silence. Sometimes she even thought he was at ease with it, though it was possible he was simply relieved that when she didn't speak, she couldn't make discomfiting observations about his private life.

She remembered Mrs. Watson again. For her sake, the silence ought not to stretch much longer. "I didn't explain to Inspector Treadles what I thought to be the significance of the discrepancy concerning the curtains."

"I noticed."

"But you understood?"

He hesitated briefly, then nodded.

It was Charlotte's estimation that when Inspector Treadles married a woman from a family far wealthier than his own, he consented to have his clothes made at one of the best tailors' in London to honor and respect his in-laws, so as to not appear as if he didn't belong. It was also her estimation that Mrs. Treadles, who married down, would have opted to run a simple household, leaving behind the more luxurious style she'd known, to honor and respect the man to whom she had made the commitment of a lifetime.

Charlotte didn't believe Inspector Treadles's maid came into his bedchamber in the morning on a regular basis and his inexperience in the matter caused him to miss the clue in Mrs. Meek's description of the events.

"I called on your sister this afternoon, by the way," said Lord Ingram.

Her fingers tightened around the half-eaten madeleine in her hand. "How is she?"

"Doing her best to hold herself together."

Oh, Livia. "She knows about our father's quarrel with Lady Amelia?"

"Everybody knows."

Was there a more terrifying phrase in the English language than "unintended consequences"?

"Did you see him?"

"He wasn't at home. And your mother was not receiving visitors."

Meaning she had taken to her bed—after another hefty dose of laudanum, no doubt.

"But Miss Livia did ask me to tell you, should I run into you, that she is grateful for what you have done. She emphasized that you couldn't possibly have foreseen that—"

"That by connecting the deaths of Lady Amelia, Lady Shrewsbury, and Mr. Sackville, I would double the number of Holmeses suspected of homicide?"

"Inspector Treadles will find something tomorrow."

She almost dropped the madeleine in her surprise. He was consoling her—and he'd never consoled her in all the years they'd known each other. "You don't believe it."

"I often question your actions, but rarely your reasoning. And this isn't one of those rare instances."

She took a deep breath: She had fallen so far that he of all people felt the need to comfort her. "Thank you. Very kind of you."

Mrs. Watson stuck her head out from the bedroom. "Beg your pardon, miss, but Mr. Holmes, he's fast asleep. Do you still need me to keep an eye on him?"

"That won't be necessary, Mrs. Hudson. Thank you."

Mrs. Watson bobbed a curtsy and left, galumphing down the stairs. When the house was quiet again, Lord Ingram asked, "Is that the actress who took you in?"

His voice was carefully neutral, but nothing could disguise disapproval of this magnitude, so she pretended not to have heard it. "She's very convincing, isn't she? And she's the one who identified the inspector's origin by his accent. I must have her train me to better hear the differences in regional accents."

"I don't like this arrangement. You know nothing about her."

At least now he was sounding more himself. "I happen to think I know a great deal about her."

"That you can deduce someone's circumstances doesn't mean you can read all their thoughts and intentions. Ask yourself, if this had happened to someone else, to Miss Livia, for example, wouldn't you point out that she is enjoying an unlikely amount of luck?"

"Sometimes luck is just luck."

"And most of the time, what seems too good to be true generally is."

Disagreement, their usual state of affairs. A bittersweet sensation, this familiarity. Sometimes it was more sweet than bitter, but not tonight.

She rose and walked to the desk at the back of the parlor. "What would you have me do? Leave my benefactress?"

"Yes."

"And then what?"

"Let me help you," commanded her old friend who had become so proper and decorous, every inch the future pillar of Society. "You always said you wished to be the headmistress at a girls' school. You can still achieve that."

"How?"

He joined her at the side of the desk. "Move to America. You can invent a new identity and start a new life there, with nothing to prevent you from going to school, receiving training, and ultimately finding a good position."

"With you bearing all the expenditures in the meanwhile?"

"Pay me back once you are self-supporting. With interest, if you'd prefer."

"But there will be no consequences whatsoever if I do not or cannot pay you back. Am I correct?"

He did not answer.

The direction of his gaze: somewhere over her right shoulder. The placement of his hand: braced at the edge of the desk. The rise and fall of his chest with every breath—beneath his dark grey coat, his waistcoat was silk jacquard, silver tracery upon the blue of deepest twilight.

"I assume you've heard from Mr. Shrewsbury?"

His jaw tightened. "I have."

"Did he offer me the position of his mistress?"

"He did."

"I hope you didn't decline on my behalf."

At last he looked directly into her eyes. "I would not presume to speak for you."

His dark eyes were solemn, almost antagonistic. Yet heat prickled her skin and charred her nerves. She set the last bite of madeleine on her tongue. "Aren't you going to ask whether I will consider it?"

His gaze dipped to her mouth before meeting hers again. "I won't presume otherwise. You have demonstrated that you will consider—and do—just about anything."

She tilted her chin up. "Are you angry with me?"

He again did not answer, but looked at her as if taken aback at how close she was to him, even though they were separated by a chair.

"I'm sure you would prefer for me to remain with Mrs. Watson," she murmured, "rather than take up Mr. Shrewsbury's offer?"

The direction of his gaze: the pulse at the base of her throat. The placement of his hand: a hard grip on the back of the chair. The fine white linen of his shirt rose and fell with every quickened breath.

The next moment he was ten feet away by the grandfather clock, standing with his back to her. "And when have you ever taken my wishes into consideration when it comes to making your choices?"

She exhaled slowly, unsteadily. "I won't apologize, you know. Going to Mr. Shrewsbury was the only choice I could live with, the only way to break through this wall that my family would keep around me all my life."

"Have I asked you to apologize?"

"No, but you are angry with me. Furious."

He turned around halfway. If glances could take physical form, his would have speared her to the wall. "There isn't a single person with the slightest interest in your well-being who isn't furious with you, Charlotte."

"But I'm fine now."

"You are not starving in the streets, but you are not fine. You are a lady's companion, for God's sake—there is no one worse suited to being a lady's companion. Today you may rejoice in escaping worse misfortunes. Tomorrow, too, perhaps. But in a week you will be bored out of your mind.

"When you were living under your parents' roof, at least you had the possibility of an independent future to look forward to. What do you have to look forward to now? Let me be generous and attribute only the best of motives to this Mrs. Watson. Still it remains

198 · *Sherry Thomas*

that now you are an employee at a position that provides nothing of what you seek—no independence, no intellectual stimulation, and certainly not anywhere near five hundred pounds a year.

"How long can you last? How long before it sinks in that you have exchanged one cage for another? How long before your mind rebels against listening to the same anecdotes for the fifty-eighth time?"

She leaned against the desk, needing its support. "You make it sound so bleak."

"What did you think it would be? A rich and fulfilling life?"

This time it was she who did not answer.

He exhaled. "I will see myself out."

He was retrieving his walking stick from the stand when she said, "I will let you sponsor the cost of my emigration and education if you will agree to one condition."

"No."

"But you haven't—"

He set a hand on the door. "I may not be able to tell what your mother had for lunch yesterday by the color of your hat ribbons, but that doesn't mean I can't extrapolate what you are about to demand. It will be the same . . . service you tried to extort from me by threatening to go to Roger Shrewsbury if I failed to provide it."

She slanted her lips. "You should have heeded that threat. We'd all be much better off if you'd come off your high horse and done some yeoman's work."

"No, we'd all be much better off if you'd stuffed your idea exactly where I told you to."

"I can't live the way you want me to, all bottled up and pretending that everything is all right."

"It's how the rest of us live. Why can't you?"

This debate was inching dangerously close to the lines of their previous conversation, which had flared into a heated argument, and ended with her shouting that no, they *really* would have all been much better off if he'd taken her advice and never proposed to his wife, an I-told-you-so she had refrained from lobbing at him for six long years.

They had not parted on the best of terms.

She sighed. "Fine. Don't take me as your mistress then, even though you want to."

He set his hat on his head. "Good evening, Miss Holmes."

She hated it when he called her *Miss Holmes* in a private conversation. Hated the distance it implied. The gulf that he would not cross.

"I apologize for being such a trial when you are only trying to help. I'm sorry."

He was quiet for a long moment. "You don't try me, Charlotte. You discomfit me. You make me question things that I would otherwise have happily accepted as given. But that is not your fault. Not the preponderance of it, anyway."

He opened the door and left. By the time she reached the stair landing, he was already halfway down. "Now I'm safe with Mrs. Watson," she called after him. "You don't need to have me followed anymore."

He stilled—and answered without turning around, "Miss Holmes, I have no idea of what you speak."

Charlotte opened *A Summer in Roman Ruins* to her favorite page.

My aunt delighted in the entertainment of her progeny and not infrequently hosted children's parties that were almost bacchanalian in their duration and intensity. The energy and volume of two dozen boys and girls did not bother me—I had been guilty of spurring them to ever greater levels of boisterousness. But that summer I slept fitfully, worried that one fine day a gaggle of youngsters with too much cake and orangeade in their bellies would break away from the vicinity of the house and stumble upon my wondrous and fragile site.

In fact, a reprobate thirteen-year-old preyed on my apprehension by threatening to do exactly that: drive a herd of wild children across the estate to descend upon my dig, wreaking as much havoc as Hannibal had done in Italy with troops and elephants brought across the Alps.

What I had to do to preserve the integrity of my site, I wish upon no one.

What memories. An excellent day's work, blackmailing his fifteen-year-old self into kissing her.

I don't want a genteel peck, she'd told him cheerfully. *I want you to live up to your scabrous reputation.*

He'd scowled. *Do you even know what* scabrous *means?*

Indecent and salacious.

That's the kind of reputation I have?

He was usually spoken of as "that troublesome young Lord In-gram." And the other children whispered about him as if he had horns and a forked tail: He had been smoking cigarettes since he was nine; he had caused a dozen governesses to be dismissed; he had got a serving maid into terrible trouble during his very first year at Eton.

Charlotte didn't consider any of the rumors credible, except the smoking part—a hint of Turkish tobacco clung to him, not an unpleasant scent for a glowering boy.

Yes, that's your reputation.

He looked at her askance. *And you want an indecent and salacious sort of kiss?*

Is there any point to any other kind?

This last she might or might not have said out loud: the kiss that followed caused a minor malfunction in her brain. She didn't re-member their exchanges afterward either, if anything at all.

Present-day Charlotte sighed softly. They'd contemplated each other with so little regard on the day they had first and last kissed, he as a target to exploit for her, and she as merely a very strange girl for him.

If only they could have seen the future.

———— ❊ ————

"Miss Holmes, you mustn't worry so much. Everything will be all right," said Mrs. Watson.

They were at the tail end of a late supper and Charlotte was eating without her usual gusto.

She sometimes thought of her mind as bearing a certain resemblance to the post office, a complex system that sorted and conveyed packets of information with speed and efficiency. But at the moment her most prized asset was more comparable to an automobile, a machine liable to break down every few miles and strand the hapless motorist by the side of the road.

She smiled weakly at Mrs. Watson. "I never used to fret about anything—and didn't understand why anyone would. If there was something that needed to be done, that was different. Worrying about outcomes over which I have no control is punishing myself before the universe has decided whether I ought to be punished.

"Now I realize that in my former life I worried about nothing because I feared nothing. That equanimity, which was but a false sense of security, evaporated the moment true consequences appeared. I was unnerved by what might happen to me. Or my sister. And now, my father."

She dipped her spoon into a bowl of fruit compote. "You're right, Mrs. Watson, I mustn't worry so much. But at the moment I don't know how to stop."

"You are looking at me with hope, Miss Holmes." Mrs. Watson sighed. "It's all I know how to do, saying 'you mustn't worry so much.' I haven't the slightest idea how to nip useless fretting in the bud. In fact, I sometimes wake up in the middle of the night and worry, even though I am in circumstances that I would have considered enviable in my youth."

They fell silent for some time. It was still raining, the rain drumming steadily upon the roof.

Charlotte speared a morsel of peach and pushed it around in the syrup. "In any case, much uncertainty will be removed tomorrow. Inspector Treadles will let us know the moment he learns of anything."

Mrs. Watson likewise stirred the contents of her compote bowl. "Now that you've met the inspector in person, what do you think of him?"

"I like him. He is more or less the man he ought to be, though I hadn't expected he would be so deferent to his 'betters.' Perhaps he conducts himself in such a manner because he doesn't want it said that he forgot where he came from. Or perhaps he sincerely believes in the validity and authority of the hierarchy in which we live."

"In other words, you believe you were right in continuing the pretense that Sherlock Holmes is a man."

"Yes."

Inspector Treadles was most respectful to Charlotte. But it was a respect that stemmed from gallantry, the kindness the strong owed to the weak, not the regard one held for an equal, and certainly not the admiration he felt for Lord Ingram, whom he clearly considered his superior.

"What about your friend, Lord Ingram?" asked Mrs. Watson. "He must know that you have no brother named Sherlock Holmes. Yet he seems to have no trouble accepting your powers of reasoning."

"He's long been a victim of my powers—he's grown inured."

"I've seen him at polo matches. The ladies are always fanning themselves—some men have that effect on women, even if they aren't classically handsome."

"Well, he's married."

Her statement sounded more like a grievance. An accusation.

"But not happily so, from what I understand."

His marriage was his great mistake. But now that someone who only knew him via gossip had commented on his private life, Charlotte felt obliged to defend that mistake. "Happiness has never been the goal in a Society marriage."

"Oh, I have long observed that. They are very much business arrangements, sometimes absolutely cold-blooded ones. But occasionally one comes across a union that has no reason to exist except for love and that overwhelming optimism love inspires. It's for those matches that I hold my breath. And it is when they do not succeed that my heart breaks a little, for what might have been."

Would there have been a might-have-been in Lord Ingram's case? If Charlotte hadn't warned him before his wedding that a perfect woman did not exist except in a man's imagination, if she hadn't pointed out that anyone who took the trouble to appear flawless must have an ulterior motive, would he have tested his wife, upon his godfather's passing, by telling her that he received only a five-hundred-pound annuity, instead of the fortune stipulated in his godfather's will?

For it was certain that had he told Lady Ingram the truth, she would have been overjoyed, rather than cold with disappointment and then hot with rage, blurting out that she only married a man known to have resulted from his mother's affair with a Jewish banker because of what he stood to inherit. Why else would she have sullied the bloodline of her own children?

The question Charlotte asked herself concerned the weight of her own words. Had they planted the seed of doubt in his mind—or would the same suspicions have formed by that point in the marriage, regardless of whether Charlotte had said anything years before?

She took a deep breath. "His children are lovely, at least."

Mrs. Watson ate a piece of strawberry from the compote, chewing thoughtfully. "Have you ever been in love, Miss Holmes?"

"No."

It would probably have been more convincing if her answer hadn't been as quick or emphatic, but Mrs. Watson only nodded slowly. "Sometimes that is a blessing, Miss Holmes. A blessing."

Fourteen

A t noon the next day a cable arrived for Charlotte, sent to 18 Upper Baker Street.

Dear Mr. and Miss Holmes,

I am beyond pleased to inform you that the supply of strychnine at both Dr. Birch's and Dr. Harris's had indeed been compromised. The bottles contained no strychnine at all. We now have a case of clearly premeditated murder.

Robert Treadles

By evening the news was all over London. The mysterious Sherlock Holmes had been vindicated—at least with regard to his suspicions concerning Mr. Harrington Sackville. Lady Shrewsbury's family still maintained strenuously that she died of natural causes and that anything else was malicious slander. Lady Amelia's family, on the other hand, seemed stunned by this latest development. They were muted in their response.

"You should relish the moment, Miss Holmes," said Mrs. Watson the next morning. She was in a dress of printed silk, a summery pattern of pastel paisley on a creamy background. "For someone who has the greatest city on earth agog in wonder and speculation, you are far too contained in your reaction."

Charlotte spread a little too much butter on her roll. "I would feel better if all the hubbub had made a bigger difference to my family."

Wild theories continued to abound as to what exactly linked those three deaths. Speculation continued as to the identity of Sherlock Holmes. At the same time, however, people were also wondering what connections, unknown to the general public, the Holmeses might have to Mr. Sackville.

But the continued attention to the Holmeses wasn't solely responsible for Charlotte's subdued reaction. There were also Lord Ingram's dire words. Must she leave behind everything—and everyone—she knew for an uncertain future far away? And if she must ultimately make such a decision, did it not behoove her to make it sooner rather than later?

"Miss Holmes, you are fretting again."

The butter disappeared into the soft, spongy interior of the warm roll. Such a sight had always comforted Charlotte before—and turned her mind blissfully empty when she bit into it. But this was her third roll this morning and, as Mrs. Watson had observed, she was still fretting. "I'm sorry."

"No, don't apologize. Do you know what you need, my dear? You need a proper occupation."

"I have a position."

Mrs. Watson waved her hand. Morning light streaming into the room caught the lacy cuff of her sleeve. "We both know that being a lady's companion is not a good use for your time."

"But what *is*?"

"Think about what you told me in the tea shop, your ability to distill what others fail to see into startling insights." Mrs. Watson's eyes shone. "You lamented that it was a talent of no use whatsoever to a young lady who has been expelled by Society. Which, alas, is still true. But things have changed for *Sherlock* Holmes. That enigmatic gentleman is now famous in London—and beyond. And *his* talents need not go unexploited."

Charlotte forgot all about the roll half an inch from her lips. "Are you suggesting that . . ."

Mrs. Watson pushed a piece of paper across the table to Charlotte. "Tell me what you think."

Sherlock Holmes, celebrated consultant to the Criminal Investigation Department of the Metropolitan Police, makes available his services to private clients. Reasonable fees. Inquiries received at Box _____, General Post Office.

"You do not have a private box at the post office yet, but we will remedy that before we send the advert to the newspapers."

The concept shocked Charlotte—her parents would perish on the spot if they learned that she was advertising herself to the *public*.

"Unless we can individually contact those who might have problems for you to solve," said Mrs. Watson gently, "how else will they know that they can benefit from your help?"

The idea made sense. Of course she had to proclaim her services far and wide, in order to result in even a trickle of paying customers. And of course it had to be now, before the name Sherlock Holmes faded from memory.

"But I am your companion, ma'am. How am I to fulfill my duties if I meet with clients and whatnot?"

"Ah, but this is so much better than having a paid companion. It would bore you to no end to do nothing but read to me and then listen to me ramble on. And frankly it wouldn't be all that interesting to me either. This way we embark on a venture together, a venture that has a fair chance of being profitable, too."

Mrs. Watson all but rubbed her hands together in anticipation. "Beyond paid advertisements, you will need an office, some cards and stationery, three quid a year to rent that private box at the post office, and of course all manner of incidentals—people always fail to plan for the incidentals. It is beyond your means now to set yourself up properly, but not beyond mine. The flat can be your office. I will foot the rest of the upfront expenses and take a cut of your fees as my recompense."

"But we don't know if I'll have significant enough fees for you to recoup your cost."

"It's business, my dear Miss Holmes. Every investment carries a risk, but this one is a risk I'm more than willing to bear. In fact"— she winked at Charlotte—"you need to be careful in your negotiations, to make sure I don't take too large a share of your future earnings."

"Ma'am—"

Mrs. Watson's expression turned solemn. "Miss Holmes, I was in the theater. I have seen talented actresses hand over a shocking percentage of their earnings to men who took them on when they seemed to have few prospects. Do not make that mistake, my dear. Do not undervalue what you are ultimately worth because you are at a momentary disadvantage."

The sensation of having at last met her real mother returned. Charlotte swallowed an unexpected lump in her throat. "Yes, ma'am. I will remember that."

"Good." Mrs. Watson laid her hands over her heart. "Oh, Miss Holmes, we are going to have so much fun."

—❖—

My Dearest Robert,

I know I wrote only two hours ago, but I must let you know that a most delicious box of little cakes has arrived for me, compliments of Mr. Sherlock Holmes and his sister. The note that accompanied it explained that you had very much wished for me to have a taste of these madeleines. My sweetling, how I adore you for always thinking of me. (And marvel, as usual, at Holmes's astuteness, as you would not have expressed that desire aloud.)

Now to business. Holmes asked that I convey to you the significance of the maid not having opened the curtains. He wrote that he had not wished to say too much, in case the chemical analysis came to naught. But now that you have a mandate to investigate, you will want to know that such a thing hints strongly at improper relations between the maid and Mr. Sackville.

I have never witnessed such goings-on in my father's household and I dare say that my brother, for all his faults, is not one to take physical advantage of his staff—he would be afraid of catching some dread disease. But too many young girls who toil in domestic service must deal with unwelcome advances, as a cost of employment.

Although, as much as I hate to cast aspersion on someone I have never met and of whose circumstances I know very little, Becky Birtle, the young girl in question, seems to have been a willing participant, if indeed there were advances on Mr. Sackville's part.

Had she entered the chamber to relight the fire before her master awoke, it would go without saying that she need not have approached the curtains—but then neither should she have disturbed him in his rest. But since her purpose was to give him his morning cocoa, she ought to have first opened the curtains and possibly the windows, to let light and fresh air into the room.

That she had approached and touched him without doing so first indicates her duties were hardly foremost on her mind. In fact, it might be the most charitable thing to be said under the circumstances.

But I do hope that this was not the case. Such a scenario makes me worry for the girl and feel all too cynical about the world.

I believe I shall comfort myself with a fresh cup of tea and a scrumptious madeleine that tastes as bright and lovely as a summer day in Tuscany.

> *All my love,*
> *Alice*

Inspector Treadles tapped a finger against his wife's letter and tried to decide whether the information that he had been provided was useful.

Or, rather, whether it was useful in the correct direction.

The discovery that the supply of strychnine had been tampered with at both doctors' places, along with Lord Ingram's disclosure that Lady Sheridan had been seen at Paddington Station, had firmly settled his suspicion on the Sheridans.

The possibility of questionable conduct on Becky Birtle's part threw a wrench into his theories.

The Sheridans made for great suspects. By ridding themselves of a brother they no longer loved, they would put an end to their perennial monetary worries. They had the sophistication and—despite the hollowness of their financial situation—the means to choreograph an intricate murder that presented as an accidental overdose.

But lucre as a motive did present its problems. The Sheridans' shortage of funds was chronic rather than acute. They had dealt with it for decades without murdering anyone. Why should they start at this late stage in life?

On the other hand, improprieties between Becky Birtle and Mr. Sackville were far more likely to ignite murderous passions in the here and now. Someone else could have been competing for Becky Birtle's affection. Tommy Dunn, the manservant who worked outdoors, perhaps. He was much closer to Becky Birtle's age and a spurned young man could very well turn into a dangerous beast.

Except no one flew into a rage and throttled Mr. Sackville. And Treadles couldn't see Tommy Dunn as the sort to arrange for an elaborate scheme that would leave no trace of his involvement.

What about the other female servants? What if one of them had believed that she had an understanding with her master, only to discover he was also having his way with Becky Birtle? Might that not provoke a fury that had no equal in hell?

"Inspector, there's a message from the chemical analyst for you," said Sergeant MacDonald.

Treadles read the cable. *"What?"*

"What is it, sir?" asked MacDonald, wide-eyed.

Treadles needed a moment to gather himself. "Remember that I asked for Mr. Sackville's tissue to be tested for other poisons besides chloral?" He glanced at the telegram again. "They found arsenic."

Fifteen

A very different-looking Curry House greeted Inspector Treadles upon his return. A fog had rolled in. The house drifted in and out of billows of vapor, a pale, ghostly vessel in a sea of mist.

The character of the interior had changed, too. With the beauty of the coast obscured, it did not have the same airiness and sparkle. Instead Treadles felt an intense isolation, made only more stark by the unrelenting prettiness of the décor.

Before Treadles's arrival, Sergeant MacDonald, with two local constables in tow, had made a search of the entire property. Two sources of arsenic had been found. One, located in the kitchen, had been dyed red—as required by law to prevent accidental misuse. The other, a box of white arsenic kept for killing mice, was in the storeroom.

This was more or less normal for a household of this scale and provided no immediate clues as to who might have used it. Not to mention, even though one had to sign for the purchase of white arsenic, with forethought, a would-be poisoner could always find an unscrupulous chemist some distance away and make the transaction untraceable.

For this *was* a poisoner with forethought. No arsenic had been found in the contents of the dead man's stomach, but it had seeped into his hair and nails, indicating a long-term poisoner at work.

Then what happened? Why did the poisoner change tactics? What made it imperative that Mr. Sackville must die immediately, rather than at an indeterminate future date?

And did it have something to do with Becky Birtle having been a rather impertinent girl?

"Can you tell me something of the traffic into and out of the storeroom, Mrs. Cornish?"

They were again in her office, but the housekeeper didn't radiate as much command over her fiefdom as she had the previous time—knowing that Mr. Sackville had been murdered couldn't possibly be easy on anyone at Curry House. "The storeroom is usually locked," she said, with determined self-possession. "Cake and biscuits are kept inside and we don't want Jenny Price getting into them. But Mr. Hodges has a key—he took cocoa and sugar for making Mr. Sackville's morning cup. Mrs. Meek, too, when she wanted a nice tureen for soup.

"And sometimes I give Tommy Dunn my key. The staff receive three meals a day and tea besides. But it's hard work he does. I don't mind him taking a few extra biscuits for himself."

"So everyone, other than Jenny Price, goes in and out of that room." This wasn't helpful to Treadles's investigation at all.

"That's right. There's no wine or beer in it—those are in a locked cellar. No silver either. And no one has ever taken anything they oughtn't from the storeroom. But Inspector, why are you interested in who can pinch arsenic when Mr. Sackville died of too much chloral?"

Treadles glanced down at his notes. "You didn't mention Becky Birtle. Did she have access to the storeroom?"

"From time to time I asked her to fetch something for me. But surely you can't suspect a child?"

Treadles didn't answer this question either. "The morning of Mr. Sackville's death, when you went into his room, had the curtains been opened yet?"

Mrs. Cornish blinked. "I'm sure I don't remember. There was Mr. Sackville so cold and all. I paid no mind to the curtains."

"Had the curtains been closed, you would have needed to open them to see."

"I don't remember anything about the curtains—they must have been open."

She exuded respectability. It demanded nothing of Treadles's imagination to envisage her picture gracing the cover of *The Experienced English Housekeeper.* Would she lie?

And more importantly, if she lied, what was the reason? What would impel her to spare him the impression that the housemaid might have been up to no good?

"I would like to see a photograph of Becky Birtle."

The abrupt change of subject had Mrs. Cornish reaching for her teacup. "She didn't leave behind any."

"Tell me something of her character then."

Mrs. Cornish added what appeared to Treadles an excessive amount of sugar to her tea. "Becky is at a . . . trying age. She thinks she's a woman full-grown and doesn't care to be told different. But she has a good heart. In a few years she ought to turn out a fine young woman."

"When do you expect her to return to Curry House?"

"Oh, I can't tell you, Inspector. Now that her parents know Mr. Sackville was murdered, I dare say they wouldn't like for her to come back at all."

Did Treadles hear a note of relief in Mrs. Cornish's voice? She had reasons to be concerned for her own respectability—it would not reflect well on her, as head of the staff, if it became known that Becky Birtle had conducted herself in a questionable manner. But was that Mrs. Cornish's only worry?

"You asked earlier, Mrs. Cornish, why I'm inquiring after arsenic when Mr. Sackville died from an overdose of chloral. The answer is we have found arsenic in Mr. Sackville, indicating that someone has been poisoning him."

Mrs. Cornish started violently. "No!"

Treadles went on. "That someone most likely had frequent access to him. Since Mr. Sackville was more or less a recluse, that limits the suspects to members of the household."

"But—but what a horrible thought."

"Unfortunately that is the case."

"But he died of chloral. And no one in this house knows how to burgle two different doctors' places."

That was the puzzling part. But Treadles had learned, in his years as a detective, that those in service were a far more diverse lot than commonly presumed. It was not unheard of for the servant hall to harbor a few who had known the shadier side of life.

"It is what every housekeeper supposes—and hopes for—that those who serve under her are a meticulously law-abiding lot. But you do not know the background of everyone here, do you?"

Reluctantly Mrs. Cornish shook her head.

"Who in this household would wish Mr. Sackville harm?"

"No one!"

"You know that is not true: Someone under this roof very much wished the master harm. You are responsible for the running of the place. You should know of any domestic tension that had the potential to mutate and fester."

Mrs. Cornish gripped her teacup with both hands. "Sir, you

mustn't think this house was a hotbed of ill will. It was nothing of the sort."

"It would be a thoughtless poisoner who makes his hatred widely known. Have you observed subtler signs of discontent and resentment?"

"I've never had any complaints against Mr. Sackville. Becky thought him a fine gentleman. Jenny Price adored him. Mrs. Meek is new here and she's anyway the cheerful sort, always a good word for everything and everyone."

This did not sound to Treadles like a compliment, more the politeness of someone who could do with a bit less of that determined agreeableness.

"Tommy Dunn thought the sun rose and set on Mr. Sackville's shoulders. And Mr. Hodges . . . Mr. Hodges holds his cards close to his chest."

Treadles raised a brow but only waited.

Mrs. Cornish took a large gulp of her tea. "I used to think that he and Mr. Sackville rubbed along just fine. But last Christmas, when Tommy Dunn had the fob from the master and couldn't stop taking out his watch to check the time, Mr. Hodges looked at him as if he were an idiot. I thought maybe he was a little jealous—Tommy Dunn had no reason to receive a gift almost as fine as the one he himself got.

"When Mrs. Meek came, she was impressed with everything. Mr. Hodges would have this stony look on his face when she and Tommy Dunn agreed on how fine the house was and what a grand gentleman the master was. One time he even got up and left the servants' hall."

Hodges, when called in to the drawing room to answer questions, immediately repudiated Mrs. Cornish's claims. "Maybe I did roll my eyes at Tommy Dunn a few times, but only because it was bordering on unseemly, how often he showed off that watch fob. A grown man ought to know better. I left the servants' hall that day after supper because it was about to rain and I remembered I'd left my window open a crack—I was back five minutes later. And it wasn't Tommy Dunn Mrs. Meek was talking to at that time, it was Becky Birtle."

A thought came to Treadles. "You are sure it wasn't Miss Birtle speaking with Mr. Dunn?"

"As far as I could tell, those two had nothing to say to each other."

This was odd. In a household full of older people, they were the only two youngsters. "Has it always been like that?"

"Not always. When Becky first arrived, she talked a good deal to Tommy Dunn. And he was helpful to her. But then it all changed. He used to stay after supper to hear us talk—never said much himself but wanted to listen, especially if we brought up places we'd been and sights we'd seen. Not long after Becky came, he stopped. Just left at the end of supper and went back to his own room."

This fit with the supposition that Tommy Dunn had perhaps been sweet on Becky Birtle—and disappointed in his affection.

"Is there anything else you can tell us, Mr. Hodges, that might help us in our investigation?"

Hodges thought for a moment. "When I came back from my holiday for the inquest, the whisky decanter in Mr. Sackville's bedroom was gone."

"Did you look for it?"

"I asked Mrs. Cornish. She said she'd looked all over the house and couldn't find it."

Whisky would have been a good means of administering arsenic. In fact, anything would have been a good means of administering arsenic. It was not for nothing that arsenic had been a favorite weapon in the poisoner's arsenal. The powder was odorless and tasteless, easy to disguise in food and beverage. Not to mention, the symptoms of arsenic poisoning closely matched those of cholera—and in places where the water supply was not in question, could be blamed on gastric attacks.

"I might as well let you know, Mr. Hodges, that arsenic was found in Mr. Sackville's body."

Hodges's hands closed into fists. He exhaled heavily a few times. "The tricks with the strychnine were ghastly enough. Arsenic, too?"

"Arsenic, too. How frequently did Mr. Sackville take his whisky?"

"Almost—" Hodges blew out another shaky breath. "Almost every day, but he never took more than a thimbleful or two."

"On what occasions did he not take it?"

"When the weather was warm, he might ask to have a glass of wine instead. The cellar keeps the wine cool."

"I believe I've asked you this before, but let me ask you again, Mr. Hodges. Do you know of anyone—specifically, anyone in this house—who might have wished Mr. Sackville dead?"

A muscle leaped at the corner of Hodges's jaw, but his answer was firm. "No."

"Do you know of anyone who might have wanted him to *suffer*?"

The gastric attacks Mr. Sackville had endured in recent months were most likely not gastric attacks at all, but the effects of arsenic.

Hodges unclenched and clenched his hands again. "No, Inspector. We don't have that sort of lowlife in this house."

Tommy Dunn echoed that opinion. "Ain't no master more generous than Mr. Sackville. And a new master mayn't even want us to work for him. Why would anyone hurt him?"

He made a valid point. For a servant to poison the master of the house was for him to endanger his own livelihood, especially in a hired house like this, with no one coming to inherit the property. The next tenant might very well bring a full complement of retainers.

Treadles asked Dunn about Mr. Hodges leaving the servants' hall while Mrs. Meek and someone else discussed the merits of the house and of the master.

"Was that you or was that Becky Birtle?"

"Must have been Becky. Don't remember nothing like that."

"Weren't you there?"

"No. Went back to me own room after supper."

"I understand you didn't get on with Becky Birtle."

Hostility darkened Tommy Dunn's face. "She thinks too much of herself, that girl."

There was an excess of antagonism in his expression; a high opinion of herself couldn't be the only thing that bothered him about Becky Birtle.

"Did you feel a sense of affection for her before your sentiments turned?"

The young man snorted. "What? You asking if I fancied her?"

"Yes."

"Never. She's a scrawny girl—bony like a goat. Didn't do a thing for me."

"Then why did you come to dislike her?"

Dunn shrugged, but his jaw was held so tight a vein bulged on his neck. "Like I said, she gave herself airs."

Something had happened to derail a once friendly enough association, but Treadles was not going to get it from Dunn.

"Do you know anything about a whisky decanter that's gone missing?

"Caught Mrs. Cornish in my room looking for it. She said she didn't think I took it, but someone might have hid it under my bed or something. Can't say I believe her."

Treadles did not enjoy this aspect of his work. A murder investigation unearthed not only deeply held, obsessively nursed grievances, but a plethora of everyday resentments. The undercurrents that would have otherwise remained beneath the surface for the foreseeable future.

One didn't need to be naive to enjoy the idea of a harmonious household, where the master was gentlemanly and considerate and the servants dutiful to their employer and kind to one another. To not believe in the possibility was to become the kind of cynic who suspected every ordinary establishment of seething with acrimony and discontent.

And Robert Treadles had been such a fortunate man—he owed it to himself not to go down the all-too-easy route of skepticism and disenchantment.

⁎

As there was nothing to be gained by interviewing Jenny Price again, Treadles called in Mrs. Meek, who arrived in a high state.

"Is it true, Inspector, that Mr. Sackville had been poisoned with arsenic?"

Treadles had expected that the news would have spread. "I'd like to know who came to you with the information."

It might help him judge the differing degrees of rapports among the servants.

"Nobody *came* and told me. Mrs. Cornish looked all shaken when she walked past the kitchen. So I followed her and asked what was the matter. She told me. It was such awful news that I asked both Mr. Hodges and Tommy Dunn, too, because I didn't want to believe it."

She stared at Treadles, as if still hoping that he would reassure her otherwise.

"It is true," he said softly.

Immediately her gaze shifted to Sergeant MacDonald. The latter nodded, closing the last avenue of denial.

Mrs. Meek slowly sank into a chair. "But that's evil. Evil."

Treadles gave her a moment to collect herself. "According to the answers you provided last time, when you reached Mr. Sackville's bedroom, one of the first things you did was to open the curtains. Is that correct?"

She looked at him in bafflement. "What does that have to do with anything?"

"Please answer the question. Did you open the curtains?"

"I did."

"You are sure they weren't already open?"

Mrs. Meek sat up straighter—she bristled with the injured dignity of someone about to defend her integrity. "I am completely sure, Inspector. We all rushed to Mr. Sackville's bedside. 'Feel him, feel him,' Becky was yelling. So I did, and his temperature was all wrong. I looked up at Mrs. Cornish. But she wasn't looking at him. She was looking at the curtains. I remember this very clearly. It was still dim inside the room, but light was already seeping in around the edges of the drapes, halolike, if you will. Then Mrs. Cornish pulled open the curtains on her side and I did the same on the window closer to me."

There was an innocence to Mrs. Meek's reply, a resolute lack of insinuation.

Treadles was reminded of his own obliviousness to the significance of the curtains. A thought occurred to him. "Have you ever worked in any other position in a household, Mrs. Meek?"

"No, Inspector. I was always the cook. Cook's assistant early on, and then the cook."

Perhaps she truly was plainly stating the facts. Perhaps she herself didn't understand the import of what she had revealed.

"How would you describe Becky Birtle?"

"Becky? She's a bit of a handful. I don't mind a high-spirited girl myself but I think Mrs. Cornish was frustrated with her."

"Is she an attractive girl?"

"Not beautiful, but most girls that age are rather pretty—first bloom of youth."

"Is there a picture of her anywhere in the house?"

Mrs. Meek frowned. "N—oh, wait, I remember now. A traveling

photographer came through recently. Mr. Hodges said that Mr. Sackville had paid for a photograph for the servants only the year before and wouldn't pay for another one so soon. But Mrs. Cornish said she'd pay for one herself. So we dragged some chairs outside and sat for the photographer and he came back a few days later with a copy for Mrs. Cornish."

"Was Becky Birtle in the picture?"

"Yes she was. Standing right behind me."

And yet Mrs. Cornish had been firm that there was no photograph of the girl in the house. Treadles made a note to speak to the housekeeper again before he left.

"Mr. Hodges tells me that a whisky decanter went missing. Have you heard about it?"

A knock came on the door. Even before Treadles answered, Constable Perkins, who had been assigned to accompany the detectives from Scotland Yard and facilitate matters for them, peeked in. The young man's face was flush with excitement.

"Inspector, Sergeant, a word please."

Treadles raised a brow. For the constable to interrupt an interview, it had better be important. He murmured a word of apology and left the room, MacDonald in his wake.

"Inspector, the name Sergeant told me to check—"

"What name, Sergeant?"

"When I was searching Mrs. Meek's room, sir," said Sergeant MacDonald, "I found letters addressed to a Nancy Monk. The name sounded familiar, but I couldn't quite remember. So I asked Constable Perkins to see if he could find out something more."

"One of the men at the station remembered right away," said Perkins. "But we didn't want to rush, so we sent a cable on the Wheatstone machine to Scotland Yard. And they cabled back and confirmed our suspicions.

"Nancy Monk was the defendant in an arsenic poisoning trial twenty-five years ago. Everyone in the family died, except the master of the house, who was away on business. She took the stand to testify on her own behalf and the jury came away convinced that she cared a great deal for the little children. And since there was never any evidence of anything between the cook and the master—she had a young greengrocer she was planning to marry—she was acquitted."

And a quarter of a century later, she turned up in another case of arsenic poisoning.

When Inspector Treadles returned, Mrs. Meek was rocking back and forth on her seat, her fingers clutched tightly around the armrests.

Treadles got to the point. "Mrs. Meek, have you ever gone by another name?"

All the blood drained from her face. "Why do you ask?"

He simply waited.

"I was framed!" Her voice shot up an entire octave, giving her words a jagged edge. "The man I worked for—it was him. His cousins had a sheep farm and they kept white arsenic for dressing the wool. A month before everyone died he visited his cousins. He mixed that arsenic into the spare jar of snipped-and-pounded sugar I kept in the cupboard. And of course he made sure to be away on business when the sugar in the kitchen jar ran out and I started using sugar from the other jar.

"I brought the children milk with sugar and hot cocoa for the missus, like I did every morning. They also had buttered toast sprinkled with sugar. You can't imagine their suffering that day. I was frantic with worry. But I never thought they were poisoned. And I never thought I'd be charged.

"She wasn't a pretty or clever woman. But she tried to make the best possible home for him. And the children were sweet and loved everything I cooked. I was happy to hear that their father, when he proposed to the daughter of a business associate less than a year later, was turned down. I was even happier to learn that he'd died on his cousin's sheep farm, after he was gored by an angry ram. Perhaps God wasn't blind and deaf after all."

She knotted her fingers together, fingers that were large and rough from work. "But if that was justice from above, it came too late for me. My young man, he believed that I was innocent, but his mother wouldn't let him marry anyone who'd been through such a public trial—not to mention she was afraid I'd poison *her*. And I couldn't stay in Lancashire anymore. I had to say good-bye to him, move far away, change my name, and make a new life for myself.

The former Nancy Monk looked up at Treadles, her gaze direct and earnest. "I did *not* poison Mr. Sackville. And if you check with my previous employer—I served her for twenty years—you'll find that I told the truth. She was sorry to see me go. And I'd have stayed on, but I'm not so young anymore and it was too much work feeding two dozen dyspeptic ladies day in and day out."

"We will most assuredly be checking with your previous employer," said Treadles.

Her distress was so palpable that he found it difficult to breathe. He wanted to believe her, but he could not allow his own sympathies to muddy the investigation.

"And what do you intend to do in the meanwhile, Inspector?" Mrs. Meek's shoulders slumped. "Arrest me?"

Treadles sighed inwardly. "I do not plan to—yet. But I strongly caution you to remain in this house—or be considered a fugitive from the law."

—❧—

Treadles did not forget about the photograph, but Mrs. Cornish had a ready explanation. "Becky took it with her when she left. She wanted

to go home, but she was afraid her parents wouldn't let her leave
again. So she asked for the photograph as a memento."

Treadles nodded. "During my interviews with other members of
the staff, I learned of a whisky decanter that you were searching for,
Mrs. Cornish. You failed to mention it to me."

Mrs. Cornish sucked in a breath. "But that had nothing to do
with the case. There's never been any theft in this house for as long
as I've been here and I was upset that as soon as Mr. Sackville died
somebody thought it was all right to swipe something of his."

On the face of it, this was a plausible enough explanation. But
then again, if one merely went by appearances, there would not be
an investigation into Mr. Sackville's death. "Did you ever find it?"

"No," said the housekeeper immediately.

"Do let us know if it turns up."

"Of course, Inspector." Mrs. Cornish smiled tightly. "Of course."

Sixteen

The response to Sherlock Holmes's advertisement in the papers was beyond anything Charlotte could have anticipated. Even Mrs. Watson declared herself more than gratified by the influx of inquiries.

There were, as she had cautioned Charlotte, a number of letters that had nothing to do with perplexing issues that needed unraveling. Several missives scolded Sherlock Holmes for interfering in matters that were none of his concern—one purporting to be from a friend of Lady Amelia's, another a relation of Lady Shrewsbury's. A few others claimed friendship—and kinship—with the fictional Holmes, expressing hope for renewed acquaintance and perhaps some financial assistance. The ones that amused her the most were a half dozen or so marriage proposals, from women who didn't want the singular genius of their time to lack the warmth and solicitude of a good wife.

There was even a gentleman convinced that Holmes must be of the Uranian persuasion.

*Great men, in my observation, are more likely than not to harbor a deep love
for other great men. I therefore urge you to join our society and together strive*

to overturn the prejudices that would condemn us and the barriers that would have us always be outsiders, fearful of discovery and banishment.

"I would join his society in a heartbeat," said Charlotte to Mrs. Watson, "but I fear I shall disappoint him bitterly."

A portion of the remaining inquiries were rejected right away as spurious.

"This man asserts that he has an income of four thousand pounds a year and wants to know whether his fiancée is sincere in her affection for him or only for his money." Mrs. Watson scoffed. "Look at this paper. I should be surprised if he has an income of four hundred pounds a year."

Another letter, from a young woman who worked in a florist shop and was puzzled by the conduct of a customer who always bought a single rose but suddenly bought a bouquet of yellow zinnias, seemed legitimate enough to Mrs. Watson. But Charlotte, after looking at it, declared it fabricated. "Lord Ingram is an accomplished calligrapher. And he has taught me that while it is possible for a person to master more than one style of handwriting, it takes a great deal of practice to achieve fluidity in the flow of the letters. And even when one does, there might still be noticeable hesitation at the beginnings and the ends of words. In fact, looking at the script, I would guess the writer to be working for a newspaper."

Mrs. Watson's eyes widened—there had been a number of inquiries from the papers, wishing for a word with Mr. Holmes, which they'd promptly discarded. Charlotte grinned. "No, his handwriting didn't tell me that, but the letter is postmarked very close to the premises of *The Times*. Our would-be trickster didn't realize that he had better be more committed to his fraud if he wanted a face-to-face meeting with the mysterious Sherlock Holmes."

Their first actual client at 18 Upper Baker Street was a young man with a pink, eager face. He had been courting a lovely young lady. Her birthday was in three weeks and he had asked what he ought to give her. In response she had given him a riddle to test the depth of his devotion.

What I'd like to receive is to be found at the beginning of the year, in the middle of the longest word in the dictionary, at the bottom of the stairs, and the end of eternity. Does this turn you upside down? Then you must flip yourself the right way around.

Charlotte disappeared into "Sherlock's" bedroom for three minutes, then returned with a big smile on her face. "My brother has solved the riddle for you. If you take the letter at the beginning of the word 'year'—"

"I did try that route earlier," said the young man. "The beginning of the word 'year' yields the letter y. Bottom of the stairs would give me s, and end of eternity another y. But what's the longest word in the dictionary?"

"That would depend on the dictionary, wouldn't it? But the longest word in the word 'dictionary' is itself."

The young man gasped with delight. "And the letter in the middle of the word is . . . ah . . ."

Charlotte waited patiently until he exclaimed, "O! It's o."

"I do believe you are correct, sir."

"But what do y, o, s, and y give me?"

"Your young lady did warn you that everything might be upside down, did she not? So let's reverse her directions, the ones that are reversible in any case. If we take the end of the year, the top of the stairs, and the beginning of eternity—middle of the dictionary is still middle of the dictionary—then what do we have?"

The young man thought for a minute. "R, o, s, e. Roses, she wants roses! I can get her roses!"

He left beaming. Mrs. Watson, who had volunteered to look after the administrative aspects of their enterprise, accompanied him out.

Since neither Charlotte nor Mrs. Watson had any firsthand knowledge of what would be a fair price for Sherlock Holmes's services, the latter had decided to make it seven shillings for a meeting that solved the problem. *It's a bit more than what a doctor would charge for a call, but not much more. And there's only one Sherlock Holmes.*

Mrs. Watson returned, beaming from ear to ear. Charlotte rose from her chair. "I can't believe it. He paid!"

Mrs. Watson had reassured her that of course her clients would pay. But to Charlotte the entire enterprise still felt like a mirage, an elaborate fata morgana castle in the sky. That she might turn nothing more than a few minutes of time and a bit of thinking into actual money—enough money for a week of room and board in a halfway-respectable place!

"Oh, yes, he paid. Most willingly, too."

The mischief and satisfaction on Mrs. Watson's face . . . Charlotte's jaw dropped. "What did you tell him my fee was?"

"A guinea."

A guinea was twenty-one shillings, three times what they had agreed to charge. Charlotte gaped at Mrs. Watson. "But that's a fortune!"

"Yes, but allow me to know better in this case. He confirmed that he is very well off, did he not, when you told him what you knew about him?"

The young man's family was successful in manufacturing. But still, a guinea. "It isn't so much about what he can afford but more about, well, not overcharging."

Mrs. Watson pressed the heavy coin into Charlotte's palm and closed her fingers around it. "Remind yourself that you're far more likely to undercharge than overcharge, my dear, because you don't yet understand your own value and you've never been taught to demand your full worth." She smiled. "That's why I appointed myself the bursar of this operation, because I've had to learn both."

———— ❈ ————

Their second client was a timid woman of about thirty who had misplaced an emerald ring her husband had given her and was desperate to find it before he returned home from a business trip. Charlotte located the ring at the bottom of the woman's hatpin holder. Mrs. Watson charged her nine shillings plus outlay for their return trip in a hansom cab, which the client was more than happy to pay, besides gifting them with a ham pie, for "poor Mr. Holmes, who can't leave his room."

"If this keeps up, we might bring in more than five hundred pounds a year," Charlotte marveled, as they settled into a cab.

Mrs. Watson patted the aigrette on her bonnet. "Five hundred pounds isn't an astonishing sum, my dear Miss Holmes."

"But it's as much as I ever hoped to make, after many years of school, training, and experience!"

"Well, we may not bring in five hundred a year, since we may not always have a steady supply of clients. Or we could bring in much more, if we have a few dukes and princes whose secretaries I'll bill fifty quid a piece," said Mrs. Watson with great relish. "And don't you worry that I'll overcharge them. Not every nobleman is in dire financial straits. The Duke of Westminster has an income of two hundred fifty thousand pounds a year."

Charlotte couldn't help laughing. "My dear lady, I feared to impose on your kindness. I see now that I needn't have worried. You are a shark!"

Mrs. Watson preened a little, evidently pleased by Charlotte's observation. "A shark with a good nose for money in the water but, let's say, rather soft teeth."

—❊—

"Miss Livia," said the maid, "there's a woman to see you. She says her name is Rajkumari Indira."

Livia looked up from the frame of embroidery on which she hadn't made any progress in days. "What?"

Occasionally one did see an Indian princess in London, but the Holmeses had few ties with the subcontinent and did not move in the kinds of circles that hobnobbed with foreign dignitaries. Why in the world would one call on her?

In the parlor, a woman draped in scarlet and gold silk stood at the window, her back to the room, her hair covered by a very long shawl that had already wrapped around her person once. At Livia's entry, she turned around, the shawl drawn across her face, concealing everything except her eyes.

When she saw that Livia had come alone, she dropped her hand from the edge of the shawl. Charlotte!

Charlotte placed a finger over her lips, signaling Livia to be quiet. Livia ran across the room and embraced her sister.

"Oh, Charlotte!" Then she pulled back. "My goodness, you are practically naked!"

The blouse Charlotte wore ended just beneath her breasts. The shawl, drawn diagonally across the body from hip to shoulders and then back around, covered most of the exposed portions of Charlotte's torso, but from the side one could easily see four inches of skin.

"It's so nobody looks at my face." Charlotte laid a hand on Livia's arm. "Are you all right, Livia?"

"I'm well enough. People don't actually *believe* that I did away with Lady Shrewsbury, but it gives them something to speculate about in the meanwhile."

The situation was a little less promising than that. The discovery of arsenic had tongues wagging that while Mr. Sackville might have been murdered, he had to have been done in by someone local, most likely one of his servants—leading to the current consensus that his death had nothing to do with Lady Shrewsbury's and Lady Amelia's.

With the suspicion for those latter deaths once again falling squarely on Livia and Sir Henry, respectively—which must be the reason Charlotte had taken the risk to come see her.

"You've become too thin," said Charlotte softly.

"It was always more enjoyable to watch you eat than to eat myself." Livia took Charlotte's face in her hands. "At least you haven't become too thin."

"Mrs. Watson feeds me 'round the clock and I haven't turned anything down. But at the rate I'm going, within the week I'll reach Maximum Tolerable Chins. Then I'll be obliged to give up this reckless dining."

Livia chuckled.

Charlotte took Livia's hands in her own. "If only there had been an inquest, at least in Lady Shrewsbury's case."

Livia sighed.

"Don't worry." Charlotte came beside Livia and placed an arm around her shoulder. "Inspector Treadles will get to the bottom of this. He is very good at what he does."

Charlotte didn't possess the instinct to comfort. Livia well knew this: When they'd been girls, Charlotte remained in her corner of the room and observed as Livia battled with her sometimes overwhelming feelings of inadequacy and insignificance. But over the years her sister had learned that it made Livia feel less alone, less despair stricken, to be gently stroked on the back. Or embraced. Or patted on the arm.

Really, any kind of contact at all.

And the odd thing was, knowing that Charlotte was not naturally inclined to physical closeness made her touches not less effective, but more—they were not a reflexive reaction to the distress of another, but a considered one.

Livia leaned on her sister and finally gave voice to the fearful thought that tumbled day and night in the back of her head. "What if Inspector Treadles gets to the bottom of it, only to find out that Mr. Sackville's butler did it?"

Leaving Livia forevermore known as the woman who probably had something to do with Lady Shrewsbury's death.

Her entire life she had been frustrated by her invisibility. At home she was the last daughter her parents remembered. In Society the women were prettier, livelier, younger, cleverer, or even more pathetic—she knew of at least one instance in which a widower offered for a plain, penniless spinster who would otherwise have to endure a lifetime under the thumb of a tyrannical brother. Whereas Livia always seemed to carry her own special shield of obscurity everywhere she went, behind which she could stand in the middle of a room and not be noticed.

How she'd yearned to be the center of attention.

And how cruel to be taught this way that she ought to be careful what she wished for.

"Inspector Treadles will apprehend real suspects in no time," said Charlotte. "You have my assurances as a consultant to the Criminal Investigation Department."

Livia snorted. "This reminds me. I saw the advert for Sherlock Holmes's services. Are you really taking clients? How do you keep up the pretense?"

Charlotte explained the procedure she and Mrs. Watson had established. "I saw my first two clients this morning. We already made thirty shillings."

"So fast?"

"Yes. And I have another client lined up for the afternoon."

She opened her reticule, took out a small pouch, and put it in Livia's hand. Livia didn't have to open the pouch to know it was the jewelry and money she'd given Charlotte the night she had run away.

She gave it back. "It's too early. You don't know that you'll still have clients in a week—or a month. And I still have reservations about this Mrs. Watson."

Charlotte shook her head. "I'm more worried about you now than I am about myself. You take it. Mrs. Watson has invested her own funds to set up Sherlock Holmes's operation, so she has every motive to keep me around and in good shape until she at least recoups her cost."

Livia stared down at the pouch. "Oh, Charlotte, what is going to happen to all of us?"

"According to my crystal ball, Mrs. Watson will make a fortune. I will make a name. You will clear your name, as will Papa. And Mamma will feel relieved for a short while and then more aggrieved than ever."

Oh God, if only. If only. "While we are looking through your crystal ball, can you tell me if I'll always be stuck at home with Mamma and Papa?"

"Only if you want to be, Livia," said Charlotte softly. "Only if you want to be."

———※———

"Lady Sheridan, thank you for seeing me on such short notice," said Inspector Treadles.

Lady Sheridan smiled without warmth. "Your note did not leave much room for refusal or delays, Inspector."

She was a small, fine-featured woman, her grey hair swept back in a precise and severe chignon. But whereas her husband was hale and vigorous, Lady Sheridan reminded Treadles of nothing so much as her town house, a once-beautiful entity made worn by time and adverse circumstances.

"I apologize for the necessity of the intrusion," Treadles said as gently as he could. "But we have an eyewitness account of your return to Paddington Station from a Great Western train. The eyewitness, who has been interviewed by my colleague, is entirely certain that she saw you on the day Mr. Sackville died—and even produced her diary entry to bolster her claim."

"Lady Avery kindly sent a message to that effect." A note of irony lined her words. "I did return to London that day. I am one of the patronesses of the Young Women's Christian Association and attended the opening of a new center in Bath, which took place before numerous witnesses. Then I got on a train the next day and came back."

"You didn't go to Stanwell Moot?" It would have been a fairly convenient side trip from Bath.

"I assure you, Inspector, I never set foot in Stanwell Moot."

Unfortunately, that was probably true. Constable Perkins's conscientious legwork had not produced a shred of evidence that either of the Sheridans had ever visited the village or its vicinities.

"I was also told that you were once very fond of Mr. Sackville. That you lamented that he had drifted away from the family. Lady Avery said you claimed not to know why he cut off contact, but there is a very real possibility that you knew and chose not to tell her, as she was liable to repeat what she learned to others."

"An astute observation." The expression on Lady Sheridan's face was almost a smile.

Treadles found himself warming up to the old woman at this sign of almost approval. He had to issue a stern reminder to himself that she was still a prime suspect. "Can you elucidate us as to why Mr. Sackville drifted away from the family?"

Lady Sheridan waved a weary hand. "One of those tedious

arguments between brothers about their manly honor—I can't recall how it began."

Her dismissal of the matter seemed genuine enough. Treadles tried a different angle. "Lord Sheridan insisted that there was no estrangement."

"And I believe that he believed so. Until Harrington died he was probably still expecting his brother to ring the bell and admit he'd been wrong all these years."

Could it truly be so insignificant, an argument that caused formerly affectionate brothers to become strangers?

"Mr. Sackville's passing does not seem to have grieved you, my lady."

"I have been brought up to never grieve in public. In any case, we lost him long ago—my husband might not have realized but I did, eventually. I already grieved."

Her voice was hard.

Inspector Treadles rose and inclined his head. "Thank you, my lady. That will be all."

"Breathe in," Mrs. Watson ordered.

Charlotte sucked in hard. Mrs. Watson yanked on the laces of her corset. On Sherlock Holmes's supposed sickbed lay a tangle of scarlet and gold silk, the blouse, skirt, and scarf of the *ghagra choli* that she had just taken off. With Mrs. Watson tying the corset laces, Charlotte stepped into her petticoats and peeked at the street below from behind the curtain.

She had been followed from the Holmes house to 18 Upper Baker Street, she was fairly certain of that. But now there was no one—and no carriages—loitering below.

The doorbell rang just as she finished dressing. Charlotte put the pile of *ghagra choli* into an armoire and took a seat in the parlor; Mrs. Watson went down to open the door for Mrs. Marbleton.

Her inquiry had been one of the earliest Sherlock Holmes responded to.

Dear Mr. Holmes,

I am concerned for my husband.

Mr. Marbleton writes twice a day when he is away. If he feels postal services are too slow, he cables in addition. And anytime circumstances permit, he telephones, in spite of my protest that it is hardly the thing to do for the lady of the house to stand in a passageway and shout her more tender sentiments for all to hear.

I have not heard from him in thirty-six hours. Instead, a strange letter bearing no return address has come. I cannot puzzle out what it is trying to tell me: The sentences make sense, but why would anyone think that I have the remotest interest in animal husbandry?

The letter is typed, on plain paper. I enclose a replica I have made of this letter in the hope that you may be able to advise me.

Yours,
Mrs. C. B. Marbleton

Charlotte had written back immediately.

Dear Mrs. Marbleton,

I am very sorry to hear about your husband. Although I cannot ascertain his whereabouts, I can tell you something of the note you received.

The text, while coherent, has no significance. However, by examining the punctuation—namely the hyphens and the full stops—it emerges that the letter contains a message in Morse code.

Decoded, it says Call for me at general.

Should you have further need of my service, you are welcome to call upon 18 Upper Baker Street at four o'clock tomorrow afternoon.

Your servant,
Sherlock Holmes

And now Mrs. Marbleton had arrived, a woman who had been without news of her husband for more than seventy-two hours, when she normally heard from him several times a day when he was away.

She was pale and tense, but otherwise willowy and handsome, a woman in her forties, her visiting dress of an elegant simplicity that Livia would have much lauded. Pleasantries were exchanged. Charlotte gave the by now standard speech concerning her "brother" in the next room. Mrs. Marbleton, with hands clutched tightly together in her lap, tendered her best wishes for Mr. Holmes's health.

Charlotte let the silence that followed linger for a few seconds before she asked the by now also standard question, "Would you like to know for certain that Sherlock's powers of observation and deduction are very much intact?"

"I was at the General Post Office this morning and retrieved a letter meant for me. I have been plentifully assured of Mr. Holmes's mental acuity," said Mrs. Marbleton, already holding out the letter. "Would he mind taking a look at this new one?"

This letter was not typed. Instead it was pasted with individual letters—letters cut out from books, rather than newspapers, judging by the thickness of the paper. The text praised the material and workmanship of boots cobbled by a Signor Castellani of Regent Street.

"I already asked around," said Mrs. Marbleton. "There is no establishment by that name or owned by anyone of that name. I checked for the hyphen-and-full-stop code from the previous letter, which didn't appear to be the case. I also tried using the crossbars on the t's and the dots on the i's, to see whether it was a variation on a theme—that doesn't appear to be the case either."

She'd spoken in a near monotone, as if regurgitating facts that had nothing to do with herself. But Charlotte heard the quaver in her voice, the fear and anguish.

She made the usual pilgrimage to "Sherlock's" bedroom. Mrs. Watson, seated inside, looked almost as tormented as their client. Had news of Surgeon-Major Watson's death reached her in a state of unsuspecting naivety, or had she been dreading that terrible confirmation for days on end?

Charlotte didn't know what to do, so she placed the cup of tea that had been brought for "Sherlock" into Mrs. Watson's hands and sat next to her for a bit.

Upon her return to the parlor, she told Mrs. Marbleton, who had been staring at her own untouched tea, "My brother is of the opinion that this should be a straightforward Bacon's cipher."

"What is that?" Mrs. Marbleton's gaze was dark and intense—an intensity that derived not from hope, but despair.

"It's a system devised by Francis Bacon to hide a message in relatively plain sight. If you'll examine the letters that have been pasted, they are of two different typefaces, Caslon and Didot—and only those two."

Mrs. Marbleton looked closely at the note. "I didn't notice that earlier."

"The message starts with a Caslon letter, so that makes Caslon letters A, and Didot letters B. If we go through the entire message letter by letter, we would end up with a string of As and Bs. Mrs. Marbleton, will you write down the As and Bs as I read them aloud?"

Mrs. Marbleton peeled off her gloves. Charlotte handed her a pen and a notebook. "Have you contacted the police by any chance, ma'am?"

Mrs. Marbleton shook her head. "I do not know everything

about my husband—there is a time of his life that he never talks about. I've been glad to leave it alone as there are years of my own life I would rather forget. For as long as I've known him, he has been a diamond of the first water—a complete gentleman, adored by his friends, admired by his business associates. But if I were to go to the police, I'm not sure what might be dragged up—in public, no less."

"I understand, Mrs. Marbleton. You may be assured of our complete discretion."

When the a's and b's had been set down and double checked, Charlotte said, "Now we divide this long string into segments of five letters each, and those sequences ought to correspond with the sequences Bacon had set out as representations for each letter."

Entirely translated, the message read *package browns*.

The fine grooves beside Mrs. Marbleton's mouth etched deeper as she studied the words. Then she swallowed and looked up at Charlotte. "I hate to admit it but calling for this letter at the General Post Office was . . . nerve-racking. May I engage you to come with me to Brown's Hotel, Miss Holmes? I would feel less deprived of courage if I didn't need to do this alone."

Charlotte shivered. But it was only Brown's, and in broad daylight no less. "Yes, I will accompany you."

———※———

Mrs. Marbleton already had a hansom cab waiting below. But since Mrs. Watson also wished to come along, in the end Charlotte and Mrs. Watson took another cab and followed behind.

"What did you hear from her accents?" Charlotte asked Mrs. Watson, as their vehicle veered around a large town coach.

"English. Or at least she grew up English. But she has spent time on the Continent. America, too—at least ten years there," answered Mrs. Watson. "What do you know about her?"

"She was born into generous circumstances. But there was a

reversal of fortune in her youth, of such severity that she didn't fade into genteel obscurity, but plunged down to outright penury. She had to work at menial positions."

Asking Mrs. Marbleton for help with writing down the a's and b's would make her think she was at least doing *something* for her husband. But just as importantly, it allowed Charlotte to observe her hands, which had been well cared for. But the repeated burns a young woman unaccustomed to work suffered in a kitchen did not fade away so readily, not even with the help of the best emollients.

"Obviously at some point her fortunes improved markedly. I can't be sure whether it happened before or after she left England, but my guess would be after. And this is—or should have been—a triumphant return for her, until her husband's disappearance."

Mrs. Watson glanced outside before she looked back at Charlotte. "Will you be all right if it turns out we won't be able to help her?"

Will you be all right? Charlotte wanted to ask. But it seemed far too intrusive a question.

"I should manage," she said.

⁎

The package at Brown's Hotel contained a key, along with a note that stated a room number.

Mrs. Marbleton gripped the key, seemingly paralyzed. Mrs. Watson was similarly immobile, peering at her anxiously. Charlotte mustered a big smile for the clerk. "We were told there would be a prize waiting here, but we haven't the least idea who has prepared it for us. Would you happen to have a record of the person who left this package?"

The pimply young man reddened. "Ah, yes. Yes, of course. If you'll give me a moment, miss."

He brought out a book of registry. "This was left behind by a Mr. York."

Charlotte glanced at Mrs. Marbleton. The name didn't appear to signify anything for her. "Is Mr. York still here?"

"He left for Paris two days ago."

"Was his luggage sent ahead to Southampton, then? Which liner did he take?"

"I believe porters came for his luggage. And I'm almost sure he left on a steamer of the French line."

Mrs. Marbleton recoiled at this answer. Charlotte smiled again at the clerk. "It's possible we might need to retrieve some heavy items. Won't you be so kind as to send a pair of your stoutest porters?"

She didn't anticipate an ambush but it didn't hurt to be careful.

"Of course, Miss. I will have the porters wait outside the room. It might be a minute or two before they arrive."

Charlotte guided a stricken-looking Mrs. Marbleton and a pale Mrs. Watson to a chaise. After a few minutes, she shepherded them to their destination. The porters were in the passage when they arrived, standing with their backs to the walls and tugging respectfully on their caps.

Charlotte turned the key and opened the door slowly. The sitting room was empty. But Mrs. Marbleton gasped, rushed toward the mantel, and clutched a fountain pen that had been left behind.

They searched the rest of the suite, but no more of Mr. Marbleton's belongings were found. Charlotte tipped and dismissed the porters, then took out her magnifying glass and examined the entire suite square inch by square inch.

"I gave this pen to Mr. Marbleton as an engagement present. He wrote all his letters with it," said Mrs. Marbleton to no one in particular.

The rooms had been cleaned thoroughly, probably by the maids in the morning. When Charlotte had satisfied herself that she would not learn of anything else—other than the fact that no one had slept in the suite overnight—she whispered to Mrs. Watson to keep an eye on their client, while she went down to the lobby and spoke with a different clerk.

"The gentleman who stayed in this suite last night"—she showed him the note with the number on it. "I might have found something that belongs to him. Do you know if he has already left?"

"Let me check for you, miss," said the clerk, an older man with a portly figure. He pored over the columns of the registry. "Let's see. You are in luck, miss. Mr. Marbleton will be with us for another several days."

Seventeen

"How perfectly diabolical," murmured Mrs. Marbleton, when Charlotte told her that the suite in which they stood was registered to a Mr. Marbleton.

"You don't seem terribly surprised by this particular twist of events," said Charlotte.

"Only because I now have an idea who might be behind it. And it isn't anyone from Mr. Marbleton's past, but my own." Mrs. Marbleton smiled grimly. "Thank you, Miss Holmes. And you, too, Mrs. Watson, for your company. But I'm afraid there isn't anything else you can do."

"Surely we haven't exhausted all avenues of inquiry. Mr. York's movements can be traced. The steamers have passenger manifests and—"

"I understand, Miss Holmes. But you are assuming it isn't a false trail that has been laid for me."

"Even if that should turn out to be the case, the account on this room probably hasn't been settled yet. Not to m—"

"No!" The syllable ricocheted around the room. Mrs. Marbleton took a deep breath, a deathly pallor to her cheeks and a near-frantic look in her eyes. "Please listen to me, Miss Holmes. You do not wish to go anywhere near this man. You simply do not. Do you understand?"

Mrs. Watson gripped Charlotte's arm and answered for them. "Yes, we understand."

With flawless courtesy, Mrs. Marbleton saw them out. Charlotte and Mrs. Watson remained silent as they made their way to Albemarle Street. But as soon as they got into a hansom cab, Mrs. Watson blurted out, "Heavens, what is going to happen to that woman?"

Charlotte had no good answer for her.

The rest of Inspector Treadles's afternoon was spent at Scotland Yard, conferring with Sergeant MacDonald and Superintendent Croft, Treadles's superior. Sergeant MacDonald had made little headway in discovering the purpose of Mr. Sackville's London trips. But now, with Superintendent Croft's blessing, they would publish the dead man's picture in the papers, ask for help from the public, and hope that those who came forth would offer useful information.

"And we'll have to verify Lady Sheridan's claims of her whereabouts, too," he said to his wife, when he was at last back home.

They would be verifying a great deal more than that. His latest conjecture was that Lord and Lady Sheridan might each have been plotting against Mr. Sackville, without the other's knowledge. And they each had an accomplice at Curry House—though the possibility existed that they counted on the same person.

This dual-conspiracy scenario would explain the usage of both arsenic and chloral: One of the Sheridans might have opted for a slow poisoning, the other, a rapid one. Neither of them needed to be in Stanwell Moot to carry out their schemes. And their accomplices could honestly state that no one at Curry House wanted Mr. Sackville harmed.

"Have you arranged to see Mr. Holmes again?" asked Alice. "Or to be in the next room, at least, while the great man remains shrouded in mystery?"

"No, I haven't." He leaned in and kissed her on her jawline. "Sometimes I'd rather spend more time in my wife's company than that of any man's, however great."

What he didn't say was that he was reluctant to consult Sherlock Holmes again so soon. He couldn't quite explain this reticence—after all, he'd been desperate to speak with the man only days before.

A rare instance of proprietary sentiments regarding his own case, perhaps. He was a thorough and competent investigator and ought to be able to handle the rest of the work without constantly leaning on someone else.

Alice returned him a kiss on the cheek. "Ha! And here I was hoping that I might receive more madeleines, if you would but pay another visit to Upper Baker Street."

"What maddening inconstancy, Mrs. Treadles! Is your heart so easily given to a box of baked goods?"

"I never knew it either, sir. But now I at last understand the power of seduction inherent in French pastry." She handed him two fresh shirts and a pair of beautifully shined shoes—he would be on the overnight train to Yorkshire. "So what is this Miss Holmes like? I'm curious. You saw the notice in the paper, didn't you? Holmes is taking private clients. I'll be surprised if Upper Baker Street isn't inundated. And Miss Holmes is the one who must handle this tide of visitors."

How *would* one describe Miss Holmes? "Do you remember the time we speculated on Sherlock Holmes's appearance?"

"We concluded that he is likely to be dark-haired, pale from spending his days reading by a lamp, with piercing, intelligent eyes, and a somewhat impatient demeanor, since he must find the rest of us trying." Alice thought for a moment. "I believe we also thought that he'd be dressed well but simply, since he wouldn't preoccupy himself with frivolous concerns."

"And if we'd known he had a sister, we'd have expected her to resemble him to a high degree, wouldn't we?" Treadles accepted several handkerchiefs and two pairs of socks from his wife and dropped them into his travel satchel. "A mind as great as Holmes's must be both magnetic and charismatic. A lesser sibling, without necessarily being aware of it, would choose to imitate the greater sibling—to echo his physical qualities, since those are much easier to emulate than his cognitive prowess."

"A very fair assumption."

"Which leads me to conclude that either Miss Holmes possesses an ironclad concept of her own self—or that Sherlock Holmes, before his misfortune, had been a popinjay of the first order."

Alice's eyes brightened with excited interest. "Goodness. Do you mean to tell me Miss Holmes dresses extravagantly?"

"When we were engaged, you took me to your favorite shop for trimmings and garnishes."

She laughed. "And when we left you said you feared for your manhood because the place was so overwhelmingly feminine."

"If that place came to life, it would resemble Miss Holmes exactly. I counted sixteen rows of bows on her skirts."

"How extraordinary. I'm not sure I'd be able to take a woman like that seriously."

"I'm not sure I did at first. But by the end of that meeting . . ."

"Yes?"

Treadles recalled all the things she had told him about himself—and the single word in her notebook, *Barrow-in-Furness*. "By the end of our meeting I knew I would never think lightly of her again."

❖

As Charlotte's hired hackney approached, Lord Ingram looked up. Livia was not the only one who'd become thinner—his eyes, too, had become more deep set. The light of a distant street lamp illuminated dramatic hollows underneath his cheeks.

The carriage stopped. He opened the door, climbed in, and settled himself on the backward-facing seat.

"Good evening, my lord," said Charlotte when the hackney was on its way again, "and thank you for coming."

"Tell me what happened—in detail."

He listened to her narrative without any interruptions, one hand set lightly on top of his walking stick, the other beside him on the seat, his face largely invisible in the shadows.

A silence rose at the conclusion of her account. She sighed inwardly—she couldn't remember the last time he *wasn't* displeased with her for one reason or another.

In her mind's eye she saw him down on one knee, chipping away at the dirt encrusted inside an old Roman urn, while she slowly flipped through the pages of the *Encyclopedia Britannica*—after he'd kissed her, she'd felt quite free to show up at his ruins and he'd felt quite free to ignore her. What a beautiful silence that had been. What a lovely era.

Looking back on those halcyon days made her feel old. Certainly enough time had passed for many, many things to have gone wrong . . .

All at once she became conscious that he was studying her. Throughout her recital of the events of the day he had been looking at the top of his walking stick—and occasionally out of the windows. But now his attention was squarely upon her.

She, on the other hand, had been half staring at the carriage lantern outside. Carefully, she held still and did not glance toward him. She wanted to go on luxuriating in the weight and intensity of his gaze. To go on wallowing in that bittersweet mingling of pleasure and heartache.

How had they managed to not realize, for so long, what they meant to one another? And why then must they see the light when it was too late, when they could possess no more than a few moments of ferocious mutual awareness?

He tapped his walking stick against the floor of the hackney, a dull echo that signaled the end of the silence. She inhaled quietly, deeply.

"So . . . the villain in Mrs. Marbleton's case is too mannered for your taste." His voice was perfectly modulated.

She, too, took on a brisk, efficient tone. "I've constructed Bacon's ciphers before. It's tedious work. If I were holding her husband hostage and wanted her to worry, I'd let her stew in her own anxiety rather than dispatch all these clever but not that clever puzzles."

"You imply this Mrs. Marbleton staged an elaborate ruse. Why?"

"That's what I intend to find out. I'd like for you to forge a letter for me."

"You can do that yourself. I've taught you well."

"You are still far better than me."

He snorted. "I'm better, but not that much better. Whom do you want this letter to be addressed to and what do you want it to say?"

It was not a promise to help but it was a step closer. "I noticed something odd about Mrs. Marbleton: Everything she wore was new. Or at least everything that was visible to the observer.

"I dearly love clothes, but I don't remember ever going about not only in a new frock, but new gloves, new boots, a new hat, *and* carrying both a new reticule and a new parasol."

"Maybe she suffered a fire at her place of domicile."

"In my former life I happened to be a devoted browser at Harrod's and saw many of the items she wore on offer there. This evening

I made a pilgrimage to that temple of commerce and asked after the newcomer to London who had bought those items, on the pretense that she had given me a card with her address and invited me to call but I'd lost the card and was quite distraught."

"If God doesn't want people to lie, he shouldn't have given the best liars such earnest and innocent faces," murmured Lord Ingram.

For a quick second, it was almost all incandescent pleasure in her heart. She smiled into the dark. "Precisely. Since God obviously intended for me to prevaricate, to do otherwise would be to thwart His purpose. And so I've learned that Mrs. Marbleton currently resides at Claridge's, as that was where her purchases were delivered.

"Here's something else I suspect about Mrs. Marbleton: She and I might have a great deal in common. The kind of reversal of fortune she suffered, which caused her to fall from the lap of ease, if not of luxury, straight into a scullery—I can think of very few other instances. Even if she lost her parents and had no older siblings who could look after her, what about aunts and uncles and cousins and grandparents? What about family friends? What about more genteel employment as a governess or a lady's companion?"

"You are saying that she, having been caught in a compromising position, chose to run away?"

"There can't be too many of us. And I'll wager someone like Lady Avery or Lady Somersby would know the circumstances surrounding every last one. If you write an anonymous letter to—since Lady Avery is already involved in the Sackville case, let's spread the wealth and send it to Lady Somersby, and tell her that a lady who has had a tremendous fall from grace years ago has returned to London and can be found at Claridge's. I dare say within two days we'll have her identity."

"No."

His answer was quiet but implacable. Charlotte tilted her head. "Why not?"

"You've not thought the matter through, Charlotte. Setting Lady Somersby loose on this woman and having the former announce her true identity from the rooftops? Should Mrs. Marbleton happen to be in real danger of any kind, you will do her a great disservice."

"Oh," said Charlotte. She truly had not thought the matter through.

"However, there is a premiere performance at Covent Gardens. I can still make the intermission if I hurry. Since it's a night to see and be seen, one of our Ladies of Gossip should be there."

"Make sure you aren't too obvious. Don't let them realize that you've approached them only to ask this question."

He scoffed. "Haven't you deduced that these days *they* approach *me*, and not the other way around? They're still trying to find out what happened to you, and anyone who knows you to any extent is subject to regular interrogations."

Charlotte, for the moment, had forgotten about her own scandal altogether. "What do you tell them?"

He leaned back in his seat. Once again she felt the impact of his gaze. What did he think when he looked upon her? What did he want? What pain or pleasure unfurled in the deepest part of his heart?

"I tell them that I don't know anything," he said quietly. "And that I never expect to hear from you again."

<hr/>

When Charlotte returned to Mrs. Watson's house she found her business partner in the parlor, wrapped in a man's smoking jacket and nursing a glass of claret.

"Château Haut-Brion, the '65 vintage." She held up the darkly scarlet liquid to the light. "My husband adored this wine. When we married, we bought four cases, with the intention of opening a bottle each year for our anniversary."

Mrs. Watson turned around. "Would you like to have a glass, Miss Holmes?"

"Yes, thank you," said Charlotte, sitting down.

The wine that John Watson would never taste again was velvety yet potent. Mrs. Watson refilled her own glass and took a long draught.

"I don't usually have reason to consider myself terribly naive. But goodness how naive I've been, to think that this would be all fun and games.

"I keep wondering what must be going through Mrs. Marbleton's mind," Mrs. Watson said, her gaze focused on some distant point. "After the telegram came, informing me that my husband had been killed by a stray jezail bullet, I refused to believe it. I thought they had mistaken a different man for him, that he might be injured and lying somewhere delirious, even that he'd been captured by the Afghanis and held in a dreadful prison—but I couldn't contemplate his death. Couldn't accept it until men from his regiment, men who saw him die before their own eyes and laid him to rest in Kabul, came to offer their condolences.

"But at least then I knew where he was and what happened to him. Mrs. Marbleton, is it even worse for her because she doesn't know? Is she imagining the most horrific scenarios before telling herself that all would be well, that she would see her husband in one piece again and this would all turn out to be but a stupid prank? How she must be seesawing between hope and despair—ever diminishing hope and ever proliferating despair."

Charlotte took another sip of her wine. If she gave voice to her suspicions concerning Mrs. Marbleton, then Mrs. Watson might stop worrying about Mrs. Marbleton, but she would instead worry about Charlotte. (*But it's perfectly fine for me to worry about you?* said an imaginary Lord Ingram. *Yes*, she replied, *not only fine, but good and proper.*)

"Would you—would you like to go to Kabul someday, Mrs. Watson, and visit your husband's grave?"

Mrs. Watson sat down. "I've often thought about it—sometimes I wish I hadn't left India so precipitously. That I'd made the trip while I'd remained on the subcontinent. But it's such a long way to go to look at a headstone."

And to be reminded of all the years that had been robbed.

"If ever again you think of going, ma'am, know that I'd be honored to accompany you."

Mrs. Watson smiled very slightly. "And what would London do without Sherlock Holmes?"

"London has managed for millennia without me. I'm sure it can hobble on in my absence for a few months." Charlotte set down her wineglass. "Good night, ma'am."

As she reached the door, Mrs. Watson said, "Thank you, Miss Holmes."

Charlotte paused briefly, then resumed walking.

❈

Lord Ingram's letter came the next morning, on the early post.

Dear Charlotte,

As expected, Lady Somersby and Lady Avery approached me at the opera. After demurring all knowledge of your whereabouts, I asked them, naturally enough, whether they knew of any precedents like yours, of a young woman who not only defied the rules but also the consequences.

With very little hesitation they brought up the name of Sophia Lonsdale, though they believed that she did not so much run away as was outright disowned. It has been nearly twenty-five years, but they agree that

she found a position working in the refectory kitchens at Balliol College,
not too far from her ancestral home. They were certain that she later
married a young tutor, shortly before he left the country for a post
overseas.

Here they became embroiled in dispute over where the young couple
had been headed. Lady Avery insisted it was Vienna; Lady Somersby
would not budge from Budapest. And there was not enough time to resolve
the debate before the curtains rose again.

But what they told me of Sophia Lonsdale matched closely with your
description of Mrs. Marbleton.

> *Your servant,*
> *Ashburton*

Charlotte grabbed Mrs. Watson's copy of *Burke's*. The Lonsdales were a prominent family in Oxfordshire, the most distinguished branch being the one that produced the Earls of Montserre. Sophia Lonsdale probably came from a cadet branch of the family, but still, terribly respectable stock.

Alas, there was no time that morning to look further into the matter of Sophia Lonsdale: Charlotte had clients with whom she must meet.

By the time she had solved, for a pair of ancient spinster sisters, why their equally ancient butler didn't seem quite himself—the man had died years ago, but one of the sisters kept forgetting the fact and becoming startled by the sight of a stranger in the house, that the new butler gave up, found a white-haired wig, and with the complicity of the other sister, began passing himself off as his predecessor—another letter arrived from Lord Ingram, much to her surprise.

He, unlike Sophia Lonsdale's purportedly missing husband, did not write more than once a day.

Certainly not without compelling reason.

Dear Charlotte,

A message arrived from Lady Avery just now. She had checked her diary from years ago and admitted that she and her sister were both incorrect as to where the tutor Sophia Lonsdale married went for his next position. It was neither Budapest nor Vienna, but Berlin.

The far more important part, however, was buried near the end of her note: Because of the third act starting, she did not have the time to tell me that Sophia Lonsdale died more than twenty years ago while on holiday in Switzerland.

Your servant,
Ashburton

Eighteen

"Bony like a goat" was an unkind description for Becky Birtle. But she *was* waiflike in appearance: small and thin, with big brown eyes and surprisingly pink lips.

Not beautiful, as Mrs. Meek had said, but pretty enough with the smooth skin and good health of youth.

And oddly familiar in her features.

She sat with her shoulders hunched, her teeth clenched over her lower lip. "Is it true, Inspector, that Mr. Sackville—someone poisoned him with arsenic?"

"Yes, it's true."

A hollowness came into her eyes. "I thought—when it came out that he'd been murdered, I thought it had to be his brother. But arsenic—that's someone in the house, isn't it?"

"Most likely."

"But why?" That question was uttered so softly it was addressed more to herself than anyone else. "He was such a nice person."

"How was he nice?"

She looked toward a row of postcards on the mantel, which was but a length of darkened wood beam that must have been salvaged from some other structure. The Birtles' ancient cottage was a far cry from the modern splendor of Curry House. The ceiling was so low Treadles could scarcely stand straight. The smoke-darkened walls and the scarcity of windows gave the entire interior an air of permanent gloom.

"Mr. Sackville talked to me." Again she seemed to be speaking to herself. "He was the only one who did. Everybody else only told me to do this and that."

"I thought young maids had no leave to speak to the master. How did you and Mr. Sackville become so friendly?"

"We met on the coast path. I took a walk one Sunday afternoon and so did he. When I saw him, I said I was sorry to be in his way. He said a young lady never needed to apologize for going about her business. Then I told him that I worked for him and that Mrs. Cornish would have my hide if she knew I spoke to him.

"He laughed and said, 'Never mind Mrs. Cornish.' Then he asked me if I wouldn't walk with him for a bit and tell him about myself."

That easy demeanor and friendly curiosity must have made a powerful impact on the girl. "What did you tell him?"

"Hardly anything. He asked 'bout where I was from. How I liked Curry House. If the others treated me proper. And I said Yorkshire, yes, sir, and yes, sir. He said then if I was too nervous to talk I didn't need to say ought else."

"How much distance do you think you covered?"

"A mile. Maybe a mile and a furlong."

Around twenty-five minutes then, depending on the terrain and their walking speed. "So you said nothing else the rest of that time?"

"No. But two days later I was in the study dusting. He came in for some papers and saw me with a book in my hand. I thought he'd be angry at me for touching his things, but he only asked what book was it. I told him it was a book about Japan. He asked if I liked it." She emitted a wistful sigh. "And we started talking."

"Was it always questions on his side and answers on your side?"

"He let me ask him questions, too. If he read all the books in the house. If he'd ever touched an electric switch. If he remembered a time before the queen was the queen."

"He answered everything you asked?"

"Not everything. Not when I asked him why he went to London."

Treadles's ears perked. "How—and when—did that come about?"

"It was my fourth week at the house. Mrs. Cornish made me clean the upstairs sitting room again. Said it weren't done proper the first time. That was when Mr. Sackville came in. He asked me why I looked put out, I explained, and he said it looked perfectly proper to him. I said it was a right travesty"—the girl pronounced the word carefully and with relish—"that what was good enough for him weren't good enough for Mrs. Cornish. He laughed and said that of course a housekeeper was a greater expert on the cleanliness of the house than the master and I ought to listen to her. But he was going to London that day. Was there anything that he could get for me from London, to make me feel better about having to clean the sitting room twice?

"I said I didn't have enough money to buy anything. He said it would be a gift. So I told him that I didn't get a good look at London when I passed through and I'd like a nice postcard—then it'd be like I got to see at least one good place. He came back with half a dozen for me. Real pretty ones."

Treadles glanced at the mantel. "Those ones?"

"Yes, Inspector."

Treadles moved to the fireplace and examined the postcards. They each bore puncture marks at the corners. "You had these on the wall of your room at Curry House?"

"Yes, Inspector."

"Did Mr. Sackville acquire anything from London for anyone else?"

"I don't reckon so. He said not to say anything to anyone or they'd all want him to fetch things."

"Why do you suppose he did that for you?"

The girl blushed. "He said it was because he was a person to me. That to the others he was only the master of the house, the one they must serve for their wages."

"Did he bring you back other items?"

Becky Birtle's lips protruded. "No. He didn't. Next time he was to go, he asked me if I wanted anything. But he didn't go in the end—had an awful stomachache the day of. The next time he did go, but he had to get off the train at Exeter and spend the night, because he had such a horrible gastric attack."

She gasped. "You don't suppose those gastric attacks—don't they say arsenic poisoning don't look that different from bad tummy troubles?"

"Did these attacks happen before Mrs. Meek became the cook?" Treadles already knew the answer; it was the reason he hadn't arrested Mrs. Meek.

"For sure they did." Becky Birtle gasped again. "Stacks of Bibles! I was sick as a dog that night. You don't suppose, Inspector, that I got poisoned, too?"

Treadles sat up straighter. "Did Mr. Sackville eat the same food as the staff?"

"No, his food was cooked and served separate from ours. But wait—" she thought for a moment. "That was when we were still getting food from the inn. And that week there was a wedding and Mrs. Pegg was cooking for it too. I think everyone at Curry House did eat the same food that week, soup and fish pies and boiled beef."

Mrs. Pegg was born and brought up in Stanwell Moot. By all accounts, she'd had no dealings with Mr. Sackville whatsoever.

"Was anyone else sick that day?"

"No, only me."

"Was there anything that only you and Mr. Sackville ate?"

She hesitated.

"What was it?"

"Before he left that day, he was in a good mood. When I ferried up a scuttle of coal, he saw that my fingers were stiff cold—Mrs. Cornish loaned me to help with the wedding and I was caught in the rain coming back to Curry House. So he asked if I wanted a bit of whisky to warm up."

Treadles's brows shot up. "Mrs. Cornish has been looking for a whisky decanter, missing since Mr. Sackville's death. She couldn't find it anywhere in the house. Did you take it?"

Becky Birtle, who had a very direct gaze for a young girl and had been looking at Treadles for some time, lowered her face.

"I'll take that as a yes. Have you drunk from it again?"

"No! I don't even like whisky."

"Then why did you take it?"

"Because—because he was really lovely to me that day and I wanted something to remember it by."

"Wasn't he always very nice to you?"

"Yes, but I didn't see much of him after that."

"And why is that?"

Becky Birtle flushed to the roots of her hair and shook her head.

"This is a murder investigation, Miss Birtle. Do answer my question."

"But this is . . . private."

"A great many murders have been committed because of what people do in private."

"But—but I didn't *do* anything, this is just . . . private."

Her reluctance seemed deep-seated. Treadles went on to the next item on his list. "The morning you went to give Mr. Sackville his morning cocoa and found him unconscious, why didn't you open the curtains?"

"What does that have to do with anything?"

"So it's true, you didn't open the curtains."

"I mayn't have."

"I have been given to understand that it would be highly inappropriate for you to approach him while he lay in bed. And yet you stated this is what you did."

"I didn't do anything bad. My first few weeks at Curry House I ran into him at every corner. I thought we were friends. And then I don't see him for a good long time and I thought—I thought I'd take his hand and jiggle it. A good-morning-surprise-it's-me. Like you would with a mate, if you went to visit them and they was still asleep."

"So there was nothing illicit going on between you and Mr. Sackville?"

"No! That'd be—he must be even older than my dad and my dad is old!"

Her incredulity seemed genuine. "Is there anyone in the house who might believe that your rapport with Mr. Sackville isn't quite so innocent?"

The girl recoiled. "What? Why would they think like that?"

"Because it isn't normal for the master of the house to develop a friendship with a young maid."

"But why are you asking—you think it has something to do with Mr. Sackville's murder?"

"A number of things could have happened if one of the other members of the household believed that something illicit went on

262 · *Sherry Thomas*

between you and Mr. Sackville. That person might be enraged on
your behalf, convinced that you'd been taken advantage of. That
person might be enraged on her own behalf—what if she thought
she had a romantic understanding with Mr. Sackville? It could be for
monetary reasons, too. The person might believe he is to be the chief
beneficiary of Mr. Sackville's will—and didn't want him getting
close to anyone else. Do you see what I mean?"

"I—I guess so."

"Then can you tell me who might have had suspicions?"

She twisted her fingers. "Will that person become a suspect?"

"With no obvious motives, and in a household this small, everybody already is a suspect. You wouldn't be broadening our field of
suspects, Miss Birtle, but narrowing it."

"I suppose that's all right then," she said uncertainly. "And it
really wouldn't make him a suspect, I don't think."

A *him*. "Was it Tommy Dunn?"

"Tommy?" she laughed. "Tommy wouldn't care if I fell off the
cliffs."

"I understand he was initially receptive to having another young
person at Curry House. What changed?"

"Ask him." Amusement flashed in Becky's eyes. And a trace of
smugness.

"I have. He refused to answer. Perhaps you could help him out—
tell me why and eliminate him from suspicion."

This was not strictly true. Even if Tommy Dunn's dislike of
Becky had nothing to do with what went on between the latter and
Mr. Sackville, he could still be an accomplice, albeit an unlikely one,
for Lord or Lady Sheridan.

"Only if you swear never to tell anyone."

"I can only promise that if it has nothing to do with the case."

"It has nothing to do with anything. I caught Tommy with Mr. Weeks, the sexton from Barton Cross, when I was out on a walk." Her expression turned more somber. "You truly mustn't ever tell anyone, Inspector. I teased Tommy—and told him I had a hard time keeping secrets. I didn't mean it. But he was so scared. I was put out that he thought I would tell on him. But he must have been mad with fear—he didn't have anywhere else to go and Mr. Weeks has children to support. He didn't believe that I'd keep him safe."

Treadles couldn't understand such goings-on between men, but he well knew the consequences of exposure. "His secret is safe with me."

"Thank you, Inspector," Becky Birtle said softly.

Treadles let a minute of silence pass. They sat, almost companionably, he drinking his tepid tea, she nibbling on a biscuit that looked rock hard.

"So it was Mr. Hodges who noticed something about you and Mr. Sackville?"

The girl nodded. "The next day after my horrible stomachache, Mr. Hodges asked if I'd pinched Mr. Sackville's whisky. I asked him if he was calling me a thief. He said Mr. Sackville is careful about his tummy and don't take more than a few sips but twice that much was gone from the decanter—and that I was the only other person to go in that room.

"So I told him that I did drink but only because Mr. Sackville offered, and it would have been rude to refuse. Mr. Hodges scowled something mighty and said gentlemen was different than regular folk. Nobody holds them accountable and I better have a care for myself."

She turned her face to the side. With a start Treadles understood why she had looked oddly familiar when he met her for the first time: the picture of a young Mrs. Cornish that he had seen at Curry

House. There was a good resemblance if one happened to see Becky from certain angles.

He had considered Mrs. Cornish from the perspective of a scorned lover, an angry bystander, and opportunistic collaborator. But Mrs. Cornish as a deeply concerned kinswoman opened an entire new vista of possibilities.

"When you left, Mrs. Cornish said you took a photograph of the staff as a memento."

"I didn't leave, Mrs. Cornish dismissed me—said I was making too much of a nuisance of myself, fainting and crying." She flattened her lips. "Maybe I was. And I never took that photograph—the only person I'd have wanted to remember was Mr. Sackville and he wasn't in it. I found the picture in my suitcase after I came home."

The discrepancies made Treadles's heart pound: having Becky hundreds of miles away—and the only image of her exiled from the house—would ensure that no one suspected any blood ties between the two. "I'd like to see the photograph. And I'll need you to hand me the decanter of whisky."

Becky Birtle excused herself and returned with both items.

Treadles examined the decanter, which still contained two inches of intoxicant. It occurred to him that Becky Birtle could have emptied and replaced the contents of the decanter. But a quick sniff was enough to let him know that the amber fluid inside was no cheap grog, but the best Scotland had to offer.

He next turned his attention to the photograph. The captured images of Mrs. Cornish and Becky Birtle did not show much likeness, but all the same Treadles asked Becky Birtle to fetch her parents.

Mr. Birtle, a former gamekeeper who could no longer work on account of his arthritis, was indeed old for someone with so young an only child. His wife was a square slab of a woman and possibly even older than he. Becky Birtle closed the door and left, her foot-steps fading away on the squeaky floorboards.

Treadles waited until she was out of hearing range. "Mr. Birtle, Mrs. Birtle, I understand that the questions I am about to ask will seem intrusive. I hope you will forgive me."

The couple looked at each other.

"Yes, Inspector?" Mrs. Birtle sounded as if she rarely spoke, her voice resembling the rasp of rusted gears forced to rotate.

"I must ask whether you are Becky's natural parents."

Another look exchanged between the Birtles. Mrs. Birtle wiped her hand on her apron. "Why do you need to know, Inspector?"

"I am investigating a murder. None of the suspects with the means to have committed it appear to have concrete motives. There-fore I must get to the bottom of every possible connection among all parties involved. If you are concerned the information might get someone into trouble, please consider that withholding the necessary intelligence from me may result in an innocent bystander being charged with the crime."

Mr. Birtle placed his hand atop his wife's. Mrs. Birtle glanced at her husband and then looked Treadles in the eye. "We took Becky in the day she was born and raised her as if she were our own."

Treadles let out the breath he didn't realize he was holding. "And is Mrs. Cornish of Curry House Becky's natural mother?"

Mrs. Birtle nodded.

"Thank you for your trust in me." Treadles inclined his head. "I will do my best to keep this from becoming public knowledge."

❦

It felt almost unsettling to finally have a prime suspect, but the scenario made sense. Mr. Hodges must have told Mrs. Cornish about the closer-than-necessary rapport between their employer and Becky Birtle. Mrs.

Cornish would have become more and more concerned about her daughter's involvement with Mr. Sackville. At an impressionable age, she herself had been taken advantage of by a man who refused to marry her and look after their baby—possibly an unscrupulous employer—and she was desperate for the same not to happen to her child.

Becky Birtle returned to the parlor. Treadles had asked for her—he still had one last point he wanted to clear up. But one look at the girl's face let him know that she had heard everything. How? The floorboards would have squeaked had she snuck back to eavesdrop.

As if she heard his question, she pointed behind his head. He turned around to see a small, half-open window—she had eavesdropped from outside.

"Mrs. Cornish can't be my mother," she said, her voice barely above a whisper. "She doesn't even like me."

"I can't speak to the state of her affection, but I have no doubt she feels a tremendous sense of responsibility toward you."

"Enough to kill Mr. Sackville when he did nothing wrong? That can't be."

"If she was the one who poisoned Mr. Sackville, she wouldn't be the first to have attempted murder for what she *perceived* he did."

"But what could she even perceive?"

Treadles could not have asked for a better lead-in to his question. "Perhaps unbeknownst to you, she witnessed the incident that caused Mr. Sackville to no longer be there everywhere you turned."

Becky Birtle squinted at him. "That's ridiculous."

"Is it? I can't tell since I don't know what happened."

"*Nothing* happened. *Nothing.*"

"It might not have been nothing to Mrs. Cornish."

Becky Birtle threw up her hands. "Fine. I'll tell you. It was a few days after Mr. Sackville and I had those horrible tummy troubles. I—I had my monthly and it was an awful one. I could hardly stand, but Mrs. Cornish said it was no excuse—the other women in the house didn't take to their beds during their time.

"Mr. Sackville saw that I was in pain and he was worried. He thought maybe it was something I ate. So I told him the truth, that it was only my monthly."

Treadles could only hope he wouldn't stammer—his face scalded with embarrassment. "That was it?"

"That was it. Mum—my real mum, not Mrs. Cornish—always told me that men hate it when women bring up their menses. I thought it was ridiculous. They love to moan about their own aches and pains, why should they begrudge us a little complaining about ours? But Mum was right. That was the end of anything between Mr. Sackville and me." The light dimmed in Becky Birtle's eyes. "Guess he wasn't a real friend after all."

Charlotte twisted the black handkerchief with her black kidskin-clad fingers and reminded herself that she must give the impression of frailty and forlornness. It would not do for her to swivel about, scanning the guests who moved through the lobby of Claridge's: The widow's veil might obscure her face, but it couldn't completely disguise the set of her shoulders or the angle of her head.

She glanced discreetly toward the front entrance, followed it with a sideways glimpse toward the staircase. Perhaps now she should lift the handkerchief and give it a helpless flutter. Maybe even—

"My condolences on your loss, my dear lady."

Her heart thudded—Lord Ingram had materialized out of nowhere. "What are you doing here?"

One corner of his lips lifted. Her heart thudded again: She couldn't remember the last time he smiled—or half smiled—at her. "And I thought you'd be glad to see me, since you're always scheming for it."

"Yes, when I've nothing better to do."

He sat down next to her on the chaise longue. The half smile had disappeared but no forbidding look took its place. How rare and incomprehensible: at the moment he was not actively displeased with her.

"With your penchant for diminishing a man to little more than a shell of his former manhood, it never ceases to amaze me that you managed to receive all the proposals you did."

She had indeed reaped her fair share, including one from his brother, Lord Bancroft, her favorite proposal of them all.

"It's my décolletage—when gentlemen stare at my bosom, they don't hear a word I say. I strongly believe that if trees sprouted breasts tomorrow, they would soon be wearing wedding rings."

He chortled.

Her nerves tingled.

Some men had that effect on women, as Mrs. Watson declared. But it was Charlotte's obligation not to respond to said effect when she was in the middle of a surveillance mission—or at least not to respond to such a degree as to diminish her concentration. "So what *are* you doing here?"

He blew out a soft breath. "You are many things, Charlotte, but terribly experienced you aren't. It was almost too easy to predict that you'd be setting up shop at Claridge's to see what you can find out about your Mrs. Marbleton."

Had he come to put a stop to it or . . . "Don't tell me you mean to keep me company."

"Easier than bailing you out of trouble later."

She wondered whether she ought to object to his presence, but he was right that she had no experience in this sort of thing. And if he was going to take the trouble to make sure she was all right, she'd rather he sit next to her than lurk somewhere unseen.

She smoothed her gloves. "I won't be here for much longer. I've a client to meet."

"A less troublesome one, I hope."

"Don't be such a constant killjoy. If nothing else, my association with Mrs. Watson has already made us five pounds—and we've clients lined up for the next fortnight."

Five pounds! The thought never failed to make her giddy.

But he would not let go of his entrenched cynicism. "She has certainly been quick to exploit your acuity for her own gains."

She peered at him through her veil. "What's the matter, your lordship? Usually you are a bit more generous in your opinion of people, especially when you don't know enough about them."

"I can afford to be more generous when those hypothetical people aren't essentially in control of your life, Charlotte. I still think it w—"

But she was no longer listening to him.

"What is it?" he asked softly, taking her by the hands, so that to passersby they would appear deep in conversation, a bereaved young widow and a gallant friend trying to comfort her.

"Do you see the man in the gold paisley waistcoat?" She indicated his location with a tilt of her head. "I know him."

Lord Ingram glanced unobtrusively at the man. "Who is he?"

"The first time I went to Mrs. Watson's place, before I arrived, she had let in another young woman, thinking she was me. But that caller turned out to have fraud in mind, claiming kinship with Mrs. Watson where none existed."

"And?"

"And she had an accomplice, a young man." Charlotte took one more look at Paisley Waistcoat. "That one."

Nineteen

By the time Inspector Treadles reached the closest police station to Curry House, Mrs. Cornish had already been brought in and put into an interrogation room.

He wasted no time. "Mrs. Cornish, you said nothing about the fact that Becky Birtle is your daughter."

Mrs. Cornish flinched, as if he'd thrown sand in her face. "That's—that's—"

"I wouldn't try to deny it, not when I already have confirmation from Mrs. Birtle."

Mrs. Cornish glanced at the door.

"I've dismissed the constable who stood guard outside," said Treadles. "I gave my word to Mrs. Birtle that as much as possible, I would keep Becky's true parentage a secret."

Mrs. Cornish stared at her hands—she'd come to the police station in a pair of kid gloves, probably her best pair. "Surely you must understand why I couldn't possibly bring it up, Inspector. It took years of hard work to rise to where I am.

"After Mr. Sackville passed, Mrs. Struthers wrote me and said if the next tenant at Curry House didn't need a housekeeper, I was welcome to go work for her. But if word got out that I have an illegitimate child, she won't want me anymore. No one will want me anymore. Respectability is everything in my line of work."

The anxiety in her voice was overwhelming.

"Then why bring her to your place of work at all?"

"Mrs. Birtle was worried that Becky was getting too headstrong and restless. The Birtles don't have much. Becky would have to go into service. And service can be . . . it can be a small, closed life. I remember how bored I was as the underhousemaid, how little there was to look forward to. I never wanted to get into trouble, but a flirtation here and there was the only cure for boredom.

"And then I fell in love with the son of the house and he promised to look after me. It's that same old story. But when it happened to me, I thought he was special and I was special. And it turned out that neither of us was special at all.

"I didn't want that to happen to Becky. Here I am in a position of some authority. I could look after her. But more than anything else, I felt Curry House was a safe place. Mr. Sackville never made any advances toward me or any other women in the house. And he treated Jenny Price with more care than most able-bodied folks did."

Treadles pulled out a chair but did not sit down. "And then he proved himself not quite as above reproach as you had thought."

Mrs. Cornish's lips quivered. "You think . . . you think . . ."

"You failed to inform Tommy Dunn of details of Mr. Sackville's condition that would have let a physician know that he was in need of strychnine. You said Becky requested to take the photograph when instead you stowed it among her things so that no one else would find out that she is your daughter and that you had a strong motive to protect her. Not to mention that you were, according to everyone else, desperately searching for a missing whisky decanter."

"Are you implying there was arsenic in the whisky?" cried Mrs.

Cornish, her gloved hands gripping the edge of the desk that separated them.

"Becky suffered a gastric attack the same day Mr. Sackville was forced to spend the night in Exeter. The only thing they both had was whisky from the decanter."

"If there was arsenic in the whisky, I didn't put it there. I might not have been completely truthful earlier, Inspector, but it was to save my position and my reputation, not my neck!"

Her breaths echoed harshly in the small room. Treadles waited until she had regained a measure of her composure. "Did Mr. Hodges tell you that Mr. Sackville offered Becky some of his whisky?"

"He did—and said I ought to keep a closer eye on the girl. So I snuck by when Becky cleaned abovestairs. Several times a day I did this and never once did I see Mr. Sackville with her. I kept it up until the day before Mr. Sackville died. What reason did I have to poison Mr. Sackville, when I'd no evidence that he took advantage of Becky, or even thought about it?"

"Then why were you scrambling for the whisky decanter, going so far as to snoop in Tommy Dunn's quarters for it?"

"I didn't want to believe that Becky took it." She looked at him beseechingly. "I didn't want to believe that my own flesh and blood was a thief."

"Why did you secret the photograph in her luggage then?"

"Before Becky came, I was afraid I'd never want her to leave again. But she came and . . . she was a stranger. She thought a little too well of herself. She didn't like to work too hard. And she didn't care a whit for life in service except that she was in the household of a real gentleman."

Mrs. Cornish sighed. "I remember the housekeeper at my first place scolding the maids and I remember thinking how unsympathetic and needlessly strict she was. But I've become that woman. I

can't understand why Becky doesn't take greater pride in her work
and I can't understand why dust on the mantel doesn't feel like dust
in the eyes to her. She was a disappointing housemaid to me and I
must have been an ogre of a housekeeper to her.

"But I wanted her to have the photograph. I didn't offer it to her
because I thought she'd find that offer strange. But I figured that if
she had it, she'd keep it. And maybe someday, when she's a good deal
older herself, she'll look back and understand that I wasn't being
unreasonable, but responsible."

A knock came on the door, startling her. She looked fearfully at
Treadles.

Treadles rose. "If you'll excuse me."

On the other side of the door was Constable Perkins. "Sir, the
results from the chemical analyst."

Treadles took the cable—and swore. The whisky he'd retrieved
from Becky Birtle contained no trace of arsenic. Nor any trace of
chloral.

"I also have a message on the Wheatstone machine from Sergeant MacDonald," said the young constable.

Dear Inspector Treadles,

Dozens showed up at Scotland Yard to testify to Mr.
Sackville's movements in London—the hazards of soliciting
help in the paper. One man seems credible.

According to him, Mr. Sackville regularly visited the
house across the street from his in Lambeth, usually
shortly before dinner. He remarked Mr. Sackville because
he was a fine-looking gentleman and didn't seem to belong
to the district. The most interesting thing he said,
however, was that the house burned down some six weeks

ago—which fits nicely with the occasion of Mr. Sackville's final trip to London, the one from which he returned early and distraught.

To be thorough, I showed the man a picture of the staff at Curry House. To my surprise, he immediately identified Hodges the valet. I asked if Hodges ever accompanied Mr. Sackville, he said not that he'd ever seen, but he remembered Hodges because once Hodges knocked on his door and asked if he knew what went on in the house Mr. Sackville visited.

I will interview others in the neighborhood to see if they have seen either Mr. Sackville or Hodges.

MacDonald

Clandestine entry into a suite of rooms at Claridge's should be a straightforward affair: One bribed a porter or two and proceeded.

Apparently not, especially if one's debut in breaking and entering was to take place under Lord Ingram's watchful eyes. There was a protocol, which consisted of handing the matter over to Lord Bancroft Ashburton, Lord Ingram's second-eldest brother and Charlotte's one-time suitor, a man of many responsibilities and almost as many means of achieving his ends—and waiting until Lord Bancroft issued a suitable time for the burglary to take place.

"It takes the fun out of the thing to have approval from high places," Charlotte complained to Lord Ingram, as they walked into Mrs. Marbleton's large, empty suite. "This ought to feel more . . . illegal."

Instead they'd been given a perfectly safe window of three-quarters of an hour from the man who defended the empire against threats from without and within.

Lord Ingram only shook his head.

"I don't mean to sound ungrateful," Charlotte said, feeling a little apologetic. "You called in a favor, I take it?"

In spite of his brother's assurance that no Marbleton would return during the allotted forty-five minutes, Lord Ingram approached a window and peered down to the street. "It's the only currency Bancroft understands."

"You can't possibly have that many favors left to call in." Charlotte knew something of this trade between brothers.

A faint regret tinged his answer. "Used my last."

From time to time he would leave England for a while, ostensibly for a dig. But Charlotte could always tell whether he'd been to an excavation—and when he'd been somewhere else entirely.

Archeology, as it turned out, was an excellent excuse for all kinds of foreign jaunts. Once he returned on a crutch and attributed his injury to a large statue falling over. Another time he came back with a heavily bandaged hand and said that there had been feral dogs at the site.

The scar on his hand hadn't remotely resembled the marks of canine teeth or claws.

Does your wife never have any suspicions? she'd asked him once.

No.

To have suspicions, one would have to pay attention. After their falling out, Lady Ingram had not bothered with any more false affections.

There must be ways to find temporary escape without risking your life, Charlotte had told him.

You have fewer choices, Charlotte, he'd answered. *It doesn't mean I have many.*

She let her gaze linger on him another second, then ventured farther inside the suite, carefully opening drawers, wardrobes, steamer trunks. When she'd taken a mental inventory of everything, she went back to a cupboard that housed a portable darkroom, several cameras, and a large stack of photographs.

Mrs. Marbleton did not stay alone. Also registered to the suite were two young people, Stephen and Frances Marbleton, her children, ostensibly, with Frances Marbleton being none other than Miss Ellie Hartford from the Dog and Duck in Bywater, the woman who had wanted to claim Mrs. Watson as her mother.

And judging by the photographs, the young Marbletons had been traveling.

Many of the pictures featured only scenery but some had captured one of the young Marbletons in the frame—they were probably traveling alone, taking each other's pictures.

In those images they seemed to have deliberately chosen not to include any landmarks. There was the sea and there was open landscape. But the coast could have been any stretch of British headland. And the rolling countryside was as likely to have been plucked from Sussex as Derbyshire.

"If you can afford to live at Claridge's Hotel," called Lord Ingram from the next room, "would you still seek employment?"

He had found a list of employment agencies. "I believe they specialize in helping women, don't they?"

Charlotte sucked in a breath. On the list was Miss Oswald's employment agency, where Miss Oswald had all but accused Charlotte of being a journalist going about trying to write an exposé on similar agencies.

Briefly, she recounted that conversation to Lord Ingram. "I wonder whether Frances Marbleton went around to all these fine establishments—and what she might have been doing there."

"Since they have a portable darkroom, they must have photo-negatives. I can make prints of her images and find out."

"You do that, dear sir. I'm afraid I must go and prepare for my next client," says Charlotte.

"A client you need to *prepare* for?"

"Oh, yes. At least an hour of preparation."

He rolled his eyes. "You are up to no good, Charlotte Holmes."

"You should try it sometimes. Or more precisely, you should return to it sometimes—you used to be excellent at being up to no good, your lordship."

He did not rise to her goading, but asked, "Why did you ask me to wait for you on a street corner last night? And why did you look back several times after I got in the hackney? Are you again suspecting that you might be followed?"

"I *was* being followed. I changed vehicles three times before I could be sure I'd shaken my tail loose."

"You think it's the Marbletons?"

"I'd much rather it be someone you hired. Why would the Marbletons follow *me*?"

"Why did Mrs. Marbleton counterfeit a case for you to begin with? It isn't safe, this Sherlock Holmes business."

"Well, this next client is definitely safe," she promised him. "Sherlock Holmes would give up the business altogether if this one proves anything but safe."

⸺⁂⸺

A subdued Roger Shrewsbury walked into Sherlock Holmes's parlor.

In advance of his visit, a hole had been drilled in the wall between the parlor and the bedroom—then concealed in such a way as to allow Charlotte to see into the parlor without herself being seen. But all that had been completed the day before, with help from a friend of Mrs. Watson's who invented magic tricks. The one hour's preparation Charlotte mentioned to Lord Ingram involved no further work on the flat, only further work on Mrs. Watson, begging her to not to be too hard on Roger Shrewsbury.

Mrs. Watson took on the role of Holmes's sister. She briskly explained to the client the infelicities of the great detective's health and the necessity for her to act as a go-between. Then, without asking Shrewsbury whether he needed to be reassured Holmes still had all his faculties, she said, "I can see that you have rarely been a man of your own mind, sir—you are surrounded by those accustomed to imposing their will on you, and you have been content to let them make your decisions. This then is quite a leap for you."

"Yes," came Shrewsbury's hesitant words. "Yes, I suppose."

"You mentioned nothing of what you wish to see Sherlock about, but he has hazarded that it has something to do with the circumstances surrounding your mother's death." Mrs. Watson smiled. "It couldn't have been an easy decision to trust a stranger. My brother commends you for it."

Her smile was so warm and encouraging, Charlotte would never have guessed that she had been adamantly against speaking any kind words to their caller. *No, Sherlock Holmes ought to give him hell, expose him for the spineless cad he is.*

The man probably believed, for at least forty-eight hours, that his conduct had been directly responsible for his mother's death, Charlotte had explained. *He's useless, not heartless—not to mention we don't want him to run out in mortification.*

"I'm beyond gratified by Mr. Holmes's understanding," said Shrewsbury, sounding almost teary.

Charlotte sighed. The poor man, so unaccustomed to receiving a bit of compassion.

"He's right—I've indeed come about my mother," Shrewsbury continued. "When Mr. Holmes's letter came about, linking her death with Lady Amelia's and Mr. Sackville's, everyone in the family was furious. But I—I couldn't help wonder whether there wasn't some truth to it, some nefarious conspiracy at work, if you will. My mother had the constitution of a camel. She could hike fifteen miles in the country, summer or winter. She never suffered from any aches or pains. And her physician, twenty years her junior, always said that her heart would keep on ticking long after his had given out."

"So you agree with Sherlock's assessment that hers hadn't been a natural death."

"I haven't told anyone this, but the night before we found her dead, she went out. Now you must understand that it had been an awful evening. Nobody said anything at dinner. My wife was terribly upset because my mother scolded her for failing at her duties to keep me on the straight and narrow. I hadn't received any lecture myself, but I was on pins and needles: It would be only a matter of time before mine crashed over me like an avalanche.

"As soon as dinner ended my wife retired for the evening. I hovered around my mother for a while, until she told me to go away— she'd deal with me the next day. It was oppressive at home, so I went out for a walk. And as I was coming back, I saw the most amazing sight, my mother getting inside a hansom cab.

"A *hansom cab*! She had never used a public conveyance in her life. She used to say that they smelled of unhygienic drunks and that she shuddered to think about the encrusted grime and filth. I couldn't imagine what would have prompted her to get into a hansom cab when she was in town, with her own carriage parked in the mews behind the house, a quick summons away."

"Did you ever ask?"

"No. Even if she hadn't died I wouldn't have dared. She was the one who asked the questions and pointed out where we fell short— not the other way around." He was silent for a few seconds. "That was the last I saw her. I returned home and proceeded directly to the whisky bottle. I didn't even hear Miss Livia Holmes and Mother having a row outside. The next thing I knew was my wife shaking me, trying to make me understand that Mother was no more."

He clasped his hands together, as if trying to hold on to his courage. "Since then I've been trying to find out where she'd gone that evening and whom she'd seen, if anyone. So far I've managed to eliminate a few of her closest friends—but I always knew it couldn't possibly have been them in the first place. She'd call on them in sackcloth before she would in a hansom cab."

"Sherlock believes you would like for us to pass on this information to Scotland Yard—without revealing the source, of course. Is he correct?

Shrewsbury grimaced. "Mother would be turning over in her grave if she knew what I was doing. But I don't want to accept that she died of an aneurysm of the brain. I don't want to accept that I was the one who sent her to her grave."

Mrs. Watson smiled again. "You have done very well to bring the matter to Sherlock's attention."

"Will it—will it help solve what happened to my mother?"

"Let me confer with Sherlock first."

Charlotte already had her questions written down in a notebook. *See*, she mouthed to Mrs. Watson, *he's not so bad*. To which Mrs. Watson responded with a dramatic roll of her eyes before taking the notebook and returning to the parlor.

"Sherlock has a few questions. First, Mr. Shrewsbury, where exactly did you see Lady Shrewsbury get on the hansom cab?"

"Near the corner of George Street and Bryanston Square."

"And which way did it go?"

"Toward the east."

"Did you watch it for some time? Did it turn onto any other street?"

"It kept going for a while and then it turned south. I think that was at Montague Street."

After he left—with a full slate of compliments for Mr. Holmes—Charlotte emerged from the bedroom, poured a cup of tea, and helped herself to a slice of the cake that he didn't touch.

Mrs. Watson stood by the window, looking at Charlotte one moment, out of the window the next, then again at Charlotte, peacefully enjoying her cake.

"You're awfully unsentimental, Miss Holmes, about the man who was your first."

"It was a purely strategic decision." Charlotte took another bite. "I like him, but not enough to stand at the window and watch him leave."

Mrs. Watson sighed. "Young ladies these days. But I must admit, he isn't as despicable as I thought he would be."

"He isn't despicable at all," Charlotte said. "His misfortune is that he was born fun-loving into a tribe that doesn't understand fun. They require him to be serious and ambitious, to have a lofty reputation, an enviable family, and an illustrious career in politics, of all things. He's never been allowed to decide anything for himself, and therefore has never developed either confidence or judgment. So it really was remarkable that he would go against the will of his entire clan to tell us what he knows."

"But does it help, what he has told us?"

Charlotte looked longingly at the rest of the cake on the plate. Alas, she was already at one-point-four chins and must refrain from a second slice. "We now know that something extraordinary took place the night before Lady Shrewsbury died. We only need to find out what it was."

Twenty

Hodges, when he'd been brought into the interrogation room Mrs. Cornish recently vacated, betrayed no hint of anxiety. He nodded pleasantly at Treadles. "Evening, Inspector. Constable Perkins says you have some questions for me?"

Treadles regarded him for some time without speaking, a tactic meant to intimidate. From time to time suspects broke down under the weight of his gaze. Often they fidgeted in discomfort, eyes darting everywhere. But occasionally a suspect would stare right back at him with defiance. Or, even more rarely, with a great display of equanimity.

Hodges fell into this last category. He met Treadles's gaze with a calm fearlessness that early Christian martyrs would have prayed for. But tranquility before an interrogator did not necessarily imply innocence: It could just as well indicate an arrogance bordering on pathology—or a complete lack of conscience.

Treadles tapped his knuckles against the cable from Scotland Yard. "Mr. Hodges, you said you didn't know where your late employer went in London or what he did. But now we have a reliable eyewitness who placed you at exactly the same place as Mr. Sackville, asking for his purpose. How do you explain that?"

"Fairly simple," said Hodges, as if he'd long expected the question and had the answer ready. "I was a boxer before I entered service, and lived in London for twenty years. Sometimes when Mr. Sackville went off to London, I did, too, to see old friends in the area.

"One day I saw him in Lambeth and I was curious—wouldn't anyone be, under the circumstances? So I knocked on a few doors and asked if anyone knew what went on in the house Mr. Sackville entered. Nobody was sure but they all thought it a little dodgy. Gambling, most likely. Probably loose women, too. I was frankly disappointed. It was too . . . common. I thought Mr. Sackville would have had some more gentlemanly vices."

Treadles didn't believe him. "If they were truly such pedestrian sins, why did you keep them a secret?"

"Mr. Sackville can't defend his good name anymore, so it's up to the rest of us. Men have sinned much worse. But when they die of natural causes, nobody cares what they've done in their spare time. Mr. Sackville ought to be given the same privacy—he'd have wanted it."

Treadles raised a brow. "You didn't have as high a regard for his good name when you insinuated to Mrs. Cornish that he might be taking advantage of Becky Birtle."

"I said no such thing." For the first time, a note of vexation crept into Hodges's voice. "I warned Mrs. Cornish that the girl was taking liberties with Mr. Sackville's expensive liquor—and made up the nonsense about Mr. Sackville offering it to her. Told Mrs. Cornish she ought to have a stern word with Becky. Even an amiable gentleman wouldn't hesitate to give the sack when his whisky is endangered."

A former boxer. A man accustomed to dodging and counter-punching. And conditioned by years in the ring to keep a cool head under pressure. "What else have you been keeping from us, Mr. Hodges?"

"Nothing, Inspector," said Hodges evenly. "Nothing."

"Very well, Mr. Hodges. I will need a written statement of your whereabouts during the twenty-four hours leading to Mr. Sackville's death."

Hodges inclined his head. "And you'll have it, Inspector."

—❧—

Hodges was not the only liar. Lady Sheridan's story, too, turned out to be less than entirely truthful. The YWCA had indeed dedicated a new center, and Lady Sheridan had indeed been there—rather unexpectedly, as she had cabled her regrets only two days prior, citing ill health.

But she had not left Bath the next morning, as she'd informed Inspector Treadles. Instead, she had departed immediately after the evening reception, even though she had paid for a night's lodging at the hotel.

"How do you explain the discrepancies, Lady Sheridan?" Treadles demanded.

He was tired: He'd returned to London on the early train. But more than that, he was frustrated. The investigation had uncovered an abundance of information that seemed promising, only to then never lead anywhere. He wanted a suspect. He wanted proper answers. He wanted the case solved so he could sleep in his own bed—and wake up with his wife in his arms.

Lady Sheridan, however, displayed no inclination to help him achieve his objectives. "What does it matter when I left Bath, Inspector? An old woman is entitled to change her mind and head home earlier."

She was even thinner than Treadles remembered, her voice scratchy and weary. He felt an onslaught of self-reproach. She was clearly not well and he'd fallen barely short of discourtesy.

"You had every right to modify your plans, ma'am. It is not that you changed your mind that brought me back, but that you failed to disclose the truth."

Lady Sheridan sighed. Treadles had the strange sensation that her skeleton might rattle apart even with such a miniscule motion. "The truth is I had nothing to do with Mr. Sackville's death."

"Then, ma'am, you can have no objection to making your itinerary known—to remove yourself from suspicion."

Lady Sheridan regarded him with something close to approval. "Very well then. I left Bath that evening, but had a spot of discomfort along my return route. I got off at the next stop, took a room at the nearest railway inn, and continued my journey the next day, when I felt more equal to the challenge."

"Can anyone at the inn corroborate your account?"

"I'm afraid I didn't pay much attention to where I was. All I needed was a bed that didn't sway—it could have been any inn at any station along the line."

It took a great deal of cheek to give such an answer. And a great deal of dignity to endow it with even a semblance of seriousness. "Ma'am, I'm afraid I can't take that for an answer. Why wasn't your maid with you?"

"When I decided to leave Bath she wasn't feeling well. I told her she could follow the next day. But of course, en route I succumbed to the same thing."

Treadles studied this frail yet formidable woman—and asked her the same question he'd asked Hodges. "What else have you been keeping from us, Lady Sheridan?"

The answer he received was also the exact same. "Nothing, Inspector. Nothing."

❋

Treadles did not neglect the servants of Lord and Lady Sheridan's household. But her maid unhesitatingly confirmed that she had

286 · *Sherry Thomas*

stayed overnight in Bath by herself. And none of the others could tell him anything more of Lady Sheridan's precise itinerary—the majority had never even heard of Mr. Sackville.

Only the two senior-most staff recalled the days when Mr. Sackville had been a frequent and esteemed guest. "He'd bring friends. The friends would bring their friends," said Mrs. Gomer, the housekeeper. "I used to complain about how much more work it was when he came around. But then he didn't come around anymore and it was never the same. A house without young people is just not the same."

"I was still a footman in those days," said Mr. Addison, the butler. "A very young footman."

They stood in the butler's pantry, a small space allotted to Mr. Addison's use, as he cleaned the tap meant to sit on top of a gasogene.

"Everybody looked forward to Mr. Sackville's visits," Mr. Addison continued, "especially Miss Clara—he was more a big brother to her than an uncle. And of course her friends visited—her cousins, too. It was a lively house then, the place in the country."

"Mr. Sackville was well-liked?"

"Oh, yes."

"Did he have any vices that you know of?"

Mr. Addison was filling the lower globe of the gasogene with water. He paused for a moment. "Not me, Inspector. He didn't drink too much or gamble too much. Never made unreasonable demands of the staff. Never took advantage of us, if you know what I mean."

Treadles nodded—he did know what Mr. Addison meant. "Would you happen to know why Lord Sheridan and Mr. Sackville fell out?"

Mr. Addison did not answer immediately, but concentrated on tapping scoops of white powder through a small funnel into the gasogene's upper globe. "Inspector, I ought not say anything about it, but I'll tell you because you're looking for Mr. Sackville's murderer in the wrong place."

"Please do. I'll be more than delighted to eliminate your master and mistress from the list of suspects."

Mr. Addison peered at Treadles. When he was satisfied that Treadles had spoken in complete sincerity, he set aside the funnel. "The last time Mr. Sackville came to visit, I overheard an argument between the brothers. You probably know that Mr. Sackville was a great deal wealthier than his lordship. Well, Mr. Sackville's advisors encouraged him to make certain investments. He passed on the suggestions to Lord Sheridan. The investments turned out badly. Mr. Sackville insisted on compensating his lordship for his losses and his lordship wouldn't have it—said nobody forced him to put money in any ventures and he deuced well could take his losses on the chin, like a man.

"But Mr. Sackville wouldn't let it rest. He went on insisting until his lordship exploded and told Mr. Sackville that Mr. Sackville understood the world only through the lens of his fortune. So his lordship was now poor as a church mouse, but what did it matter when his only child was dead and nothing would bring her back. Why couldn't Mr. Sackville at least let him have his pride?"

So Lady Sheridan had not been lying when she'd characterized the spat as an argument about manly honor.

Mr. Addison carefully fitted the long-tubed tap on top of the gasogene and shook the entire apparatus for the powders—tartaric acid and bicarbonate of soda, if Treadles remembered correctly—to react with water. The contents of the gasogene bubbled, hissing faintly. "Mr. Sackville left that day itself. I always felt bad about their estrangement. It wasn't really any kind of insurmountable dispute. But Mr. Sackville never came back. And I guess he had the last word after all, when he left his fortune to his lordship."

Sometimes, the more you know, the less things make sense, Treadles's father-in-law had once said. If it had been the other way around, if Lord Sheridan had insisted Mr. Sackville compensate him for soured investments and Mr. Sackville had refused, then the Sheridans would have been much more likely to hold a grudge all these years, a grudge that could have turned cancerous.

But why would anyone kill a man who wanted to make it up to them, even though strictly speaking he hadn't been at fault and had suffered his own losses?

"I think Lord Sheridan always expected that Mr. Sackville would come striding back someday—and it would be as if there had never been a quarrel," said Mr. Addison, setting the gasogene aside for the gas to percolate into the water. "A shame that didn't happen—and won't ever happen now."

Treadles thanked the butler. And then, out of personal curiosity, he said, "I rather like that gadget, the gasogene. But the missus won't allow one—she says too many of them explode and she has no desire to be married to a one-eyed policeman."

Mr. Addison chuckled. "Well, gasogenes don't come wrapped in wicker for nothing. They will explode if they aren't handled carefully. That's why I make the soda water myself, instead of giving the task to a footman."

The gasogene didn't look as if it would hold more than two quarts of water and it needed to sit for a considerable amount of time to complete the carbonation. "I can see that it makes enough for a small family, but what about when you have guests?"

"We have another one. And we can always store water that's been carbonated in bottles for a short while. But you are right, this wouldn't have been enough in the old days. When we used to have a house full of guests we had gas delivered in canisters—but then again, canisters have their dangers, too. Any gas under pressure does."

"Very true." Treadles glanced at the gasogene again, still tempted. Perhaps Alice might relent if he could find a way to further reinforce those glass globes. "And if you don't mind one last question from me, Mr. Addison, do you have any theories as to why anyone would wish Mr. Sackville harm?"

The butler shook his head. "It's been decades since any of us last saw him. He could have met all kinds of unsavory characters in those intervening years. All I can tell you is that his death has nothing to do with anyone in this house."

A knock came on the door of Lord Ingram's darkroom. "My lord," said a footman, "Mr. Shrewsbury to see you. Are you at home to him?"

That ass. "You may show him in here."

Shrewsbury knew enough to enter quickly, closing the door behind himself. "Oh, good. This place doesn't stink as badly as I'd have expected."

"It's ventilated," Lord Ingram said coolly, as he pinned another photograph to a cord strung across the width of the room. "What can I do for you, Mr. Shrewsbury?"

"Ah . . . you wouldn't happen to have heard from Miss Holmes, would you, my lord? The rumors are growing wilder every day and I'm beginning to really worry about her."

"Only beginning to?"

"Well, I thought she'd have come to me by now."

"That foolish woman. What good reason could she possibly have for not seeking your aid?"

In the crimson glow of the small, red-glass-encased lightbulb, it was impossible to tell whether Shrewsbury flushed. But the scrape of his heels across the floor was quite audible.

He cleared his throat. "I'm also beginning to see that maybe she might not want to be my mistress. If you hear from her, will you please tell her that I'm offering help, plain and simple, whatever she needs, and no conditions attached. I only want to make sure she's all—wait, who's that?"

Lord Ingram followed the direction of Shrewsbury's gaze. The prints had come out well. Despite the dim, reddish light, Stephen Marbleton's features stood out in relief. "I don't know—I'm developing someone else's negatives. Have you seen the man before?"

"The man? No, never seen the man. But the woman looks familiar—even though I'm certain we've never been introduced."

Lord Ingram unpinned a print of Frances Marbleton, taken at some seashore, and handed it to Shrewsbury so he could take a closer look. "Have you gone tramping over the summer? Perhaps you passed her in some field."

"No, I haven't been anywhere near Devon this summer."

The hairs on the back of Lord Ingram's neck rose. He exhaled carefully, so he could continue to speak with some semblance of detachment. "This is Devon?"

"There must be pebble beaches elsewhere in Britain, but this looks a good deal like the one at Westward Ho!. What a name, eh, exclamation supplied. Went there with my mates a few times when I was at university. You've a house somewhere in the vicinity, don't you?"

"My place is near the Hangman Cliffs. Never been to Westward Ho!."

"I know what you mean. Too many tourists—I mean, it's the only reason the place exists in the first place."

Lord Ingram was suddenly in a hurry. "Anything else I can do for you, Mr. Shrewsbury?"

"Umm, no."

"In that case, please excuse me. I have an urgent appointment."

Inspector Treadles was not proud of himself, but at some point his curiosity got the better of him—and he decided to burgle 18 Upper Baker Street.

It wasn't terribly late yet. But from where he stood in the alley behind the house, number 18 was completely dark, not a fleck of light coming from behind the curtains. He had already circled the block of buildings twice. Now he slipped into the shadows of the back door—and quickly picked the lock.

The ground floor was silent, the caretaker's room furnished but empty of occupants. The stairs did not creak as he climbed up, not did the stair landing groan.

He was not surprised when the door of the parlor opened quietly at his touch—why should it be locked, when most likely no one lived on these premises? Still his heart pounded a little as he tiptoed to the bedroom.

He pulled on a curtain. Light from the street lamp streamed inside, illuminating a perfectly made and perfectly empty bed. He shut the curtain and lit a match. No, nothing else that a perennially bedridden man would need.

Was there even a chamber pot under the b—

A heavily bearded man stared back at him from under the bed—and yanked Treadles by the ankles. Treadles went down hard. The man scrambled out and ran, stepping over one of Treadles's hands, causing him to yowl in pain.

Fortunately, nothing was broken. But by the time Treadles made his way down the stairs and out the back door, the man had disappeared.

"Don't make any sounds."

Charlotte's heart jumped to her throat before she realized the voice, though kept to a vehement whisper, belonged to Lord Ingram. "What are you doing here? And don't make the joke that I should be overjoyed to finally have you in my bedroom."

She'd been out of her room only a few minutes, getting ready for bed. He was the last thing she expected to find upon her return.

"Why should I joke about how overjoyed you must b—"

292 · Sherry Thomas

"There is a tear near the knee of your right trouser leg. Bits of grass and leaves are stuck to the edges of your shoes. And what's—" She grabbed her magnifying glass and studied his jacket, and then she knelt down to examine the wool of his trousers with the same rigor.

"You always did tell me you had perverse predilections," he murmured.

"I've never told you any such thing. And I have lost all respect for you, since you think my merely being on my knees in front of you is perverse." She pulled a pair of forceps out of a penholder and removed several small, gleaming objects that had been embedded in the fabric near his cuff and dropped them onto a table.

"I see you have been to Claridge's again." The bits of glass weren't ordinary shards, but fragments of photographic plates. "There was some sort of struggle, plates shattering all over the place. And then you ran—I assume you made your way out from a service door, to avoid being recognized running through the lobby. But you were pursued. You leaped over a gate into Grosvenor Square Park. Did your trousers get caught on a finial on the gate? No, that's not it. I see what must have happened. You looked back as you ran and tripped over a root. But eventually you shook loose your pursuer and came here. You do know, I hope, that I'm the youngest child at home and have no idea how to dress a skinned knee for anybody?"

"Of course I know that. I came not to get a bandage, but to sleep with you, since I almost died tonight."

She blinked—was that her brain melting from a surge of extreme internal heat?

He laughed softly.

She rolled her eyes. "Very funny. So you came to warn me that they knew the plates had been stolen and were lying in wait for you?"

"Roger Shrewsbury called on me earlier. I happened to be in the darkroom. He saw the photographs I was developing"—Lord Ingram took out one from an inside pocket and handed it to Charlotte—"and said he thought the pebble ridge was near Westward Ho!, which isn't at all far from Mr. Sackville's house."

Didn't one of Inspector Treadles's reports state that a photographer and his assistant had come through the nearest village to Curry House, in the week before Mr. Sackville's death? If those two were Stephen and Frances Marbleton, then . . .

Charlotte set aside her magnifying glass and forceps. "Now I know why Mrs. Marbleton came to see me: Sherlock Holmes interfered with her otherwise perfectly orchestrated plans. If I hadn't written that letter, there would have been no scrutiny of Mr. Sackville's death, and certainly nothing linking his death to the other two."

"There is *still* nothing linking those three deaths, other than that they knew each other in life."

"There's something else now. There's Sophia Lonsdale."

"Who is dead."

Charlotte tapped her finger against her lips. "Unless she isn't."

Inspector Treadles lost count of the number of times he'd paced the street before Lord Ingram's town house. He was about to give up and leave when a hansom cab disgorged his lordship, who seemed not at all surprised to find Treadles loitering and immediately invited him for a stroll.

Treadles gave a quick account of what happened at 18 Upper Baker Street. He braced himself for mortifying questions as to why in the world he had chosen to break into the home of an acquaintance, but Lord Ingram only nodded. "If you'll permit me a few minutes, Inspector, you might find that what took place tonight on Upper Baker Street has some bearing on Mr. Sackville's case."

At first his narrative of Sherlock Holmes's mysterious client only baffled Treadles. But when Lord Ingram reached the part where Frances Marbleton was identified to have been in Westward Ho!, Treadles stopped in his tracks. "The photographer and his assistant—the two young people who had come through the village five days before. I'll bet they were the ones who swapped out the strychnine in the doctors' dispensaries."

"That is Holmes's and my thinking also. And Stephen Marbleton broke into 18 Upper Baker Street in an attempt to retrieve the photonegatives they found missing."

"That part makes sense. But what does Mrs. Marbleton, who may or may not be Sophia Lonsdale risen from death, have to do with anyone in this case?"

"We are still trying to find out. Will you meet with us tomorrow afternoon at two?"

"Yes, of course."

Lord Ingram took out one of his cards and scrawled something on the back. "This is the address. I hope to know more by then."

When Treadles at last reached home, his wife was already in bed. "Welcome back, Inspector," she murmured as he slipped under the covers next to her. "Busy night?"

He exhaled. "I'll tell you in the morning."

"Everything all right?" asked Alice, wrapping an arm around him.

"I think so."

A thousand and one questions swarmed in his head. His kingdom for a few absolute certainties!

But he did arrive at one definite answer: Nobody in Sherlock Holmes's "condition" ought to be moved about willy-nilly. If he wasn't there in his bed at night, then he most likely hadn't been there during the day.

Treadles knew something of the circumstances of Lady Shrewsbury's death. He knew about Miss Olivia Holmes, who had, in a drunken rage, called for Lady Shrewsbury's imminent demise. He knew that when Sherlock Holmes's letter to the coroner took effect, Miss Olivia Holmes had been the chief beneficiary. He also knew that Miss Olivia Holmes had a younger sister, who happened to have fallen from grace the exact same day disaster struck Sherlock Holmes.

Why he hadn't put two and two together earlier he didn't know. Except that the mind did not go where the mind did not want to go.

"You are wound up tight," murmured Alice.

He stared into the dark. "Do you think an extraordinary woman ought to be treated differently, my dear?"

"Where did that question come from?" Alice chuckled softly. "And treated differently from whom? Other women?"

"Yes."

"And how will this extraordinary woman be treated? As well as a slightly better-than-average man?"

"Better than that, I hope."

"The extraordinary will always be treated differently—they're extraordinary, after all. What *I* wonder is whether a not-so-extraordinary woman will ever be treated the same as a not-so-extraordinary man."

Something in the tone of his wife's voice made him turn toward her. "You wonder just now—or you've long wondered this?"

It caused a strange sensation, almost like panic, to realize that he didn't know this about her.

She was silent for some time. "When I was ten, I told Father that someday I would like to run Cousins Manufacturing. He said that would not happen. I loved my father, you know that, and he was a wonderful man. But he was old-fashioned in this matter—he wanted his son to carry on his life's work, even though Barnaby isn't remotely suitable for it.

"It helped in a way, I suppose, that Father was firm and clear from the beginning that the business would go to Barnaby. And he did give me the latitude of choosing my own husband, instead of ordering me to marry a lordship for aristocratic connections. But yes, I have long wondered why I must content myself with being a spectator to the family enterprise, when I would have much preferred being a participant."

"I . . . thought you were happy with what we have." Treadles's throat was suddenly dry.

"Of course I'm happy with what we have. You are the man I want by my side all my life. But that is not to say I wouldn't have been good at managing and growing the business—and enjoyed that, too."

Why didn't you tell me earlier? he wanted to ask. *Four years we've known each other, three as man and wife.*

His heart was somewhere past his spleen. He felt small and lonely, even though nothing had changed.

Nothing at all.

Except the idea that he—and their life together—was enough for his wife.

And so much for his hope that someday he would be able to give her everything she had ever wanted.

Twenty-one

The note from Lord Ingram came early, before Charlotte had even sat down to breakfast. And it wasn't delivered by post, but via courier.

Inspector Treadles's decision to burgle 18 Upper Baker Street did not startle her, though she was surprised by his timing—she'd thought it would be a while longer before he questioned something as fundamental as Sherlock Holmes's gender. The presence of the other intruder, however, did give her pause.

Mrs. Marbleton was nothing if not thorough.

Sophia Lonsdale was nothing if not thorough.

But why? What was the purpose of her involvement? If only Charlotte had access to Ladies Avery and Somersby and could pick their brains of everything they knew about Sophia Lonsdale.

"Good morning, my dear," chirped Mrs. Watson as she sat down and reached for the teapot.

She sported a day dress that made Charlotte think of a field of buttercups: spring, hope, renewal. Being Sherlock Holmes's business partner had made Mrs. Watson busy—and buoyant. It gladdened Charlotte to no end that—

She mentally smacked herself. How sloppy of her to overlook a potentially tremendous source of information. Mrs. Watson had told her that the divide between Society and the demimonde was porous. She knew who Charlotte was. She knew the state of Lord Ingram's marriage. Why hadn't Charlotte asked her about Sophia Lonsdale?

"Do you know, Mrs. Watson, I recently learned of someone who went through a similar experience as I did, but a generation earlier. She came from a background more prominent than mine. Her family, instead of exiling her to the countryside, disowned her altogether."

"Are you speaking of the Lonsdale girl? Yes, I remember. Quite the scandal back then." Mrs. Watson's teacup stopped halfway to her lips. "How curious that you should bring her up."

"Oh?"

"Guess who was the man responsible for ruining her."

Charlotte's heart skipped a beat. Could it be? Was Mrs. Watson about to give her the one link that would crack this case wide open? "Who was it?"

Mrs. Watson took a sip of her tea. "Lord Sheridan."

For the first time in her life, Charlotte encountered a drawing room that was too gaudy for her. She ran her fingers along the gold tassels of a bright purple lampshade, lifted the edge of a tiger-skin rug that draped the back of a red velvet chaise, and tested an even dozen orange and blue pillow cushions for fluffiness.

Yes, definitely too gaudy. But if one removed the pillow cushions, not all of them, just five or six . . .

"This is one of Bancroft's places?" she asked Lord Ingram.

"Correct."

"Tell me the truth. Was it a whorehouse under previous owner-ship?" she asked.

"No, it was a very dull dwelling. Very respectable, I believe." His answer came with a straight face, but something in his expression made her think that he was trying not to laugh.

"Are you saying that Bancroft's minions made changes to the décor?"

"Minions? This is Bancroft's own handiwork."

Charlotte looked around again. "Huh. I never would have guessed Bancroft had such extravagant tastes. He's so . . . colorless."

"You told the poor man to his face that he was the most boring person you'd ever met."

"It was a compliment—he is exactly the faceless bureaucrat you want to be in charge of the inner workings of the empire. But this parlor is giving me second th—wait, do you mean to tell me that Bancroft fitted out this place to appeal to *my* tastes, when he was courting me?"

"He almost succeeded, didn't he? I told him if he took away half of the cushions you'd feel right at home."

Charlotte snorted—he knew her too well.

"I also told him not to propose until after he'd first shown you the house, to stack the odds in his favor. He ignored my bang-on advice, of course." He glanced at her. "A family trait, that."

Was he referring obliquely to his own dismissal of Charlotte's counsel not to marry the mercenary Lady Ingram?

"I'm almost sorry that he joined the ranks of your rejected suitors," he went on, as if he at last heard what he'd said and needed to shift the subject. "It would have been a sight, the two of you thrown together for eternity."

"Well, I always say that of all the proposals I've ever received, Bancroft's was my favorite."

Not because of Bancroft, per se, but because of the effect his suit had on his brother. She would never forget that first simmering silence between them, those ever-expanding ripples of pleasure and pain in her heart, as she listened to the uninterrupted stillness and heard everything he would not say aloud.

Sometimes such a silence descended with the grandeur of theatrical curtains, sometimes it stole upon them like wisps of morning mist. This time she exited her recollection to find herself enveloped in yet another one: He was watching her again, while her face was turned to the red velvet chaise, her fingers playing with the button on a cushion.

The doorbell rang, shattering the unquiet silence.

Charlotte sat down on the chaise. They greeted a wan-looking Inspector Treadles. Lord Ingram asked the policeman to tell Charlotte what happened the night before at 18 Upper Baker Street, to which she listened with a half-raised brow.

There was something not quite right with Inspector Treadles. It was clear he had realized that there was no Sherlock Holmes. It was also clear that he knew the scandal to Charlotte Holmes's name—and he did not approve. By extension, he must approve slightly less of Lord Ingram, whom until now he had considered a man without flaws.

But none of those reasons, singly or together, could have accounted for his disheartenment.

The wonderful, beloved wife?

Lord Ingram regarded his friend with a neutral expression—he had become much more opaque in recent years, especially since his estrangement from his own wife.

When Inspector Treadles finished relating the events of the previous evening, Lord Ingram brought out a stack of prints he'd made from the negatives he'd stolen from the Marbletons.

"Is this the man you saw at Baker Street?" he asked, showing Inspector Treadles an image of Stephen Marbleton.

"No, the man had a beard."

Lord Ingram handed over another photograph, the same young man, wearing the same clothes and standing in the same place with the same pose, only now sporting a luxuriant beard.

This caught Inspector Treadles's attention. He examined the

photograph with much greater attention. "I've heard of the manip-
ulation that can be done to photographs, but I've never seen it with
my own eyes."

"I used to distribute prints of my brother Bancroft with horns
on his head. To date I remain his favorite brother," said Lord Ingram
drily. "But I take it that's still not the man you saw."

"No, I don't believe so."

"This one?" Lord Ingram handed over yet another photograph
of a bearded young man.

Charlotte's eyes widened. This man had on a lounge suit and was
casually posed, beard and all, but his features were those of Frances
Marbleton's.

"Yes, him," said Treadles.

"I spoke to Mr. Shrewsbury this morning, before church," said
Lord Ingram. "This is also the person he believes to have been driv-
ing the hansom cab that his mother inexplicably rode in the night
before she died."

Inspector Treadles studied the photographs again, one by one. "I
will have someone show these pictures to the villagers. Do you know
yet what might have been their motive?"

"I spoke with Mrs. Watson this morning," said Charlotte, "and
learned that the lover who ruined Sophia Lonsdale was said to be
none other than Lord Sheridan."

Lord Ingram frowned. "He must be a good twenty-five years
older than her."

"She was one of his daughter's closest friends. Mrs. Watson's understanding is that their grief drew them closer and one day, mutual
comforting went too far," Charlotte explained. "But let's consider a
slightly different scenario. What if the man who ruined her had been
Mr. Sackville instead? If Lord Sheridan took the blame for his
brother, that could explain their subsequent alienation.

"Here's something else I learned from Mrs. Watson: Lady Shrewsbury had been the one to broadcast Sophia Lonsdale's indiscretion. And if Lord Ingram gets hold of Lady Avery or Lady Somersby, it's quite possible he could unearth some connection between Lady Amelia Drummond and Sophia Lonsdale, too."

In this scenario, Sophia Lonsdale would have ample reason to swoop in, cold-blooded murders on her mind, for the wrongs she perceived her victims had perpetrated against her all these years ago. For a fall from grace so complete that decades later she still carried discoloration on her hands.

Lord Ingram cradled his chin in the space between his thumb and forefinger. "This would have been a perfect explanation. Why don't you sound more convinced?"

"Because I don't understand Lady Sheridan's involvement in the present day. I feel we're still nowhere near the bottom of what she'd been trying to do on that trip to—"

She fell silent. There was something she had learned from Inspector Treadles's reports—the ones he had handed over for Sherlock Holmes to read during his first visit. What was it?

Her palm struck the tufted surface of the velvet chaise. "Inspector, when you interviewed Dr. Birch, the physician from the next village who was summoned because Dr. Harris was out, he mentioned that he had his dogcart already hitched because he was headed out to the village inn to see to an elderly traveler in need of morphine.

"I believe you can find Lady Sheridan's picture in recent Bath papers, from the opening of the new YWCA center. And I believe if you were to show her picture to both Dr. Birch and the innkeeper, they would confirm that she is the elderly traveler in question."

—❖—

Sergeant MacDonald was dispatched to Devon that same afternoon. By midmorning the following day, he was wiring back reports. The young Marbletons were indeed recognized as the traveling photographer and his assistant who had come through the village. Inspector Treadles sent a pair of constables to Claridge's, but they telephoned from the hotel, reporting that the Marbletons had already vacated their suite and left no forwarding addresses.

Within a quarter hour, Sergeant MacDonald's next report came.

Dear Inspector Treadles,

I spoke to Dr. Birch and his sister, Miss Birch. They both identified Lady Sheridan as Mrs. Broadbent, the elderly patient staying at the inn in Barton Cross. Since Dr. Birch had to rush out to Curry House, Miss Birch was the one who took the morphine to the inn and administered it to Lady Sheridan.

When Dr. Birch came back from Curry House and called on Lady Sheridan, she was better, thanks to the morphine, though still in a state of great suffering. As he recounted what had kept him from seeing her sooner, she became more animated and asked a number of questions.

Dr. Birch doesn't recall whether he used Mr. Sackville's name in his exchange with Lady Sheridan—he thinks he might have. Miss Birch had this to add: After she administered the morphine, Lady Sheridan asked her to retrieve a framed photograph of her daughter from her reticule. And when Miss Birch reached in, the first thing she felt was not a photograph, but a pistol.

Yours truly,
MacDonald

When Inspector Treadles arrived at the Sheridan town house, Mr. Addison conducted him not to the drawing room, but Lady Sheridan's bedroom.

"The doctor has just been. She doesn't have long to live," said the butler, looking much less spry than Treadles remembered from mere days ago. "Please be brief, Inspector."

Lady Sheridan lay in a half recline, a hillock of pillows behind her back. Her grey hair was loose, her cheeks waxy, her eyes deeply sunken. At Treadles's entrance, she signaled a white-capped nurse, who had been feeding her spoonfuls of broth, to leave.

"I'm afraid I won't be able to answer many questions, Inspector," she said slowly. "I've had quite a bit of laudanum."

"I'll be quick then, ma'am. How do you explain your presence in the next nearest village to Curry House at the same time Mr. Sackville died?"

"Coincidence. I might die any minute. For old times' sake, I wished to see my brother-in-law one last time."

"Why did you choose to do so alone? Why not bring along Lord Sheridan?"

She snorted, a sound of bitterness. "He isn't about to die."

"If a social call had indeed been your only purpose, why lie about something so simple and understandable?"

"If I didn't, Lord Sheridan would know, wouldn't he?" Her eyelids drooped. When she looked at Treadles again, the simple action seemed to require superhuman effort. "He'd have asked me why I must undermine his proud estrangement from his brother and I hadn't enough time left to bother with that sort of nonsense."

"And the pistol you carried with you on the trip?"

This time she closed her eyes, a strange little smile about her lips. "A lady must take care when she travels by herself."

Shortly after Treadles had been promoted to sergeant, he returned to Barrow-in-Furness to visit his mother. She had been in robust health, but as he said good-bye to her, he'd had a sense of foreboding. That it would be the last time he saw her. She'd died mere weeks later from a sudden and fierce fever. In the hours before his father-in-law drew his last breath, everyone had been convinced that he would fully recover, especially Alice. But Treadles had the same premonition. Mr. Cousin had died that night.

There would be no further questions for Lady Sheridan; their final meeting was at an end.

He bowed. "Thank you, ma'am. Good-bye."

�֍

Upon Inspector Treadles's return to Scotland Yard, he found Hodges's written statement at his desk. Treadles filliped the piece of paper. Something about the handwriting snagged his attention, the oddly crooked g's, the squashed o's, and the majuscule a's that were more ambitious than necessary.

Where had he seen this handwriting before?

Then he looked at what Hodges had actually written. He'd been staying at an inn in Camberwell, which was in *London*, very far from Isle of Wight, the supposed destination for his holidays.

But very close to Lambeth, where Mr. Sackville had visited twice a month for at least seven years running.

Treadles leaped up and pulled open the file case where he kept his official correspondence. Yes, there were those two letters he'd received about the house of ill repute in Lambeth. The exact same handwriting. The first letter was rather vague. The second, which he'd received two months ago, was full of anger and anguish, all but screaming into the void, warning of pure depravity, the exploitation of the most innocent and helpless, etc.

He rushed out to Lambeth, to the lane named in the letter, and stood before the skeletal remains of what must have been a structure big enough for a family of twelve. He'd been there no more than a few minutes before he realized that the house next door had an unusually large number of men hurrying in and out.

Not that news from home is much better, Alice had said on the night of Holmes's "misfortune," sitting at the edge of Treadles's desk and flipping through the evening papers. *Recriminations over the failure of the Irish Home Rule bill. Police still looking for suspects in the fire in Lambeth that destroyed a building and killed two.*

And what had he said to her? *I know about that building in Lambeth. Every last inspector in Scotland Yard got letters about it—and it isn't even a copper hell, but a bookmaker's. You close one down and it opens right back up two streets over.*

The *neighboring* house was the bookmaker's place, and the men who barged in and out the runners who collected bets and settled winnings.

What then had been the depravities committed in the house that had been burned to the ground? What kind of depravities would turn a man like Hodges, who must have seen a fair bit of the seedier side of life, into a rabid crusader?

—❈—

Treadles ordered Hodges arrested and brought to London. Sergeant MacDonald delivered the valet into Treadles's keeping late that evening.

This time Hodges didn't look so natty. There was something about being arrested and put under the power of the Crown that stripped jauntiness from a man. A state of vulnerability that was not helped by the blank, sterile walls of an interrogation room.

"Mr. Hodges, you were the one who poisoned Mr. Sackville. You were outraged at what went on in that house in Lambeth he visited. You gave him arsenic, coinciding with the timing of his trips to London, so that he would suffer and not be able to achieve what he set out to do."

"You can't prove anything."

The absence of jauntiness did not imply the absence of defiance.

"No, but I have here a sample of your writing, and every inspector at Scotland Yard has received letters from you, screaming about the intolerable deeds that went on inside the house. And then the house mysteriously went up in smoke, resulting in two deaths. That is enough ground to charge you with arson and murder, Mr. Hodges."

Scotland Yard certainly didn't have any other suspects. The investigation had been ongoing for weeks and the officer in charge still couldn't be sure how many people had lived inside or what it had been used for before it was reduced to ashes and rubble.

"I didn't burn down the house," Hodges answered through clenched teeth.

"You will have a difficult time proving that."

"I was in Devon."

"You could have had accomplices in London."

"I would never do such a thing. There were children inside. Little children!"

Hodges's outburst ricocheted in the room. His hands balled into fists. And he panted, as if he'd run all the way from Curry House.

Treadles felt as if he'd been picked up, turned upside down, and shaken violently. "Tell me about those children," he said, his voice sounding curiously disembodied.

"The little girl they brought me wasn't even nine. She said she'd been in that house for a whole year, at least. And she told me that there were boys and girls at least three years younger than her." Hodges's throat worked. "Yes, I gave him arsenic before his next trip. But I didn't want to kill him—I am not a murderer. I wanted to buy some time for the police to do something. Anything."

"You had the wrong house number in your letters."

Hodges dropped his head into his hands.

It had been an easy enough mistake. Of the two houses, only one had its number on the exterior, and though it seemed to be right in the middle, between the two entrances, the number had belonged to the bookmaker.

"When did you decide to change to chloral?" Treadles still sounded dispassionate.

Times like this, it was as if some mechanism deep inside him roared to life and insulated him in a thick layer of numbness.

"I never had anything to do with the chloral. I was gone that week. In London. I went to see if there was anything I could do to close the place down, but when I got there, it had already burned to the ground." Hodges wiped the heel of his hand across his eyes. "And no one knew what happened to the children. No one."

The next morning, Treadles returned to 18 Upper Baker Street. He noticed that the manservant who conducted him to the flat was the same one who had opened the door for him the other day at the lurid house where he last met with Lord Ingram and Miss Holmes—on loan from Lord Ingram to keep an eye on Miss Holmes's safety, no doubt.

Miss Holmes greeted him solemnly. It had been excruciating to come before her at their previous meeting, knowing that her wide-set, innocent-seeming eyes would have remarked every last ounce of his inner distress. But now he barely cared.

Now the numbness reigned.

He stated what Hodges had revealed at Scotland Yard, something his normal self would have tried his best to shield from the hearing of a lady. She listened without moving, not even to pour tea, and remained still for long minutes afterward.

Vaguely he wondered whether it had been too much for her—whether her woman's mind could not handle iniquities of this magnitude without going to pieces.

"What Becky Birtle said," she murmured. "It's so obvious in hindsight. Mr. Sackville was only interested in her because she was small and underdeveloped and he thought her still prepubescent. When it turned out she already had menses, he lost all in—"

She sprang out of her chair. "The Sheridans' daughter. How did she die?"

He rose hastily. "Sergeant MacDonald looked it up and copied down what had been written on her death certificate. I have it with me." He opened the document case he carried. "Congestive heart failure, signed by—Dr. Bernard Motley. But he is Mrs. Treadles's family physician."

Miss Holmes all but ripped the piece of paper from him. She stared down at it, a fierce frown on her face. "Do you remember the case you had sent me via Lord Ingram, the curious death of a young girl related by none other than this Dr. Motley?"

"The one you believe to have killed herself by smuggling frozen carbon dioxide to her room?" What did that have to do with anything?

"Did the Sheridan household have a ready supply of carbon dioxide?"

"I spoke to the Sheridans' butler. He mentioned they used to have canisters of gas for carbonating water."

"It was her. Clara Sackville killed herself." Her voice was firm, implacable.

The implication of her words at last penetrated past the shield of numbness. "Are you saying that Mr. Sackville did something to his niece? His own niece, when she was a little girl?"

Miss Holmes returned to her seat, lifted the teapot, and poured, her hands perfectly steady while Treadles scrambled to reassemble his protective cocoon. "And Sophia Lonsdale was one of her best friends."

Treadles was still reeling. "She killed Mr. Sackville for Clara?"

"It would explain the pistol in Lady Sheridan's reticule, wouldn't it? She would have done it herself, but he already died before she had the chance to confront him."

A knock came at the door. "Miss Holmes," said the manservant, "something came in the post. You said to bring everything to you right away."

"Yes, thank you, Barkley." She scanned the envelope. "Mrs. Marbleton—my name and address have been typed on the same typewriter she used to produce her first cipher for me to solve. Let's see what she wants to tell me."

Dear Miss Holmes,

Two months ago, I returned to Britain for the first time in many years, to see an old friend on her deathbed. Before she passed away, she gave me a diary from another old friend who departed many years ago. My dying friend had never read Clara Sackville's diary, as Clara had asked her not to open it until her parents had both passed on. No other person of my acquaintance holds to her word as firmly as my friend did—I know because she had long kept my secrets.

But I have never been as resistant to curiosity. After my friend's funeral, I read Clara's diary. As I did so, I wept, screamed, threw an inkwell across the room in anger, and shook at the cruelty and injustice in this world.

And despised myself for having never guessed anything remotely near the incestuous truth.

Clara loved and trusted her uncle. He exploited that trust and love and twisted her innate desire to please. I cannot bear to think of how lonely and frightened she must have been. When he used her to satisfy some warped part of himself, he forever isolated her from everyone and everything else she held dear.

The more she descended into her private hell, the more she tried to love him. Love was her defense against the judgment that was to come. Love was the only excuse.

But as soon as she entered puberty, he had no more use for her. It annihilated her: the betrayal of trust, the belief that she had done the abominable in the eyes of God, the knowledge that she would have carried on doing the same if he hadn't abandoned her. Not to mention the fact that he was family, and that everyone, especially her parents, still expected her to be terribly fond of this uncle.

That she did not destroy the diary tells me that she wished for the truth to be known someday. So I proceeded accordingly. The choice was left to Mr. Sackville. He could choose to face exposure, or he could choose to not face it.

As for the women whose deaths you've connected to his, yes, indeed there was a connection. Lady Amelia and Lady Shrewsbury came upon Clara and Mr. Sackville. Clara recorded that she was terrified they would inform her parents, but her uncle assured her that it would not come to pass. Lady Amelia's husband owed Mr. Sackville a ruinous amount of money. Lady Shrewsbury was not in financial distress, but she was a social-climbing toady who didn't have enough character to gainsay Lady Amelia.

The incident took place when Clara was a few months short of eleven. These women failed her utterly. They did nothing to protect her from Mr. Sackville's predation, then or ever.

I offered them the same choice as I did Mr. Sackville.

They all chose chloral. Cowards, one and all.

Lady Sheridan died in the night. Expect the matter to be made public soon.

Yours truly,
An admirer

P.S. Best of luck with life as Sherlock Holmes.

P.P.S. I have taken temporary custody of the children from the house Mr. Sackville frequented in London. I hope they—or some of them at least—will grow up and be well.

P.P.P.S. Lady Sheridan and I ran into each other quite by chance. I have the habit of investigating establishments that purport to help women. She had long been a patroness to the YWCA. We met each other outside the association's institute in Bethnal Green, not a place I expected to encounter Society ladies.

Recognition shocked us both. But almost immediately we began to speak. I had always regretted the injury I must have caused her. Unbeknownst to me, she had devoted herself to the welfare of vulnerable young women because of the harsh fate I had met with—which she felt was far more punishment than I deserved.

At some point in the conversation we began reminiscing about Clara. She told me that she had never believed in the explanation the physician had offered, but only pretended to do so for her husband's sake. Clara had been far from well. Lady Sheridan had tried everything in her power to uplift the girl's spirit and blamed herself for failing.

I debated with myself, but in the end decided to tell her the truth—and assured her that I would not let the guilty parties go free.

But Lady Sheridan had decided to take matters into her own hands anyway. And it was only the full execution of Sophia Lonsdale's plan that had prevented her from committing murder at the end of her life.

"So all three of them took the chloral themselves," Treadles heard himself murmur.

"Sophia Lonsdale must have been in the hansom cab Lady Shrewsbury got into the night before her death," said Miss Holmes. "I wonder that she didn't also confront Lady Amelia in person."

"But there is no evidence of her having been in the vicinity of Curry House."

"I believe when the young Marbletons reported on how difficult it is for a stranger to go unnoticed in the area, she opted for the postal service instead—it can't be difficult to have her package resemble, from the outside, a wrapped magazine or some such, so that the servants would pay it no mind. The worst that could happen would be that someone finds a typed, unsigned letter detailing Mr. Sackville's perversions. But of course Mr. Sackville would have destroyed everything."

Treadles nodded. "Do you think Sophia Lonsdale was in a hurry at the end? Almost a fortnight passed between Lady Amelia's death and Mr. Sackville's, but only a day elapsed between Mr. Sackville's and Lady Shrewsbury's."

"It's possible she became impatient. It's also possible she wished to take advantage of my scandal." Miss Holmes smiled slightly. "Seems more plausible to have a healthy woman die in her sleep when she'd been greatly angered by her son than for no reason at all."

Treadles had no idea what he could say in response. He did not understand Miss Holmes's scandal. It made no sense how such a diamond-bright mind could have made such foolish, downright immoral decisions.

She took a sip of her tea. "What of the valet, Hodges? What will happen to him?"

He was glad to move away from the subject of her carnal weakness. "I do not believe Lord Sheridan, when he learns the truth, will wish to prosecute. And if he declines, I have no reason to believe Scotland Yard would take on the task."

Miss Holmes folded the letter and carefully placed it back in its envelope. "I have a presentiment that in revealing Clara's tragedy, Sophia Lonsdale will credit her dead friend, the one who had held Clara Sackville's diary for many years, with the plan for vengeance, so as to keep her own name out of the news.

"No woman goes to the trouble of staging her own death without a compelling reason. Inspector, would you please keep her involvement in the case out of public knowledge?"

Treadles considered a moment, before saying, "I will."

"I am greatly indebted to you, Inspector, for your gallant assistance in this case."

Treadles inclined his head and rose. It was not Miss Holmes's fault that what he'd always believed about his wife turned out to be not exactly the case, but all the same he was ready not to have anything to do with Sherlock Holmes for a good long while.

As if she'd heard every thought in his head, Miss Holmes set a prettily wrapped package in his hands. "The madeleines are for Mrs. Treadles. Please convey my warmest regards to her."

Twenty-two

"You know what I have been thinking?" asked Livia.

They were seated at the refreshments area set aside for the Reading Room patrons at the British Museum. Charlotte had resumed her weekly trip to the Reading Room, and Livia had snuck out of a skull-numbing garden party to visit with her favorite sister.

"What have you been thinking?" asked Charlotte.

She looked well, her serene, cherubic self—more than one gentleman had walked past their table unnecessarily, studying her out of the corner his eyes.

Life had improved drastically for Livia, too, since it finally became known that Lady Shrewsbury and Lady Amelia had committed suicide to avoid public shame. Of course, Charlotte's absence was always an ache in the heart and Livia dreaded the long months in the country after the end of the Season. But to be free of suspicions at last, to no longer live under that dark cloud hanging over her head—it was a pleasure well worth savoring.

And of course, Charlotte now had an income—her latest case earned a whopping four quid ten shillings, much to Livia's heart-palpitating joy. *I have become much thriftier*, Charlotte wrote in one of her letters. *I'm determined to accumulate enough to provide for all of us—you, me, and Bernadine.*

Livia wiped her fingers on a napkin. "I think you should publish some of Sherlock Holmes's cases. Those accounts would be far better publicity for your services than newspaper adverts."

Charlotte put another half sandwich on Livia's plate. "But by coming to a private consultant, my clients expect a certain amount of privacy."

"Change their names, then no one will be the wiser."

Charlotte shook her head. "The only case I've been a part of that has the makings of a proper narrative is the Sackville case. Even if I change the name of everyone involved, people would still already know what happened. Not to mention, magazines that might want to publish such accounts would shy away from that particular one, for fear of offending the sensibility of their readers."

Livia was undeterred. "Then fictionalize it. Take the bones of the story and rebuild it. Sherlock Holmes is asked by Scotland Yard to help with a suspicious death. You can keep the method of the killing, but change chloral to some other poison. And you can also have the murderer come to you by means of a newspaper notice, except somewhat differently, of course."

"I like it." Charlotte grinned. "And what would this person be avenging?"

At the bright interest in her sister's eyes, Livia's mind suddenly swarmed with ideas. "That would be the easiest thing to come up with, wouldn't it? People are always doing horrible things to each other. In fact, last week I read a book by Mr. Twain and it mentioned a massacre that took place in Utah a generation ago. The local militia killed more than one hundred people from a wagon train headed to California. You can have someone who survived the massacre tracking down those responsible for it."

"All the way to London?"

"Why not?" Livia reached for the half sandwich Charlotte had given her and took a bite. Ah, everything tasted so much better when Charlotte was at the table. "The world is a small place nowadays. And it would also be in keeping with the spirit of the original case, that of an avenger coming from abroad."

"A workable idea," Charlotte pronounced, taking a sip of her lemonade.

Livia almost preened. Charlotte didn't give false compliments. If she said the idea was workable, then it was workable. "You will do it then?"

Charlotte shook her head. "*You* should write this story, Livia."

"Me?"

"Yes, you."

"But I've never written anything before."

"That isn't entirely true."

Of course Charlotte would know about Livia's notebooks filled with half-germinated ideas and stories that had fallen apart a few pages in. Livia's face heated—she ought to have burned those notebooks. It was too embarrassing for her amateurish efforts to have been seen by anyone, even if it was only Charlotte.

"Remember when you read Poe's 'The Murders in the Rue Morgue'?" asked Charlotte. "Remember how outraged you were that after all the tension and excitement of the premise, in the denouement Mr. Poe couldn't do better than a crazed orangutan? You were scribbling in your notebook for days afterward."

"Yes, but it's much easier to condemn him for using a crazed orangutan than to come up with a better story myself."

Charlotte refilled Livia's glass of lemonade. "I never told you this but some of your openings were more than decent. I wish you'd have continued with those stories."

Livia's heart thudded. She was good at something?

"Anyway, give this Sherlock Holmes story a try," Charlotte said firmly, as she pushed a plate of sponge cake in Livia's direction. "You'll surprise yourself."

⁂

Charlotte returned from the British Museum in time for her last appointment of the day at 18 Upper Baker Street. At precisely half past seven, the bell rang. A few seconds later, a cheerful-looking young woman entered the parlor.

"Miss Oxford, how do you do?"

"Very well, thank you." Miss Oxford shook Charlotte's hand vigorously and with a wide smile. "I'm pleased to be here."

Her unencumbered high spirits struck Charlotte—her clients typically betrayed *some* signs of anxiety. The usual pantomime about Sherlock Holmes's disability ensued. Miss Oxford, after expressing her sympathy, declared emphatically that yes, she wished for a demonstration of Mr. Holmes's mental prowess.

Charlotte looked her over. Then she walked to the sideboard and poured two glasses of whisky. "You're a Londoner, born and brought up in this very area. But you've been abroad recently and only just returned. Paris, I would say. You weren't a tourist there. You didn't hold any positions. Nor were you living with family or friends. Which leads me to conclude that you are a student of medicine at the Sorbonne."

She handed a glass of whisky to her "client" and raised her own. "Welcome home, Miss Redmayne."

Miss Redmayne burst into a peal of laughter. "What gave me away? Is it the family resemblance? Everybody always says I take after my aunt."

"There is a good likeness."

The more Charlotte looked at her, however, the more Miss Redmayne began to resemble someone else: the late Duke of Wycliffe, Lord Ingram's father—or at least his official father.

Charlotte had always assumed that Miss Redmayne wasn't Mrs.

Watson's niece, but the latter's daughter—easier on everyone that way, and the girl could go about with a gloss of legitimacy. She had further assumed that Miss Redmayne's father was a man of considerable wealth—John Watson, an army doctor, would not have been able to provide for his widow in as comfortable a manner.

She had, however, never imagined there to be connections between Mrs. Watson and the Ashburtons.

Miss Redmayne merrily chatted away. Charlotte knew she must be making the correct responses, for Miss Redmayne laughed and continued talking. But Charlotte's head spun.

It wasn't uncommon for children to develop a rapport with their father's mistress, especially if they had already lost their mother. J. H. R., the mysterious entity to whom Lord Ingram's book had been dedicated, was none other than Joanna Hamish Redmayne, otherwise known as Mrs. Watson. She wasn't someone he disapproved of hugely, but a friend and confidante of long standing. And Mrs. Watson hadn't run into Charlotte by accident at the post office. She had been *sent*.

Miss Redmayne stopped and looked at Charlotte expectantly. Charlotte made a concerted effort to recall what had been said to her. "I can't declare with one hundred percent confidence that I would have enjoyed dissection, but I'd like to think I wouldn't faint more than two or three times before I became used to it."

Miss Redmayne chortled and launched into another anecdote from her anatomy class. Charlotte forced herself to pay attention and keep up with the discussion. A quarter of an hour must have passed before Miss Redmayne said, "Well, shall we go home? My aunt promised there will be a magnificent bottle of champagne waiting."

"Why don't you go first? I have a bit of preparation that needs to be done before I'm ready for my first client tomorrow."

After making Charlotte promise she won't be long, Miss Redmayne flounced down the steps. Charlotte returned to her seat and sank down heavily.

A knock came at the door. Charlotte started. "Who is it?"

Lord Ingram walked in.

Charlotte was instantly on her feet. "What are you doing here?"

"You wrote me."

He studied her closely, but with a measure of caution. Did he know? Had he taken one look at her and realized that she now knew what he had orchestrated?

She searched his face, but it did not reveal what he was thinking. "Yes, I wrote you but I didn't request to see you."

She had gone to Somerset House, found the name of Sophia Lonsdale's husband in the wedding registry, and asked Lord Ingram whether he knew anything about the man Sophia Lonsdale had taken such pains to leave behind.

"I met with Bancroft just now." He spoke with an exaggerated calm, as if he were bracing himself for trouble. "What he told me you need to hear right away."

She didn't give a farthing for what Lord Bancroft had to say. Instead she closed the distance between them and jabbed a finger into his chest. "You lied to me. You did have me followed."

He did not answer immediately, but looked at her—not scrutinizing her for clues, just taking her in feature by feature. "I have said a great many things to you that are convenient, rather than truthful."

His dark eyes were turning darker. His gaze traveled from her eyes to her lips and back again. She was even closer to him than she'd thought: They were practically touching, separated by scant molecules of air. She inhaled the sandalwood scent of his shaving soap and the fragrance of clean, warm skin.

"And I only had you followed until you became Mrs. Watson's

companion. After that it was all Mrs. Marbleton, or I should say, Mrs. Mo—"

She kissed him.

He stood stock-still for a moment. Then he yanked her to him, cupped her face, and kissed her back with the force of Zeus's thunderbolts striking ground.

Sweet. Bitter. Pleasure. Pain. And then only fierce, mindless sensations, only heat and electricity.

She was panting for a while before she realized that the kiss had ended, that she stood with her cheek against the lapel of his coat, listening to the fast, strong beat of his heart.

He took a step back. She sighed—every sublime moment must come with a bereft hour. He didn't need to address the matter for her to understand that even though everything had changed, nothing had changed.

"I hope you will not be angry at Mrs. Watson," he said quietly. "All I asked was that she pass on some funds to you. Welcoming you into her house and then taking you on as a business partner—those were her own decisions."

The direction of his gaze: on the floor next to her feet. The placement of his hands: gripping the gloves he'd taken off as he came into the room. The rise and fall of his chest was rapid, agitated.

He was waiting for her verdict.

"I am not angry at Mrs. Watson."

He did not relax. In fact, he appeared more tense—they both knew she could never be angry at Mrs. Watson.

But what about at him, her former partner in silence? Was she angry that he thought nothing of overstepping his bounds when he believed it necessary, only to now withdraw behind long-established lines of separation?

She sighed again. "What was it you were going to tell me about the tutor Sophia Lonsdale married?"

He gazed at her another moment. "Moriarty? Only that it gave Bancroft quite a turn to hear that name. He kept asking how I'd learned about the man. And when he was finally convinced that I wasn't personally embroiled with Moriarty, warned me in no uncertain terms never to be."

Charlotte's heart stopped momentarily—thank goodness he'd said no to her idea of writing to Lady Somersby and having her identify Mrs. Marbleton.

"And this reminds me, Holmes," he reached into his pocket and pulled out an envelope. "Bancroft asked me to give this to you."

Her heart thudded—she'd feared he would never call her Holmes again.

"Hmm, *he* is not in need of a mistress, is he?" she murmured, just to see Lord Ingram roll his eyes.

The note read,

Dear Mr. Holmes,

I have watched your consulting service with great interest and would like to call on you tomorrow morning at ten to discuss a matter of great delicacy and importance. Should you choose to accept the commission, it would require you to work closely with my brother, Lord Ingram Ashburton.

I hope I will be able to secure your assistance.

Yours truly,
Bancroft Ashburton

Trust Lord Bancroft to know how to set a lure.

She burned the note—because that was what Lord Ingram had told her one did with any communication from his brother. Then she said to Lord Ingram, "Tell Lord Bancroft that he had better keep his promise. And that I will see him not at ten, but at eleven."

He shook his head, but his expression was gentle, almost affectionate. "I was always afraid this day would come. That Bancroft would discover you for your mind."

"When did *you* discover me for my mind, Ash?" she asked impulsively.

He already had one hand on the door. Looking back at her, he said, "From the beginning, Holmes. The very beginning."

Don't miss the next exciting book
in the Lady Sherlock series,
coming from Berkley in Fall 2017!

USA Today bestseller **Sherry Thomas** is one of the most acclaimed historical romance authors writing today, winning the RITA Award two years running and appearing on innumerable "Best of the Year" lists, including those of *Publishers Weekly*, *Kirkus Reviews*, *Library Journal*, Dear Author, and All About Romance. Her novels include *My Beautiful Enemy* and *The Luckiest Lady in London*. *A Study in Scarlet Women* is the first in the Lady Sherlock Series.

She lives in Austin, Texas, with her husband and sons. Visit her website at sherrythomas.com.